SPECIAL MESSAGE TO READERS

THE ULVERSCROFT FOUNDATION
(registered UK charity number 264873)
was established in 1972 to provide funds for research, diagnosis and treatment of eye diseases. Examples of major projects funded by the Ulverscroft Foundation are:-

- The Children's Eye Unit at Moorfields Eye Hospital, London
- The Ulverscroft Children's Eye Unit at Great Ormond Street Hospital for Sick Children
- Funding research into eye diseases and treatment at the Department of Ophthalmology, University of Leicester
- The Ulverscroft Vision Research Group, Institute of Child Health
- Twin operating theatres at the Western Ophthalmic Hospital, London
- The Chair of Ophthalmology at the Royal Australian College of Ophthalmologists

You can help further the work of the Foundation by making a donation or leaving a legacy. Every contribution is gratefully received. If you would like to help support the Foundation or require further information, please contact:

THE ULVERSCROFT FOUNDATION
The Green, Bradgate Road, Anstey
Leicester LE7 7FU, England
Tel: (0116) 236 4325

website: www.foundation.ulverscroft.com

An author, journalist and screenwriter, Robert Ryan was born in Liverpool and moved to London to study natural sciences at university. He began his writing career in the late 1980s for *The Face, Arena* and the US edition of *GQ*, before moving to a staff job at the *Sunday Times*. After the publication of his first novel, he left to go freelance.

While learning to play the trumpet for his third book, Ryan met Guy Barker who, as well as being a great jazz trumpeter, had worked with Anthony Minghella, notably on *The Talented Mr. Ripley*. After reading the novel, Guy wrote a musical theme for the book, which opened his Mercury-nominated album *Soundtrack*.

Robert continues to contribute to *The Sunday Times* and collaborate with Guy on further jazz projects. He lives in North London with his wife, three children, a dog and a deaf cat.

Find out more at robtryan.com

THE SIGN OF FEAR

London, 1917: Terror has come from the sky, and Londoners are scurrying in fear. A twin tragedy strikes Dr John Watson: an old friend, Staff Nurse Jennings, is on a boat-ambulance torpedoed in the Channel with no survivors. And his concert-going companion, Sir Gilbert Hastings, is kidnapped. Then comes a gruesome ransom demand, for Sir Gilbert and four others, which will involve terrible mutilation unless the terms are met. With his old companion Sherlock Holmes otherwise indisposed, Dr Watson is on his own in a race against time . . .

Books by Robert Ryan
Published by Ulverscroft:

EARLY ONE MORNING
THE BLUE NOON
NIGHT CROSSING
AFTER MIDNIGHT
THE LAST SUNRISE
DYING DAY
EMPIRE OF SAND
DEAD MAN'S LAND
THE DEAD CAN WAIT
A STUDY IN MURDER

ROBERT RYAN

THE SIGN OF FEAR

Complete and Unabridged

CHARNWOOD
Leicester

First published in Great Britain in 2016 by
Simon & Schuster UK Ltd
London

First Charnwood Edition
published 2019
by arrangement with
Simon & Schuster UK Ltd
London

A catalogue record for this book is available
from the British Library.

ISBN 978–1–4448–4027–8

Published by
F. A. Thorpe (Publishing)
Anstey, Leicestershire

Set by Words & Graphics Ltd.
Anstey, Leicestershire
Printed and bound in Great Britain by
T. J. International Ltd., Padstow, Cornwall

This book is printed on acid-free paper

For Deborah once more

Our Little Funk Hole in the Vaults (1917)

When the Kaiser's sun shines in the west,
And the reign of the tyrant is o'er,
Worse than ever was known of before;
For 'gainst babies his battles are fought,
And Humanity's law set at naught,
So for safety's sake, I run from the bomb
  of the Hun,
To my Little Funk Hole in the Vaults.

There's a bleak little hole at the bank,
Where we rush when we hear of a raid,
All helter and skelter, before any damage
  is made.
There we sit and count our sins,
And decide to redeem our faults,
Till we hear it is done,
Then we all make a run,
From our Little Funk Hole in the Vaults.

Part of a song written by staff of the Bank of England after bombs fell in nearby Lothbury and Coleman Street

Prologue

13 June 1917

'Have you seen this man?'

The words sounded stale in Major John Watson's mouth. He must have uttered the phrase a thousand times in the past few weeks, always accompanied by a showing of the now-creased photograph of the square-faced Irishman he was seeking.

The elderly jeweller repositioned his pince-nez on the bridge of his nose and leaned over the glass-topped counter. 'Buying or selling?'

Watson looked around the shop. There wasn't that much to buy in the sad, dusty cases, unless you were in the market for second-hand. The war had made diamonds scarce, and what was Hatton Garden without its stock in trade?

'Selling,' Watson said. 'A diamond star and a diamond badge. Either complete or broken down into sapphires, emeralds, rubies and pink diamonds.'

The man's eyes narrowed a little as he recognized the description. 'The Irish Crown Jewels?'

Watson nodded his assent and jeweller looked at the photograph again. 'Is that — '

'No. It's his brother, Frank,' pre-empted Watson.

'Of course. I heard he was acquitted by the investigating committee.'

Doesn't mean he's not guilty of the crime, thought Watson. Just that he is a very slippery customer.

1

'I haven't seen him, no.'

'Thank you for your time. If you hear any-thing . . . ' Watson slipped the photograph back into his jacket pocket and laid his calling card down on the table. 'Perhaps you could ring me.'

'Ah. I see,' the jeweller said, recognizing the name on the card. 'And how is Mr Holmes? I met him once, you know, during that Blue Carbuncle affair.'

'He is well,' said Watson drily. In fact, he was in bed at the Connaught, having spent the night trawling for their quarry in the Tick-Tock Club and the back room of the Orinoco, a mission not without its risks, given the clientele of such places. How would he explain himself if there was a police raid? Not, as Holmes had pointed out, that a raid was too likely, given the paucity of policemen in the city. Conscription had winnowed the ranks considerably.

'Let me tell you something, Dr Watson,' the jeweller said, his eyes scanning from side to side as if worried he might be overheard. 'There are merchants along here who would kill for a sniff of a pink diamond right now. But you couldn't keep something like that secret for long. If this man is trying to sell the Irish Crown Jewels or their component parts, it isn't in Hatton Garden. I'd have heard.'

Watson thanked him and walked out into a bright summer day. *Dr Watson* — it was some years since he had been anything other than a major and the title sounded at once comforting yet alien. He supposed he was, dressed in his civilian clothes and working on behalf of

2

Sherlock Holmes, back to his old ways. He was, temporarily at least, Dr John Hamish Watson once again. Which, he thought, might be the whole object of the exercise.

He crossed the road to the teahouse on the corner of the Garden and Greville Street. It was a neat place, with bentwood chairs and lace tablecloths, and was around half full, although the customers were mostly the old, the infirm and the war-damaged. He took a place at the window and ordered a pot of tea and a currant bun. And, a hasty addition, two of the establishment's homemade biscuits. Perhaps, he thought, his appetite was coming back.

It was several months now since the incident that had robbed him of his ability to enjoy everyday sensory pleasures. If he found himself revelling in the sun on his face, the wind in his hair, the smell of freshly brewed coffee, the nose of a fine claret, he was whisked rudely back to a rusting bridge in Holland. There, in the midst of a prisoner exchange — in which he was one of the captives to be swapped — he had seen his friend and companion Mrs Gregson shot down in front of him. Murdered. Executed. Killed by the hand of the egregious Miss Pillbody, a German agent whose intention had been to hurt Watson by snatching away something he had grown to . . .

Grown to love.

Yes, perhaps. Since their meeting in Flanders in 1915, where, as a VAD, she had assisted him in his medical work, he had certainly become fond of Mrs Gregson. But, in the mêlée that followed the shooting on the bridge, Watson had been deprived of any chance to comfort her in her dying moments. Or to find comfort himself. It was while he was recovering from his ordeal as a POW in Germany — and the events in Holland — that Holmes had arrived at the convalescent home, claiming that an old nemesis, the thief who had walked free after stealing the Irish Crown Jewels from Dublin Castle, was in London once more.

Watson took out the photograph of the Irishman and laid it in front of him. It was like chasing smoke, looking for this one. A whisper here, a rumour there, that was all they had to go on. Was the man even in London? Or had Holmes simply engineered this whole business to try to shake Watson out of his lassitude? To make him *Dr Watson* once more?

He was aware of the waitress at his shoulder, a stout middle-aged woman who clearly had nothing wrong with her appetite. She laid the biscuits in front of him, but stayed at his side.

Watson looked up at her. 'Thank you.'

'You looking for him?' she asked, nodding at the picture.

'As a matter of fact, I am. And it isn't Ernest, if that's what you are thinking. It's Frank, his brother.'

'No matter who he is, he was in here, 'bout half an hour ago. With another gentleman. Foreign, the other man. American, I think.'

'Are you certain it was this man?'

She peered down at the grainy portrait. 'I'd bet ten bob on it.'

4

Watson began to fumble for his pocket for coins, all thought of tea and buns gone. 'And which way did he go when he left?'

'I don't know. I was out back.'

Watson groaned. More smoke to slip through his fingers.

'But I heard him tell his companion to fetch him a taxi to Liverpool Street Station.'

It took Watson ten precious minutes to find a motor cab to take him east to Liverpool Street. In the end, he had resorted to breaking the law to get the attention of a cabby, emitting a loud, piercing whistle that wouldn't have been out of place at the docks or at the end of a saucy show at the Alhambra. You could be fined for making such a sound in the street, in case it was mistaken for a Zeppelin air-raid warning. Still, this illegal blast of air did the trick in procuring a metered taxi and, within fifteen minutes, he was dropped at the rank in front of the terminus of the Great Eastern Railway.

As he stepped across the open concourse of Edward Wilson's Gothic confection, he was aware of a strange, tightening sensation in his chest and the feeling that his hatband was several sizes too small. He paused to take stock. The physician in him quickly dismissed any notion of a heart attack. Yet, whatever it was, the affliction was making him feel nauseous. He looked around at the porters and travellers — many of them soldiers heading out to the barracks in and around Colchester or for embarkation in Harwich — and they looked similarly discomforted by the strange thrumming that agitated

5

the atmosphere around them.

His brain, initially confused by this disturbance in the air bouncing off the red-brick
façade before him, finally determined the noise
was coming from the sky. He looked up through
a gauze of wispy clouds, and his first thought
was: dragonflies?

★   ★   ★

The man whom Watson had spent fruitless weeks
chasing was unaware of what was happening
back at Liverpool Street Station. He had bought
a single ticket and caught the train to Colchester
without mishap. From there, he had taken a
connecting service to a village on the edge of the
militarized zone around the Combined Services
Signal School, which everyone knew was the HQ
for the Government's code-breaking and wireless
interception organization. It was the second time
he had made the journey and he knew it was but
a brisk ten-minute walk down the gentle hill to
Dr Bradford's house. Bradford had a motorcar
he was determined to use for the return journey,
hence the single. It would also thwart anyone
who had tried to follow him into the Essex
countryside. He had heard that Holmes and
Watson were taking an interest in him. Good. It
would be a real pleasure to wrong-foot them
once again. But he had to be careful. They might
not be at the height of their physical or mental
powers, but he shouldn't underestimate the pair.
Still, twisting the tail of that insufferably
self-important sleuth and his unctuous little

lapdog would give him considerable pleasure.

The Irishman straightened his clothes, took off his hat and smoothed down his tar-dark hair, before he yanked on the bell pull. The visitor could see a familiar spark of recognition in Dr Bradford's face when he opened the door and squinted in the noonday light at the stranger standing before him.

'Dr Bradford?'

'Yes.' The physicist instinctively pulled the dressing gown tighter around his waist and refastened the cord. 'Can I help you?'

'Are you alone?' the visitor asked, looking over the man's shoulder into hallway.

'Quite alone.'

'Have you had breakfast?' The Irishman tried to keep the disapproval from his voice. What sort of hour was this to be rising?

'I was just about to . . . I'm sorry, you are . . . ?'

The Irishman passed over his official identification and a letter asking for all assistance to be given to him under DORA, the Defence of the Realm Act.

'I knew it!' Bradford said excitedly as he read the name. 'I guessed you were related the moment I set eyes on you. But I expect you get that all the time. You're — '

'His brother,' he confirmed. 'Frank.'

'Come in, come in. Will you take tea?'

'Thank you, yes.'

The visitor took off his hat and examined the interior of the house as he followed Bradford through. It was built in the Arts and Crafts style

7

around a square hallway with a central staircase that looked as if it could withstand an earthquake or a German bomb. Everywhere was wooden panelling and twee little carvings or bold William Morris wallpaper. It smelled strongly of polish and fresh flowers.

Bradford indicated his visitor should wait in the sitting room. In it, he found four gramophones of different sizes and a collection of drums, some vividly decorated, others plain and unadorned, some intricately shaped, while others were simply hide stretched across a wooden frame. He tapped one of the larger examples and was surprised at the depth of sound and the deep resonance that came from it. It took an age before the air in the room returned to normal.

'North African,' said Bradford as he entered with a silver tray, which he placed on a low, carved table. 'The Atlas Mountains. Lovely sound. Drums are something of a hobby of mine.' He nodded towards the gramophones with their flared horns staring at him like a row of Cyclopes. 'And recorded sound, as you can see.'

'Yes.'

Bradford had a reputation in this village — which was a few miles from the government installation where he worked — for eccentricity, a notoriety fuelled by his housekeeper. He was vegetarian, she told the locals, she had once caught him rolling naked in the snow, he stored his urine in jars, which he sometimes struck with a stick to make a noise, he played the viola at all hours of the day and night; that young men came from London sometimes, and stayed the night, and him almost forty and not yet married . . .

For the price of a few pints in the Dragon Inn, the Irishman had heard it all on his previous visit to the village, albeit mostly second- and third-hand, and doubtless accumulating more sordid detail with each telling.

'Sugar?'

'No, thank you.' In fact, he liked his tea over-sweet, but it had become the polite norm to refuse other people's sugar, as it was on the list of 'voluntarily' rationed foodstuffs that the nation was meant to cut down on.

'Sure?'

'Ah, just the one then, to be going on with.'

Bradford passed him the sugared tea. 'How is your brother?'

'Well, his heart isn't what it was.' This was the truth, the hours in an open boat in particular having put a terrible strain on his organs.

'I'm not surprised, after all those adventures. He is a brave man. A hero. Saving all those men.'

'Ah. Although there are those who said if he hadn't got them into that pickle in the first place, he wouldn't have had to rescue them, now, would he?'

Bradford gave a nervous laugh, unsure whether his visitor was being serious. It seemed disrespectful to a national hero. Perhaps the man was jealous of his famous sibling. After all, one of them was a household name every schoolboy admired, the other . . . well, who even knew he had a brother?

'What can I do for you?' Bradford asked.

'We have a rather delicate situation.'

9

'How's that?'

A lengthy pause followed. 'The father of a young friend of yours . . . '

The teacup froze halfway to Bradford's lips and his eyes swivelled shiftily, as if looking for an escape route.

'Please relax, Dr Bradford; I'm here to help. You could say I'm, well, sympathetic to your tastes.'

The cup rattled slightly in the saucer as Bradford put it down, the tea untouched. 'I am very discreet.'

'That's as may be. But you recall a rich, idle young man called Tyler hanging around the Jermyn Street Baths and the tables of the Orinoco? His father found some letters.'

Bradford let out a groan. 'He was meant to burn them.'

'In my experience, those are exactly the kind of letters that end up not getting burned. Anyway, the son confessed all, his tale being that it was you who seduced him. Not vice versa.'

'The lying toad,' the doctor hissed.

'That's as may be. But you know who his father is?'

Bradford shook his head.

'He never mentioned that his father is Lord Brigham?'

Bradford looked glum. 'He never did, no.'

'Now, the Government, and DORA, can suppress a lot of things, but a court case for indecency — '

'It can't come to that!' Bradford was genuinely horrified. The blood drained from his face, leaving him looking waxen. 'My mother — '

'It won't come to court, you have my word. You're not exactly Oscar Wilde.'

Bradford shuddered, no doubt thinking of what a stretch in prison would be like for a convicted 'nancy boy'.

'But we have to take steps, radical steps, to make sure this is . . . hushed up.'

'Radical? I don't know if you realize this, but I am involved in some very sensitive work for the Government. Very sensitive. To do with the Zeppelins and — '

'Which is exactly why I am here, Doctor. It's not my place to know what you do, other than it is vital to the defence of London. Now, we will need that work to continue while we make certain, um, overtures to the family of this boy . . . '

'Young man,' Bradford objected.

'The law does not care about the ages of those involved, Dr Bradford, you know that. A perversion is a perversion . . . I'm just saying what they think, not my own personal opinion. The lad is of an age to know his own mind, as far as I am concerned. We are all victims of our urges and it seems to me we can't choose what those urges are to be. Am I right? Yes. So — ' he clapped his hands together as if he were a teacher settling down a group of naughty boys — 'we have set up a laboratory where you can continue your work in complete privacy and safety.'

'Where?'

A wave of the hand dismissed the details. He

11

used the usual panacea of the country's secret services. 'A safe and secure location.'

'For how long?'

A shrug. 'Till we are certain you can return to work hereabouts, totally . . . unencumbered from any concerns about your private life.'

'But you can definitely make this go away?'

A nod. 'Definitely.'

Bradford let out a sigh of relief. 'I've been a fool.'

'Neither the first nor the last. You know, my brother once said, 'Difficulties are just things to be overcome.' We have some difficulties, we will overcome them. It is the work that is important now. My brother also said, 'Superhuman effort isn't worth a damn unless it achieves results.''

It was Bradford's turn to nod. 'I need to go to the laboratory, to pick up — '

'You don't. All will be done for you. You just need to get dressed, pack a few clothes and we'll be on our way. We'll take your vehicle, if that is agreeable, rather than public transport.'

'Yes. Of course.' Bradford stood, his eyes glazed and hooded, as if he had been fed opium, and hurried out, his slippers slapping on the polished wood of the stair treads as he ascended to his bedroom.

After Dr Bradford had gone, Frank Shackleton drained the by-now lukewarm tea and smiled to himself. A job well done. And he hadn't needed to use the leaded cosh that weighed so heavily in his jacket pocket after all.

★　★　★

12

The impact of the object on the pavement almost lifted Watson off his feet. It was as if a giant gavel had come down next to him. He was holding Shackleton's photograph in his hand, ready to show the clerks in the booking hall, but the shock of the crash plucked it from his fingers. It took him a second to gather his wits and look to his right, where something had buried itself in the tar of the roadway. A few spirals of grey smoke marked the spot and it took another moment before Watson appreciated what he was looking at. Four black fins. A bomb. High explosive, by the size of it. And either it was defective or it was on a time-delay fuse. Either way, it could go off in an eye-blink.

He fumbled for his officer's whistle before realizing it was still in his RAMC tunic, so put his fingers into the corners of his mouth and, for the second time that day, broke the law with a roughneck's whistle. 'Get back!' he yelled, once he had gained the attention of the people around him. He waved his arms over his head, knocking his hat off. 'Bomb! Get back!'

Not dragonflies, Watson. German bombers! Sherlock's voice in his head chided. He ignored it.

Now a real whistle blew. 'Clear the area! Take cover.' A policeman was striding towards him, pointing at the entrance to the Metropolitan railway and its Underground platforms. 'Get underground!'

The next bomb to fall on the station from Ernst Brandenburg's fleet of twenty Gotha G.IV bombers circling over the East End of London

13

was neither a dud nor a delayed fuser. It passed through the four-arched roof of the station and detonated next to a full passenger train. Outside, Watson didn't even hear the explosion before the station appeared to exhale an enormous breath of super-heated air, mixed with steel, iron, dust, glass and body parts. This percussive wave lifted the policeman off his feet and carried his full body weight into Watson, spinning the pair of them over the concourse, a tangle of limbs, rolling like tumble-weed, until they came to rest, unmoving, against the wheel of an abandoned taxi.

1

September 1917

They had run out of clean water a good two hours before sunset. The ambulance train had been sitting in a siding for most of the day, the September sun still strong enough to heat the metal and roast the inside of the carriages, nearly all of which had non-opening windows. Above the stationary train, seagulls whirled and screeched as if to taunt them about how close they were to the coast, to the Channel and to the boats that would take them to Blighty. Fully loaded troop trains occasionally crawled past on the main line, wan young faces at the windows looking out at the long row of Red Cross carriages, the soldiers no doubt wondering if that would be how they would return from the front — full of sepsis or devoid of limbs. Only the raw recruits did that, of course. Those returning from leave, the veterans of months or years of war, knew better than to speculate and averted their gaze from the marooned ambulance train.

Even as the sun began to fall towards the treeline, promising a respite from its warmth, Staff Nurse Jennings decided that her Gurkha had to have water. A stoical young man with very little English, he had lost both feet and the fever that had him in its grip suggested his suffering wasn't over yet. Major Ramsey, the chief MO on the train, suspected that they would have to amputate to at least below the knees.

Staff Nurse Jennings was only on the train because it seemed a useful way to travel back to England for her first proper leave in almost two years. Why not volunteer for a shift on the ambulance train? Do some good while she made the journey to see her parents. But what should have been a ten-hour journey had stretched through delays and reversals into almost thirty-six. And now there was no water.

Almost as bad as that, she had sent a telegram to her old friend Major John Watson and informed him she expected to arrive at Victoria sometime in the next twenty-four hours. It was unlikely she would make even that vague appointment. She had started a correspondence with the major when she had heard that Mrs Gregson, a VAD of her acquaintance, had been killed in action while working with him.

She had sent her sympathies, he had replied and they had continued to exchange letters. In truth, it wasn't an entirely innocent arrangement on her behalf. Mrs Gregson had seemed invincible to her, a force of nature who could never die like a mere mortal. Staff Nurse Jennings would very much like to hear the truth about her fate from the horse's mouth. And it would be grand to see Major Watson again, of course.

The train was twenty-six carriages long, with the final carriage reserved for infectious cases — mumps, measles, scarlet fever — the rest a mix of sitting-up cases and compartments

16

adapted for the stretchers. It was an old-style ambulance train, where the carriages did not connect, which meant that when she went in search of water, she had to climb down onto the track to access the next carriage along. While the train was moving, of course, it was that much harder to move between carriages, as scrambling along the outside and trying to leap between coaches was strictly forbidden. But she knew that nurses and orderlies, for the sake of their patients, often disobeyed that order.

Jennings lowered herself onto the gravel and looked along the length of the train, towards the stream of white smoke that showed the position of the locomotive. It wouldn't do to hesitate and take in the view or enjoy the cool air on her face after the stifling heat and the smells of the interior. Ambulance trains had a tendency to move off without warning, and there were many tales of nurses, doctors or orderlies stranded as their transport chuffed off into the distance. She could see other figures at the side of the track a few carriages along. She could make out an orderly — the wall-eyed Beckett, judging by the size of him — and some of the less injured men, all smoking as if it might help get up steam for the loco.

'Have you any clean water in there?' she asked as she approached the cluster of men. New Zealanders, she noted. Mostly with head or shoulder wounds.

Beckett shook his head. 'Thimble full is about all, Nurse. We should be movin' soon, though, shouldn't we?'

17

'I have no idea, Beckett. That's in the lap of the gods and the French railways. It is hard to say who is more inscrutable.'

He rolled his eyes in sympathy. 'You're not wrong there, miss.'

As she passed she was aware of the men's heads swivelling to follow her. There were muffled words and what could only be described as a filthy laugh. She turned and stared at the group, holding their gaze until, one by one, they broke away and examined their boots or cigarette ends. 'Fag break over, I think, Beckett,' she said. 'Don't you?'

'Yes, Nurse. Come on, let's be havin' you.' He prodded one of the soldiers — his cranium swathed in stained bandages that needed changing — who flashed a sly smile that might have been an apology for whatever crudity they had shared.

Jennings waited, hands on hips, secretly pleased with herself, as they hauled themselves back up inside. The Jennings of two years ago couldn't have faced down lewd soldiers. She would have blushed and flustered. But there was little about these boys in men's clothing that could intimidate her now. And, despite the roughness of some of them, she always had to remember what they had been through.

She smiled at a young lad who had pressed his face to the window, flattening his nose into a grotesque shape, but he didn't respond. Becket appeared behind him and peeled him off the glass, leaving a fat streak of slobber and mucus, as if two amorous slugs had indulged themselves on the pane. The orderly made the universal symbol for someone who wasn't quite right in the head. Poor boy, she thought, returned to his mother in that state.

As Jennings turned to continue on down the line, she was confronted with a RAMC colonel and two adjutants stepping between the coaches. He stopped when he saw her and pointed with his swagger stick towards the carriages behind her.

'Any Chinkies up there?' he asked without anything approaching a preamble.

'Sir?'

'Chinese?' the colonel said. 'Do you have any Chinese on this train?'

She shook her head. 'Gurkhas. Sikhs, Mussulmans. Some Canadians and New Zealanders. The rest British.'

'No Orientals?'

She paused, as if considering this, but took the opportunity to look him up and down. Around forty, trim, with a rakishly thin moustache, but with broken veins on his face and nose, suggesting a fondness for the bottle. What have we here? she wondered.

'None that I can recall, sir.' She indicated the front of the train. 'Although I haven't seen in some of the compartments down there.'

The colonel slapped his thigh with the stick and turned to his young adjutants, both of whom looked as if they were clenching their buttocks very tightly. 'Well, that's a first-class cockup, isn't it? You've managed to lose a whole train.'

'Colonel Hartford, sir, the bombing at

Boulogne has disrupted everything — ' one of the adjutants began.

'Quiet! I don't need excuses from you.'

'Sir,' offered the second adjutant. 'This clearly isn't the right train. It was a six-carriage unit — '

'And you've never heard of two trains being linked together? Eh?' demanded Hartford.

The adjutant lowered his voice. 'Not one subject to an EXTO, sir.'

'What's an EXTO?' Jennings asked.

Hartford turned back to Jennings after she had spoken, as if he had forgotten she was there. 'Don't let us keep you, Nurse.'

'I need some fresh, clean water, Colonel. For my patients. We have been sidelined here for many hours now. Perhaps you can help us get a move on?'

The colonel looked as if she had asked for a slice of the moon. 'Help? I'm sorry, young lady, we have more important things to worry about. We've mislaid a train.'

Jennings felt a glow of anger. 'Yes. You said. Full of Chinese. From Noyelles-sur-Mer, I suppose.'

The colonel's eyes narrowed slightly. 'How on earth could you know that?'

'Well, it's common sense — '

'Yes, but how do you know there was a train from there?'

'I didn't know anything about a train, till you mentioned it,' Jennings said with some exasperation. 'I just put two and two together.'

'Did you? Did you indeed?'

'Look, if you would excuse me, I have a very

20

sick man in need of water. I hope you find your Chinese — '

As she tried to step round him, the colonel raised his stick so that it lay across her breasts. It felt like a terribly insulting and demeaning thing to do and she shuffled backwards on the gravel. 'Colonel, please. If you will let me pass, or I'll be forced to . . . '

Forced to what? She could think of no threat likely to dent this man's air of authority.

The loco emitted a quick, perfunctory whistle and, without warning, the train gave a lurch. Chains rattled and couplings groaned as the tension was taken up along the length of the train. Another jerk, a squeal of reluctant metal and within a few seconds it had accelerated to walking speed.

'Oh, no.' Nurse Jennings reached up an arm and readied herself for the jump, but as she did so, hands gripped her shoulder.

'Sorry, miss.' It was one of the adjutants.

She twisted away. 'Let go of me. How dare you?'

She could feel the breeze from the moving metal whipping at her face and her uniform. Already it was going too fast for her to risk jumping on board. She felt tears of frustration sting her eyes.

There was Major Ramsey at the window, face agog as he looked down at her. She tried to raise an arm, but it was slapped down.

In despair, she watched the terminal carriage of the train, the coach containing the infectious cases, disappear into the distance, a final whistle from the loco seeming to mock her.

'What are you doing?' she demanded. 'Why are you behaving like this? I am a British nurse — '

'That remains to be seen, doesn't it?'

'What on earth do you mean by that?'

'Lurking around trains, armed with information you have no right to.' The colonel touched his moustache and pointed to the staff car parked on the far side of the tracks, now revealed by the departed train. A driver stood to loose attention next to the front wheel, his fiercely polished buttons glinting with the rays of the dying sun. 'I think you'd better come with us, Nurse, so that we can get to the bottom of this.'

'What are you talking about, you pompous man? The bottom of what?'

The colonel was unfazed by her outburst. 'What exactly you know about Noyelles-sur-Mer.'

2

London was like a frightened child: cowering in the dark beneath the stairs, hands over eyes, hoping that the bogeyman who was out there would not find it. That is how it felt to Dr John Watson as he stepped out of the Wigmore Hall and into the last glow of twilight. Normally, the streetlamps would have been lit by now, but since the night raids on Chatham and Margate, the authorities had decreed the greatest city in the world should be plunged into darkness to foil the German bombers. Those few lights that were illuminated had to be blackened or greened, for it was indeed obvious the Germans weren't going to stop at coastal towns. They had already shown they could get through by day. Sooner or later, they would come for London by night.

Watson looked up at the sky. Not a star was to be seen. The thick, dull cloud was London's friend. It meant the Germans could not see the river, which pointed like a wayward silvered arrow to the beating heart of the metropolis — the city, the docks and the warehouses. So they were likely safe from the Hun's bombs that night.

As the concertgoers swirled around him, Watson turned to his companion for the evening performance, Sir Gilbert Hastings. Watson was wearing his RAMC uniform; Sir Gilbert was dressed as if for a night at the opera, one of the few men in the audience in full formal evening wear. As with any public gathering in the capital, military outfits predominated and any civilian men increasingly wore the modish lounge-style suits.

'Splendid,' said Sir Gilbert. 'Especially the Elgar.' He leaned in and lowered his voice. 'But, Lord, I do miss some Beethoven.'

Watson could only nod his agreement. Rationing extended as far as music — there would be no works by German or Austrian composers performed for the duration, by popular demand. And by popular threat. An attempt to play a Bach recital in an East End church the day after a Gotha bombing raid had killed eighteen schoolchildren at Upper North Street School had caused a riot. It had resulted in a badly damaged organ and a very traumatized organist.

But in truth, Watson hadn't particularly enjoyed any of the concert. Although his appreciation of good food and strong drink had returned over the months since the incident at Liverpool Street, it was still as if some key ingredient for his appreciation of music had been snuffed out. Before the war, he could remember being thrilled by the *Enigma Variations* and the Tallis *Fantasia*, both of which had been on the programme this evening. But, while he appreciated the precision of the playing, a rarity these days when the ranks of musicians had been depleted by conscription, he was not moved. He had forgotten what it was like to be moved. He remembered how a sublime passage could

24

transport him beyond quotidian cares. Now, all he could hear was artifice, the cheap manipulation of notes and chords creating false sentiment or an illusion of transcendence. But he knew the music hadn't changed. He had. Some capacity for pleasure had died on a bridge in Holland.

Watson held out his hand and Sir Gilbert took it. 'Same time next week?' Sir Gilbert asked. 'Chopin.'

'I'll check my duty roster,' said Watson. He liked Sir Gilbert's company. He was an excellent surgeon, based at Moorfields, and a man who appreciated a comfortable silence and was not prone to mindless gossip. Watson had met him when he had been giving evidence about so-called shell shock and psychological damage to the War Injuries Compensation Board, on which Sir Gilbert served. They had continued the discussion over dinner at the Criterion, and Watson had found him a convivial companion. But Watson was in no frame of mind to be tied down by rigid social engagements. Sometimes only the work kept him sane. And he was not sure his fragile soul could take an evening of Chopin.

'ONE HUNDRED PER CENT!' The cry made Watson start and he turned just in time to see the crude missile arc over his shoulder and land in Sir Gilbert's chest, where it exploded with a whoosh, covering both of them with a fine patina of white powder.

Sir Gilbert, stunned by the impact, staggered back, but was saved from falling by members of the crowd.

Watson turned to confront the assailant, who was dimly illuminated by the foyer lights of the Wigmore Hall. He was young, under thirty, with untidy hair and a look of ragged hatred on his face. He was wearing a tweedy lounge suit, dusted with some of the flour he had thrown, with a medal ribbon in the buttonhole. Watson went to reach for the man's lapel, with a view to detaining him, but a remarkably strong blow dashed his hand away.

'One hundred per cent!' he yelled again and turned on his heels. One brave soul, an elderly gentleman of seventy or thereabouts, tried to block his path, but again the arm lashed out and the man stumbled backwards, blood oozing from an eyebrow. Nobody else attempted to apprehend the crazed assailant after that and he was able to sprint off into the darkness that was wrapping itself around the streets of London.

Watson quickly examined the wound of the brave old man, but it was simply a split in thin skin. 'I'd have knocked him down ten, fifteen years ago,' he said, as Watson mopped up the blood. 'And boxed his ears to boot.'

'I think we are both too old for this malarkey, don't you?'

'What was it all about?' the man asked. 'Robbery?'

It wasn't such a foolish question as it seemed. The blackout of London had seen a surge in petty crime. Watson instinctively checked the pockets of his tunic, but his wallet, cigarette case and army pay-book were all in place.

After delivering his patient to a doorman at

the Wigmore — the venue had a first-aid kit containing small adhesive bandages that would do the trick — Watson turned back to Sir Gilbert, who was busy trying to dust his ruined topcoat. 'Bloody fool.'

'Do you know him?' Watson asked.

'I know his type,' snarled Sir Gilbert.

'You all right, sir?' A policeman about the same age as Watson had emerged from the gloom. Watson felt at a pang of guilt, as he always did at the sight of a uniformed bobby, remembering the poor chap whose body had saved him from the worst of the blast at Liverpool Street.

'Yes, officer, yes. Can you fetch me a taxicab?'

The policeman looked around, bemused. Thanks to the petrol shortage, motor taxicabs were rare beasts, even in the West End.

'Underground's best bet. Although the stations are filling up fast, even around here.'

Sir Gilbert's expression showed what he thought of that suggestion of using the Tube system. Platforms were increasingly crowded with families seeking shelter from the yet-to-materialize night raiders. The thought of the mass of commoners congregating down there was enough to keep respectable folk like Sir Gilbert firmly above ground.

'I'm only round the corner in Wimpole Street,' offered Watson. 'My housekeeper will help clean you up or you can borrow a coat of mine. And there's brandy to steady the nerves.'

The thought of alcohol seemed to lift the surgeon's mood. 'Ah. Very well. Lead on. Thank you, Officer.'

The darkness had congealed in the short time since the attack, so the air resembled a shroud of thick black velvet cloth. The walk to Wimpole Street necessitated stepping very carefully, with slow, exaggerated motions, through the unfamiliar blackness, avoiding the self-absorbed figures that occasionally loomed out of the shadows. Sometimes the glow of a cigarette, the rustle of a dress or the tap of a cane was the only warning of the presence of a fellow pedestrian, and in some places, Watson was reduced to groping along the wall, even though he knew these streets well enough in daylight. How he missed the fluidity of his youth at times like this, a body seemingly built of elastic, able to swerve around opponents, leaving them grasping air, almost dancing along the rugby pitch, knowing there was an explosive burst of energy still in reserve if needed. His stock of spare energy, these days, was very depleted.

Crossing the street was particularly hazardous; one had to wait at the kerbside, ears pricked for the clop of hoofs, the clatter of a motor engine or the bell of a tram, for any lights on vehicles were meagre indeed — a slit of illumination at best. Then it was a headlong dash, as if running over no man's land, Watson thought, hoping not to get cut down halfway across.

'One hundred per cent of what?' Watson asked once they were heading north. 'That young man and his flour grenade, he kept saying one hundred per cent.'

'Compensation,' Sir Gilbert replied. 'The board has decided to offer a hundred per cent of a pension only to those who have lost two limbs or more.'

'Yes, I read something of the sort,' said Watson, recalling a *Times* leader on the subject. 'But one hundred per cent of how much? I mean, what is the core figure? What is the most a soldier can expect?'

'Ah, well, we await the Treasury's decision on that. You remember Lord Arnott? Of the Bank? He's the Treasury liaison. There's a lot of argy-bargy at the moment — what we think is fair, what the Treasury claims it can afford, that sort of thing. We have settled on forty shillings a week for an enlisted man, although we are still arguing about the rate for officers, but there are already those who feel our new sliding scale is unfair. As if it were possible to please every — ' He stumbled slightly on an uneven pavement and Watson steadied him. 'Some would say that, I don't know, blindness should carry equal weight to the loss of a limb. Not that the hooligan tonight was blind.'

'No, I would say your attacker has lost but one limb.'

'How do you know that?'

'Well, my thumb is still throbbing from the blow he struck. Yet it was hardly delivered with any great force. And the chap who tried to stop him from fleeing? Opened his brow up like one of those hookless fasteners. Wood or ceramic, I would say. His false hand, I mean.'

'Well, he won't be getting anything close to a hundred per cent for that, no matter how much he protests. And he can't be that poor if he can afford to throw flour around in these straitened times.'

'I don't envy you the job of deciding men's fates. Just on the left here, there's a corner.' He steered Sir Gilbert around the junction. 'It can all seem very arbitrary to an outsider. One arm is worth this, an eye that.' And, he thought, what was psychological trauma worth in the grand scheme of things? But he didn't want to raise that subject just now. His view that it should be considered every bit as debilitating as physical injury had caused some violent disagreements within the Board.

'Somebody has to make these decisions,' snapped Sir Gilbert. 'It's very simple — how does it affect your manliness? Are you one hundred per cent of a man? Fifty per cent?'

Watson considered again the neurological cases he had witnessed and sometimes treated, their 'manliness' stolen by the intense mental damage the war had wrought. Sir Gilbert, he knew, was one of those sympathetic to soldiers suffering non-physical damage, and had lobbied to have it included in the compensation tables. Others on the War Injuries Compensation Board, however, believed the only wounds that counted were those that destroyed flesh and bone, those that they could put their fingers into, like some latter-day Doubting Thomas.

'Not too far now,' said Watson, taking the surgeon's arm. 'So you know who did this to you? Who that fellow represented?'

'I have a suspicion. They picketed the Board last week.'

30

'Hush,' Watson said, harsher than he intended. 'What is it?'

'Listen.'

A bell, tolling frantically, but some way distant. Not a church bell. A tram? No, there were no tracks allowed in the West End. It was a handbell.

Watson stopped and waited, and it was but a few moments before he heard the sound that would soon freeze all of London's blood in its veins. It was coming from high above the blanket of cloud, the layer he thought might offer some protection. But no, they had come anyway. The low thrum of engines announced their arrival. To the north, the gun battery known as 'Union Jack' opened fire, a jagged pyramid of light signalling the first discharge. Windows rattled nervously in their frames with each boom. The battery was firing blind, but then the bombers about to drop their loads were also trusting to dumb luck to make their aim true. 'Honeysuckle' battery offered a sustained salvo, the sky above the rooftops shimmering bright with the muzzle flashes. Next came the searchlights, probing upwards like spokes of a wheel, but finding only the featureless underside of the clouds.

'Take cover!' Another handbell rang from just behind Watson and Sir Gilbert and a police whistle sounded. There would be no maroons, the roof-fired rockets that alerted the populace during daylight — the authorities considered the sleep of munitions workers to be sacrosanct. Quite how they would sleep through the subsequent detonations of bombs wasn't clear.

31

'Take cover!' the policeman yelled again.

From every direction, or so it seemed, came the slap of leather soles and the ring of hobnails on pavements as the spectres around them broke into a run. One of them careened into Sir Gilbert, spinning him around. Watson gathered him close and propelled him forward, goaded into an undignified sprint as the air pulsed with the sound that London — and Watson — had learned to dread ever since the first bombing raid in June. That had been in daylight; the throbbing somehow seemed far more sinister at night. It was the Gotha Hum.

3

It wasn't a squadron or even a half-squadron of Gothas generating the hum across central London that was often likened by those below to the noise created by a monstrous bee trapped in an enormous bottle. It was a single solitary plane, but it sounded like a whole squadron of Gothas.

High above the clouds that blanketed London, the lone bomber that had caused panic on the streets was not a Gotha, but the first of the latest German bombers. The four-engined, Maybach-powered Zeppelin-Staaken R.VI was better known as a *Riesenflugzeug* — a 'giant aircraft' — or R-type. And giant it was. With four engines, a wingspan of 42 metres and a crew of nine, chosen from the elite of the England Squadron, it was a monster of the night sky.

Above the cotton-wool layer that sealed in London, the night sky was blazing with stars, bright enough to cast a faint shadow of the plane on the tops of clouds that glinted like new marble. It was a feeling of both great power and great solitude, thought Oberleutnant Schrader, the man chosen to command this first, tentative mission over the enemy capital by an R-Type.

Using primitive radio-beacon navigation, Oberleutnant Heinrich Schrader of the *Englandgeschwader*, the England Squadron, had nursed the enormous creature over the North Sea, making landfall just south of Margate and then turning north-west, floundering a little until, thanks to a rip in the clouds, he managed to find the Thames. Then he directed the senior pilot, Leutnant Hermann Deitling, a foul-mouthed but talented Swabian, to keep the river on the port side of the bomber, navigating by gyrocompass and the star Arcturus, a celestial body that always seemed to favour the German's missions.

The commander had his orders: he was under no circumstances to bomb Buckingham Palace — the Kaiser would not countenance his relatives being killed in an air raid. But anything else was considered a legitimate target. 'Fortress London,' they called it. Every sweatshop down there was making uniforms, boots, webbing, bullets, bicycles — all the machinery of war. The whole city was militarized, all of it fair game.

At least, that was what Schrader told himself; had done so on every Gotha raid. The commander had been a fighter pilot, a hero of Bloody April when the German high-speed, twin-gunned Albatros fighter had blown the RFC out of the sky, but a shrapnel wound to his shoulder had left him with limited movement. Hence his transfer to bombers. Fighting one-on-one with the British had seemed a very different kind of war, nobler and fairer than bombing. And besides, he had a secret. He liked London. Schrader had visited as a young boy with his father, who had been almost over-whelmed by the demand for black cloth from his factories in the wake of Queen Victoria's death. He had brought Heinrich across with him to witness the funeral and the vast inland sea of mourning clothes that the city became. Schrader had liked London, loved its energy and its centre-of-the-world arrogance.

And now he was helping destroy it.

The British newspapers would have them believe that every bomb hit only hospitals, schools and churches, but he hoped that was just propaganda. Besides, if his raids shortened the war, then he was doing some good. The fact a machine as vast as the R.VI, with a wingspan that made it look like some prehistoric bird, could fly over and bomb London would surely dent the British sense of superiority. U-boats at sea, R-types in the air, and the likelihood of tens of thousands of German troops released from the Eastern Front now that Russia had problems at home — the war was definitely going the Kaiser's way. Perhaps, Schrader thought, he would be seeing London again soon, this time as a victor of war.

At seventeen thousand feet, even travelling at a ponderous 130 kilometres an hour, Schrader knew his Giant was immune to enemy fighters. As with the nimbler Gothas, it would take night-fighters too long to reach a height where they could be a threat. In their enclosed cockpit, plugged into electrically heated suits, with oxygen bottles to gulp on, the R-type bomber crew felt invincible in a way the Gotha fliers never could. Not that the Gothas were done yet — it was rumoured to cost half a million marks to produce one R-type. Which meant the fleets of bombers the England Squadron planned to send over London before the month was out would have to be a mix of the cheaper Gothas and the new Giants.

Schrader looked down the bombsight tube but, apart from the odd flicker of an explosion from an anti-aircraft gun or a sudden finger of light from a searchlight poking through cloud, there was little to see.

He checked the map again. By his reckoning, he was over the East End and the docks. Time for the R-type's other innovation. Bomb doors, electrically operated. To think, just a few years before, they had been tossing grenades and sticks of dynamite out of aircraft by hand. Now there was a dedicated bomb bay, racks with release systems and a payload of a ton, including incendiaries.

When the England Squadron had been formed to succeed the Zeppelins, its mission had been to set London ablaze — the so-called 'Fire Plan'. But the incendiaries had proved unreliable at best, so they had added High Explosive to the mix once more. In truth, Schrader didn't want to burn the city to the ground. But he did want Germany to win the war.

'Bomb doors open,' the commander said, and felt the aircraft judder slightly as the metal flaps lowered into the night air, increasing drag.

Schrader pressed the button that opened the clamps holding the mixed payload in place. The commander's stomach somer-saulted as the plane leaped upwards.

'Bombs released.'

4

'And how is Mr Holmes?'

Watson took a piece of cheese from the tray and popped it into his mouth. He and Sir Gilbert were in the basement of his Upper Wimpole Street apartment, which in turn sat above an ophthalmic practice. The cellar was low ceilinged but dry, lit by yellow-flamed paraffin lamps that emitted threads of black smoke into the air, like a fine cotton yarn. It was furnished with two rather threadbare but comfortable wing chairs. Mrs Turner, Watson's housekeeper, had her own area next door, equipped with a single gas ring, table and bentwood chair, where she was busy dealing with Sir Gilbert's flour-splattered outer clothes. They could hear the rhythmic shushing of the brush, interrupted every now and then by a loud tut from Mrs Turner.

'Holmes? As well as can be expected,' Watson said flatly before taking a sip of cognac from a balloon glass.

'Oh dear, that doesn't sound encouraging,' said Sir Gilbert, helping himself to a Bath Oliver and snapping it in half.

Watson was tired of answering questions about Holmes. Leave the man be. When they had been unable to locate Frank Shackleton — Watson had tended to the dying and injured at Liverpool Street in the aftermath of the bombing and the

37

trail had gone cold — Holmes had returned to his bees, where he was content. He sent the occasional letter to confirm that, no, he did not miss London or his old life at all. Not one bit of it. But if there was anything vexing Watson, perhaps he'd get in touch . . . ?

Watson lit a cigarette, wondering while he did so what was going on above ground. If there was, indeed, anyone left above ground. It seemed to him that London was in danger of becoming a troglodyte city, where people lived and died in the Underground stations or the tunnels under the Thames that had been colonized ever since the Zeppelin raids of 1915. Hadn't H.G. Wells prophesied something like that? Watson sometimes felt he was living in that damned man's fiction, especially after nearly losing his life in a 'land ironclad', as Wells had called the tank.

Watson could feel the cloud of gloom creeping over him, as insidious as any poison gas. The sensible thing to do now was to be quiet, to pretend to doze. Instead, he felt something sparking in his brain, goading him towards confrontation.

'Have you ever loved anyone, Sir Gilbert?'

Sir Gilbert, about to light his own cigarette, paused, his brow furrowed into sharp ridges. 'Not even my wife asks me that question,' he said, once he had put match to tobacco. 'And very few Englishmen would broach the subject. I love my country, if that's — '

'Anybody,' insisted Watson. 'Not anything. Not any high-falutin concept of patriotism. People, I mean.'

Sir Gilbert shrugged, his eyes betraying the confusion at the turn the conversation had taken. 'As men, I don't think we examine such things too closely — '

'Perhaps not closely enough,' suggested Watson. 'I have loved several times, I believe, and always had it snatched away from me. If one were a superstitious man, one might think it a curse. Perhaps those who are incapable of love have it easier.'

Sir Gilbert sucked on the cigarette and shifted in his seat. He wondered if Watson was referring to his old colleague, whom he had, after all, once described as an automaton. 'Are you talking about *Holmes?*'

Watson gave a hollow laugh. 'I am talking about Mary and Emily and . . . ' just a beat of hesitation, ' . . . Georgina, if I am frank.'

Sir Gilbert had heard something of what Watson had suffered as a prisoner of war in Germany the previous year and of the strange aftermath to his incarceration that took place on a bridge in Holland, when a friend of his had been shot by a sniper. He had also noticed the man's rather peculiar mood swings of late, which he put down to these events and the trauma of being caught up in the first Gotha bombing raid on London. In his experience, nobody came back from the war unscathed, although that was not always a popular position with the other members of the War Injuries Compensation Board.

'Unlucky, perhaps, rather than cursed. And you have been through a lot.'

'Not just me.' Watson smiled. 'You asked how Holmes was and I said, 'As well as could be expected.' What I meant was, as well as could be expected after facing up to his own demise.'

Watson stubbed out his cigarette and took some more of the excellent brandy.

'He's ill?'

'No, but he has stared death in the face, felt its warm breath on his cheek. He knows it is waiting for him now.'

'You'd best explain,' said Sir Gilbert huffily, not liking the glazed look in Watson's eyes.

Watson blinked as if he knew what Sir Gilbert was thinking and fixed him with a steady gaze. 'Not so long ago, Holmes was willing to lay down his life for mine. I was in a POW camp in Germany. A very wicked place. He planned to deliver himself into the arms of the German Intelligence machine in exchange for my release and then, when they were poised to crow about it, to snatch victory away from them by committing suicide.'

'Good Lord. That's a strange way of winning.'

'But I have no doubt he intended to go ahead with it. Had I known this then, perhaps I would have taken the honourable course and removed myself from the equation.'

'Also by suicide?'

'By taking my own life, yes.'

Sir Gilbert gave a grunt. 'I can't say I approve of such thoughts.'

Watson nodded. 'There was a time when I would have agreed with you. But how long do I have left on this earth, Sir Gilbert? Five years?

Ten?' He looked up and pointed at the ceiling. 'Even now, a bomb could be on its way down, ready to drill through Number 2 Upper Wimpole Street, as it did through Upper North Street School those few months ago, and reduce us to dust.'

Sir Gilbert took solace in a large gulp of cognac. 'I rather hope not.'

'Well, right at this moment, so do I.' Watson smiled. 'Mainly because of you and Mrs Turner. My point is, if it did happen now, or in five years or ten minutes, what is the difference in the long run? My work, my small contribution to this world, is over. It might be time to make a dignified exit.'

Sir Gilbert, much concerned at such maudlin talk, reached across and put a hand on Watson's knee and squeezed. 'Surely not, Watson. Surely there are more stories you need to tell? The world is hungry for Holmes. I heard the new *Strand* sold out in hours and had to be reprinted. All because it contained the first Holmes story for quite some time.'

'The first short story, yes, since before the war. But I did not call it 'His Last Bow' for no reason.' This was the tale of Holmes and Von Bork, the German agent, whom the detective had thwarted on the eve of the war. Watson had been contractually obliged to write it, or at least had been fulfilling a promise made by Mrs Gregson to the editor that he would deliver another adventure for publication. Now it was out there with the public, he felt no urgency to write up any more of the handful of untold tales

41

in his possession. 'There will be no more Holmes stories.'

What? No 'Thor Bridge', no 'Mazarin Stone', no 'Sussex Vampire'?

Of late, Watson had ignored the spectral voice in his head. Now he answered: No, Holmes, those tales can die with us.

Sir Gilbert leaned forward, concern etched on his features. 'Are you feeling all right, Watson? I have a colleague in Harley Street who deals with melancholia . . . '

'Take no notice of the major,' said Mrs Turner, as she came through, holding a severely brushed topcoat. 'He gets these black moods now and then. They come like rain squalls, and then they're gone.' She glared disapprovingly at Watson, her eyes bulging from her bony face. 'Mostly, whenever cognac is involved. It's a wicked kind of balm, if you ask me.'

'Morlocks!' Watson exclaimed.

'I beg your pardon?' Mrs Turner asked, taken aback by the force of the exclamation.

'Morlocks,' Watson continued in a softer tone. 'H.G. Wells postulated we might turn into troglodyte cannibals if we spend too long underground. Morlocks, they were called.'

Sir Gilbert caught Mrs Turner's eye and noted the landlady's almost imperceptible shake of the head. 'Well, I wouldn't have too many ideas about eating a stringy old bird like me, Major Watson.' She held up the garment. 'I've got most of it out. I'm sure your valet will complete the process, Sir Gilbert.'

'Thank you, Mrs Turner. A splendid job. At

least, I think a cabby might pick me up now.' His eyes flicked to the ceiling. 'Do you think it's . . . ?'

'Safe?' asked Watson. 'I don't know.' He stood, not at all steady on his feet, and his companions realized that a hefty proportion of the brandy bottle had disappeared without their really noticing. 'But I've come to a decision tonight.'

'What's that?'

'No more lurking in basements. What will be, will be.'

Mrs Turner smiled. 'Well, if you don't mind, sir, I will stay down here for a few more hours. I'll put some cocoa on.'

'I'm going up top. No more Morlocking down here for me.'

'Are you absolutely sure you're feeling all right, Watson?'

'Yes, Sir Gilbert,' he declared with an intensity that took the surgeon back. 'Never better! Never better. Shall we go and take some air and see if the bugles have sounded and procure you a motor taxi?'

5

They found the missing train in another siding, where leggy purple-flowered weeds grew confidently between the sleepers. It had been abandoned by its locomotive, dumped like an unwanted child. Six carriages, the windows barred on the outside, the glass steamed up with hot breath from within.

Colonel Hartford ordered his driver to pull over and leaped out, his face close to puce with anger. Nurse Jennings twisted away, breaking the adjutant's grip on her arm, and followed the colonel into the clearing. The sun was falling fast, the shadows of the trees that enclosed most of the siding lengthening, the air taking on a grainy, photographic quality as dusk approached. She could hear, even at a distance of several hundred yards, the low chatter and the moans of pain coming from within the train, even if she could not see clearly what it held. There were other sounds, too: the chirp of evening birdsong and, a constant low note, the grumble of the guns at the front.

'How long has that been there?' Jennings asked as she walked up behind the colonel, who stood with his hands on hips, as if surveying a battlefield.

'I have no idea. But it went astray this morning.'

'They'll be thirsty in there. Frightened.'

44

'That is the least of my worries.'

'Because they are . . . ' she let her disapproval wrap around the word, ' . . . Chinkies?'

'Because I have my orders!' the colonel said heatedly. 'Heads will roll for this. Shaw! Shaw!' One of the adjutants appeared. 'Go back to that station we passed and get me a locomotive. At once.'

'Sir.'

'And, Shaw.'

'Sir?'

'Use your revolver if you have to. I don't care how many Frenchmen you have to shoot — just get me a loco to take this to Calais and the *Dover Arrow*.'

The *Dover Arrow*? She remembered that from before the war: one of those boats where the whole train could be rolled onto the ferry without having to disembark the passengers. It had operated for a scant few months before the war intervened. If only they could do that for every ambulance train, the amount of distress from loading and reloading the wounded — and time men spent suffering on quaysides and platforms — would be greatly reduced.

As Nurse Jennings walked towards the carriages, she heard the slap of palms on glass. Faces were appearing from the gloom within and pressing at the steamed-up windows as sleeves wiped crescents of glass clear. They were indeed Chinese faces, their features almost comically contorted as they shouted at her. One of the carriages began to rock as the bodies threw themselves at the side closest to her. A pane of

45

glass cracked with the sound of a whiplash under the press of bodies. Nurse Jennings felt a flash of fear and took a step backwards before she composed herself.

She turned slightly and yelled to the colonel, 'What's wrong with them? Why are they in there?'

'Wrong? Nothing's *wrong* with them. They mutinied. Refused to move our dead. Some superstition about restless spirits following them around. They are being shipped back home.'

The Chinese, so she had heard, were being used as manual labourers — some as trench-builders and gravediggers, other to construct or extend the narrow-gauge railways crisscrossing the hinterland of the trench system. As she had explained to the colonel, she knew about Noyelles-sur-Mer because there had been talk of setting up a Chinese-only hospital there and a call had gone out for Mandarin and Cantonese speakers. The best she could manage was St Kitts patois.

She moved closer and within six feet she could smell them. There was a thin, brown liquid running from the train, no doubt from a makeshift latrine of some description. Yet there was more than just excrement, she could smell something more corporeal, unmistakable after her years in the canvas wards of the CCS: the stench of high fever. And here and there on the windowpanes, she could now make out the tell-tale splatter pattern of coughed-up blood. There was more banging. Another of the panes cracked and this time a sliver of glass fell free.

Now she could hear the pleas to open the carriages, the tone clear even if she didn't understand the language.

She retraced her steps. 'Colonel? These men are sick.'

'Well, they might be now.'

'They need water. Lots of it. That station you mentioned will either have clean water or it will have the facilities for boiling it. I shall distribute it among the men.'

'You can't go in there.'

'And why not?'

The colonel rubbed his chin, perplexed. 'This is not your concern.'

'You made it my concern by kidnapping me.'

'I did not kidnap you.'

From beyond the trees came the sound of a locomotive whistle.

'Believe you me, Colonel, I know nothing about these men. I am not, as you seem to think, some sort of spy. I am a nurse. And as a nurse my job is in there.' She pointed to the carriages.

The colonel shook his head and muttered to himself.

'What?'

'I can't let you in. The doors are locked.'

'And you have a key?'

'I do.'

'Then I suggest we get the water, you open the door — '

'And let these mutineers escape?'

'And then lock me inside.'

The colonel looked at her as if she had quite taken leave of her senses. 'Why one earth would you do that? They're savages — '

'Who are the savages here, Colonel? The men locked in the carriages? Or the men who put them there?'

'They'll tear you limb from limb.'

'I'll take my chances.'

'Or they'll do worse than that.' He flushed slightly. 'You are a white woman — '

'I am an Englishwoman!' she snapped, reverting to language he might understand. At times like this, she only had to ask herself one question: what would dear Mrs Gregson say? 'And, by God, I shall do my duty as one. You lend me your revolver if it will help salve your conscience, but believe me, one way or another I am going in there and I am going to do my job. I am beginning to think it was no accident that God brought me here, Colonel. He moves in mysterious ways.'

'He's not the only one. Bradley!' Colonel Hartford turned to the second adjutant. 'Take the car. Go to the station, bring as much clean water as you can carry.'

'Sir.'

'And I'll need lamps, in case the power supply has failed. It is pretty dark in there now,' Nurse Jennings interrupted.

'And, Bradley?'

'Sir?'

'Find out what's happened to our bloody loco, will you?' He turned back to Jennings. 'And let me make one thing clear. Once you step into those carriages, you are no longer my responsibility. On your own head be it.'

'Would you like that in writing?'

The colonel unbuttoned his tunic pocket. 'As a matter of fact, I would.'

6

There had been a time when the ambulance trains arrived in London by day. There would be brass bands, flag-waving, crowds of welcoming relatives and well-wishers. Despite the terrible injuries of the men being unloaded, a party atmosphere prevailed. People were proud of what these men had achieved, of the punishment they had taken for their King and Country. Well, the party, if that's what it had been, was well and truly over. Now, the troop trains taking those to the front left in daylight; the ambulance trains skulked in at night, as if, Watson couldn't help but feel, they carried a shameful secret.

Watson accepted a cup of tea from the VAD who was serving at Lady Limerick's free buffet at Victoria Station, which offered complimentary refreshments to those coming from or going to the front, as well as to the odd doctor on duty.

'Have you heard?' the young woman asked.

'About?' replied Watson.

'Liverpool Street Station. Hit by firebombs earlier tonight.'

'What, again?' Watson said.

'Yes. Direct hit on an ambulance train as it pulled into the platform. Incinerated the lot.' She gave a shudder and wiped her hands on her once-white apron.

So the bombers he and Sir Gilbert had heard had already shed their lethal load by the time

50

they came overhead and caused the panic on the streets of the West End. A railway station, he supposed, was at least a legitimate target of sorts. But the horrible irony of the wounded making it home to London, only to be immolated by a German bomber, was not lost on him.

'You all right, sir?' the VAD asked.

Watson had spilled his tea in his anger. 'Yes, sorry.'

He turned back and looked around the station concourse. The ambulances were waiting, so were a few forlorn-looking relatives, although such was the volume of casualties, one could never be certain which station any given ambulance train would arrive at. Charing Cross, Victoria and Waterloo were the main termini but last-minute diversions to Blackfriars or London Bridge were quite common.

He watched Captain Trenchard, an RAMC medic, emerge from the dispatch office and limp over towards him. Shrapnel, shattered femur, Ypres, he reminded himself. Though not yet twenty-five, his hair was streaked with grey, and he spoke with the weariness of an old man.

Trenchard was waving a sheaf of papers at him. 'Tonight's vacancies, sir,' he said, handing them over. 'Lady Cottle's been closed down, I am afraid. JJs.' Lice.

Many of the private hospitals that had opened at the start of the war in a flurry of charitable hubris — most of them aimed solely at officers and funded by well-to-do women — had found it hard to continue as the war dragged on. Watson knew of several where cleanliness was questionable, the care sporadic and the heating

51

unreliable, and he avoided sending men there unless the other hospitals were overflowing. He quickly examined the list that Trenchard had passed to him. Millbank had a decent supply of beds, as did Roehampton House and The Burlington Clinic, the latter being two of the better-funded private establishments.

'How many trains due?'

'Two tonight. Been some chaos on the other side, apparently.'

Trenchard checked his watch against the station clock and stifled a yawn. It was getting on for two in the morning. Watson could see he was thinking of his bed. 'Late tonight.'

There was a similar sense of restlessness coming from the ambulance drivers and their orderlies, who were standing around their machines, impatient for their customers to arrive. Many were on their second pack of Woodbines, judging by the litter of butts at their feet.

Watson wondered if Staff Nurse Jennings would be on one of these trains, as her telegram had suggested. What would the war have done to that fresh-faced nurse he had met at the field hospital in Flanders? It had changed them all, most physically. The obvious manifestation of the conflict could be seen on the streets, the disgrace of disabled soldiers reduced to begging while the Government squabbled over pensions and compensation. But it had altered the entire country mentally, possibly for ever, for the nation that once ruled most of the globe now knew the fear of an enemy — first with Zeppelins and now

52

by the hated Gothas — that could fly over it with impunity and kill its citizens in their beds.

What would two years of nursing on the front line have done to Staff Nurse Jennings? Put new lines on her face and scars on her soul, no doubt. He must not expect the bashful young girl of old, with her coy, dimpled smile and the light in her eyes. The war had a way of extinguishing such a blaze, replacing it with cold cinders. Still, it would be good to see a familiar, friendly face, and someone who had known, no matter how briefly, Mrs Gregson, the woman who had proved such a loyal and devoted friend that it had led her to a terrible death.

The thought of her caused him a spasm of pain and he quickly examined the list of hospitals again. Stay busy, that was his mantra. The stations at night, the hospitals by day, a petition to the compensation board here, attending lectures on new medical procedures at the Royal College of Physicians or a debate on the *Psychology of the Unconscious* at the University of London, writing a letter to his old friend, then some Elgar . . . and keep away from those idle moments when you find yourself on a bridge in Holland once more, unable, no matter how you try, to change the outcome —

It wasn't your fault, Watson.

It was nobody's fault but that damnable woman Miss Pillbody. Evil in a dress.

Quite.

Watson let out a long sigh and caught Trenchard's look of concern. 'I'm all right, lad. Just a bit tired.'

53

Watson took out a pack of Joy's Cigarettes — the ones that claimed to cure wheezing and asthma, although he had his doubts — and offered one to Trenchard. He lit both of them with a single match.

'How much will you get for the leg?' he asked. 'Compensation?'

'Gosh, I don't know. Haven't had my Board yet. Not much, I suppose. Not compared to some of these chaps . . . '

'And your brother,' Watson said, recalling what Trenchard had divulged one night as they had shared a flask of brandy.

Trenchard nodded. His brother was in Netley Hospital, a victim of vicious shrapnel burst. 'I don't know how he stays so optimistic. I'm not sure I would want to live like that.'

'You'd be surprised how much people want to live.'

'Why do you ask?'

Watson explained about the man shouting, 'One hundred per cent!' to Sir Gilbert earlier that night.

'Well, I have some sympathy. But you can't give everyone the same, can you? There isn't enough money to go around, is there? And I can still walk, after a fashion, and there is talk about perhaps a special shoe to help alleviate the limp.'

'What will you do? After the war?'

'I'm only qualified in battlefield medicine. I'd like to take the training further. That or the family business.'

'Which is?'

'If you lived in Berkshire, sir, the chances are

54

at least someone you knew would have been laid to rest by James Trenchard and Co. Undertakers. But part of me thinks perhaps I should switch sides — try to keep people out of my father's clutches for as long as possible.'

'How would your father feel about that?'

'Oh, as he always said when a new undertaker opened in the vicinity, there's always enough dead to go around.'

The truth of this made them pause and ponder for a while. It will seem strange, Watson supposed, going back to the rituals and homilies of the individual burial, when the passing of one single human is given such pomp and ceremony. How over-earnest and self-indulgent that seemed now after years of the lime pit and the 'Known Only Unto God' mass graves. Then again, perhaps when death became less commonplace, more noteworthy, it would be an important step back towards the world they lost in August 1914.

'Train coming,' said Trenchard, and sure enough, there was a multi-pointed star of light moving along the tracks towards them. Watson began to sort the sheets out, readying himself for the rapid assignment of hospitals and wards that was needed to make sure the platforms didn't become clogged with stretcher cases and walking wounded.

Already the stretcher-bearers were moving forward, trying to ascertain which platform the train would pull into. Ambulance engines were quickly cranked into life by the drivers, spewing fumes up into the cast-iron girders of the concourse roof as they waited at idle. There were fresh volunteers at Lady Limerick's free buffet, lining up mugs of tea for the traditional British welcome home for the wounded.

'Just the one?' Watson asked, throwing down his cigarette and stubbing it out with the toe of his Trenchmaster.

'Looks like it.'

'Might not be another tonight, not here. They've closed Dover and Folkestone harbours,' said a concerned voice from behind them.

Watson turned to be confronted by the elaborate grey moustaches of Sir Francis Lloyd, the man who effectively ran London these days, like a military governor. The ambulance trains only entered when he said so, spies were only shot when he agreed, anti-aircraft guns were sited only where he indicated, no free buffets or soldiers' rest houses opened without his approval.

'Why's that, Sir Francis?' Watson asked.

'Bloody Hun. They've sunk a boat-ambulance out of Calais. Fully marked up with its red crosses, clear as day, apparently. Can't reopen the ports till we're certain the bugger's not still out there, lurking like the dog it is. You know the drill — sink one ship, then wait till the rescuers come and sink them, too.'

'So we didn't send rescue ships out to this boat?'

Sir Francis avoided his gaze. 'I gather not.'

Watson closed his eyes, thinking of the wounded trying to tread water, weighed down by casts and bandages, incapacitated by fever, disease and amputation, desperately holding on for saviours who never came. 'Damn them.'

Sir Francis assumed he meant the German U-boat crews. 'Damnation is too good for them, Watson.'

The air was full of wet smoke and cinder now as the train approached, belching a plume of steam. Watson felt a growing sense of panic. He had to go and help with the trainload of sick and wounded, but some feeling of dread made him want to know more about events at sea. 'So no survivors?'

Sir Francis shook his head. 'Torpedoed. Out in the Channel, in the pitch-dark. Didn't stand a chance. All hands,' he said angrily. 'All hands.'

'Will there be a passenger manifest?'

'I expect so. I don't know.' Sir Francis caught the desperation in Watson's voice. 'You suspect someone you know was on there?'

'I can't be certain,' Watson said, the image of Staff Nurse Jennings unloading his blood transfusion kit, and of the distinctive little scar on her throat, flashing into his mind. But it'll be just my damned luck, he thought, but didn't say. Is anyone safe around me?

'Does the boat have name?'

Sir Francis consulted a telegram. 'Yes. The *Dover Arrow*.'

7

Fatigue had infected the crew by the time the coast of Belgium came into view. With the bomb load gone, on paper the R-type should have been capable of much more than 200 kilometres an hour, but truculent winds had buffeted the machine, making progress both slow and queasy.

Once they were clear of England and its defences, and had passed over *Tongue* lightship, Oberleutnant Schrader had ordered the pair of pilots — the R-type required two of them at the controls — to take the plane down to an altitude where the oxygen bottle was no longer needed. All they had to do was nurse her in and land. *All they had to do*, he repeated to himself, as if it were nothing. How many planes had been lost on the final approach? More Gothas than the British could claim, that was certain. And as for this unwieldy beast, with its 18-wheel under-carriage, one mistake and . . .

He broke out the coffee as they approached land, real coffee, strong enough to jolt them all awake, to give them the alertness that might mean they would survive to drink a schnapps in the mess before turning in.

'Eyes sharp, everyone,' Schrader said.

The British, unable to catch the bombers, had taken to attacking the home airfield, so the landing lights were kept extinguished at night. They would only be switched on when the Giant identified itself. The radio operator, therefore, began sending out a pulse of radio signals in the direction of the strip.

The pilots, Deitling and Fohn, took the plane down, and Schrader's ears popped. As they pierced the clouds he could see the dark, broiling waters beneath them. More than enough Gotha crews had ended in those unforgiving waves. Rescue was possible, thanks to fast search boats from Zeebrugge, but in practice it was a rarity.

'There!'

One of the pilots had spotted something. Schrader stood and peered into the darkness. Yes, a light — long, short, long, short. The Ostend Beacon. The Flanders coast was ahead.

As if over-excited at the news, one of the engines began to miss a beat, its steady pulse replaced by a jittery rhythm. All heard it and Schrader saw Fohn and Deitling exchanged glances as the aluminium sides of the Giant's cabin began to vibrate in sympathy. 'Too much coffee, perhaps,' he said, breaking the tension.

He could afford to be flippant, with a few dozen kilometres left to run. If the engines malfunctioned on the way out or some distance from the base, they had mechanics who would climb out on the wing, into the darkness, to be plucked at by the icy slipstream, and service them. Not a job for the faint-hearted. He wasn't going to send Rutter or Borschberg, the upper gunner/engineer, out at this point; with a trio of engines left they could glide in if need be, but it wouldn't come to that.

They ploughed on in silence, all alert to the

sound of the three healthy Maybachs, waiting for more evidence of malfunction, but none came.

'Ahead, skipper,' said Fohn eventually. A row of green lights flashed off and on three times, a brief come-hither from the Ghent airfield.

'Circle at five hundred metres,' Schrader instructed, 'until they give us the full set.'

He drained the last of the coffee and screwed the cup onto the flask. Mission almost accomplished. Soon he could let the tiredness wash over him. He could almost taste the welcome schnapps as the great biplane lurched into its holding pattern over the strip, waiting for the main landing lights to illuminate for just long enough to get them down. There was only one slight fly in the ointment of elation. The thought that tomorrow, they would have to go back to London and do it all again.

8

Three days after the sinking of the *Dover Arrow*, the event, along with the after-dark raid on London, still dominated the newspapers, driving even the new offensives in Flanders from the front pages. After a lengthy all-night shift settling the wounded into Millbank, many from those under-reported skirmishes around Ypres, Watson bought a *Pictorial* on the Embankment and set off to walk through Mayfair and Marylebone to his rooms in Wimpole Street.

The sun was up, and London's soot-stained buildings seemed a shade lighter as the rays probed the façades. It was hard to imagine this was a city that all but shut down once the sun had completed its arc through the sky and began to fall towards the horizon. Night had rarely been so unwelcome in London.

As he walked towards the park, he scanned the pages for more information on the sinking of the boat-ambulance. 'What happened to the Dover Light Barrage?' demanded a leader writer. A system of ships equipped with powerful searchlamps, magnesium flares and a drape of steel antisubmarine cable had been established between Dover and Calais. It was designed to deter U-boats, and had apparently worked until now, but one daring *Kapitan* had apparently crept in and done for the *Dover Arrow*.

The number of casualties — 139 — had been

published, but no full passenger list. Watson had no way of knowing if Staff Nurse Jennings was among those who had perished. The newspapers were claiming the names of the dead were being held back as a matter of 'national security' and so as not to give succour to the enemy. Which suggested some bigwigs had died in the attack — when Kitchener's ship hit a mine there had been a small but vocal minority in the cabinet who had wanted the news suppressed, fearing the impact on the public's morale. There was even talk of producing an impersonator to deny Kitchener had been killed at all. It was unlikely, however, that anyone as important as the Secretary of State for War was on the *Dover Arrow*. But whoever had perished, it was clear that a notice under the Defence of the Realm Act — DORA — had been served on newspaper editors, effectively muzzling them. To Watson, the thought that he might never know if Staff Nurse Jennings was on the *Dover Arrow* was almost unbearable.

The other topic exercising the contributors to the *Pictorial* was the weather. Nothing unusual in that for the British, except now London had started praying for *bad* weather. Watson looked at the sky as he crossed St James's Park. The clouds were mostly bone-white, but to the east was an ominous band of dark pewter and the *Pictorial* was forecasting strong winds out in the Channel and the North Sea and moonless nights. London could breathe easy, for a few days at least.

Still, there were obvious signs of government

jitteriness. The park was dotted with great mounds of sandbags, to be supplied free to Londoners. The night-time raids of the Zeppelins had caused a certain amount of consternation, but they had proved vulnerable to the incendiary shells of the ack-ack batteries and the phosphorescent bullets of the night fighters. These Gothas, however, flew high and fast, and apparently fearless, and were more robust than gasbags filled with flammable hydrogen. No, Watson was sure, the bombers would return. He just hoped the Government was using the lull to do more than fill sandbags.

The strain of the night had begun to seep into his bones by the time he let himself into 2 Upper Wimpole Street and climbed the stairs, one weary step at a time. His tread was heavy, as if the Trenchmasters had leaden soles.

He was halfway up when he realized he could hear voices, real ones, not those that sometimes played in his head these days. He could make out the high, fluting tones of Mrs Turner, but there was another, pitched at a far deeper register. Watson removed his cap, slicked back his hair and rose to his full height before opening the door to the sitting room.

Mrs Turner had served tea and was standing pouring a cup for the man who was perched on the edge of Watson's favourite armchair, one of the few items he had rescued from Baker Street.

'Ah, there you are, Major,' she said. 'I was just telling the inspector that you were a little late this morning.'

Inspector. There was a time when Watson knew almost every senior policeman in London, but this one was a stranger. He was early forties, barrel-chested, clean shaven, with calm, heavy-lidded eyes that suggested — erroneously, Watson was sure — a sleepy, docile personality. Very useful in a copper. The man sprang to his feet with an effortlessness Watson could only envy. No aching joints or stiff muscles there.

'George Bullimore,' the policeman offered, along with his hand, which Watson took.

'Major John H. Watson at your service, Inspector. How can I be of assistance? It's a long time since Scotland Yard came calling.'

'Bow Street, actually,' Bullimore corrected. 'And I am not calling upon you to engage you in your former capacity.'

'Please, sit down. Thank you, Mrs Turner,' Watson said as she handed him a cup of tea.

'I'll leave you to it, gentlemen. I'll run a bath, Major Watson, and prepare breakfast.' She turned to the policeman. 'Will thirty minutes be sufficient?'

'I'm sure my business will be complete by then,' said Bullimore.

Watson took a place on the couch and Bullimore fetched a notebook and pencil from his inside pocket. 'Firstly, Major, I hope you don't mind me asking . . . how is Mr Holmes?'

'Content in his retirement,' Watson said.

'Very good. He deserves it. Now, I am here about Sir Gilbert Hastings. You know the gentleman, I believe.'

'We share an appreciation of music, yes.'

'And you saw him, let me see, three nights ago?'

'The night of the air raid, yes. Why? If I might ask?'

Bullimore looked pained. 'Major Watson, we believe you were the last man to see Sir Gilbert before his disappearance. The final item in his appointment book was a night at the Wigmore with you.'

'Disappearance?'

'He failed to return home that night.'

'But I put him in a motor taxi.'

'What time was that, sir?'

'Just gone midnight, I think. The 'All Clear' bugles had been blown.'

Eyes flicked to the notebook. 'That was at eleven forty-seven. And how was his temperament?'

'Temperament?'

'Did he seem angry, depressed, agitated, worried?'

Worried about my state of mind, perhaps, Watson thought. I'm the one who is all of those things. 'As even-tempered and level-headed as always.'

'Did anything untoward happen during the course of the evening? Anything out of the ordinary.'

Don't give me that innocent look. You know damn well it did, thought Watson.

'One thing before I get to that. Three days have apparently passed. Why have you only just contacted me?'

'A number of reasons. Sir Gilbert was often enough in the habit of spending a night or two at his club and his failure to return home raised no eyebrows.'

65

'Not even from his wife?'

'Sir Gilbert had sent her to the country, along with the children. Evacuees, you might say . . . not uncommon among those that can afford it.'

'What about work? Didn't one of his hospitals miss him? Surely they noticed when one of the top surgeons failed to appear in the theatre?'

'He had taken a few days off. The final reason is . . . well, the police are ruinously understaffed at the moment, as you know. It is taking us two or three days to get around to most incidents. And a gentleman being a few hours overdue, having dispatched his wife to the country and booked some leave . . . '

'You thought a mistress might be involved.' It was a statement, not a question.

A nod of confirmation. 'Wouldn't be the first time.'

'I don't know him well, but I have no reason to believe Sir Gilbert kept a mistress. He didn't seem the type.'

That doesn't mean he didn't, Watson. Some men boast of such things, others prefer a little . . . discretion.

'Oh, be quiet.'

'Sir?' asked Bullimore, a concerned expression on his face.

'Nothing, Inspector. Just dismissing a theory. I speak out loud, sometimes. It's an affliction of age.' And an affliction of having a fictitious Sherlock Holmes inhabiting his cranium. 'Who raised the alarm then?'

'His valet, concerned that his clothes were

66

untouched and he must still be wearing evening dress. Can you tell me more about the night you had at the concert? Anything unusual happen?'

'There was one strange incident that night. It was outside the Wigmore Hall, following a concert we had attended. Elgar, Vaughan Williams, Dvorak . . . Debussy, yes. Debussy. The latter not entirely to my taste. Anyway, a young man . . . youngish anyway, attacked Sir Gilbert. With a sack of flour.'

'Flour?'

'Not a whole sack. There is rationing on, you know.'

Bullimore gave a wry smile. 'But it was only flour?'

'I'm almost certain. I didn't think to have it analysed. It smelled like flour, tasted like flour.'

'And were you hit with this floury substance?'

'A little light dusting . . . Do you think it may have been noxious in some way?'

Bullimore didn't reply.

'I have had no ill effects. Nor Mrs Turner, who must have breathed a considerable quantity when she was brushing down Sir Gilbert's coat.'

'We'll assume it was simply flour then. Tell me about the assailant.'

'Protestor as much as assailant.'

'Protesting about?'

'The deliberations of the War Injuries Compensation Board. I, we, had the impression he was disaffected, perhaps because his own injury was relatively minor.'

'Injury?'

'A false hand. Wood or ceramic. He struck me

67

a blow with it.' Watson held up his right hand, showing the faint blue bruise that remained. Old skin, he thought, marks more easily and heals much more slowly than the elastic covering of youth.

'Can you describe him?'

'Late twenties. Brown hair. Brown eyes. A chipped front tooth. Tweed lounge suit, not of the best quality, perhaps.' Oh, Holmes, you would have been able to pin him down to address, hobbies and occupation.

Once upon a time, perhaps. What about the medal?

'Ah, yes,' said Watson, as if the memory had just come flooding back to him. 'He had a medal ribbon in his buttonhole.'

'I don't suppose you know which one?'

'Which medal, you mean?' Watson said, playing for time.

'Yes.'

Watson squeezed his eyes shut and pictured the man stepping from the crowd, the yell of 'One hundred per cent!' on his lips. He urged his mind's eye to move down towards the collar of the jacket, and it did so but reluctantly. There was the ribbon . . .

In what colours?

They came into focus. A central band of golden yellow, with three stripes of white, black and blue running down each side. 'Mons,' Watson blurted.

'Mons?'

'The Mons Star,' explained Watson. 'Yellow, white, black and blue. That means it must have been the 1914 Star.'

68

Bullimore wrote this down. 'Forgive my ignorance, awarded for . . . ?'

'Those who served in France or Belgium between the 5th of August 1914 and midnight on the 22nd of November 1914 inclusive.'

'Ah. I didn't get out there until the end of 1915. Then got myself gassed. So, really it was for those in at the beginning. The Old Contemptibles.'

'It's broader than that. It covers British and Indian Expeditionary Forces, doctors and nurses, as well as anyone from the Royal Navy, Royal Marines, Royal Navy Reserve and Royal Naval Volunteer Reserve who served ashore in France or Belgium.' Mrs Gregson would have been due one, he thought, for she had spent time with a volunteer ambulance brigade in 1914, one of the first British women to see action near the front line. It had been a baptism of fire but, like tempered steel, she had come out of it harder and tougher.

Bullimore let out a sigh. 'Well, that hardly narrows it down. There must be hundreds, thousands, out there.'

'Yes, I think you have a pool of many thousands to fish in. But you think this attack is somehow linked to Sir Gilbert's disappearance?'

Bullimore scratched the corner of his eye. 'It's possible.'

'Are you suspecting foul play? Or an abduction?'

'There has been no demand, ransom or otherwise. I had the valet who reported him missing open all Sir Gilbert's correspondence. Nothing. I don't suppose you caught the number of the cab that picked him up?'

Watson shook his head. 'No. But . . . '

'But?'

'In hindsight, it was remarkably easy to find a taxi. Considering there had been an air raid. They tend to make themselves scarce when bombs are falling. It was outside here and put up its flag when we emerged onto the street.'

'Did you see the driver?'

'No. Not clearly. It was dark and he was wearing a muffler, as I recall. As we have established, I'm not a very good detective.'

The policeman stood. 'You've been most helpful, sir. Would you be amenable to a police artist making a sketch of this flour man?'

Watson also rose to his feet. 'Of course, Inspector, although sketchy will be the word. But any way I can help . . . '

Bullimore consulted the notebook one last time. 'As well as Sir Gilbert, do you perhaps know Professor Anthony Holbeck? Or Dr Adrian Powell? Or Lord Henry Arnott? Perhaps Professor Carlisle?'

'I know of them, have met them, in fact, but I can hardly claim acquaintance. Why?'

The notebook snapped shut like a bear trap. 'Thank you for your help, Major. If you think of anything else this is my number at Bow Street.' He laid a card next to the teapot. 'Just one word of advice . . . '

'What's that?'

'Knowing your reputation of old, I must remind you this is a police matter. Sir Gilbert may be a friend, but perhaps you and Mr

70

Holmes could leave this to the police?'

'Inspector, as I said, I am hardly the detective type and, as I also noted, Mr Holmes is contently retired.' Except in my head, he thought. 'You will not be tripping over us.'

When he had seen him out, Watson quickly scribbled the three names the inspector had mentioned on the back of the policeman's card. Holbeck, Powell and Arnott. There was another, wasn't there? Yes, Professor Carlisle of The London. He added that name to the list.

'The inspector has gone, has he?'

'Yes, Mrs Turner. Can my bath wait? I have to make some telephone calls.'

'Of course. I drew it hot just in case the inspector was one of those windbags. Oh, before you place your calls, two telegrams came earlier addressed for your urgent attention.' She fetched them from the mantelpiece.

One was from Sister Spence in France, asking if he had heard from Nurse Jennings, as her parents were concerned about her whereabouts. So she had not made it home. Had she indeed been on the *Dover Arrow?* Part of him had clung to the hope that she hadn't boarded that particular train, and now his heart fluttered nervously at the prospect that she really had perished at sea. If so, she'd be on that secret passenger manifest. But he knew a man who could cut through all that 'matters of national security' horse manure and find out for him.

The second telegram was the one that caused his pulse to race. 'Your presence is requested at 221b Baker Street as a matter of some urgency.'

71

9

A return to 221b was always a bittersweet affair for Watson. Much of the fabric of their old rooms was still recognizable, the wallpaper up the polished stairs, the fireplace, but at some point it had been tidied up, the windows flung open and the delicious, and sometimes not so delicious, smells of the detective and the doctor's tenure purged. It wasn't surprising. It was some years since they had lived there. Holmes had given up the rooms when he had moved to Sussex and Watson was living at his medical practice. Mrs Hudson had subsequently retired to the North Country and the building was now managed by a nephew of hers.

Watson returned to 221b on occasion to pick up the mail that still arrived for Holmes (the Post Office assiduously delivered even those marked simply 'Sherlock Holmes, London', to Baker Street) and, he had to admit, sometimes to wallow in nostalgia for days long departed. This time, though, he approached with a spring in his step, a fresh purpose in his mind. Two mysteries! What had happened to Nurse Jennings? And where was Sir Gilbert? Had he been abducted? Or suffered an accident? A loss of memory, perhaps? Or was he simply entertaining some younger woman in an unsuspected *pied-à-terre* somewhere in this anonymous city?

And a third, Watson. There is a third question to be answered.

Yes, of course. Who, exactly, had summoned him to their old chambers? For the telegram had been unsigned.

He raised the brass knocker and let it fall, remembering that sound from the other side, the thin thud that reached their sitting room, when Holmes's nostrils would flare and his head move to one side as he waited for Mrs Hudson or Billy to show the visitor up. The squeaky tread on the stairs. The protest of deliberately unoiled hinges. In some ways it was the most delicious few moments of any case: the anticipation of a singular problem that would engage that great mind for days or weeks to come.

The woman who flung open the door was neither landlady nor servant. She was short, perhaps not five foot, but she radiated an energy that Watson could feel across the threshold. It was like being under a radium lamp. Her blond hair was piled on top, adding a few precious inches, and she was wearing a modish wrap-around tunic in a bold chequered pattern. He caught a hint of citrus perfume.

'Dr Watson, I presume!' she exclaimed in an accent he placed as East Coast America. It was quite brash to his ears.

'Major Watson, yes.'

'Oh, come in, come in.'

He removed his hat and stepped inside the hallway.

'You know where to go.' She pointed up the stairs.

'I am afraid I am at a loss, Miss . . . did you send the telegram?'

'Forgive me. Yes. Elizabeth Buck.' She held out her hand. 'Of the *New York Reporter*. You can call me Betsy; everyone does.'

'Betsy Buck?' It sounded like a name from a theatre poster.

'My editor's idea. Thought it sounded more fun than Elizabeth. I told him, I'm not in this business to do fun. I want to do real journalism. But Betsy kind of stuck.'

'What happened to Mr Hammond? He was in residence on the last occasion when I called.'

'Gone. A mine in Rhodesia or some such. I rent the rooms now. While I'm in London, that is. I hope, of course, to go to France.'

'France?'

'To the war! I am a reporter, Dr Watson, and I intend to cover the entry of our boys into the war. Go on up . . . Oh, that's your mail; you can collect it later. You get rather a great deal, huh? Or rather your old friend and colleague does. Hup, come on.'

Watson barely managed a glance at the stack of papers before he was driven up the stairs like an errant sheep by a keen collie. He would have to deal with that teetering pile at some point. He had a standard card: 'Mr Sherlock Holmes appreciates you getting in touch with him concerning your problem, but unfortunately he is not in a position . . . '

Most of the conundrums the correspondents sent were nothing of the sort, being more often than not merely vague accusations (Mr X is a

74

German spy, Mrs Y murdered her husband). But there was normally one that caused something to twitch inside, that bore reading once or twice . . . Eventually, though, Watson would always sign the standard card and slip it into the reply envelope. They simply weren't in the detection game any longer, no matter how intriguing the puzzle.

There were three shocks awaiting him when he stepped into the old sitting room. The first was the colour of the walls, a rather startling canary yellow; the second was the paucity of furniture, a brace of armchairs and a writing desk and chair, the former with a typewriter sitting on it. There were no paintings hanging from the rail, no shelves of books, no Bradshaw's, no Persian slipper. The old Holmes room had been, well, gutted.

The third surprise rose to greet him as he entered. She was a tall woman, towering over the American, wearing a black veil and bodice — partial widow's weeds. With so many bereaved, the convention for full mourning was no longer *de rigueur* for a wife; in fact, it was considered too self-centered in some quarters. It was felt a less formal approach recognized that the woman was not alone in her loss, and acknowledged that a whole nation mourned.

'Dr Watson. Thank you for coming.' It was a London accent, East End, but softer than the lowest classes. 'I was hoping for Mr Holmes.'

'Aren't we all?' he said wearily. 'And it's Major Watson.'

'This is Mrs Violet Crantock,' said Betsy. 'Who

75

has been coming here day after day demanding an audience with Mr Sherlock Holmes. I have no address for him, but I found one for you and — '

'You have to help me, Dr Watson. I'm at my wits' end.'

This wasn't what he expected at all. Part of him had hoped that, somehow, the telegram was a summons from Holmes himself. Not from a widow with, no doubt, some case of merely passing interest. He had two mysteries already. He didn't need a third.

'Please, sit down, Mrs Crantock.'

As she did so, she removed her hat and veil.

'I'm sorry for the loss of a loved one,' he offered.

'That's just it, Dr Watson. I'm not sure I have lost him. Not now.'

'You'd best start from the beginning,' suggested Betsy, taking her place at the writing desk.

'The Upper North Street School bombing. You remember it?'

'Who could forget such a terrible act?' Watson said truthfully. It was the same raid that had caused the carnage at Liverpool Street, the first time London experienced the Gotha Hum. 'Eighteen dead from a single bomb. Mostly mere babes.'

'Eighteen children. And my husband. John Crantock. He was killed by falling masonry.'

'I remember, yes. But he was not discovered until the next day, as I recall.'

'That is correct. John is, was, a sergeant in the London Rifles, until he lost an eye. And the hearing in one ear. So he was invalided out. He was given a job at Old Street, St Luke's.'

'The Mental Hospital for Lunatics?' he said, giving it its full title. 'I have had dealings there.' The first cases of shell shock had been dispatched to the rather grim asylum, for a regime of electro-shock and cold baths, which did nothing for their mental state.

'Well, it ain't a loony bin no more, it's a printing works. My husband was a nightwatchman there. A trusted employee, given his military record an' all.'

'I am sure he was. And he was unfortunate enough to be walking home when the bomb struck?'

'Yes. Night shift, you see. Thirty-three hours sometimes they make them work. Understaffed, y'see. Use girls of thirteen now, to do a man's job. So I wasn't worried he was late — overtime, I thought. First I know is when I get a messenger boy round in the morning asking if John was unwell, on account of him not turning up at St Luke's as expected. Two hours later, I'm down the morgue identifying him.'

'A tragic case,' said Watson. But, he failed to mention, hardly unusual or noteworthy.

The widow reached down, unclipped her bag and handed across a folded piece of paper, which Watson took.

'John was killed in June. June the 13th. Last month, my mother, who is in service in Derbyshire, said there was an opening up there for a lady's maid. Now, I'm not trained, but, as you know, there's a shortage of domestic staff

77

now the munitions pays so well. But I've never fancied being on the shells — all that yellow skin. And once Silvertown went up . . . not likely. I don't want to leave Georgie — that's our boy — an orphan. Plus the Germans aren't bombing Derbyshire, are they? We'd be safer up there. So I gave notice to our landlord and wrote to my mother. And then, four days ago, that was on the doormat.'

Watson unfolded the paper. It was written in a slow, deliberate, highly cursive style, as if copied from a book of calligraphy.

'John didn't learn to write till he was in the army. So it's very distinctive.'

Watson looked down again and read out loud: 'Do not leave. Wait for me. It won't be long now.'

'What do you think it means?' Betsy asked Watson.

'It means,' interrupted Mrs Crantock, 'that me and George are going to join John in heaven.' She put her lace-gloved hands over her face and began to sob. 'And I don't want to go.'

10

After Mrs Crantock had composed herself, Watson questioned her further on the circumstances of John Crantock's death and the identification procedure at the morgue. Satisfied she had nothing left to furnish him with, he promised he would give the case some consideration.

She took her leave, having written down her contact details — but taken the note from her husband with her — and Betsy made some tea for Watson.

'Well,' she said, once she had poured, her eyes wide with excitement. 'What do you think?'

'I don't think he is trying to entice her to heaven, if that's what you mean,' replied Watson. 'That is no note from beyond the grave. And trust me, I have experience of such things. If the dead do send notes, they are not as neatly packaged as that one. No, a human hand put that on her doormat.'

'So what's it all about?'

'Well, if he was insured for a small fortune, I would suspect a man who had faked his own death. But I am of the opinion he might have shared such a plan with his wife before now. Besides, as she assured me, there was no great insurance pay out. And if I am not mistaken, she was genuinely taken aback and puzzled by the note.'

Betsy sipped her tea. 'Is there another

possibility? A hoax, perhaps?'

'Yes, a malicious hoax is a possibility. A neighbour, perhaps? A work colleague? It would have to be someone who knew Crantock's writing style and could imitate it.'

'Perhaps an admirer who doesn't want her to leave? She is a handsome woman beneath all that black.'

'Whoever it is, he is keeping a close eye on her. He — '

'Or she.'

'Or she,' Watson admitted, 'clearly knew that Mrs Crantock was considering leaving London.'

'So someone is spying on her?

'Or opening her mail.'

'Are you interested?'

No, Watson. We aren't.

'The truth is, I have other problems to occupy me.' The whereabouts of Staff Nurse Jennings being his primary concern.

Betsy looked disappointed. 'Well, of course. What's one woman's happiness in the grand scheme of things, huh?' She sipped her tea. 'But you did promise to consider the matter.'

'I am considering it now. I also told her to put her trust in the police.'

'And she told you they laughed at her.'

Watson put the tea down and sat back, the better to appraise his hostess. There was something doll-like about her, but Watson suspected a core of steel was at the centre of that apparently delicate frame. 'Are you interested in this because of Mrs Crantock's wellbeing or because you smell a newspaper story, Miss Buck?'

80

She seemed to relax a little and her voice was softer when she spoke. He wondered what her tale was — it can't have been easy getting accreditation as a female reporter in Europe. 'Oh, I have my newspaper story — plucky doughboys arrive in England to win the war for the Allies. A few words with General Pershing, if I'm lucky. That's what my readers will want to hear: how we pulled England's chestnuts out of the fire. No offence intended.'

'None taken,' Watson sighed. He knew right enough what the coming of Americans meant — industrial might, an army of fit young men, overwhelming numerical superiority, a fresh perspective on the stalemate of the Western Front. 'Right now, we'd be grateful for anyone winning the war for us. So, why are you interested in Mrs Crantock?'

'OK, honest Injun.' Betsy beamed at him. 'I can think of a better catch than the doughboys. Every American scribbler in London will be filing that story once the troop ships dock. But here, I have one that might make my editor sit up and take notice of little Betsy Buck.'

'And what's that?'

She mimed the banner headline with her thumbs and forefingers, as if it were written across the sky: ' "The Return of Sherlock Holmes".'

11

The Northumberland Arms, near Charing Cross, was not the sort of establishment that Watson frequented on a regular basis. He was more at home a few hundred yards to the east at Simpson's, sitting in the window, watching the stream of humanity ebb and flow along the Strand.

The Northumberland hadn't been a rough pub/hotel before the war — Watson could remember it well from the affair of The Hound — but its proximity to the railway station now made it a favourite for the working girls and the sort that preyed on gullible soldiers, often using prostitutes as bait.

That afternoon, the air in the pub was chewy with thick yellow smoke and the sound of gulping as pint glasses were emptied in double-quick time. Soon, last orders would sound, closing the pub for two or three hours, encouraging those who had work to return to it. Few in the pub, however, kept what could be called regular hours. Fewer still could be accused of assisting the war effort directly.

Watson, dressed for once in sombre civilian clothes, pushed his way through the crush to the bar. Snippets of conversation caught his attention as he progressed through the packed bodies.

'Ten months, she got, for deliberately sleeping with a soldier knowing she was infected.'

'Hardly seems fair. Y'pays y'money . . . '

'The Germans are droppin' poison sweets on Paris — '

'Pontefract cakes.'

'Madeleines or macaroons. French don't eat liquorice . . . '

'Everyone who ate them died . . . '

'Go on.'

'Poison gas — '

'That *Dover Arrow* hit a mine, one of ours, mark my words.'

'I read it in the *Mail*, so it must be true.'

'Full moon due soon. Harvest moon. Then the hunter's. They'll be over then.'

'You read that in the *Mail*, too?'

'Nah, *Express*.'

The thought of the bombers returning seemed to lower a small cloud of gloom over the group. Watson took advantage of the sudden stillness as they contemplated the Gotha Hum, placed his elbows on the polished wooden bar top and ordered a pint of mild from a barman with a nose like fleshy cauliflower.

'Make that two, Dr Watson.'

Watson didn't have to turn. He would recognize that sandpapery rasp anywhere. He changed the order to two pints.

'No treatin', I'm afraid, sir,' said the barman, as he pulled the pints, reminding Watson that the buying of 'rounds' was forbidden under wartime regulations.

'I'll be payin' my way, don't you worry, Derek,' said Porky.

That would be a first, thought Watson. 'I would have stood you a decent lunch somewhere, Porky.'

83

He could feel warm breath on his ear when the man laughed. 'I don't like to move much out of me old haunts these days. Even this is a bit far south for me. Here, hand me one of those; there's a room out back where we won't be disturbed.'

It was less a room than a wood-panelled, three-sided cubby-hole or 'snug', but with its opaque glass panels, red-cushioned benches and polished table, it did feel a world apart from the throng in the other bars.

Shinwell Johnson raised a glass. 'Your good health, Dr Watson.'

'And yours.' The man known for years as 'Porky' no longer deserved that old nickname. He was lean and lined, the face weathered by a life on the fringes of respectability, and some periods when he had crossed over fully to the criminal side. There had been prison time, too. The skin never seemed to shake off that pallor entirely.

'*How is Mr Holmes?*' said Watson.

Porky froze, the glass halfway to his lips. 'How should I know, Doctor?'

'No, I mean that is your next question: 'How is Mr Holmes?''

Porky laughed, showing stained tombstone teeth that appeared to have developed an aversion to each other. 'What, you a mind reader now?'

'It's just the normal sequence of events,' said Watson with a sigh.

'Still playing second fiddle to his nibs, eh? Well, I wasn't going to ask you about Mr Holmes, 'cause I saw him not that long ago.'

Now Watson was on the back foot. 'Really? Where?'

'Here. Not in here, exactly, but London.'

'Well, I'll be . . . ' Watson gulped the warm liquid to cover his annoyance. 'What was he doing here?'

Porky winked in an exaggerated fashion. 'Well, you'll have to ask him that, won't you? I'm like a priest or a lawyer when it comes to confidentiality.'

Watson had to laugh. 'Porky, you are as far removed from either of those professions as I can imagine.'

Porky joined in with a throaty chuckle. 'Maybe. But I still have me uses. First Mr Holmes and then you come calling.' Porky drained half the pint in one. 'Probably get another in before the bell goes if we don't hang around. What can I do for you, Dr Watson?'

'I have three problems. Two of them, I need your help with.'

Watson quickly outlined the case of Sir Gilbert and his disappearance after an evening at the Wigmore.

'Do the police suspect you?'

'I doubt it. But these four names . . . ' He passed the policeman's card across.

'Arnott, Holbeck, Powell and Carlisle. Firm of solicitors?'

'All members of the War Injuries Compensation Board. As is Sir Gilbert. Eminent surgeons and psychologists all, except Lord Arnott, who is a money man, holding the purse strings for the Board's ruminations. Between them, they decide on the level of compensation for war injuries, juggling what is fair with what the country can afford.'

'I'll wager I know which side of that wins. I'm glad I was too old to serve.'

'That's as may be, but I placed telephone calls to all of the committee members at their places of work this morning. None has been in. There was a level of evasion about the replies I received, too.'

Porky caught on quickly. 'Ah. You think they've been disappeared, too?'

'It's possible.'

'Kidnapped, like?' The rest of the pint disappeared and Porky licked his lips.

'Again, we have to consider that possibility.'

'And it's something to do with this compensation board they all serve on?'

'I would say it was a mighty coincidence, if not. I can't see what else connects them.'

Porky nodded his agreement. 'What do you want me to do exactly?'

'Confirm that they have all gone missing. And find out what the police are doing about it.'

Porky scratched his neck beneath his collar. 'I've a few contacts at the Yard left . . . not as many as I did have, but I can get the s.p. on it. Is that it?'

'Not quite.' Watson explained about Mrs Crantock and her husband who apparently wrote messages from beyond the grave.

'What're your thoughts?' Porky asked.

'That he faked his death. She identified him only by his boots and clothing. His facial features were smashed by falling masonry. For some reason he wanted to disappear.'

'And you think he's watching her?'

Watson nodded and rose just as the bell rang for last orders.

'Don't rush. We'll be all right in here. What do you want me to do about the haunted widow?'

Watson sat once more. 'Put a man on her. Try to find the watcher.'

'You have an address?'

Watson handed it across.

'Two men, Doctor, in shifts.' Porky rubbed his thumb and forefinger together to show it would cost.

'Agreed.'

'What's the third thing? You said you had three problems.'

'Don't worry about that, Porky,' he said. 'The *Dover Arrow* is mine.'

'The *Dover Arrow*? I tell you they should string those submariners up by their balls if they ever catch them.'

Two fresh pints were delivered by the big-nosed barman, who took Watson's proffered coins and removed the empties without a word. Porky took the glass and raised it to Watson. 'Nice doing business with you again, Dr Watson.' He took a sip. 'You know, it's just like old times.'

Watson was about to object when he realized what had been bothering him for most of the day, ever since he had called in at 221b Baker Street. For the first time in what seemed an age, he was actually enjoying himself.

A sly grin split his face, as if he was holding back a guilty secret. 'Yes. It is, isn't it?'

12

Beneath the billowing square of green camouflage netting that hid the Giant from prying
Allied eyes, Oberleutnant Schrader crouched
down in front of the undercarriage. He used a
knuckle to rap on one of the main spars that held
the multi-wheeled contraption together. It rang
sonorously and, satisfied, he stood. The original
wooden stay had cracked on landing. He had
been dismayed to find that only a few intact
millimetres had separated him and his crew from
disaster. That spar had been milled from a piece
of cheap softwood. As if that would last more
than a few landings, given the weight of the
R-type. It was, he thought glumly, typical of the
poor workmanship and materials being used in
all the aircraft being delivered to the front.

He walked from under the shroud of
camouflage and examined the sky. A uniform lid
of Dreadnought grey pressed down on them.
The sun was low now and, as if peeking under
curtains, part of its disc had appeared in the gap
between cloud and horizon. There, the sky
glowed red, as if it were being annealed.

Schrader looked back at the enormous
bomber. Were the British building an equivalent?
A vast war machine capable of flying to Berlin? It
was likely, because the whole war in the air had
been a game of leapfrog, each side gaining the
upper hand before the enemy came up with its

own innovation that gave it a temporary advantage. The thought of his mother and sisters running like frightened rabbits into holes in the ground, cowering in *U-Bahn* stations, depressed him. It was why they had to smash London and the morale of its inhabitants as quickly as possible. Before they did the same to Berlin.

'Oberleutnant Schrader!'

It was Feldwebel Rutter, his ventral gunner — an unenviable position, crouching on a ramp lowered beneath the belly of the beast — and engineer. 'What is it?' he asked.

'Leutnant Trotzman requests your presence in his office, if it is convenient.'

Schrader glanced once more at the sun, the disc now fully bridging the gap between the ragged cloud line and the horizon. 'Good news?'

A shrug. 'I don't know, sir.'

Schrader felt a flutter of something in his stomach, a mix of apprehension and excitement at the thought that Trotzman was about to authorize a mission to London that night.

The former wasn't cowardice. He had examined his feelings carefully. Only a fool wouldn't be concerned about the quality of the planes he was expected to fly. Setting off in a Giant to England was every bit as hazardous as Heinrich Barth heading off to map the Sahara or those Englishmen who insisted on trying to walk to the South Pole. A voyage into the unknown. Although he wasn't one of those flyers who feigned engine trouble when conditions looked bad, he was a man who insisted on stacking the odds in his favour as much as possible.

89

He pointed at the bomber. 'Run the engines on her. Fifteen minutes. Make sure the fuel lines are clear.'

'Sir.'

'And Rutter . . . '

'Sir?'

'From now on, I want all fuel filtered through the finest mesh before it goes into the tanks.'

Rutter nodded. The engine malfunction on their return flight had been caused by flakes of rust in the fuel line, probably from a storage tank or the bowser. Now, so he had been told, they would fit superchargers to two of the engines, an experiment in giving enough boost to enable them to fly higher than the Gothas. Superchargers. Something else to go wrong.

Trotzman was the England Squadron's chief weather officer. It was, Schrader mused, as he hurried across to the meteorological hut where Trotzman was based, the most thankless task in the unit. Trotzman was meant to work miracles. Using information from weather balloons released on the Belgian coast, from German shipping and the occasional air patrol, he was meant to predict what conditions would be like over the North Sea, London and south-east England over a twelve-hour period. You'd have to be Freyr or Zeus to do that.

It meant every unexpected airstream blowing them off course, every unanticipated cloudbank, was reason to curse Trotzman and his stupid, useless charts. It had been so much easier when the British newspapers had published detailed weather forecasts. Now, aware that the 'other

90

side' was reading them, they produced puzzles or cartoons instead, which were little use to Trotzman and his ilk.

He opened the door to the hut and stepped in. To his surprise, Hauptmann Rudy von Kahr, the squadron's leader, was already in there, pouring himself a coffee from a pot on the stove. Trotzman was leaning over a map spread out on the table, the familiar rectangle of Belgium, France, North Sea and England in which the Giants and Gothas operated.

'*Oberleutnant*, come in. Coffee?'

Schrader closed the door behind him and saluted but was ignored by the captain, who handed over his tin mug of coffee and then poured himself another. Schrader sipped the coffee and then addressed Trotzman.

'Is it clearing?'

The weatherman shook his head, his expression as jowly and hangdog as ever. He looked like a depressed bloodhound. 'My guess is it'll be another four or five days. In time for the full moon.'

'I see.' Except he didn't. Why were they bothering him with no news?

'How is the shoulder?' von Kahr asked him.

Instinctively Schrader rotated it, feeling it click and crunch in the socket. 'Not bad.' He tried to raise his arm above his head. 'Movement still limited. The doctors reckon — '

'You could still fly a plane, though? A real plane? A fighter?'

Schrader hesitated, gathering his thoughts by drinking some more of the bitter coffee. 'I could fly one. I'd have trouble with some actions.' He

91

mimed reaching forward and felt a twinge. 'Clearing the guns, maybe. Depends on the model. Why, might I ask? Sir.'

Von Kahr moved to stand next to Trotzman, his sharp, handsome features and meticulous grooming making the weatherman look like he was built from sacks of potatoes. The squadron leader was of impeccable Prussian stock, and the holder of two Iron Crosses and an Order of Hohenzollern at the age of thirty 'Can it be done?'

'It is possible,' Trotzman said, tracing a line. 'For a good pilot.'

They both looked up at Schrader.

'Why do I feel like I am being measured for my funeral suit?' he asked.

Von Kahr laughed and waved the suggestion away. 'The England Squadron has been selected for a highly prestigious mission. They wanted the best pilot — '

'And naturally you volunteered,' said Schrader, regretting the words as soon as they had left his mouth. 'I mean. You are the best pilot.'

Von Kahr's eyes narrowed somewhat. Trotzman, a step behind the squadron leader, grimaced as if in warning.

'Your family is in Berlin, aren't they?'

That wasn't a bad guess. Schrader had a Berlin accent as thick as the porridge they served in the mess. 'Yes.'

'Cardboard boxes, wasn't it? The family business?'

'Textiles, sir. We make uniforms for the army now.'

'Good, good. You speak English, I hear.'

'I do. A slight accent, apparently, but not too bad. My father exported a lot of items to Great Britain. He insisted we children all learn the language, in case we followed him into the business.'

'Well, it's about to come in very useful. But . . . ' he drained his coffee, ' . . . this is the sort of mission you will never be able to tell your tailoring family about. Yes, I did volunteer for it, of course. But they said the squadron leader was too valuable to lose. Especially after what happened to poor Brandenburg.'

Schrader didn't like the sound of that. It seemed that 'losing' the chosen pilot was a distinct possibility.

'So, my thoughts turned to you.'

'Thank you, sir.' He wasn't sure whether he managed the inflection of genuine gratitude he was striving for.

Trotzman spoke now. 'The weather isn't suitable for bombers. The winds above three thousand metres are wicked. But lower down, at cloud level, five or six hundred metres, bumpy, yes, but manageable. There are places . . . ' he jabbed the map, ' . . . where you might have to skim some waves, but you're used to that. Although your passenger might not be.'

'Passenger?'

'I think we can bring in the admiral now,' said von Kahr.

Trotzman left the hut and Schrader said, 'I don't like the sound of this. Admiral who?'

Von Kahr lowered his voice. 'Admiral Hersch,

a senior commander in the Nachrichten-Abteilung.' This was Naval Intelligence.

'But we are air force,' protested Schrader.

Von Kahr looked sympathetic for once. 'Apparently, we are all just performing dogs for men like Hersch.'

Hersch stepped in, looking like a caricature of a Prussian aristocrat, with his expensive leather coat, broad shoulders, cropped steel-grey hair and a duelling scar. Introductions were made. The admiral's manner was brusque and workmanlike. 'Your mission is to fly to England, with a passenger, and land on English soil. Once the passenger is out, you fly back home.'

So simple, Schrader thought. Fly in shitty weather across the North Sea and land — land! — in England and then take off again. Even if he wasn't shot down by the guns or a patrolling fighter, where was he meant to put a plane down? He could hardly ask to use an RFC airstrip.

Trotzman spoke again. 'We have identified an area near Colchester where you can set a plane down, turn and take off again. A cricket pitch. Nice and smooth.'

'But what about landing lights?'

'You'll be going in by day,' said Hersch.

The temperature in the hut seemed to drop by a few degrees. Schrader couldn't help it, he let out a bark of a laugh. 'By day? Are you . . . ?' Careful, now. 'Are you sure that is wise?'

Von Kahr also laughed, but mainly at Schrader's discomfort.

Hersch, though, bided his time. 'Don't worry,

94

Schrader. You'll be in a captured Bristol two-seater. British markings. It's at Nieumunster.' This was where the Gothas often landed if they weren't able to make their home base on their return after bombing England.

'How the hell did you get a Bristol?'

'Low on fuel. Fog. Pilot mistook the strip for Furnes. Absolutely intact.'

'And a doddle to fly, apparently,' added von Kahr. 'Once you get used to the fact that some of the controls are back to front. Also the armament is a Lewis gun on the upper wing on what is called a Foster Mount. But I don't anticipate you using that. You'll have an hour or two to get used to it all.'

That long? Schrader thought. 'When do I go?'

'Tomorrow.'

'I'll give you up-to-date weather and optimum routing at first light,' said Trotzman.

'Then you'll be ferried over to familiarize yourself with this F.2,' said Hersch. 'Your passenger arrives at noon. We've taken off the observer's gun to give more room. The passenger is a non-combatant anyway.'

'And we'll give you an Albatros escort for the first section, so you don't get shot down by any of ours,' added Hersch. 'We've fitted one of the bomber's beacon guidance systems to the plane.'

'So when we get your radio signal on the return, you'll be shepherded home.'

'Exactly,' agreed Hersch, his face relaxing into an expression of concern. 'I can tell you're the perfect man for the job. Any questions?'

There were so many queries that they were

95

jostling to get out of his crowded mouth. Schrader took a breath. 'Who is the passenger, sir?'

Hersch's expression of kindly concern was replaced by something altogether steelier. 'What I meant was: any questions, Oberleutnant Schrader . . . other than that one.'

13

The five members of the War Injuries Compensation Board all came back to their senses within half an hour of each other. Not that they could share their thoughts on the ordeals they had been through. Each man was in a separate cubicle, chained to an iron bedstead by wrists and ankles. They were also tightly gagged and blindfolded. The only sound each could hear was the squeak of bedsteads as their colleagues struggled to free themselves. One by one they became still, from exhaustion or a sense of futility.

Once it was clear all were back in the real world, the voice came over the loudspeaker system. The crude paper cones in the speakers distorted the voice, making the identification of any accent impossible.

'Welcome, Professor Anthony Holbeck, Dr Adrian Powell, Sir Gilbert Hastings, Professor Horace Carlisle and Lord Henry Arnott. It's an honour to have such distinguished company. Please forgive the manner of your abduction and your incarceration. You will be released shortly for a period of exercise and any calls of nature you might have. I suggest you obey whatever instructions you are given to the letter, for there will be three orderlies with you at all times. Each one is armed with a cosh and, sad to say, not afraid to use it.'

The man addressing them cleared his throat. 'Now I am sure you are wondering why you have been gathered together. But I am equally certain you would have recognized the names of your fellow . . . um . . . inmates. You are, of course, as I said, the senior members of the War Injuries Compensation Board, convened by the Ministry of Pensions to ascertain the level of payment due to those of us who have sacrificed part of ourselves, our manhood, in the service of this country. And I have to say, gentlemen, we don't like what we are hearing. Oh, it's very easy to be generous when it comes to men like Captain Harold Swain. Three limbs missing? Blind in one eye? Half-crazed in the head? A hundred per cent compensation. After all, if that man lives another two years before taking his own life, well, that'll be a miracle. Or Sergeant Seymour Webb. Paralysed from the neck down. No longer a man, by your lights. Hundred per cent of the disability allowance.

'But what about Lieutenant Jeffrey Tasker? Right arm blown off from the elbow. Well, that leaves him one good one, eh? And, as luck would have it, he is left-handed. Ah, but dig a little deeper. Tasker was a talented violin player. The Westminster String Quartet. How does your precious 'manliness' rule apply now? One arm, now what's that worth — twenty per cent? Thirty?'

A drink of water.

'The truth is, none of us knows about an individual's suffering, about what percentage of the man is left. Yet you want to reduce it to actuary tables, mere mathematics. And why?' Without warning, the voice rose to a distorted scream. 'TO SAVE A FEW MILLION POUNDS! The cost of twenty aeroplanes or a week's output of shells or ten of those tanks everyone thought would win the war.

'You, Professor Holbeck, did you not suggest that those suffering from mental incapacity should receive nothing but room and board in a lunatic asylum until they were cured by electrotherapy? Dr Powell, is it really true that this country cares for its blind and deaf so well, they need little in extra compensation? Sir Gilbert? I quote: 'We cannot look after our soldiers to the extent that we bankrupt the entire country. Therefore, difficult decisions must be taken and the cloth trimmed to fit.'

'Lord Arnott, I believe you suggested a three-tier level of remuneration, with officers reaching the highest settlement, NCOs the next and the men able to apply for roughly half what an officer would receive for an equivalent injury. Interesting, that. All men are equal under the law, although some have limbs worth far more than others.' A brief pause. 'You, gentlemen, are a DISGRACE.

'So . . . here's what we are going to do. I, and my like-minded friends here, have decided we need to show you what, exactly, these men are going through. It is, apparently, the only way to elicit sympathy. Or perhaps empathy is a better word. Yes, empathy with our plight. You will form a unique group, ones eminently capable of deciding how much 'manliness' remains after terrible injury. You will no longer be able to stand aloof and you will no longer be simply the War Injuries Compensation Board, but will have become members of another elite group, one every man here is a part of. Nobody volunteers for membership, yet it grows day by day.'

A silence, broken only by the crackle of electricity trapped in wires. Then: 'Welcome to the Guild of Disaffected Servicemen.'

14

Mycroft Holmes was waiting in the Conversation Parlour of the Diogenes when Watson arrived for their appointment, and he was relieved he didn't have to send one of the irascible porters to fetch Mycroft from the silent, sepulchral rooms of the main club. The senior Holmes was standing at the window, feet planted widely apart, puffing on a cigar. With his muttonchop whiskers and long frock coat he looked every inch the Victorian gentleman. Which he unapologetically was.

'Ah, Watson. Have a seat. Forgive the cigar. I have found myself much taken with them again.'

Watson sat and Mycroft did the same.

'Thank you for seeing me.'

'I have little to do these days other than receive visitors. And I have precious few of those. You look better than the last time I saw you.'

'Physically, I am,' Watson admitted. At that point, he had been in a convalescent home, broken in both mind and body following the affair on the bridge in Holland when he was to be exchanged for Holmes.

'I can tell. Damnable business, all that. You have seen my brother?'

'Not since the trail of Shackleton went cold.'

Mycroft blew out a thin stream of smoke. 'You know the public will find it hard to believe that Sir Ernest has a brother, a man from the same stock, who is the absolute converse of the hero.'

Watson kept his council. Ernest Shackleton was indeed a national hero, thanks to his survival on the ice, but Watson knew he had a strained relationship with money, as his creditors and backers could well testify. His brother was cut from the same cloth, but with an added streak of larceny.

'Well, I think the fact that he stole the Irish Crown Jewels gives an indication of Frank Shackleton's character.'

'A crime of which he was acquitted.'

'A crime for which there was insufficient evidence of his involvement,' corrected Watson. 'They have still never been found. Holmes's theory was that if Frank Shackleton had stirred himself to come to London, something was afoot and it wouldn't be legal. We have no reason to disbelieve that was the case.'

'But you aren't here about a rogue Irishman, are you?'

'No,' Watson admitted. 'I need your assistance on something that seems to have been cloaked in DORA. I need your help in unwrapping that cloak.'

Mycroft smiled. 'Ah, those were the days, when I could stride into the inner sanctum of government and — '

'Mycroft!' Watson said, leaning forward. 'Are you having trouble with bright lights at night? Some difficulty focusing in dim lights?'

Mycroft examined the questions for some devious trick. 'A little. Why?'

'Your eyes are cloudier than when we last met. You have the beginnings of cataracts.'

'It is my seventieth birthday next week. Is it surprising?'

'No, but if it gets any worse, I can recommend — '

'I am not going under the knife, Watson.'

'Well, that's your decision, Mycroft.'

Mycroft made a grunting sound. 'I appreciate your concern. But you doctors never know when to leave well enough alone. My eyes are failing. So is my bladder. These things are the natural order. We decay, Watson, and railing against it will do no good. Better to accept it. Now, this DORA business.'

'You've heard of the *Dover Arrow?*'

Mycroft exploded to his feet and moved to the window once more. 'Heard of it? Good God, man, who hasn't? Yet another hospital ship deliberately sunk without warning. For a German U-boat captain to deliberately sink a boat of wounded and injured . . . inhuman, that's what it is. It shows why we are fighting this war — we are against a nation that can bomb school children and send a Red Cross ship to the bottom of the ocean.'

He was right about the *Dover Arrow* not being the first hospital ship to fall victim to enemy action. Already that year they had lost the *Gloucester Castle*, although all 450 wounded were saved, and the *Asturias*, with 35 fatalities, to torpedoes, and the *Salta* to a mine. Again, all the wounded were recovered in the latter incident, but 5 doctors, 9 nurses and 38 RAMC orderlies drowned.

'I think a friend of mine might have been on the *Dover Arrow.*'

'Really?'

103

'A Nurse Jennings. I met her when I was carrying out blood transfusion trials in Plug Street. She was on her way home and had volunteered for ambulance train duty rather than take the easy passage. She was due in Victoria that night.'

'And never arrived.'

'That's correct. And that very evening, the *Dover Arrow* went down.'

'But you don't know for certain she was on board?'

'I do not. No passenger manifest has been published.'

Mycroft considered this for a moment. 'Well, it's possible the authorities are waiting until they have notified the next of kin before releasing any names to the press.'

'I suppose it's conceivable that the Government has developed a new-found sensitivity in these matters,' said Watson. 'But the names are being withheld for reasons of 'national security', according to the press.'

'The press? I wouldn't put my faith in the press.' Mycroft shook his head, cheeks wobbling. 'And these days 'national security' can mean anything any government department wants it to.'

'Still, her parents, her colleagues, have no idea where she is. They — and I — would like to know if she was on board.'

One of Mycroft's eyebrows arched up. 'And what is she to you?'

'Young enough to be my daughter. You can put that eyebrow down now and take that look off your face.'

104

Mycroft laughed. 'I am only going by what Sherlock always said about you. Experience of women on five continents, wasn't it?'

'A mere three,' admitted Watson. 'And there was nothing untoward in this case. Nurse Jennings is, was, a close acquaintance and I am keen to establish her whereabouts.'

'And you think I can help?'

'A man who still has the ear of Churchill and Kell and Fisher? Who managed to bring a submarine full of Royal Marines deep into enemy territory? Who saved my life and that of his brother on that damned bridge? Don't tell me you've retired, Mycroft; I simply won't believe it. And the Government wouldn't allow it.'

Mycroft looked out of the window to hide his small smile at the flattery. 'You overestimate me, Watson. I did what I did in Holland for my brother. It's true, sometimes a politician might beat a path to my door, to ask about some piece of ancient history, the Bruce-Partington Plans, perhaps, or the whereabouts of the Skoda howitzers. But do they consult me about the current conflict?' His expression darkened at the thought and his voice became a low growl. 'I tell you, if they did, we wouldn't be in the mess we are in now.'

'I don't doubt it,' agreed Watson. 'But back to the *Dover Arrow*, if you will.'

Mycroft waved his cigar as if what, a few moments ago, constituted an impossible task was now a mere trifle. 'Leave it with me. I'll see what I can do.'

'Thank you. And if you change your mind about the cataracts ... You know the first accounts of such eye surgery were in Sanskrit? They have been dated to 800 BC And that the Romans were familiar with the removal of cloudy lens? And the Chinese in the Tang dynasty? That's how long it's been going on.'

'Well, it can go on quite happily for some more years without my participation. I won't change my mind, Watson. Not for me the knife. I shall slowly fade away into the darkness.' The last line was delivered with the fruity theatricality of William Gillette.

'Now why do I doubt that you will fade anywhere?'

Mycroft simply smiled and puffed on his cigar a little more.

Watson stood and the men shook hands.

'By the way ... ' said Mycroft, as Watson collected his hat and gloves. He turned to find Holmes tugging one of the green velvet curtains at the window, moving it aside slightly. 'Were you aware that you were followed here today?'

15

A human being cannot remain terrified for ever. At least, not at the pitch of terror that sees the mouth dry, the heart beating wildly, the stomach convulsing like a freshly captured octopus. Eventually the juice that fuels such fear is depleted. The body decides to conserve its energy. A calmness takes over, albeit with an undercurrent of apprehension running through it, a queasy vibration in the soul.

Sir Gilbert had reached that stage and recognized it. He had accepted that thrashing around and trying to scream against the wad of cloth in his mouth was a waste of time, as was trying to penetrate the wall of darkness created by the mask over his eyes. He had heard the others pass through the same cycle, the squeak of bedsprings growing erratic and then, finally, ceasing. He had worries other than mere escape now.

A full bladder, for one thing.

But how was he to signal that he needed to attend to the usual calls of nature? Never mind the hunger that had replaced the terror-pit in his midriff, or the pressure in his bowels, he was going to soil himself within the half-hour, unless he was taken to a lavatory.

But perhaps that didn't matter. Perhaps he was going to die in this room anyway. Whether he did so in stained sheets was neither here nor there. The Guild of Disaffected Servicemen? What did that mean? One thing was certain, the Government would not give in to blackmail, to anarchy like this. Never had and never would. The level of compensation would be decided by due process, not by acts of terror and intimidation.

He took heart that somebody in authority must have realized the entire Compensation Board was missing. Surely the elite of Scotland Yard were even now scouring London for them. If, indeed, they were in London, he admitted to himself. He recalled nothing much after getting into the taxicab. A feeling of drowsiness and then a stab of nausea. He remembered trying to pull the window down for fresh air, but it wouldn't come. Tapping on the partition to the cabby . . . then, nothing.

Gassed.

That was the most likely explanation. Some noxious substance had been introduced into the rear, no doubt, airtight and sealed, compartment of the cab. How clever, part of his brain thought. No struggle, no snatching from the street. You just drive on and deliver the passenger to . . .

But he knew no more than that. They could have driven for ten minutes, an hour, a day, for all he knew. He had no idea where he was. So how could even the Yard's finest locate him?

He stifled that thought immediately. He must not give in to the corrosive acid of despair. At least his wife, Margaret, was safe, with the children. She would be worried, of course, when the news reached her, but she would do the sensible thing and stay away from London, he was certain. She would leave it to the professionals. Oh, Margaret.

He swallowed back a sob. His parched throat felt as if sand had been poured down it. He needed a drink of water. But at least the pounding headache he had woken with had subsided. No doubt that had been caused by whatever crude sedative they had used to render him incapable.

He allowed himself a small feeling of satisfaction above the din of clamouring thoughts. He was thinking straighter now that the blind terror had subsided. Helped, no doubt, by his body purging the poison from his system. Like a patient recovering from anaesthesia, he felt the fog slowly lifting. He might not like what he could see — or in his case, not see — but having his wits about him was a considerable improvement, just as long as he could keep a lid on the panic he knew was waiting to spring out like jack-in-the box. Stay calm.

He only became aware of the footsteps moments before he felt the bed jerk. There was a squeak of long-idle wheels turning. Close by, a grunt of effort, followed by a slow acceleration and the sensation of moving through space. He was being taken to another location. But where? And why?

★ ★ ★

Even though the room was in semidarkness, the sudden burst of light hurt Sir Gilbert's eyes as

109

the blindfold was pushed up. Tears filmed across his cornea. He blinked. It was like viewing the world through rain on a windowpane. There were people around the bed, except they were horrible insectoid creatures: half-man, half-fly.

He swivelled his head to try to take in his surroundings. There were banks of electric lights, unlit; a wallchart of the human circulatory system. Or was it nervous system? Still indistinct. Cream-coloured metal trolleys were parked close to the bed. The glint of instruments. And the device with the bellows, cylinders and valves was an old Gwathmey's machine for delivering a mixture of nitrous oxide and oxygen.

He was in an operating theatre.

And those were . . . gas masks. Three men, all wearing gas masks. The ridged rubber tubes had reminded him of insect tracheoles, the oversized glass circles in front of the face made the eyes look monstrous. But behind the canvas, there were people. People who were intent on doing him harm in this place of healing.

Now he thrashed and tried to scream, the juices of fear once more flowing in his veins.

'Sir Gilbert,' came the muffled voice from the nearest man. 'Calm yourself. Struggling will do you no good. As I think you have guessed, I am afraid the fates have decreed, by a drawing of the straws, that you will be the first example made to the Government.'

The man stepped in closer. He was wearing a white coat a size too small, and Sir Gilbert could smell an aftershave on him. No, hair oil. A coconut macassar.

110

'Imagine the men in the trenches, Sir Gilbert. The day before, some of their comrades had gone over the top. They had walked into murderous machine-gun fire. Harvested like so much grass with a good, sharp scythe. Now, their superiors tell the next batch it is their turn. They must take that walk into no man's land. They must face the blade. And what do they do? Do they turn and run? Do they kill their officers like any sane man might? No. They write to their sweethearts, mothers, fathers, brothers. They smoke a last cigarette with their pals. They take the tot of rum, grateful for the warmth and the courage. And when the whistle blows, they climb the ladders and they die like men. And those that come back, those who have lost arms, eyes, legs, balls and pricks, are they any less men? No. We should be proud of them. Instead, we leave them to beg. To slit their own throats. To knot their sheets and hang themselves in some madhouse or throw the rope over a branch in a secluded wood. These are the men who went over the top for you and me.' He put a hand on Sir Gilbert's shoulder and squeezed. 'And I want you to be as brave as they were. Because in a way, you're fighting for them now, you are campaigning for them to win the Government's respect.'

He took a step back and, behind him, Sir Gilbert could see another of the masked men holding a device he recognized. A Pohl/ Mössinger combination cranial clamp/retractor. His eyes widened and he shook his head, silently pleading with the canvas-faced creature before him. But the eyes he could see blinking behind glass showed no sign of mercy.

'We did wonder what the first of our demonstrations should be. And then we decided, well, let the punishment fit the crime. Not that you have committed a crime, exactly. But we can clearly do something that is . . . appropriate.'

He turned and took the Pohl/Mössinger from his colleague and presented it to Sir Gilbert, like a medieval torturer displaying the instruments of pain. 'Now, we can either do this the hard way or make it as easy, if not as painless, as possible.'

Against all the odds, Sir Gilbert managed to squeeze a scream past the gag in his mouth.

16

'I have not been following you and I am mightily offended you would suggest such a thing!' exclaimed Betsy Buck.

Watson sipped his tea, unconvinced by her protests or the way her face had clenched into a low-browed frown of disapproval. 'As a journalist, isn't pursuing a story by tailing a suspect part of your armoury of techniques?' he asked.

She considered this.

If Betsy Buck had been surprised to see Major Watson on the doorstep of 221b Baker Street again so soon, she didn't show it.

'Doctor!' she had cried with what appeared to be genuine delight. 'Have you news for poor Mrs Crantock? Would you like coffee? Or tea? No, tea, of course. Come in. I've just lit the fire. Is September usually this cold here?'

Watson had looked up at the sky, thick, brooding and impenetrable, as if nailed in place. There were rumours of gales out in the channel. 'At least it means the bombers are unlikely to come tonight.'

'Amen to that. You coming in?'

And so, Watson had removed his cap and stepped into the hallway, feeling the same mix of satisfaction and regret he had on the previous occasion at being back in their old quarters. Fifteen minutes later, he was seated in front of the fire, feeling the heat of the coals on his face while dusk slid into darkness outside the window. There was efficient electric lighting in the room now, although he had to admit he missed the comforting softness of the oil and gas lamps they had used in his day. He had waited until Betsy was seated before he had made his accusation of her being the one following him.

'Yes, indeed,' she said eventually. 'I have been known to tail, as you put it, a man or a woman. But what would be the use of following you?'

'In case I meet with Holmes?' he suggested.

'Oh, pah,' she said. 'I thought that story will either come out or not. I'll know through Mrs Crantock.' She sipped her coffee. 'Besides, what makes you so sure someone followed you?'

He explained about Mycroft and his observation of a taxi that had drawn up after his own, then loitered outside and the figure inside who had peered up at the building. The cab had driven off only when the observer realized that Mycroft was busy, in turn, examining them. 'He was certain it was a woman.'

'Small, blonde, American?' she asked.

'No,' he admitted. 'He couldn't see clearly into the interior. She was wearing a hat and a veil.'

'So it could even have been a man,' Betsy said.

Watson had to admit this was true. After all, a young lad had dressed as a woman to avoid the police in the story he had called 'The Girl and the Gold Watches'.

'Well, it wasn't me in the cab,' she said. 'Barking up the wrong journalist there, Doctor.'

'Just to let you know, I have not bothered Mr Holmes with the case of the reappearing

114

husband. Mr Crantock, I mean. I think it is what he might call 'commonplace'.'

'A man writing a note from beyond the grave might be commonplace in your world, Doctor, but not in mine.'

'Nevertheless,' he continued, 'I have put a man on to it. A rather reliable chap. I expect a report within a day or two from Mr Johnson.' Porky, he was confident, would get to the bottom of the affair, even if he would charge handsomely for doing so. He supposed that he would end up footing the bill, even though the case didn't really interest him. He could hardly present it to Betsy Buck. That would be most ungentlemanly. Holmes always said he was a soft touch when it came to women.

'I look forward to hearing all about it. And if it moves from the commonplace to the extraordinary . . . ?'

Watson had to smile at that. 'If it is the work of a ghost, you mean? Then, perhaps, I shall send a telegram to Holmes.' Betsy made to speak but he raised a hand. 'I have promised myself not to disturb him unless absolutely necessary. It would have to be something quite remarkable.'

'Well, if you two ever need a place to discuss things,' she swept an arm about the sitting room, 'where better than 221b Baker Street?'

'Where better indeed.' Watson didn't add that this might have the same address as the location for many of their adventures, but somehow the spirit had flown from it. Although it was possible that the vital qualities of 221b resided not in ornate table lamps, Persian slippers and old armchairs, but in Holmes himself. Perhaps even in the combination of Holmes and Watson. Perhaps that was where the magic lay.

'You OK?'

'What?'

'Looked like you'd drifted off for a minute or two there,' she said.

'Thank you for the tea.' He put the cup down on the side table and stood. 'And I'm sorry to have . . . '

He hesitated. Something had disturbed his equilibrium.

'What is it?' Then she put her head to one side. She looked puzzled. 'Is that what I think it is? I thought you said — '

'I did. Turn out the lights, can you?'

She did as she was asked and Watson crossed to the window, pulled back the curtains and raised the sash, and now they could both hear it clearly: the low pulsing.

The Gotha Hum.

Watson went down the stairs and into the street. Betsy was close behind him and he advised her to stay indoors.

'I'm as likely to be blown up in there as anywhere,' she insisted.

Outside, the darkened streets were filled with the sound of thudding feet and shrieks of alarm. 'Take cover! Take cover!' Figures, only half glimpsed, ran past, some of the men apparently having lost their hats. Watson pressed Betsy back into the doorway as a mob bundled by, stumbling over each other. 'Baker Street is still open,' one of them shouted in his face. 'They'll

116

take you in there.' The Tube, he assumed.

In the pause that followed their passing, Watson strained his ears. The low vibration of the engines was there, all right, but nowhere as loud as on the last occasion, when he had taken shelter with the now-missing Sir Gilbert. It was coming from out to the east, the most likely target of the bombers, but seemed metronomically steady, as if the bombers were static or circling.

'I don't think they're coming our way,' said Watson.

'I think you might be right,' Betsy agreed after a moment. 'It's not getting any louder.'

It was then they heard the flat crump of the first explosion. The guns started up, stabbing plumes of light into the sky, the sound of shells detonating booming through the streets, drowning out the hum. Honeysuckle, Britannia, Wellington, one after the other the batteries began to hurl shells upwards at the invisible enemy. The individual detonations fused into a solid rumble, a continuous sound that reminded Watson of the front.

'I think we'd better go inside after all,' he said.

The bomb fragment clattered on the pavement yards away, its metal casing still glowing dull red.

'I think you're right,' said Betsy, dragging him by the sleeve back into 221b.

★   ★   ★

'The conditions over the North Sea are appalling,' Trotzman bellowed into the phone.

117

He listened for a second. 'We tried to send some Gothas over last night. All three had to turn back. One of them crashed on landing, killing the crew.'

Trotzman rolled his eyes in apology at Schrader, who waved his cigarette to show it was not a problem. The *Oberleutnant* looked at the weather updates lying on the table and reflected how lucky he had been. His own 'ultra secret' flight had taken place in a relative lull in the weather. For the most part he had nursed the Bristol — not the fastest or most manoeuvrable of planes, but rock steady — at around a thousand metres, hidden in cloud, only dropping down to check his position. Trotzman's directions and waymarkers had been clear and concise, the cricket pitch as smooth and welcoming as promised. He had even drawn some applause from a cluster of young English lads who had watched him land, unaware of his provenance.

The passenger had neither acknowledged nor thanked him but then again, hadn't been air sick all over the place either. The weather on Schrader's return leg had been less kind, and he had fought against a shearing wind not to be blown over enemy lines, which would have been ironic, considering the plane he was piloting. A friendly Fokker, sent up from Ghistelles, eventually located his beacon and shepherded him home. The flight had not been referred to since. It was as if it had never happened.

'Well,' Trotzman said, glancing over at Schrader, 'I'm looking at one of our very best bomber commanders as we speak. He is right here, on the ground. As is his plane. As are all the others planes and will be for four or five days more, as far as I can tell. Yes, *Herr Major*, my apologies for my tone. Thank you. Good night.'

The weatherman slammed the earpiece of the telephone into the cradle with such force there was the sound of something breaking. He followed this with a tirade of choice, ripe profanities.

'Trouble?' Schrader asked.

'Imbeciles. The general staff wanting to know who had ordered the bombing raid on London.'

'What bombing raid on London?' Schrader asked.

'Precisely. We are the England Squadron. And we are here.' He scratched his cheek and recovered some of his composure. 'Sorry — what can I do for you?'

'I just wanted to check it is safe to go into town, get blind drunk and wake up with a hangover and maybe a pretty girl.' Nobody had mentioned a reward of any description for his unusual cross-channel sortie, so he thought he might as well give himself one.

'Safe? Yes, it's safe to assume there will be no missions for a while. So safe, in fact, I might join you. Although I am not so worried about the 'pretty' part. Any old dog will do for me these days. But, yes, as I said, we won't be flying against London for some days.' His raised his eyebrows. 'Now, I know we weather types aren't quite as glamorous as you flyers, but would you mind if I accompanied you in this enterprise?'

119

'Not at all,' said Schrader truthfully. He knew after three drinks Trotzman would become maudlin, pine for his wife in Düsseldorf and then slope off to bed. Alone.

'I'm going to Church,' Schrader warned him. This was the most expensive of the local drinking haunts. It was, indeed, located in an old church, which had been deconsecrated in every sense. Some officers felt squeamish about what went on behind the old altar space. Schrader wasn't one of them.

'I've never been,' Trotzman admitted.

'Bring money. Lots of it. And your drinking boots.'

'And a pack of Devil Dogs?'

Teufelshunde — condoms. 'They provide their own. Kamels. Nothing but the best for those girls.'

Trotzman's eyes brightened. 'See you in the mess in fifteen minutes. I'll whistle up a car to take us.'

Schrader stubbed out the remains of his cigarette and swept up his cap from the map table. He paused halfway to the door and turned back. 'What makes them think there was a raid on London tonight?'

Trotzman shrugged. 'Agents reporting by radio, I would imagine.' He saw something darken in the *Oberleutnant*'s face, like a passing storm cloud. 'What?'

'Just a thought. If we're not bombing London . . . '

'And we're not.'

'Then who is?'

17

The young man in bed sixteen of Gordon Ward in Millbank Hospital was going to die. He had struggled against the inevitable for close to forty-eight hours, but now his internal organs had started to fail one by one. It was close to three in the morning. They were about to enter the dying hours, when men breathed their last.

Watson had come in to take a shift once the All Clear had sounded, meeting and processing three ambulance trains at Victoria. It had again reminded him that there was no news, one way or another, of Nurse Jennings. He had sent an express messenger to Mycroft's club, asking if he had made any progress and to get in touch as soon as he had anything to report. It would doubtless irritate the old grouch, but it might also stir him into action.

There were a hundred and three men — soon to be a hundred and two — on Gordon Ward, lined up in four rows, the tight, starched sheets tucked up to their chins, the fabric glowing white in the dim electric bulbs that hung above each bed. The ghostly figures of nurses and VADs were flitting about in the gloom, only seen clearly in the pool of light when they leaned over a patient to check a dressing or a temperature. No wonder the soldiers thought of them as angels, he thought, the way they seemed to materialize with drinks, bandages, medicines, a few kind words, and then melt away.

A groan escaped his patient's lips. Major Watson put his hand on the man's forehead. It was hot and slippery. A vein was pulsing in the temple, like the heartbeat of a small creature that had managed to burrow under the skin. The soldier moaned slightly and licked his lips. Watson signalled to the VAD who was reading, her voice barely above the sound of her breathing, a few beds along. She put down the book of poetry and came across.

'Yes, Major?'

'Can you spend some time with Corporal Henning here? A cold compress, please. And he might like his lips moistened.'

The young lady nodded. 'Of course.'

'And perhaps check which padre is on duty and warn him he might have some trade within the hour.'

'Oh.' She glanced at the lad. 'Oh, what a shame.'

It sounded a trite response, but he knew it wasn't meant to be. There wasn't enough time in the day to mourn properly all those who passed away. After weeks, months, years of death, that was all it seemed. Just another shame. As she turned to go, Watson put a hand on her arm. When she turned back he reached out and turned her face to the dangling bulb. 'You have an eye infection.'

'Yes, sir.'

Even in the unreliable light from an electric filament, he could see her skin was pale and a cluster of spots had colonized one side of her mouth. He took a hand and ran his thumb over a cracked and fissured palm that felt more like hide than flesh. He felt a slight resistance from her, as if she mistrusted his motives.

'How long has your eye been like that?'

'I don't know, sir. More than a week.'

'Time off?'

'Oh, I don't get much.' She tugged at a stray lock of hair. 'And we can't be seen with doctors, anyway.'

'I'm not asking you out for tea and a dance, miss,' he snapped. 'I'm asking you if you've had any rest. You seem run down. And you have the making of a sty. When did you last have a day off?'

The VAD indicated the rows of iron bedsteads and the snoring, wheezing, coughing men in them. 'They don't get a day off from this, do they?'

'No, but you must. Or I'll have a word with Sister.'

A flash of fear. 'No. Don't do that.'

'Then promise me you'll ask her yourself.' Watson made a note to follow up with the ward sister, who might resent his interference in her rosters, but who should have noticed she had an exhausted volunteer on her hands.

'I will, sir. And thank you.' The VAD hesitated. 'Anything else?'

'I hope you don't mind me saying this, sir . . . '

'Well, there is only one way to find out, isn't there?' he said, more brusquely than intended. 'And that's if you say it.'

The young woman gathered up her nerve.

123

'You look like you could use a good night's sleep, too, sir.'

He kept his features neutral for a moment and he could see in her face she thought she had gone too far. But he gave her a reassuring smile. 'I expect I do, miss. I expect I do.'

She looked over his shoulder at around the same time he heard the irregular slap of leather on wood. He turned to see Captain Trenchard limping down the aisle between the beds as fast as his disability would allow. The set of his features told Watson that something was amiss.

'Off you go now. Do what I said,' he instructed, and the VAD scuttled away. 'What is it, Captain?'

Trenchard waited while he caught his breath. 'An Inspector George Bullimore has been trying to get hold of you. Since midnight, he says. Sounded very impatient.'

'Did he?' Watson checked his Wilsdorf & Davis wristwatch. Gone three now. 'What does he want at this hour?'

'He wants you to come to Charing Cross Hospital immediately. I have a car outside.'

'Charing Cross? Why?' Watson glanced over at the dying man, feeling to leave him in his last minutes would be a betrayal. Still, that young VAD would be at his side. He might even prefer that to an old man looming over him.

'He says to tell you that they have found Sir Gilbert Hastings.'

Watson felt a rush of relief. Clearly if he was at Charing Cross there had been an accident of some description, but at least he had been

124

located. 'Well, that's good news.'

Trenchard shook his head. 'From what he told me, and the tone of the inspector's voice, I don't think it's good news at all.'

★ ★ ★

'He was found in Shoreditch Park. Not too far from City Road, in case you don't know it. No reason why you should. Good folk like yourself don't get over that way much. Now, the park is used by those who don't feel they can cope with the Underground as a shelter, or with cellars. Those that are claustrophobic, as it were. The thinking being that the Germans are unlikely to bomb parks.'

'As if the Germans have any idea where they are bombing,' said Trenchard grimly.

Inspector Bullimore nodded, no doubt thinking of the innocents blown to pieces by what the Germans would probably call 'stray' bombs, when, in fact, they were all 'stray'. The ones that hit legitimate targets were the exceptions.

Watson said nothing. He was still examining Sir Gilbert, who was lying in a private room on the first floor of the Charing Cross Hospital. A police constable stood guard outside. The inspector thought that it was entirely possible that Sir Gilbert had somehow escaped his captors and they might come in pursuit.

Although he didn't voice an objection, Watson doubted that scenario.

There were marks on the surgeon's cheeks and the corners of his mouth that suggested a gag

125

had been put in place and secured with a piece of cloth. Both his wrists and ankles showed considerable damage from ligatures. He had clearly struggled against his bonds, but to no avail. All he had achieved was chafing and cutting of flesh. There were also some marks that Watson couldn't explain, circular discolorations at the temple. Whatever they were, this man had been bound very tightly. The chances of him wriggling free, Houdinilike, were slim indeed. No, he had been released, as some kind of warning.

'So it was busy for some time? The park, I mean?' asked Watson, as he pulled the sheets back over the poor man's torso.

'Yes.'

'What hour did the All Clear bugles sound?' asked Trenchard.

'About ten thirty,' said Watson as he examined the patient's notes at the bottom of the bed, not quite certain he could believe what he was reading. 'So he would have been placed there sometime after the park emptied?'

'I would imagine,' said the inspector. 'Not that the park is ever completely empty — some stay there because they think the bombers might be back. Others, well, are up to no good. He was found by the public lavatories. Several people stepped over him, thinking he was a drunk.'

'How was he dressed?' Watson asked.

Bullimore pointed to a wooden locker in the corner of the room. 'In the clothes he disappeared in.'

Watson crossed over and opened the cupboard. Inside was the evening dress Sir Gilbert had been wearing for the Wigmore Hall concert, now sullied, stained and torn. He pulled up a sleeve and sniffed. There was an unpleasant, pungent aroma about the cloth. It was the smell of something vile and evil, impregnated throughout the fabric. 'Yet they thought he was a drunkard? Dressed for the opera?'

Bullimore gave a small bark of a laugh. 'The lavatories, and, indeed the park, where he was found are used by gentlemen who come east for . . . assignations, shall we say. With young men of the area. Rough young men. Messenger boys, porters, bookies' runners, lamplighters' apprentices, that sort of thing. Anyone looking for a few bob and not caring how they make it.'

First electricity and now the blackout had conspired to make the lighters of streetlamps — usually an old hand and an apprentice — redundant, at least for the time being. Watson had to hope that the gaslights of London would, in his lifetime, be lit by the stickmen once again and the apprentices would not have to resort to other means of making a living.

'And you don't keep it under observation?' asked Trenchard with some alarm. 'This known haunt of . . . ' he fumbled for a suitable word,' . . . sodomites?'

'First, Captain, we don't have enough bobbies on the beat to go after real criminals, let alone those whose preferences run to rather lewd tastes. Secondly, observing anything after sunset without streetlights in this city is difficult in the extreme these days. I tell you, the blackout in London has seen that sort of thing mushroom in the dark, as it were. But, to go back to my point, well-dressed gentlemen are not the rarity you might think in that part of the world. The locals have seen things a damn sight more strange than one passed-out toff.'

Watson had to admit he was warming to this inspector. Bluff and no-nonsense. Even Holmes might approve.

Steady.

'According to the notes, he had a blindfold on.' Watson looked at the patient, who now had two gauze pads over his eyes. 'Wouldn't people think it was passing strange for a drunk to be blindfolded.'

'As I say, the people thereabouts are hard to shock.'

'So what did happen?' asked Watson.

'Well, reading between the lines, one likely lad thought he would roll the drunk. There's a certain class of young man who frequent the lavatories not in search of satisfaction, but looking for victims who, they rightly perceive, might not want to kick up too much of a fuss. Often difficult to explain to the wife how you took a wrong turn and ended up in Shoreditch Park. So the chances are, this lad thought he'd steal Sir Gilbert's wallet and what have you. When he went through the pockets he found nothing, apart from a Bradbury and attached to it, a piece of paper, which had written on it: 'Call the police and this is yours.''

'A pound note?' Watson asked. At the beginning of the war the Treasury had started to print one-pound — nicknamed the Bradbury after the signature on it — and ten-shilling notes to take the sovereign and half-sovereign coins out of circulation. Although it was widely accepted, most nefarious activity in London was still fuelled by the solid reassurance of gold coins, rather than the flimsy, white promissory notes.

'A crisp new one, apparently. Now, of course, this boy's story paints him as more of a Good Samaritan than that. In his version, he was concerned and was looking only for the man's identification. Poppycock, of course.'

'However, I assume that the lad did call the police,' said Watson. 'He could have just taken the pound and scarpered. But he stood his ground.'

A nod. 'Which is why he is being let off with a very soft clip round the ear and a warning not be seen near those lavatories after dark again. And why he can keep the pound note.'

'So, Sir Gilbert was fully sedated when he was eventually discovered by the police?' Watson asked.

'Yes, although he has been topped up here, as it were.'

A silence descended on the room as each man went into his own thoughts. Eventually, Watson said, 'I'm going to take a look under the gauze. Inspector, you might want to step outside.'

'A crime has been committed, Major Watson, and I need to examine every aspect,' said Bullimore firmly.

'Good man.'

From a side drawer, Watson extracted a pair of

129

forceps and leaned over Sir Gilbert. Gently, his hand surprisingly steady given the hour, he lifted the moist covering to reveal the left eye beneath. He was about to exclaim his disgust at the perpetrators of such an abomination when he heard the thump of a body hitting the floor. He turned, expecting the inspector to have disappeared, but he had stood firm, although the expression on his face was one of horror. No, it was Trenchard who had swooned dead away.

18

It was almost noon when Watson emerged from the Tube at Oxford Circus and began his walk up Regent Street, towards All Souls, the needle-spired Nash church designed to distract the eye from the kink where Regent Street met Portland Place. Opposite that stood the grand façade of the Langham Hotel, a building for which he had an abiding affection. It seemed a lifetime ago that he had dined there with Oscar Wilde, and the playwright had told him about his plans for a novel featuring a young man who never aged but owned a portrait that showed the depravities of his existence. Wilde, in his turn, had pressed Watson to continue chronicling the adventures of Sherlock Holmes, whatever the detective's objections about elements he deemed too 'fanciful' in *A Study in Scarlet*. Such a magical evening. And without Wilde's prompting, it was possible the wider world would never have discovered more about the singular talents of the world's only Consulting Detective.

Of course, Watson didn't suspect at the time that Wilde, eccentric and theatrical though he considered him, had depravities of his own. What would the priggish Captain Trenchard make of that? Still, whatever his tastes, Watson missed Wilde; he certainly didn't deserve the ignominy and shame heaped upon him at the end of his too-short life.

There was a cluster of men outside All Souls, mostly dressed in hospital blues, the pocketless uniforms given to invalids. Some sort of remembrance service was going on within. He could hear the sweetness of the choir drifting across the street over the chuff of motorcars and the clop of horses' hoofs. The ex-soldiers outside leaned on their crutches or sat in their wheeled carriages, smoking, as if indifferent to the praise and thanks being given within.

There was sun on them and some of them raised up their pale faces to feel the warmth, no doubt quite a few of them glad they weren't still fighting among the liquefying corpses of Ypres. Some might think a leg was a small price to pay for release from that. But what did post-war Britain hold for them?

Then again, what did the future hold for poor Sir Gilbert? The irony of it was appalling. And quite sickening. Whatever the grievances of these people, they simply did not warrant the deliberate maiming of another human being. He was still sedated, thank the Lord, but sooner or later someone would have to explain.

Watson impulsively swerved sharp left and strode up to the entrance of the hotel, acknowledging the salute of the doorman as he ascended the steps. Once inside, he took a second to admire the splendour of the foyer, to try to comprehend the gilded palace that seemed to belong to another world, a place where he could smell fresh flowers, not decaying flesh and carbolic soap.

'Doctor . . . ' the voice began. 'Major Watson.

It has been too long.'

It was Herr Kolb, the assistant manager of the Langham back in the days of the Wilde dinner. He was a little more stooped and grey, but as whip-smart as ever, both in dress and mentally. The quick correction from civilian to military status showed that.

Watson beamed and held out his hand, always pleased to see another relic of a bygone age. 'Why. Albert . . . '

The man locked him in a two-handed grip and fixed him with his pale blue eyes. 'Yes, Major Watson is me, Albert Colt. You remember?'

Watson kept smiling until he realized the purpose of the charade. Herr Kolb had become Mr Colt, to save himself from the mob. 'Well, Mr Colt, it is a pleasure to see you after all this time. I thought you might be retired.'

Colt smiled. 'And I thought you might be a little too old for the army.'

'*Touché.*' Watson laughed.

'I moved from here to Claridge's. Then the Savoy. Then retirement. But hotel managers are in short supply so, here I am once more.'

'Well, I am pleased to see you.'

'And how is — '

'Mr Holmes?' Watson pre-empted.

'Mrs Watson.'

He felt like a grenade had gone off in his skull. So long since he heard that phrase. He tried to recall which Mrs Watson Colt would have known. Both of them, perhaps.

'Are you all right, Major?' Colt asked.

'Yes. Sorry. Earlier today . . . much earlier,

133

someone told me I looked tired.'

'Well,' the hotelier put his head to one side, as if examining a painting from a different perspective, 'I've seen you looking fresher. Come, what can I get for you?'

'Coffee, please.'

'Of course.'

'And a stiff brandy.'

★   ★   ★

When Colt had seated him in an almost-deserted Palm Court and taken his leave, Watson ordered his coffee and brandy from a waitress — another sign of the times, for the Langham had once employed exclusively German and Belgian waiters — who looked to be new to the position. Still, women were everywhere now — about half of the porters at the Bank of England, so he had heard, were female.

When she imagined nobody was looking, the waitress hovered restlessly at her station, eyes darting between customers as she had no doubt been taught by Colt, alert to the slightest indication of an unfulfilled need. She reminded Watson of a jittery sparrow, wary of a cat creeping up on her while she was distracted with a worm.

At intervals, probably not even aware she was doing it, she fingered the wedding ring hidden at her throat on a chain beneath the severe black uniform. Another story there, one of millions in this blighted city. A dead husband, perhaps, killed in the trenches, his loss forcing her out

134

into the workplace to provide for the children. Watson examined her rather sallow face for signs of bereavement. There were none he could discern, just a ripple of nervous energy.

The trouble was, he thought, that he himself had never really grieved. He wasn't sure how to. Of course he had been struck by the death of Mary. It had been like a blow with a hammer. The same with Emily, when she perished in the air crash. But he had done what any man of his generation would have done. He had buttoned his waistcoat a little tighter and carried on. The advantage back then was that there has been something to carry on with, something men the world over would envy. There had been Holmes.

And from this distance, he wondered how often Holmes had called upon him to rouse him from his miserable torpor in the wake of the deaths of his wives. The thought made him smile. He had tried the very same technique whenever Holmes reached for those damnable drugs. Give him mental stimulation, he had cried to himself. But Holmes had always seen the attempts for what they were. Distractions. For his part, however, when Holmes came calling he had never suspected an ulterior motive. Perhaps there hadn't been. It didn't do to suggest sentimentality was part of Holmes's make up.

There was no sentimentality. You were needed. And you dropped everything like the friend and companion you are, and my time on this earth has been the better for it.

Watson hoped that was true, not just another false emollient from the ever-unreliable voice in his head. He took a sip of brandy, allowing himself to sink further into the couch, to let the knotted tensions in his body unwind for a few moments.

Georgina.

He felt a strange weightlessness; as if the brandy were the hydrogen they pump into the Zeppelins, lifting him off the plump red cushions and the couch, his feet dangling in thin air.

I never got to say goodbye.

Watson recalled shouting the phrase at Mycroft when he was in the nursing home, recovering after the ordeal at Krok. Mycroft who, although sympathetic, was not equipped by nature to comprehend the significance of that lost moment on a bleak bridge in Holland, when the accursed Miss Pillbody, the German undercover spy, had shot the blameless Georgina Gregson in cold blood. To him, Georgina would already have been beyond goodbyes, an empty husk. But Watson would have given anything to cradle her for those last few seconds and beyond, letting her warmth, and perhaps her spirit, flow into him. But it wasn't to be.

And so that dose of grief, Georgina's, had joined the others inside, not set free or purged but tamped down like the powder in a muzzle loader. Hammered into a dense, explosive ball of sorrow somewhere in his soul. And one day it would detonate, taking his reason with it.

But not now.

Gravity reasserted itself and he felt the fullness of the over-stuffed cushions pressing against him as he sank back into the couch. His limbs felt as

136

if they had been filled with lead shot, suddenly bovine and lumpen.

No, not now. Not while there is Sir Gilbert and Nurse Jennings or even John Crantock, the resurrected nightwatchman.

'Can I get you anything else, sir? More coffee, perhaps? A sandwich?'

It was the waitress. The accent wasn't London or particularly refined, although she was trying hard to plump the vowels. He eyed the empty brandy glass, the taste on him. Instead he said: 'Your husband serves?'

She touched the hidden ring, her long fingers twitchy, unable to alight for long. 'Sherwood Foresters.'

'Ah, I know them. Knew some of them, at least. Good chaps.' Although how many of the 'good chaps' he had met in Egypt while conducting blood-transfusion trials were still alive? 'And he is safe?'

She nodded vigorously. 'Yes, thank you, sir. He's a farrier, you see.'

'Really?'

'So he's mostly behind the front. Still doing his bit, though.'

'Yes, still doing his bit,' he reassured her, cross with himself for being somewhat taken aback that a farrier's wife could find a position at the Langham. Times were topsy-turvy indeed. But it explained the flat vowels.

She patted the wedding ring again. 'Some places don't like to see married women working, as I am sure you know, sir. Mr Colt isn't like that. But I worried about Sid so much in the

137

early days, I'm not the same lass who walked down the aisle. Not as bonny, I mean. So it falls off now if I wear it. The ring. And most customers don't like finding a wedding band at the bottom of their cup.' A flicker of a smile played around her mouth but, frightened she had shared too much, she added hurriedly: 'So, another coffee, sir?'

But they both looked at the brandy glass. 'No, thank you.' After examining his pockets for coins, he handed over a ten-shilling note.

Nightwatchman where, Watson? Do you remember that? asked the voice in his head when she had left to fetch his change. *Where was Crantock a nightwatchman?*

The phantom was up to his old tricks, trying to tempt him to engage with the world and its mysteries. It was a fair point, though. St Luke's, he seemed to recall the widow had said, the place that gave the world the term 'batty', after the asylum's chief physician, William Battie. Was that right? Ah well, no doubt Porky would tell him in the fullness of time.

It was time to go home. It was time to sleep.

★ ★ ★

Autumn was in the air as Watson zigzagged through to Wimpole Street. There was the scent of wet earth, fallen leaves and mulch on the breeze, which was coming from the south. Would autumn save the city from the bombers? The sky was a cobalt blue now, clouds few and far between. The Germans had managed a raid in

138

terrible conditions the previous night. What would they send over when the skies were horribly clear and the stars shone a crystalline light down on London?

He thought of autumn in the trenches and the winter not far behind. The smell of no man's land stung his nostrils, as it did whenever he pictured the men trudging through icy water and mud, of the cold that gnawed at the bones, the clouds of corrosive gas rolling over the wire and the stench of putrefaction. Of the bodies that lay beneath that mud. Some of them his doing.

And autumn this year meant even stricter coal rationing. From October, all households had to register with a coal merchant to ensure they used only the regulation amount to heat their homes. It might be another cold, hard winter for most people in this city, perhaps even harder than 1916, and that had been bad enough. There was less food to go around now, and even in this affluent part of town there were queues at the food shops, although admittedly more often comprised of servants than the lady of the house.

He kicked at a pile of leaves in the gutter of Harley Street, as brittle as ancient paper, and the toe of his boot caught something hard and metal. He bent down, extracted it from its covering, and examined it. It was a fragment of a German bomb, a pyramid of brass, pitted and scarred, with, at the apex, a hexagonal nut. There was a number on it: '49'. It was the business end of some infernal device.

Watson placed it under his arm and continued his walk to Wimpole Street, pausing only to

139

watch a small convoy of slab-sided Pierce-Arrow armoured cars, each with a Vickers naval gun mounted on the rear, trundling towards the park, doubtless to join the anti-aircraft batteries that had been deployed around the Inner Circle.

When he reached his lodgings, Mrs Turner opened the door before he could use his key. Her face showed intense displeasure. 'You have a visitor. And he ordered me to fetch today's newspapers!'

Porky, Watson reckoned. His type would certainly offend Mrs Turner. 'Is it a Mr Johnson?'

'No, it is not,' she said through pursed lips. 'It's a Mr Holmes. And he ordered me to fetch every single one of the morning newspapers. Every one,' she repeated, as if he had requested a fan dance. 'Then some scissors and card and glue. Who does he think he is?'

'He thinks he is Mycroft Holmes,' he said, sliding by Mrs Turner. 'Once one of the most important men in England. And I am afraid I have been pestering him somewhat. But he might have important news for me about a friend who is missing.'

Watson bounded up the stairs, his weariness and the promise of sleep forgotten, and burst into the living room. As he took in those long, crossed legs, the brilliantly polished Balmorals at the end of them, the piercing grey eyes, the slightly raised, almost sardonic, eyebrow and the cheekbones you could still slice ham on, he realized it wasn't Mycroft at all. Watson couldn't help himself, he simply blurted out the name.

'Sherlock!'

140

19

Schrader was still snoozing when he heard the banging on the door of his billet. Bleary-eyed from too much beer and schnapps, he reached over to the bedside table for his wristwatch. It was just gone seven. And he had gone to bed at . . . about half-past, pissed, as he recalled.

'Just a minute.'

He still had on his breeches and singlet, so he pulled last night's shirt on and shuffled to the door. When he opened it, Trotzman was standing there, all sharp creases and bushy tail. He looked Schrader up and down with an expression that suggested he'd just swallowed a bottle of Bayer's Liquorice Expectorant.

'You carried on then? I did warn you.'

'Oh, do fuck off,' said Schrader.

'And the girl?'

Schrader gave a wolfish grin and ran a hand through his hair. 'Yes, and the girl. Worth every pfennig.' In truth, he couldn't remember much, just a blur of pale limbs and red lips, a sweaty, woozy coupling, a touch of over-acting at the pleasuring, and a much-rumpled bed. What was her name again?

'I bet you don't even remember her name.'

'Fifi.'

Trotzman barged past him and Schrader closed the door. 'Aren't they all called Fifi in that place?' The weatherman looked around the room. Apart from the thrown-back sheets, it was immaculately kept. He walked over and lifted up the book that had been left open on the desk: *The Confusion of Young Törless*, a daring racy bestseller, so he had heard. He put it back down. He preferred the elegance of weather charts to dense text.

'You have coffee?' Trotzman asked.

'I can ring for some. Madame will bring it up.'

'Another Fifi of yours? Breakfast in bed?'

He thought of the ruddy-faced Flemish woman who owned the café below and her ham-hock arms. 'You could make three Fifis out of this one. And don't speak to your superiors like that.'

'Or what, you'll find yourself a better weatherman? Good luck with that.'

Schrader pulled the bell rope twice, the agreed morning signal for a pot of coffee and a jug of warm water. 'What are you doing here so early?' he asked Trotzman, although in truth it was not early by air force standards. Just by hangover ones.

'Two new Giants are due in today. Von Kahr wants you and he to take up one apiece and then inspect them for any faults, like that cracked spar you found.'

'If you don't mind, I think I'll do it the other way around. Inspect first, then fly. Then inspect again. That way I won't get any nasty surprises at five thousand metres.'

Trotzman shrugged. 'You're the airman.'

Schrader crossed to the window, yanked back the curtains and peered upwards. 'How is the weather?'

'The same, at the moment. But the wind has shifted. It's from the south. Fine in southern England, so I hear. And the cloud seems to be breaking up over France and the Channel. And it's a full moon over London from tomorrow. A harvest moon.'

'So we fly tomorrow?'

'That's not all. You fly with a little surprise.'

'What's that?'

'The Elektrons are also arriving today from Duisburg.'

There was a sharp rap at the door, but Schrader ignored it. He couldn't keep the excitement from his voice. The Elektron bomb had been rumoured for months now. 'The new incendiaries?'

Trotzman dropped to a whisper. 'The very same. With a less than ten per cent failure rate. If God grants us clear skies and a bright moon for just three or four nights . . . '

'Yes?'

Trotzman's eyes shone. Schrader knew what he was going to say, but wanted to hear it all the same. 'Then, my dear *Oberleutnant*, London will burn.'

★ ★ ★

When the men in the gas masks wheeled Dr Adrian Powell away and then lifted his blindfold, he vomited behind his gag at the unholy sight. The resultant choking caused the leader — he could tell from the body language how they deferred to him — to undo the binding holding

143

the ball of cloth in place and yank it out. Powell heaved up his stomach's contents onto the mattress at the side of his head and followed this with a stream of pungent invective.

'You scoundrels! What do you think you will achieve by this? Scotland Yard will hunt you scum down like the animals you are. The Board is not your enemy. If it wasn't for us, you and your kind wouldn't have — '

The cosh flicked out from the man's pocket and made contact with Powell's temple. The room spun into black.

When he drifted back to consciousness, he was all too aware the gag was back in place, albeit somewhat looser. The leader was at the foot of his bed, flanked by two associates. Like Sir Gilbert before him, it didn't take long for the neurologist to appreciate he was in some kind of operating theatre. A feeling of despair and hopelessness flooded through him.

'Now, Dr Powell, this will go easier without histrionics,' said the deadened voice from behind the canvas and rubber of the mask. 'We are hoping, to be honest, that Sir Gilbert will be enough demonstration of our intent. But we suspect not. A government that can send ten thousand men to their deaths just to prove a point to the French commanders is not inclined to listen to reason.'

Powell turned as something was brought into the room on a wooden trolley.

'I do believe that you were involved in the case of Rifleman George Horrocks. No? Doesn't ring a bell? Shipped back from France, deaf as a post

144

and mad as a brush. But I think you decided that he suffered from neurasthenia — weak nerves — before he was exposed to the guns of the Western Front. Not shell shock at all, but a family trait, typical of the lower classes. And, therefore, his inherent weakness meant he and his family were liable for minimum compensation. No matter, the wife put the kids in the workhouse, anyway, you know. She's having another man's baby, too. I think you discussed all this in front of him. Deaf as a post maybe, but he could pick up the gist of things, apparently.'

Powell pulled at the restraints on his wrist and ankles, even though he knew it was to no avail. From behind the gag came a series of grunts, embryonic words that would not form.

'Rifleman Horrocks went back to his hospital and, that night, he hanged himself. No doubt due to some weakness of his nerves.' The man now spoke to his assistants. 'Are you ready? Good.' He addressed Powell once again. 'And so, in memorium to Horrocks and all the other men suffering from some congenital weakness of the nerves, a lack of manliness as you might put it, we have decided that this demonstration will involve both your ears.' He gave a nod and a low vibration filled the room. He leaned in close enough for Powell to smell his hair oil. 'And your sanity.'

20

'I was summoned by Mycroft,' said Holmes by way of explanation of his appearance at Wimpole Street. He had smoked half a cigarette. 'I have just come from him.' The remnants of an earlier cigarette lay crushed in the ebony ashtray on the table. Holmes had been there some time and had already that morning visited either the Diogenes or his brother's Pall Mall lodgings. He must have caught a very early up train from Lewes, thought Watson. 'I must apologize to your Mrs Turner for the mess I have made.' He pointed to the stack of newspapers, some of which had been snipped, leaving curls of offcuts on the carpet. 'She's no Mrs Hudson, but was useful enough.'

'Holmes, it's good to see you. How are you?'

'Greyer, older. No wiser.' He smiled, a slight, cold thing. 'Quite the contrary.'

Watson didn't comment. He knew better than to try to hurry Holmes along. He would tell him in his own good time and in his own order. Meanwhile, Watson sat, placed the bomb fragment on the floor next to his chair, unbuttoned his tunic, lit a cigarette and studied his friend. His initial thought had been how well his old colleague looked. But a closer inspection showed the dark smudges beneath the eyes, the slight yellow in the corners, the tremor in the right leg kept under control by the folding of the limbs. The comment about him being no wiser was a reference to the memory lapses that plagued him during the worst of his pernicious amnesia. Had they returned? Watson made a mental note to use this unexpected visit to give the ex-detective a full medical examination, well aware that milking a bull might be easier.

'What is that?' Holmes asked.

'What is what?'

'That item at your feet.'

'Part of a German bomb.'

'Fascinating. May I see?'

Watson handed it across and Holmes turned it over in his hands, his lips pursed. Then he seemed to dismiss it. 'Tell me everything that has happened this past week.'

'Didn't Mycroft give some of the details?'

'Hardly. A sketchy account, at best.'

'Why?'

'I never thought these words would pass my lips, but Mycroft Holmes is a very frightened man.'

'Frightened?' It was difficult to picture. Mycroft was a man who, in his day at least, did the frightening. 'How so?'

'My dear Watson, let us begin at the beginning. Tell me everything, no matter how trivial.'

'Starting from when?'

Holmes thought about this for a moment. 'Let us say, the day before the disappearance of the *Dover Arrow*.'

★ ★ ★

While Watson spoke, they consumed a pot of Empire Blend and two cigarettes apiece. Sitting in his rattan-backed chair, describing the events of the past few days, watching Holmes take each snippet of information, process and file or discard it, was as fine a tonic to Watson as a bottle of Dr Robin's.

When he had finished, Watson drained the last of his lukewarm tea. Holmes had sat back, head inclined to the ceiling, as if following the fate of the curlicue of smoke arising from the cigarette still burning in his right hand.

'It isn't a bomb.'

'I beg your pardon.'

Holmes snapped forward. 'Really, Watson, I am surprised at you. A military man and all.'

Holmes bent down and picked up the brass piece that Watson had collected from Harley Street. 'It is a shell.'

'I never had much to do with artillery,' Watson admitted. 'Only with the aftereffects of their bombardments. Are you saying the Germans are shelling us now?'

'It is,' said Holmes, turning it over in his hands, 'a British shell. The number here tells us it is a timed fuse, not a percussive one. The time is set by tightening this nut. It will have, if memory serves, a maximum of sixteen seconds from firing. That is enough to reach sixteen thousand feet before detonation.'

'It is an anti-aircraft shell.'

Holmes nodded. 'I think you will find that, all over London, people are placing parts of German bombs on their mantelpieces that are

148

nothing of the kind. As the old saying has it, what goes up, must come down. London is surrounded by guns pointing at the sky.'

'Not just surrounded, Holmes. I saw more of them moving into the park just now. The guns are in the very heart of London.'

'Then, on the next big raid, expect a steel rain to fall on the city. And not just from our enemy. And to what avail? I do believe the new bombers fly higher than sixteen thousand feet.'

'I wouldn't know about that. But the guns are for morale, to show we are doing something against the raiders.'

Holmes said nothing. His thoughts had moved on, having made his point. 'Mycroft did as you asked. He made enquiries about the *Dover Arrow* sinking and your missing friend. He was summoned that very day to luncheon with what he calls a very senior figure, at the Reform. Superficially, he says, it was a very pleasant hour or two, convivial even. The *Dover Arrow* was not mentioned at all. At least not by name. But Mycroft came away from it fully aware that if he were to pursue the matter, the doors of the Diogenes would be closed to him for ever.'

'But I thought he founded it?'

Holmes waved that away with his etiolated fingers. 'His pension would be found to have irregularities. His lodgings requisitioned. He might even find himself on a certain island off the coast of Essex.'

'Good Lord!' Watson shuddered as he recalled the aptly named Foulness, an unofficial prison colony, and the mudflats around it that had almost claimed their lives. That was during the mission he had undertaken for Winston Churchill and when he had first encountered the loathsome Miss Pillbody, the German agent who had caused him such misery. A She Wolf, he reluctantly recalled, one of a group of female spies trained to kill with impunity. As she had Mrs Gregson on that bridge.

'I can feel fragments spinning in my head, Watson, and I am waiting for them to come together. It is as if I need reversed explosion to fission them together. Have you seen the newspapers?'

'No, I haven't had time.'

'Do not ignore them, Watson. Time was when you were assiduous in your reading. There is much of interest in here.'

'About the *Dover Arrow*?' Watson asked.

Holmes shook his head. 'No. Nothing on that subject. Which in itself is of some interest. Normally the fires of war could be stoked for a good few days with such an atrocity. But the newspapers seem to have lost interest.'

'Well, I haven't,' said Watson. 'I would still like to know what happened to that ship and to Staff Nurse Jennings.'

'Your loyalty does you proud, but I think you need to prioritize, Watson. Let us consider the matter of Sir Gilbert and the others to begin with. That is where the urgency lies. First, *The Times*.' He plucked the newspaper from the floor and tossed it over. 'The classifieds.'

Watson examined the various entries on the front page.

'See anything unusual?

'No.'

'The black square.'

Watson let his eyes drop. Lower down the page, there was indeed a large, solid-black square taking up the space of several entries.

'Now turn to page fifteen. Exact same position.'

Watson did as he was instructed. He read what was printed in Baskerville bold: ' "One hundred per cent." '

'The same phrase that your flour-throwing man exclaimed, if my memory serves me.'

'It does. He did.'

'Page twenty-five, almost the same location.'

' "Justice. Fairness. Compassion," ' Watson read. ' "GODS.' Gods? What kind of Gods?'

'The mortal kind. An acronym, I suspect. An organization, of some description. London is full of leagues and legions and . . . ' a moment's thought, ' . . . guilds.'

This was true, there were leagues of various women's organizations, guilds of old soldiers, of temperance agitators, leagues of workers, and of those demanding an end to the war. Everyone belonged to one political group or another, it seemed.

'You think the 'G' is for guild?'

'Possibly.'

'Guild of . . . ? What?'

'What exactly did they do to Sir Gilbert?' asked Holmes.

Watson had spared him the grisly details. 'They blinded him.'

151

'How?'

'By removing the lens from each eye. Completely. And with less finesse than Sir Gilbert might have managed.'

'Will he ever see again?'

Watson shook his head. 'I doubt it.'

'Not much compassion or justice there, then. But the person who did this . . . would they need medical knowledge?'

'I would venture the incision and repair show some evidence of medical training, yes. But Sir Gilbert was an expert in this field. This is crude surgery, by his lights.'

'And is Sir Gilbert speaking yet?'

'Not for the moment. Still sedated.'

'When he is well enough to be questioned, we must interrogate him on every detail of his ordeal. Every detail. As you well know, Watson, people often hold the key to a puzzle without even realizing it. I would venture that the black square here represents blindness, total darkness. It is a demand, albeit a cryptic one, from our 'Guild'. The next victim will be deafened, I fear.'

'How on earth do you know that?'

'All in good time, Watson. Now, back to the news. Last night's air raid. Page five, I believe.'

'Yes, here it is.'

'Only one casualty,' said Holmes.

'It was a short raid.'

'The name is in the second paragraph from the end.'

Watson felt cold fingers playing down his spine as he read it: 'Shinwell Johnson.' 'Porky? Good grief. I . . . only just . . . how could this be?

152

Porky killed by German bombs? Of all the bad luck.'

'Luck, Watson? Luck?' Holmes dismissed fate with another wave of his fingers. 'Do you recall these words? 'Look out of this window, Watson. See how the figures loom up, are dimly seen, and then blend once more into the cloudbank. The thief or the murderer could roam London on such a day as the tiger does the jungle, unseen until he pounces, and then evident only to his victim.' Well?'

'Of course. I quoted you verbatim.'

'Not quite verbatim, but no matter. I was, of course, referring to the masking qualities of a peasouper. But this night-time blackout in London — is it not just as convenient to the ways of the underworld?'

'For the petty crook perhaps — '

'Can you,' Holmes interrupted, his voice rising to stifle Watson's words, 'think of a better way to dispose of a body than during an air raid? It is the one time we expect to see the dead in the streets. With convenient blast and scorch marks to disguise any telltale signs of fatal injury, it could be the perfect crime. Would there even be a post-mortem? Unlikely. Even the most meticulous of medical examiners would put cause of death as being due to enemy action.'

'And you think . . . ? You think it was a case of murder?' Watson asked.

'I have my suspicions, but no more. I contacted Mr Johnson some time ago, asking him to keep his ears sharp. I had . . . a feeling.' Holmes saw the surprise in Watson's eyes. 'Yes,

153

the man of science and logic, he had an instinct, a sensation, the hint of some disturbance. Don't ask me to explain. But I was unsettled, agitated, as men of our age often are. But the more I examined this perplexing perception, the more I was certain something was afoot. And then! You engage Porky to investigate a man apparently back from the dead. Next we read in the dailies that Mr Shinwell Johnson has been killed in an air raid, blown to pieces. Only identified because of the name in his hat. I would wager they stripped all documents from Porky, so he would be just an anonymous victim, but neglected to check his hatband. Porky was not a man of great refinements, but he did have his hats made at Philips in Victoria.'

'Who always sew a label with their address and the customer's name in their product.'

'Quite so.'

'This is monstrous. But, Holmes, what exactly did you ask of Porky?'

Now, Holmes was on his feet, pacing. 'I asked him to scour his contacts for news of Frank Shackleton.'

'Shackleton?'

'I was beginning to form the opinion that our wild-goose chase earlier in the year was nothing of the sort. What? What is it?'

Watson gave a smile. 'And I was beginning to form the opinion that you had designed the whole Shackleton episode as a distraction. For me.'

'Oh. Oh, I see.' Holmes stroked his chin. 'My old friend, if only I was that considerate of

154

others' feelings. No, I had genuinely heard tell of a handsome Irishman with certain proclivities who had reappeared in the capital and been seen in Hatton Garden and Leather Lane. Places where one might seek to dispose of, say, the Irish Crown Jewels.'

'Holmes, is your jaw all right?'

'Just a toothache, I think.'

'Let me have a look.'

'In a moment.' He clicked the mandible from side to side. 'We are in Wimpole Street; we cannot be far from a good dentist.'

'No, indeed. Holmes, you were going to tell me how you knew the next victim would be deaf.'

He stopped pacing and stared down at Watson. 'Yes, I — '

The pain hit Holmes like a steam locomotive ramming into his chest, crushing the ribs, bursting heart and lungs. He gripped his left arm, where hot pokers were being forced down the neural pathways.

Watson had rarely moved so quickly in years and was on his feet in a flash, or so it seemed to him, but not fast enough to prevent his old friend crumpling to the floor with the most terrible of strangulated cries.

21

'Will he recover, Dr Sykes?'

The doctor, a portly man in his late fifties with a white moustache stained by years of nicotine, looked down at the figure in the bed as he returned his small flashlight to his top pocket. He had been looking in the patient's ears. He knew he could speak openly because there was no way the man could hear him.

'To be frank, I have no idea.'

Inspector George Bullimore ran a hand through his hair. Nobody seemed to know anything. First Sir Gilbert and then . . . this. The door to the private ward opened and Captain Trenchard limped in. 'Well?'

'I called but got the housekeeper. A Mrs Turner. There seemed to be some kind of flap on.'

'Flap?' the policeman asked. 'What sort of flap?'

'I am not sure. She wasn't making too much sense. There were people there. Running up and down stairs. I could hear them. She said something about heart failure.'

This was all Bullimore needed and he barked the next question far louder than intended. 'Watson's had a heart attack?'

'No, not Major Watson.'

Well, that was a small mercy. 'So he's attending a heart attack?'

Barrhead Foundry

Tel: 0141 580 1174
barrheadfoundry@erculturueandleisure.org

Borrowed Items 11/03/2020 11:50

XXXX9094

Item Title	Due Date
* Perfect poison (text (large print))	01/04/2020
* Vendetta in death (large print)	01/04/2020
* Dead man's grip (text (large print))	01/04/2020
* Secrets of death	01/04/2020
* sign of fear (large print)	01/04/2020

* Indicates items borrowed today

Thank you for using self service

www.erculturueandleisure.org/libraries

'I think so. Someone in his building.'

'I'll send a man round later,' said Bullimore. Telephones were meant to make life simpler, quicker, but they would never replace face-to-face contact. After all, it was a relatively simple matter to determine when most people were lying during an interview. Try that down a crackling phone line.

'How is he?' asked Trenchard.

The three men examined the sleeping Powell. He seemed at ease now, a far cry from the naked, strait-jacketed man who had been brought in after shedding his clothes in Trafalgar Square. Stark, raving mad, by all accounts.

'So this man is also a member of the War Injuries Compensation Board?' asked Sykes.

'Yes,' admitted Bullimore. 'But I don't want that to go outside this room. Understood? If the press realizes what is going on . . . '

'What is going on?' the doctor asked.

Bullimore looked at Captain Trenchard, the RAMC man, wondering whether to dismiss him or not. A fainting quack wasn't much use. On the other hand, he could do with a medical man on tap in the absence of Major Watson. The armed services had taken the majority of the police surgeons he would normally rely on, leaving only the drunkards and the incompetents. 'Letters have been simultaneously delivered to the War Office, the Ministry of Pensions and Scotland Yard indicating that unless a wholesale review is undertaken, then the mutilations will continue. In an 'appropriate fashion'.'

'Appropriate to what?'

157

'War injuries,' said Trenchard, looking as if he were going to faint again. 'So Sir Gilbert is blinded, Dr Powell here driven mad.'

'And deafened,' added Sykes.

'Deafened?' Bullimore repeated. 'How?'

'Some sort of resin-like substance has been forced into his ear and it has set solid. We might be able to remove it; his mind, though, is another matter.'

'So each of the War Injuries Compensation Board is to be maimed in a way that might reflect the sort of damage our soldiers return with,' said Trenchard. 'But that's — '

'Diabolical,' completed Bullimore.

That wasn't what the young medic was about to say, but he kept quiet.

Sykes jumped in. 'Were these letters signed? I mean, is anybody taking responsibility for this outrage?'

'The same as the entries in the newspaper they directed us towards.'

'Newspaper?'

Bullimore quickly explained about the classifieds that had appeared in four of the dailies. 'GODS,' he said. 'Although we have no idea what it stands for.'

'GODS?' Trenchard repeated. 'Are you sure?'

'You've heard of them?'

'No, but I know of a similar organization. LOUGS. The League of Unfortunate Gentlemen. They had the same aims, but — '

'You know them how?' interrupted Bullimore.

'Only because of some hotheads who gave out leaflets at the station a few months back. Telling

158

the soldiers to demand more compensation.'

'Can you describe them?'

Trenchard shook his head. 'Not accurately. Not this far removed. As I said, it was months ago. I simply recall their being young, wild-eyed and passionate. One of them was on crutches. Another had an eye patch.'

'Have they been back since?' Bullimore asked.

'No, both the railway and the military police threatened them with arrest and worse. They were upsetting the men, you see. The ones coming off the ambulance trains. It's not much of a welcome to be told you've been maimed for your country and can expect little in the way of recompense, is it?'

'No,' agreed Sykes. 'I have some sympathy with their cause, but this . . . ' He indicated Powell. 'To maim other men to prove the point about an injustice . . . well, it doesn't add up, does it? Morally, I mean.'

'It's no good looking for morality here,' said Bullimore. 'We shall have to look out for what they are going to do next. Three men are left out there, to be made examples of. Before . . . ' He let it tail off.

'Before what?' asked Sykes.

It was Trenchard who answered. 'They've done eyes. Ears and brain. Men blinded by mustard and chlorine gas, men deafened and sent mad by the guns.'

'So what's next?' asked Bullimore.

'Amputees.' A pale-faced Trenchard mimed a sawing motion. 'Next, they'll start removing limbs.'

22

If you had to suffer an episode of angina in London, thought Watson, there were few more convenient addresses for it to happen than Wimpole Street. Even better, make sure your attack happens in the presence of a doctor who, though perhaps rusty in such things after years of treating the mangling of the human body by the machinery of war, still had both his full medical bag and his faculties.

Although the sudden collapse of his old friend had initiated a cacophony of conflicting advice in his head, he had concentrated on two old standbys — first, a misting vapour of nitroglycerine, followed by a dose of atropine. There were those who swore by adrenalin, but he had heard that the dosage was critical. He had been performing the crude brush strokes of street medicine, not the finesse of the doctor's surgery.

He told Mrs Turner to call the King Edward VII's Hospital for Officers on Grosvenor Gardens. It was reserved for serving officers, but Watson's name secured Holmes a bed, in a small ward that held just eight patients, all of them in long-term care. The man to the right of Holmes was engrossed in reading Aeschylus in the original Greek. The bed to his left was empty, although Watson was certain it wouldn't stay that way for long.

Watson was sitting in a metal chair at

160

Holmes's bedside, his friend's bony right hand cradled in his own, and he imagined Holmes's eyes staring at him reproachfully from behind closed lids.

'You saved his life.' It was the matron, Sybil Howard, who gave lie to the cliché that all matrons had to be as offensive and unforgiving as tanks. Sybil Howard had a lot more in her armoury than the usual matronly robustness — although he had seen her reduce young nurses to tears readily enough when they had endangered a man's life — because at fifty she was still startlingly attractive. He'd seen her use that, too, on many a stubborn, crusty major who was unwilling to submit to a bed bath or a Coudé catheter. She also had a fierce command of logic, arguing down even professors when she felt their diagnosis or course of treatment was less than perfect. The fact she survived such encounters — matrons were there to supervise nurses, not make clinical decisions — spoke volumes. She was a clever, compassionate soul, albeit wrapped in steel plate and barbed wire when need be.

'I nearly killed him,' Watson replied.

He gave a jerk when he felt her hand on his shoulder, warm through the shirt now that he had taken his tunic off. 'And how do you reach that conclusion, Major?'

He looked up at her. There was something of Emily, his second wife, about her. A heart-shaped face — plump, she might have called it when younger — that had somehow softened the inevitable progress of ageing. 'I was

161

so pleased to see him, so pleased,' he said, 'that I failed to act like a physician should. I knew he wasn't well. There were signs, but I ignored them. The jaw, for instance. It clearly wasn't toothache, but this.' He jabbed a finger at the bed. 'But to watch him attack the knot of a problem, slashing this way and that . . . well, it did me good. I was being selfish.'

Matron's voice changed to something harsher, ringing like hammer on steel. 'I think you do yourself a disservice. Major, would you come with me, please? Now. It is quite urgent.'

Bad news, he thought.

'Captain Macmillan,' she said, addressing the Greek reader in the next bed. The man looked up, his eyes rheumy in a gaunt face. Only his bristling moustache looked to be in the best of health. 'If Mr Holmes so much as stirs and Sister is not here, please pull the cord.' She indicated the rope that would summon help. 'Now, come along, Major.'

Her footsteps made a brisk drumbeat on the linoleum as she powered along the ward and out through the double swing doors, with Watson a pace behind. 'Poor Captain Macmillan. Grenadier Guards. Wounded at the Somme.'

'But that was more than a year ago.'

'Ten operations so far. His hip is still not right. Very stoic. Just reads the classics all day long. Very reliable chap. In here, if you will.'

Watson found himself in a windowless room, with a high bed — a step was provided for entry, like a horse's mounting block — screens and what looked to be a private bathroom. 'We don't

162

use this much because nurses tend to forget about it. Easier to have the men all in one place. But we do get the odd dignitary in who appreciates some privacy.'

'I see,' said Watson, although he didn't.

She pulled the curtains that covered the glass pane in the door and stepped in close. 'Nobody will disturb us here.'

'I should get back to Holmes,' Watson said, trying to step around her. A hand gripped his forearm. 'There is something we need to take care of first.'

'What is that?'

'You, Major, you. Excuse me.' Matron eased past him into the bathroom and turned on the bath taps. Pipes gurgled and banged then there was the rush of water. 'Strip, Major. Behind the screens, if you must.'

'Matron.'

She reappeared, hands on hips, eyes blazing. 'You say you missed the tell-tale signs of Mr Holmes's episode. Well, I would be failing in my duty if I did not act on the symptoms I see before me.'

'What symptoms?' Watson demanded. 'I'm as fit as a fiddle.'

'That fiddle is cracked and needs restringing, Major Watson.' She wagged an admonishing finger at him. 'When did you last sleep? Sleep properly? I have seen you here at all hours, delivering the wounded, staying with them, if need be, till dawn. I have seen your skin grow greyer and thinner by the week. Your shoulders slump. Your hands shake. You are close to

163

exhaustion, Major, and that won't do Mr Holmes any good, now will it?'

'I feel a little peaky now and then, perhaps — '

'You will get in that bath — I have put some Epsom salts in — and then you will get into that bed and you will sleep.'

'But it's the middle of the afternoon.'

'And your body has no idea what time of day it is. Two hours will do you the world of good. Strip and dip, Major, strip and dip.'

★   ★   ★

He supposed he would have to face up to life, one day, without Holmes. Lying in a warm bath, luxuriating in the heat of the water and the grittiness of the salts, it seemed impossible. But it was likely there would be consequences from the angina attack. He would have to consult the finest physicians in London, go for the most up-to-date treatment. Holmes deserved the best care. There was enough money in the Cox & Co. accounts to pay for it, too.

Matron had been right, of course. He had been running his body like a tinker flogging an old nag until it drops in the poles. Distraction, distraction, distraction. His own drug, his own version of the seven per cent solution.

Watson had a sudden vision of the slender thread by which life hangs, of the brevity of the time left to him on this earth. What was he to do with this finite allocation? He should spend it with Holmes. Because one of them would go within a few years, at most. Why waste moments

164

trying to fill up the vacuum left by the women in his life when he could spend his declining days in the company of another who had made such a contribution to his life and, yes, happiness.

He wouldn't insist Holmes came to London. He would find a cottage on the South Down suitable for two bachelors facing the accelerating years of old age. Holmes would have his bees. Perhaps he should get a bull pup. And, despite his protestations that there would be no more adventures published, he could spend the time writing the few remaining stories taken from their heyday. The *Strand* would pay handsomely for them — 'The Illustrious Client', for instance, when Holmes feigned being so near the real death that was stalking them now. And, as with poor Sir Gilbert, there was a disfiguring at the heart of it. Vitriol had been used, the same acidic solution those villains at Harzgrund had used to hide the evidence of their murderous schemes when he was incarcerated in Germany. And there was the 'Shoscombe Old Place' affair, which also involved the disposal of an inconvenient body. Worth a thousand pounds at least. They could live out their sunset years in some style.

He was jerked back from this idyll by a distant boom, and a vibration that caused the water in the tub to ripple. No doubt it was the new guns in Regent's Park being tested. It reminded him there was a long way to go, many rivers to ford and obstacles to climb, and the mystery of Staff Nurse Jennings and the *Dover Arrow* to solve before the South Downs beckoned him to retirement.

23

The new wonder weapon was laughingly tiny. Schrader had seen his mother produce bigger sausages than the Elektron bomb. It was not much more than 20 centimetres long and, judging by the way the scientist was tossing it from hand to hand, it didn't weigh much more than a bratwurst. Mind you, he thought, neither did the scientist, a weaselly little man called Grobben, who spoke in low, creepy tones that sounded as if he were whispering sweet nothings in a woman's ear. It took a while for Schrader to realize that the man was indeed in love — with his bomb.

They were in the briefing room at Ghent, a draughty barn of a place — which was exactly what it had been — that still reeked of its original occupants. It was lit by oil lamps and strings of electric lights, with a single bright spotlight shining on the blackboard onto which the scientist had drawn an exploded version of the bomb.

'Elektron,' he said softly, causing the assembled aircrew of the England Squadron to lean in to catch his words, 'is the name of the material used for the casing. It is a magnesium alloy. Inside, here,' he pointed to his diagram, 'is a thermite core. As you know, thermite burns very hot indeed, up to two and a half thousand degrees centigrade.' He smiled, smug and satisfied, like a very proud father. *Look what I made.*

Schrader raised his hand.

'Yes?'

'Oberleutnant Schrader, commander of an R-type bomber. The last type of incendiaries also had thermite in them. It burns intensely but very quickly. If they ignited at all. How long will the thermite charge last in an Elektron?'

Gröbben paused, knowing the answer would disappoint. 'Less than one minute.'

There were groans around the room and Hauptmann von Kahr swivelled in his seat and glared at the assembled company.

'You are right to be disappointed. We know you can't have the Fire Plan without fire. And we at the Hanau factory appreciate that the A-7 incendiaries, with kerosene and tar, were inadequate in every way. The A-9s, those recent models the *Oberleutnant* was talking about, had unreliable fuses and, as he suggested, a burn time that often failed to create a ground fire before it fizzled out. But the Elektron, or the B1-E to give it its correct name, has a little trick up its sleeve.'

Gröbben paused for a drink of water, knowing he had their full attention again.

'As I said, the casing is a magnesium alloy. The job of the thermite core is not to start fires, but to ignite the casing. The magnesium will burn bright and strong.' He glanced at Schrader. 'In answer to your next question, the magnesium in the outer skin will burn at around fifteen hundred degrees centigrade for around fifteen minutes. Not only is that likely to start secondary ground fires, it is almost impossible to douse the conflagration once ignited. The casing will continue to burn, no matter how much water is played on it from firefighting hoses.'

Someone gave an appreciative whistle.

'Well, let's get going then,' said Rutter, Schrader's ventral gunner and engineer. 'Trotzman says conditions are good.'

Trotzman nodded his confirmation that the weather had stabilized over the North Sea.

'Just one moment. Your bomb bays will need to be modified. There are special racks for these. They are being fabricated now and will be fitted within a few days.'

Another groan rippled around the room. It sounded to Schrader like the sound made by children who had just had their presents taken back on Christmas Eve.

Rudy von Kahr stood. 'Gentlemen, we will get a chance to use these in the coming weeks, I am sure. Let us not forget that our high explosives and shrapnel bombs with delayed fuses have a terrifying effect on the population of London. We have reports they live like moles, frightened to emerge from their holes. Tonight, we bomb with high explosive with both percussive and delayed fuses, softening them up for the real terror to come. At oh-seven hundred hours, two Giants and eleven Gothas will take off. Once over England, two Gothas will peel off and fly low towards Margate, making sure they are spotted at the coast. That will be the Gothas of Leitner and Bremmer.'

The two commanders exchanged concerned

168

glances. Being the decoy was a dangerous business, because you were inviting the whole of RFC's home defences to come after you while the main force with its defensive firepower carried on up the estuary to London.

'You will carry a fifty per cent bomb load so you can gain height quickly once the alarm has been raised.'

Leitner and Bremmer looked a little happier at this.

'Reports from over there are predicting clear skies and a full moon. Trotzman will brief you on the routing you will take over the North Sea. And tonight, the England Squadron will bomb London once more!'

An enthusiastic cheer went up into the worm-eaten rafters. Nobody appeared to notice that Oberleutnant Schrader didn't join in.

★　★　★

The public house Inspector Bullimore had chosen was one of several he deemed safe for a meeting. Close to Paddington Station, it was the sort of place used to strangers. It also had a relaxed attitude to women drinkers, as long as they stayed in the snug if unaccompanied and in one of the wooden booths if with their husbands.

His pint of ale arrived courtesy of the landlord, who scooped up the coppers he had left on the table. There had been a delay while a new barrel was put on. Bullimore held up the glass. It was still cloudy, but he said nothing. Best not draw attention to himself.

There were soldiers and some sailors in, crowded around the bar, their gaiety loud but forced. On their way back somewhere, he assumed, not just arrived in the city. Then there was a kind of hysteria that gripped fresh arrivals, the thought of a few days in the fleshpots of the capital, time for women, song, drink, shows, women again. At the end of the leave a melancholy infected them. No matter how good a time they had had, it was never enough to temper the thought of what awaited them upon their return. The war was always out there, biding its time, like a great big hungry beast that had to be fed.

Bullimore leaned out of the booth and scanned the pub. No working girls were in; the landlord kept a tight ship on that score. It was another reason why it was on the preferred list of meeting places.

One of the sailors caught his eye and he could see the man wondering how old Bullimore was. Civilians were used to that. Those in reserved jobs were often made to feel uncomfortable in public. Bullimore returned the man's gaze. He had nothing to be ashamed of. The bubbling in his lungs when he lay down at night spoke of duty done. And police inspector was a starred — that was, exempt from call-up — occupation. He smiled knowingly at the sailor and the man turned away, confused.

He sometimes wondered if he should have kept 'captain' before his name, as was the wont of many ex-military men. But 'inspector' was fine for him and, in truth, he had disliked being in

170

the provost units of the Military Foot Police. He had mainly dealt with cases of desertion or handling of POWs. For the last few months, it had been control of the chaotic traffic leading up to the front. It wasn't proper coppering. And then came the shelling and gas attacks. His behaviour during those onslaughts — getting men undercover, treating those who had breathed in the gas, neglecting to fit his own mask until all around him had theirs on — earned him the Military Cross, which, in turn, had helped him up through the ranks of the police. That, and the absence of decent men in front of him in the queue. War could prove most advantageous to career prospects.

She came in and spotted him at once. She had on a long, camel-coloured coat with a dark fur collar and a Woolland Brothers cartwheel hat with a feather in the side. He knew it was from the Knightsbridge shop because she had worn it before. She had 'dressed down', as she put it, for the assignation. The coat would be from Bourne & Hollingsworth or Barkers, rather than Madame Mercier's, but the truth was you could dress her in a munitionette's trousers and smock and she would still turn heads. It was the poise, bearing and the confidence of privilege that she exuded, which was impossible to disguise.

She did not, he noticed with some sadness, have any form of overnight case with her. Sometimes they adjourned to one of the small hotels on Sussex Gardens, where no questions were asked about marital status. Adulterers' Row, it was sometimes called. Not tonight, though.

171

Marion ignored the stares and the mumbling from the beer-swilling barflies and kept her eyes firmly on him as she slipped into the booth, taking off her gloves, but merely unbuttoning the coat, as if she wouldn't be staying. She flashed him a smile and he caught a scent of her perfume.

'A drink?' he asked.

'Lemonade,' she replied.

He fetched her one from the bar and a second pint for himself. When he returned he watched her sip daintily, her cheekbones standing out sharply as she pursed her lips, the brown eyes quizzing him. Thirty-four and beautiful. And his. Some of the time, at least.

'Not staying?'

'I can't. I have to be back. I think Charles is coming down with something.'

'Nothing serious?'

'Tonsils, I think. Dr Trellis is coming round later.'

'I'm sorry to hear that.' He tried to make it sound like genuine concern rather than selfish disappointment.

She smirked, the first sign of *his* version of Marion to appear so far, rather than the respectable figure who occupied the Big House, one wing of which was given over to the convalescence of the gassed. Which is how he had met her. 'I knew you'd be disappointed but . . . '

'Family comes first.'

'Yes.' She swirled the lemonade in her glass and examined the miniature maelstrom she had created.

He supped his pint and kept his eyes on her face while he did so, wanting to make sure he absorbed maximum pleasure from this fleeting visit.

'Are you terribly busy?' she asked when the whirlpool faded.

'I have a case I could do with Arthur's help on.'

She looked shocked at the mention of his name. 'Don't.'

Arthur, her husband, was a surgeon with the Royal Army Medical Corps, and rich from his father's invention of the Miracle Intelligent Valve, used to regulate fuel flow to engines. Every car or aircraft or boat sold in Britain put a few more shillings in the family coffers because of the patent.

'It's true, though. Bit of a medical problem.' He didn't elaborate.

'You must have police doctors?'

'Few and far between. I did have a chap called Watson giving me some advice, of Holmes and Watson fame, but he seems to have gone to ground.' He had asked Trenchard to seek out Watson and discover exactly what was going on with the man.

'Dr Watson? How terribly exciting. Arthur . . . ' She paused, before continuing. 'Arthur loves those stories.'

Bullimore drank some more. It looked as if he could be back on the Sir Gilbert case that very night.

'I'm late,' she said.

He glanced at the clock. 'You've only just got here.'

173

Her eyes widened in emphasis. Then they flicked downwards, towards the table. 'I'm overdue.'

The news took the air away from his damaged lungs completely and for a while he thought he would never draw breath ever again. Her hand flicked out and touched his.

'You've gone a strange colour. Are you all right?'

'Are you?' he finally blurted.

Is it mine? He wanted to ask, but knew, instinctively, it would be unwise to do so. It suggested he doubted her fidelity even to him. But what he meant was, *Am I really going to be a father?* He felt appalled that he had put a married woman in this situation. The potential for scandal and shame was overwhelming. Bearing another man's child? It was social suicide, even in the levels she moved in. But another part of him felt elation at the prospect of fatherhood, something he had considered in his twenties when he was engaged to Rosie, but since that had been called off, he had never even countenanced. Married to the job, his colleagues used to say. They made that jibe no longer, not since Marion appeared in his life, although none of them knew the details of the person who had put a fresh spring in his step.

'How long . . . I mean, when is it . . . ?' How ironic, he thought: the police interrogator, suddenly tongue-tied with questions.

'I'm about two months along.'

'Right.' He had no idea what this meant. Was the baby a tadpole-sized thing or fully formed

174

with limbs and eyes and a heart beating away? Was it a *person* yet? Suddenly, he felt scared. 'You're not going to do anything foolish?'

'By that do you mean anything against the law, Mr Policeman?' That smile again, tightening the band around his heart.

'I mean that in my time I have been called to many incidents, not all of them in poor districts by any means, where some woman has decided to go against nature.'

A laugh. 'Oh, how you men dress things up. A dose of diachylon or Madame Drunette's?'

'You've been researching it then?' he snapped. 'How else would you know about lead solutions or Madame Drunette's Lunar Pills? Which, by the way, are nothing short of quackery.'

A rose of colour bloomed high on her cheeks. 'Only in my lowest moments.'

It was Bullimore's turn to touch her hand, albeit briefly. 'We'll think of something. Two heads are better than one.'

'I don't think a man's head counts for much under these circumstances.'

'Maybe not. How much does a man's love count for?'

'Everything,' she said, her face suddenly taking on a glum aspect. 'And nothing.'

'Nothing?'

'Shush.'

He had raised his voice. 'What have you decided?' he asked in softer tones.

'You remember that Arthur was home on leave three months ago?'

'I do.' He certainly recalled the animal the visit

175

had unleashed inside him, a wild, snapping jealous thing that raged against having his lovely Marion back in the arms of another. He could feel the beast stirring again, as if testing its chains. 'Did you . . . ?'

'A gentleman wouldn't ask.'

'So it could be Arthur's . . . ' The thought gave him no relief.

Her lips pursed in irritation. 'The child is yours. But . . . '

'But?'

'Arthur was blind drunk most of the time. The things he had seen had affected him. Most nights he didn't so much go to sleep as pass out. He wouldn't recall a thing the next day.'

'So as far as he is concerned, you could have . . . ?'

'We could have, yes. I am sure he thinks we did. I certainly gave him that impression, even then. Just to keep him at arm's length.'

'So you could have it and . . . '

'Charles will have a new brother or sister.'

Bullimore leaned back and sighed, his mind whirling through the ramifications. He despised the slight sense of relief he could feel, despite himself. 'Well, I don't altogether approve. But the child would be brought up in rather more style than on a police inspector's salary.'

'He or she will want for nothing.'

He leaned in once more, elbows on the table. 'And we . . . '

'Shall never see each other again from this day on.'

24

Watson did not awake feeling like a new man, but he did feel like one who had been given an overhaul. A reconditioned man, perhaps. He looked at his wristwatch. It was evening and must be getting dark outside. He slid out of bed, dropping the few feet to the ground rather than using the step, and found his uniform had been sponged and pressed. He dressed quickly and hurried out to see how Holmes was getting on.

Mycroft was sitting at his brother's side now, while the former detective slept on, no doubt as a result of a sedative. An oxygen cylinder had been wheeled in, the rubber mask placed on the pillow next to the patient. Watson asked after Matron, but one of the VADs told him she had gone off duty. He made a mental note to thank her; flowers or some confectionary from Bonds.

'How is he?' Watson asked.

'He was awake briefly,' answered Mycroft. 'But agitated.'

'About?'

'He wasn't making much sense. He kept doing this . . . ' Mycroft held up fingers that looked as if they were afflicted by a spasm. 'The doctor gave him a mild sleeping draught.' Mycroft cleared his throat. 'Did he tell you about my luncheon meeting with regards to the *Dover Arrow?*'

'And you being frightened off? He did,' said

Watson, brusquely. 'I didn't think you were a coward or a man to be bullied quite so easily.'

The elder of the brothers glared at him. 'I am not, Watson. But I have sailed these choppy waters long enough to know when I have just drifted into a minefield and am likely to be blown out the water.'

'Much like the *Dover Arrow* was.'

'Quite. There is to be an official inquiry about the sinking, you know.'

'Well, that's good news,' said Watson. Even if, as he feared, Staff Nurse Jennings was on board and was therefore one of the lost, at least the truth would come out. 'When?'

'Next week.'

'I shall attend, of course.'

'It is to be held in camera,' said Mycroft solemnly.

Watson almost spluttered. 'What? Behind closed doors?'

'DORA, my dear chap.'

Watson groaned in frustration. Where was the democracy they were supposedly fighting for?

'I have walked Whitehall's ill-lit corridors of power long enough to know there is always a back door, a recondite path to the truth. Publicly, I have to be seen and heard to be chastened and to withdraw and leave it all to this inquiry. Privately, that is another matter. As the Chinese say, *ou duan si lian* — the lotus root may be cut, but its silken threads remain. I shall follow the silken threads.'

Watson felt ashamed of his earlier accusation. 'I see. I'm sorry, I didn't mean to imply . . . '

178

'Think nothing of it. I suspect, like my brother here, you are a man who wants conclusions as quickly as possible. In my area of expertise, that is rarely forthcoming. But we do need to find out what happened to the *Dover Arrow* before any inquiry buries the truth.'

'Indeed. And I have other pressing problems, not least with the maiming of Sir Gilbert and the demands of these so-called GODS.'

'Is that your problem? I would imagine MI5 and Special Branch will now be called in to take over from this policeman of yours.'

'From Bullimore? Very likely. But the fact that I witnessed the original attack and put Sir Gilbert in the taxicab that resulted in this outrage makes me feel responsible. And Holmes, here, he had some thoughts on the matter.'

They both glanced at the slumbering form. Whatever insights that great brain could offer were now locked inside a skull for which they had no key. Watson prayed that Holmes would not awake from this with his faculties impaired. He would rather die, he knew, than face life as a diminished force.

'I must go back to Wimpole Street,' said Watson. 'There were newspaper cuttings Holmes was about to show me that may shed some light on his thinking. Are you staying?'

Mycroft nodded. 'For some hours, at least.'

'I shall be back later, before my rail station duties.'

Mycroft nodded and Watson felt a terrible temptation to stay. But he knew that Holmes would want him to continue the quest for these men who thought they were GODS.

Outside, night was falling on the city. Up above, a rash of stars were sprinkled across a rapidly darkening sky and, like an old friend that one now regarded with horror, the moon was rising, ready to bathe London in its treacherous silvery glow. Watson could taste something in the air, something other than coal and exhaust fumes and manure, the usual bouquet of the streets of central London. It was the taste of fear, the sense of a city sweating in anticipation of what was to come. He could read it in the hurried steps of pedestrians, the rhythm of horses being driven that little bit faster than usual, the impatient acceleration of the almost invisible cars racing by and the irritable parp of horns.

He crossed the road and turned south, lighting a cigarette with his last match as he did so. The streets were emptying as if the air-raid alarm had already been given. Soon it would be a ghost town. He was aware of the clatter and burble of a taxicab behind him, no doubt hawking for one last fare, but he waved it on. He was but a few minutes from home.

The vehicle drove past him and stopped at the kerbside. As it did so, the rear door opened and a passenger stepped out. So it hadn't been touting for business, just looking for an address.

The man who had alighted stood to his full height. 'Major Watson?' he asked.

'Yes.'

The moonlight glinted off the barrel of the revolver that was pointing at him. Watson looked from gun to face. It was the flour-thrower, the man with the false hand. 'If you'll just step inside.'

Watson was fairly sure the man wouldn't shoot, so he simply turned on his heels, only to find himself face to face with another pistol. The owner of this one, too, was familiar. 'Best do as he says, Major,' said Captain Trenchard apologetically.

★ ★ ★

'Arm or leg?' the chief of the GODS asked, as if discussing carving up a roast.

He looked down at Lord Henry Arnott, who was in no position to answer. A muscle was twitching in his cheek, like a frog's leg under electricity. It had been firing into spasm ever since they wheeled him from the ward to the operating theatre.

'What do you offer in your scheme of things? Let me see . . . ' From the gas mask case at his hip, the tormentor took a piece of paper. 'I have the recommendations here. 'Amputation right arm through shoulder. Ninety per cent.' What's that? Thirty-six shillings a week for a private? Ever tried living on that, Lord Arnott? I thought not.' He read on: ''Amputation of leg at hip or stump not more than five inches, right arm below shoulder with stump six inches' — so precise, you people — 'severe facial disfigurement, loss of both feet.' Now what is that worth? To face the world with a visage stripped raw by gas, a jaw blasted away by bullets? Twenty-eight

181

shillings a week. Although I hear some are arguing that no compensation should be given for any wound above the neck.' He shook his head. 'Which I don't understand. And so it goes on. One leg below the knee? Sixty per cent. Twenty-four shillings. How much is a thumb worth? Well, sixteen shillings if it was on the right hand. But only twelve on the left.'

He let the paper flutter to the ground, turned, picked up a saw from the trolley and held it aloft so the electric light glinted on the blade. 'So, I repeat, arm or leg? Or perhaps both feet. Eh?'

The pungent smell reached his nostrils and he threw the saw down in disgust. 'What's that? You've shat yourself, Lord Arnott.' He was at the bedside in two paces. He punched the tethered peer once, in the face, the skin splitting like a peach under the signet ring. 'Where is your manhood now, eh?' He turned to the two men hovering in the shadows. 'We'll save this one for when we really need to make a point.' He leaned in close, certain that a dazed Lord Arnott could hear him. 'When we have to take all four limbs off.' He straightened up and shouted at his juniors. 'Right! Clean up this excuse for a man and get me another patient, quick as you like.'

★   ★   ★

The taxicab drove off with Watson sandwiched between the two men. The light of the new moon meant it was a simple matter for the driver to avoid the looming hulks of other vehicles. They turned east and then north, towards the park.

182

'Where are you taking me?' asked Watson, trying not to let the concern gnawing at him leak into his voice. Sir Gilbert had been taken by taxicab. Did that fate, that kind of mutilation, await him?

'We just want a chat,' said Trenchard. 'To clear some things up, sir.'

'At gunpoint?'

'I fear our cause has also been hijacked. We mean you no harm.'

'Tell that to Sir Gilbert,' he said, looking at the one-hander to his left. 'Am I to be blinded or maimed in some way, too?'

Instead of an answer, there came the screech of metal. Watson was thrown over on top of the man from the Wigmore and he heard the pistol clatter to the floor. There came the scream of an over-revved motor nearby and then another slam of steel into steel. The driver wrestled with the wheel, but, on the third impact, he braked to a halt. The bullet shattered the glass next to him and Watson watched his head jerk back and forward twice before he slumped forward.

More breaking glass, this time from behind, showering Watson with needle-sharp particles. He fell awkwardly to the floor as the flour-thrower tumbled out of the vehicle and Watson lost his support. Trenchard pulled him up, his voice pleading as he spoke. 'Major, you have to understand — '

The door next to Trenchard was yanked open and Watson had to watch helplessly as a gloved hand grabbed at Trenchard's hair, pulling the head back, a gun barrel was placed next to his

183

temple and the trigger pulled. Trenchard opened his mouth to scream, but the gunshot drowned him out. The boom felt as if it had burst both of Watson's eardrums and he felt warm mist spray over his face. He got a look at the shooter's face as he leaned in to drag at the dead man. It was a pugilist's face under a bowler hat.

Special Branch. MI5.

Mycroft had been right. They had sent in the heavy mob. Those boys, he knew, didn't play about.

As the limp form of Trenchard was bundled out onto the street, hands grabbed at Watson, pulling him, too, into fresh air ripe with the stench of cordite. Nearby, one of his rescuers fired into the night, the muzzle flash searing a jagged lightning bolt onto Watson's retina. Another shot followed, no doubt aimed at the fleeing flour man, who appeared to have given them the slip.

'Bollocks,' shouted the gunman and threw the pistol to the ground.

'Who the blazes are you?' Watson asked the man with the boxer's nose, his words made muffled by the roaring in his ears. His answer was a vicious blow from a cosh and the streaks of light that dominated his vision for a second were quickly replaced by darkness.

25

'Have you been drinking?' Chief Superintendent Adams asked Bullimore.

'No, sir,' he lied, then thought better of it. 'Well, just the one, sir. After I had seen what they had done to poor Dr Powell.'

His superior officer grunted. It probably, Bullimore reckoned, smelled like more than a quick medicinal one to Adams and he would be right. After Marion had left, the inspector had downed two more pints and then switched to whisky, and then had another at the Red Lion before he got home to the station house to find a message summoning him back to Bow Street and a meeting with the chief super.

'This business would drive anyone to drink, Bullimore. To one drink, I mean. You needn't worry about this case any longer. We're handing it over to Special Branch and their unsavoury friends in Whitehall. This is a government matter now.' He shook his head in disgust. 'So, I want you, tonight, to write up your notes and get them typed up, ready for a handover first thing tomorrow. Witness statements, contact details, the lot. Understood?'

'Sir. We do seem to have lost one witness.'

'Lost?'

Bullimore made an effort not to let his words slur, even though he was tired and still drunk. The thought of life without Marion, of the child he would never see — unless he ruined her reputation and marriage — had left him feeling like a hollow shell. The attempt to fill that vast void with alcohol had been both foolish and futile. 'Major Watson, who was the last man to see Sir Gilbert intact, sir. He appears to have disappeared. I sent a Captain Trenchard after him, but have heard nothing.'

'Trenchard?' Adams looked down at his desk. 'A Captain Trenchard was found dying in Regent's Park from a gunshot wound to the head earlier this evening.'

'He's dead?'

'That's what 'dying from a gunshot wound to the head' suggests, Bullimore. Tell me again how he is involved?'

Bullimore shifted his weight from foot to foot. His legs ached and he longed to sit down, but there was no sign of that invitation. 'Trenchard works with Watson on the incoming ambulance trains. I asked him to get hold of Watson, and apparently there had been some sort of disturbance at his lodgings.'

'What sort of disturbance?'

Bullimore's throat went dry. He could see himself being painted in a corner that said 'incompetence' or 'dereliction of duty'. 'It's not entirely clear. That's one of the reasons I sent Trenchard over.'

Adams looked as if he had swallowed a spoonful of cod liver oil. 'But this Trenchard isn't a copper, is he?'

'No, sir.'

'So, let me get this straight. You send

Trenchard to find out what happened to Watson, and the captain ends up dead in the street, shot through the head. Has it occurred to you that Watson might have played you for a fool?'

'How so?'

'The last to see Sir Gilbert before he is blinded. But blinded with some medical expertise in evidence. Am I right?'

'Sir.'

'And Major Watson is a doctor.'

They were interrupted by a knocking on the office's glass pane. 'Enter.'

A sergeant put his head round the door. 'Sorry to interrupt, sir, but the observers and acousticals have picked up German bombers.'

The 'acousticals' were huge concrete parabolas designed to detect the engine noise of the Gothas from many miles away. They were installed at Dover and along the Essex coast, but there was some disagreement about whether they worked better than a set of sharp human ears. 'Heading for?'

'Well, it looks like Kent, perhaps Folkestone again, but the observers at Canvey Island report bombers directly overhead as well. Headin' this way, maybe.'

'Sound the 'Take Cover'. It's a bomber's sky out there tonight. They'd be fools not to come to London.' A fleet of bobbies on bicycle with handbells and placards instructing the public to seek shelter would now spread out of the station, an action likely to be repeated across the city.

The sergeant disappeared. Adams refocused his attention on Bullimore. 'And you, Inspector,

187

go and throw some cold water on your face and put an arrest warrant out.'

'For?'

'For Major Watson, of course!'

26

Watson came back to the world shivering, his nostrils full of chloroform, his head ringing like the Great Bell of Westminster with bass notes by a steam pile-driver. He was also unable to see a thing. He managed to work a hand free, shrug off the coarse woollen blanket that had been laid over him and felt his face. His finger probed his eyes. There was no pain. He could blink. No sign of stitches. No mask.

He hadn't been blinded.

He groped around trying to get his bearings. He had been laid down on a straw mattress. Beyond that was a stone floor so cold to his touch the skin was almost ripped off his palm. He peered into the darkness, hoping for his eyes to adapt, but there was nothing but those swirling retinal patterns generated by eyes struggling to comprehend the total absence of light. It reminded him of when he been buried alive.

Don't dwell on that.

He cast aside the blanket and stood, and almost immediately his teeth started a castanet chatter. The air around him was at freezing or below. He began to stamp his feet and slap his arms, even though he knew it would do little good to his immediate outlook. The stinging on his face told him he would die from hypothermia quite quickly unless he was released from what he assumed was a prison. But how big was this room he had been incarcerated in? He had no idea. Finding out had to be a priority.

Before he began his explorations he reached down, wrapped the blanket around himself and tried to remember exactly what had happened in those last few moments in the taxi. Trenchard was dead no doubt. The man with the false hand, the flour-thrower, he was conceivably alive — the shooter had certainly been convinced he had missed him — but also possibly wounded.

Trenchard? That was a puzzle. He didn't have him down as a man of violence. Yet he obviously knew the flour-thrower. And he had the medical skills to maim the kidnapped men. And he had used a taxicab to kidnap Watson, the same *modus operandi* as the abductors of Sir Gilbert.

But who had kidnapped him the second time? And who had attacked Trenchard? Clearly, Trenchard had been in cahoots with the flour-throwing man all along. But why was he killed?

His initial thoughts that it must be MI5 or Special Branch coming to the rescue no longer seemed to hold water. Both were unorthodox organizations, but this seemed beyond the pale. Perhaps it was a rival faction within the GODS organization — someone who thought they could teach Watson a thing or two about being blinded.

And cold.

Yes, and cold. His thoughts went back to Holmes. Mycroft will think I've abandoned him, he thought. And so might Sherlock. That caused him more pain than the chill seeping through to his bones.

190

With arms outstretched he began to pace away from the mattress, counting as he did so. He had reached six when he struck the first object, solid to the touch, but also moveable. Not a wall. He pushed again and there was the squeak of metal and the restless shifting of chain links.

He used his fingertips this time, as he explored the texture. It was giving to the touch. Using both hands he found that only part of it yielded. Some sections were hard. He traced those with his fingers, trying to visualize. Then something else, crackling under his probing.

Meat, bone, gristle.

It was a body, flayed of skin.

He took a step backwards. Sniffed the air. The chloroform had initially masked any scents, but now he could smell flesh and blood in the room. He lifted his fingers to his nose. Acid curdled in his stomach at the sharpness of the scent.

Perhaps, he thought, this has nothing to do with the Sir Gilbert case. Perhaps this is personal. Someone he or Holmes crossed many years ago. After all, Von Bork had come out of the woodwork looking for revenge on the detective and had used Watson as his instrument of torture. Could it be Sebastian Moran, Professor Moriarty's blunt instrument? Or perhaps Frank Shackleton had heard Holmes was making enquiries. First Porky Johnson, now . . .

Watson moved to his left and marched forward, arms outstretched. He hit the same sort of carcass. He pushed this one harder, and again metal protested. This time, he ran his hands all over the body, standing on tiptoe to reach the top, squeezing what was left of the stubby limbs.

Pigs.

The space contained slaughtered pigs, sus-pended from hooks and chains on a metal frame of some description. It was a cold storage.

'Hello.'

His voice seemed small and lost, suggesting this was a room of considerable size. He pulled the blanket tighter and began to stride up and down, parallel with where he had found the carcasses. Stay warm, he told himself, and you might have a chance. Stay calm and you might find a way out.

He stopped when he became aware of a strange sensation. The room was moving. Then it stopped. There it was again. No, it wasn't movement as such but a vibration, a shaking, transmitted through the souls of his feet. The chains holding the pigs began to protest and he was aware of the poor animals shifting in the dark, as if waking up.

He felt something touching his head and instinctively shook it. When he ran his fingers through his hair, it was gritty to the touch. Dust. Dust was falling from the ceiling, like a fine, chalky rain.

There was a bombing raid going on. And he was right underneath it.

★   ★   ★

The boom of the guns from the park rattled the King Edward VII's Hospital's windows and the stabs of flame illuminated the wards until the

192

blackout blinds were pulled down. Bullimore looked at the two Holmes brothers. Neither of them, in truth, looked very well. The more famous of the pair was sleeping, somewhat fitfully, his face pinched and pallid. Mycroft was a rather sickly shade of grey, as if he had just seen a ghost. When Bullimore approached he rose, stiffly, and examined the policeman's credentials carefully.

'How can I help?' he asked. 'As you can see, I'm rather . . . '

'I just need to trace Major Watson's movements. We have him coming here from Wimpole Street in the early afternoon and leaving . . . ' A concentrated burst of anti-aircraft fire all but drowned out his words. The man in the bed next to Holmes pulled the sheet over his head. Others moaned in terror. The guns were meant to reassure Londoners. For some, though, they were an unwelcome reminder of what they had been through. 'When?'

Mycroft thought about this. 'I didn't make a note of the exact hour. But it was just getting dark.'

'So around seven o'clock?'

'I would say so,' said Mycroft.

Bullimore noted the time in his diary and checked his watch. It was now close to midnight. Although the guns in central London were still firing, the bombers were, as was so often the case, concentrating on hammering at the East End, Woolwich Arsenal and the docks.

'Is he in some sort of difficulty?' Mycroft asked.

'I'm not sure,' Bullimore admitted. 'Between you and me, there are those who think — '

Bullimore stopped himself. Why should he share anything with this man?

Mycroft sensed his unease. 'Inspector Bullimore, I have more secrets in here,' he tapped his head, 'than you will learn in a lifetime. You would have no trouble sharing concerns with my brother here, because, of course, he has a long history of being helpful to the Yard. Consider me *in loco* inquisitor.'

'Some hours ago an apparently abandoned taxicab was found in Regent's Park. In it were a dead driver and, nearby on the ground, Captain Trenchard, an associate of Dr Watson. An RAMC cap was found at the scene, which we believe to be Dr Watson's. Dr Watson was also the last man to see Sir Gilbert Hastings before he was savagely mutilated — '

Mycroft gave a roar of a laugh and then stifled it, remembering where he was. 'And you think that points to Dr Watson being what? A murderer? A blackmailer? A butcher? I have known the man for, let me see, when was that case of the Greek fellow? More than a quarter of a century, anyway. Do you think my brother here would have put his trust, his life, in the hands of a man who was less than honourable? Do you?'

Bullimore shrugged. He knew that human nature was not immutable, that good men go bad and, albeit more rarely, vice-versa.

Mycroft stepped closer, and raised himself to his full height. This gave him an inch or two on Bullimore. 'I ask you to examine your instincts,

194

Inspector, the ones that have got you this far in life and the police force. Do you believe Dr Watson is this scoundrel you portray? Look into your heart, man.'

Bullimore did not want to look into his heart. All he would find, he was certain, was a mass of scar tissue. 'I believe Dr Watson to be a good man.'

'And have you put out an order to apprehend him?'

'I have. Or, at least, my chief superintendent has ordered me to do so. An arrest warrant.'

'The fool. Have you done as he asked?'

Bullimore took a deep breath. 'No, not yet.'

'Then I suggest you refrain from doing so.'

'I will be in so much trouble — ' the policeman began to protest.

'Perhaps not as much as Dr Watson.'

'How do you mean?'

Mycroft appeared to deflate a little now he had won his point about the warrant. 'As my brother would tell you if he were awake, I am no detective. My forte is the gathering and analysis of facts and figures. But it seems to me there is an alternative to the ludicrous idea that Watson is not on the side of light.'

'And what is that?'

'That he has been taken by the forces of darkness. Someone, somewhere, means to do him harm.'

'But why?'

'Perhaps, without knowing it, Watson has got too close to the truth. And he has paid the price for it.'

'Watch, man.'

They both turned at the sound of the thin, reedy voice.

'Watch . . . man.'

Mycroft was by Sherlock's side in an instant and the younger brother gripped his arm. His jaw was working as if trying to masticate the words before he spoke them. The eyes bulged alarmingly.

'Calm down, Sherlock. Whatever it is can wait. Inspector, fetch a nurse, can you?'

Bullimore strode off and Mycroft laid the detective back onto the pillow. 'You must relax, my brother. Whatever it is can wait.'

Holmes gave a frantic shake of the head.

'Watch.'

'Watch what?' Mycroft consulted his pocket timepiece. He did not hold with the modish habit of wearing them on the wrist. 'Or do you want the time? Gone midnight.'

A shake of the head. 'Watchman. Watson. Tell him.'

'Tell the watchman about Watson.'

'No,' the word came out like a howl.

Mycroft rearranged the words. 'Tell Watson about the watchman?'

Now something close to a smile appeared, a brief, fleeting thing. Holmes's body uncoiled and Mycroft watched him sink back into the pillow and close his eyes once more, temporarily at ease.

Tell Watson about the watchman. Well, that was easy enough. The trick would be finding Watson to tell him.

27

It had taken Watson some considerable time to find a corner and crouch down in it. If the ceiling of this abattoir storage room was about to collapse, he reckoned he had a better change of survival on the periphery. The corollary, though, was that he might freeze into position where he sat, like an icy gargoyle, unless he kept moving. So he performed what looked like a strange series of Swedish exercises, now squatting, now standing, swinging his arms and hugging his torso.

He had checked and rechecked his pockets, but there were no matches. He had used his last one moments before the taxicab had pulled up. Even so, the chances were his abductors would have searched him and removed them before imprisoning him anyway. His cigarette case and wallet were missing, after all.

Now the sting of chloroform had completely faded in his nasal passages, the combined smell of his porcine companions and the tang of blood was almost overwhelming. Those carcasses were worth a fortune. Although meat wasn't rationed, the price had become prohibitive, more than doubling since the war began. It was possible this was a black-market operation, preparing for when full rationing was introduced. Could it be that he was simply dealing with common criminals?

When he was locked in solitary confinement in Harzgrund prisoner of war camp he had passed the time composing a new Holmes story, 'The Girl and the Gold Watches'. But he had light then and writing implements. And he wasn't in danger of freezing to death. All he had now were his mental faculties. He could use those to try to piece together what was going on. What had Holmes said? That it was as if he were waiting for an implosion, to drive all the scattered clues into one solid mass. Well, as long as his creaking knees held out, he could certainly try his best to stand in for Holmes.

It began with the attack outside the Wigmore Hall, by the man throwing flour. The man with the false hand. The man who had helped kidnap him. So, he was in league with Trenchard. The captain was obviously damaged by the war, but was a limp worth such drastic measures? Ah, but he did have a brother, still in Netley, who had suffered far worse injuries. What had he said in the cab? That they wanted to explain. Explain what? To justify the hideous, deliberate disfiguring of healthy men? Something that went against every principle of modern medicine?

Trenchard had been there when the news about the *Dover Arrow* had been delivered. But that was a sideshow, nothing to do with this.

Are you certain, Watson?

Holmes, you are lying in a bed, suffering the aftermath of a serious angina attack. Do you really expect me to believe you are in any fit state to comment on this affair?

Discard nothing for the moment. That is my advice.

198

Still, hard as he might try, Watson could see no link between the boat-ambulance and the GODS, whoever they might be. Rather a grandiose title for a group of blackmailing thugs. It suggested some sort of criminal dementia. He had seen no sign of that in Trenchard: 'We just want to explain . . . '

But how can you explain the motivation for plucking a man's eyes out? For that action also deprived hundreds of future patients of Sir Gilbert's skills at eye surgery.

And then there was Mrs Crantock and her mysterious husband, John. Apparently, like Porky Johnson, killed by German bombs. Or possibly by fragments of British shells falling from the sky. Or —

There came the sound of metal, moving.

With his attention fully back in the cold storage room, he realized that the bombing raid had moved on without causing any major damage to whatever facility he was in. He stopped his ridiculous exercises and listened hard. It had been a bolt being withdrawn, of that much he was certain. Were they coming in to check whether he was dead? To gut him and hang him from hooks like the pig carcasses?

The squeak of a handle, the sort of giant lever such meat lockers tended to have on the outside. He had found the door earlier, but there had been no equivalent handle on the inside. He supposed that was because none of the regular inhabitants of such a place ever needed to leave.

A thin sliver of white light appeared, and Watson blinked. There was smoke in front of it.

No, that was his breath in the chilled air. The slit grew to a long rectangle, and a shadow moved outside. Watson's eyes began to ache and water at the sudden illumination. He was backed against the wall, cursing himself for not having unhooked one of the carcasses and fashioned himself a weapon from a piece of metal.

Too late now.

Yes, thank you, I'm aware of that.

Now the door was fully opened and, framed in it, silhouetted by the sharp white light, stood one of his tormentors. And, judging by the hair and the skirt, it was a woman. Betsy Buck?

'I don't know if you can see this clearly, Major Watson, but I am holding a pistol pointing straight at you. Behind me, two men have rifles.'

No, not Betsy Buck. That wasn't an American accent. Besides, this female was too tall to be the diminutive New Yorker.

'I want you to approach me, hands held high. Do it now.'

He put his hands up and tried to place the voice. Mrs Crantock? No, not cockney enough. He took a step forward on legs wobbly from all his squat jumps. He stumbled a little, brushing against one of the many pigs that dangled from metal rails. He heard the hammer of a pistol click back.

'No tricks now, Major Watson. You know I will kill you without hesitation if I have to.'

The voice in his head didn't so much speak the name as shriek it, over and over again.

Miss Pillbody.

28

'You look like a pile of shit.'

Inspector Bullimore nodded his agreement. 'That's roughly how I feel.'

He was sitting at a large circular dining table, without a cloth on it. Before him was Carter Amies, an 'Agent of the Crown', the catch-all term for men who served in the Secret Service Bureau. Amies was in the section now known as MI5, headed up by Vernon Kell, and responsible for domestic security.

The room they were in was vast. A former all-male dining club, once the scene of glamorous and often raucous dinners, famed for their many-course feasts, it now showed signs of neglect. Potted plants in the corners had wilted and died. Several of the gilded mirrors that lined the walls were cracked, possibly by bomb blasts, and silvery cobwebs were draped over the chandeliers. Amies had told him that this rather forlorn space was often used for MI5 meetings. They had to assume their offices were watched, and here there was no chance of eavesdroppers because they were the only people in the room and the closed drapes deterred any observers. Although it was daytime, they were speaking under the soft glow of gas mantles.

'You keep a decent set of notes,' said Amies eventually, tapping the file Bullimore had presented him with.

'Thank you.'

'I didn't say the content was any good,' Amies added. 'Look, I know it's expected that a man work twenty-four hours a day in our line of work, but you need some sleep.' Amies himself was the epitome of freshness. Newly shaved from Austin Reed, dressed in a sharp checked lounge suit with a flower in the buttonhole, with a face handsome enough for stage or screen, he looked more like a trench-dodging fop than a spy. But the policeman supposed that was the idea.

'I know.' Bullimore also knew that sleep wouldn't come. The wriggling worms in his stomach wouldn't let him. He had passed a nanny with a baby in a perambulator on the way to the meeting and the sight had almost made him weep. He desperately wanted to see and speak to Marion, but she had made it clear that if he did get in touch, he would earn her lifelong hatred.

'I need you at your best.'

Bullimore sat up at this. 'I thought I was off the case. I thought your lot were taking over.'

'We need someone to do the donkey work.'

'Well, that's a compliment.'

'Just a turn of phrase.' Amies took out a gold cigarette case inscribed with regimental arms. So he was an army man. He offered one to Bullimore and he accepted. 'I don't look like a policeman. Anything I ascertain by questioning is not admissible in court. I am not an officer of the law, as such.' He offered a Wonderlite and Bullimore leaned in to touch the tip of his cigarette to the flame.

'What about Special Branch?'

'Oh, we have some of them on it. But remember when it was Irish Special Branch? Well, it is again now, for the time being. I shouldn't be telling you this . . . ' he puffed on his cigarette for a moment, ' . . . but those treacherous bastards are at it again. This time the rebels have threatened to execute anyone attempting to introduce conscription in Ireland. And to bomb Whitehall. They've already killed a recruiting sergeant in Galway, just as an overture, and planted a bomb at the Liverpool Irish barracks.'

Bullimore was aware of just how many thousands of Irishmen had volunteered to fight Germany, even those who hated the British establishment. 'Are the Government planning conscription in Ireland?'

'I can't say.' But his eyes said they were.

'What do you want me to do?'

'Question Sir Gilbert closely about the men who took him. He must be up to it by now.'

'And if he isn't?'

'He'll be up to it.' Amies gave a hard smile. Make him up to it, is what he meant.

'And what will you do?'

Amies opened Bullimore's own file and pushed several newspaper clippings across to him. 'Have you been following the classifieds?'

Bullimore shook his head. 'When I can.'

'Well, we have a room full of people who comb the papers every day. It is a common method of communication for enemies of the State. Our readers are women, mostly. But good, all the same,' he added, as if surprised.

'I have seen some of these.' The inspector looked down at the clippings. 'Do you know who the GODS are?'

'I gave that to the cypher department. They checked against telegraphic codes, but nothing. They suggested it is an acronym. G for 'Guild', O for 'of', the D for . . . 'Disadvantaged', perhaps, the S for 'Soldiers'.'

'Or 'Servicemen',' said Bullimore. 'There might be sailors or airmen in there.'

'True. The Guild of Disadvantaged Servicemen. It has a ring to it. There was also this.' Amies pushed another piece of paper over to the policeman. 'Published some weeks ago. A similar sentiment, but different name.'

'LOUG.'

'League or Legion of something. Nothing else that makes much sense.'

'The League of Unfortunate Gentlemen, I believe.'

Amies looked impressed for a second. 'You know this how?'

Bullimore explained about Trenchard and the men at Victoria Railway Station. 'Do you think they are one and the same?' he asked the spy.

'Possibly. GODS is a more striking name than LOUG; perhaps they changed it.' He suddenly looked serious. 'Either way, it is clear that there are people who want the Government to improve and broaden their compensation proposals or they will show the members of the board just what it is like to suffer the loss of limbs or sensation. What they are calling themselves

204

doesn't matter. What matters is stopping them.'

'I agree. And what will the Government do about their demands?'

'Nothing.'

The callousness of this remark shocked Bullimore. 'Nothing?'

'Nothing publicly, I mean. We cannot be seen to give in to blackmail by terrorists. And that is what these men are, no matter how they dress it up. We give in to such demands and next thing we know the suffragettes will be back, poisoning prime ministers and blowing up houses, and the Irish will double their efforts to cower us with gelignite. No, no negotiations.'

'And the remaining members of the board still held by these GODS?'

'We have to hope we get to them sooner rather than later. Which is why I need you to talk to Sir Gilbert. At least he is *compos mentis*. I hear Powell remains . . . incapacitated. You see to Sir Gilbert, I'll look at the other aspects of the case.'

'Such as?'

'Such as who placed these classifieds.'

'It is very simple to use a third party and a classified agent,' said Bullimore. 'And so make the booking almost untraceable.'

Amies smiled. 'True. But you'd be surprised how often people slip up.' He gathered the files together. 'We shall reconvene here at . . . ' he checked his pocket watch,' . . . six o'clock. Agreed?'

'Agreed.'

'And then I insist you get a good night's sleep.'

Bullimore rose to leave but then Amies said,

'This Watson business . . . '

Bullimore sat down again. 'I don't believe Watson is part of this gang.'

Amies shook his head. 'No, neither do I. In fact, looking at the facts, I rather think he has been taken by them. Perhaps he was getting too close? After all, he is something of a detective.'

'I think you'll find that was Holmes.'

'Well, whoever it was, Watson and Holmes have been of some assistance to my organization in the last few years. But I noticed that on the last occasion, two very good Agents of the Crown, Coyle and Gibson, ended up dead.'

'What are you saying?'

Amies tapped his ash on the carpet. 'That you should be careful if you come across him again. If I believed in such things, I'd say that this Watson is bad luck for the likes of you and me.'

★   ★   ★

Oberleutnant Schrader slept for ten hours after his return from the raid over London. He awoke in the mid-afternoon, the sun already past its peak, still feeling the slight fuzziness of exhaustion. It was as if the body burned through ten days' supply of energy in the hours spent on a bombing mission. No matter how much he slept, he never quite managed to recharge the batteries, and so he was that much more depleted each time.

But it wouldn't last for long. Winter was coming, the months when they would be reassigned to short-range bombing missions over the Western Front. So how many more sorties to set London ablaze would they have? Six, ten, fifteen at most. He just hoped they had sorted out the incendiary bomb racks. He splashed cold water on his face and dressed, before cycling to the airfield. He would have coffee in the mess.

The leaves were turning, the low sun catching the yellows and reds rapidly colonizing the branches and the ground was already flecked with gold. He thought of the hearty meals they would normally be having at home — his father liked to hunt, so there was usually wild boar and venison. How would they be faring this year? It was unlikely his father would be allowed his usual three weeks of shooting. And if he was, it would be considered bad form for a factory owner to feast while the rest of the country starved, unless you were one of the military élite, to whom the normal rules did not apply. Men like von Kahr's father, and possibly the admiral.

The Gothas and the Giants had been covered in their netting camouflage. Every plane had a team of mechanics swarming over it, busy as worker ants, as engines were stripped, fuel lines cleared, rigging wires retensioned, undercarriages inspected.

Schrader waved away several attempts to engage him in conversation as he wheeled the bicycle past them. Not yet. Not until he had coffee and bread inside him would he feel human enough. Deitling tried to wave him over but he gave the Swabian the two-minute sign.

He had the mess — a plain wooden hut, decorated by someone with posters of Asta

Nielsen and her movies — to himself, apart from the white-jacketed attendant with the hedgehog-like haircut, who served him a pot of strong black coffee — a few marks slipped onto the bar got him the good stuff, smuggled in from Holland — and some slices of dark bread and ham.

As he was eating, Trotzman came into the hut, with a snarling Deitling at his heels. Schrader reluctantly asked for two extra cups.

'Have you seen those fuckin' bomb racks?' Deitling asked.

'I think I was here first,' said Trotzman waspishly.

'My dick gets harder than those,' Deitling continued. 'They are like putty. I don't think they used metal at all, I think they're made from compressed snot.'

'I'll take a look once I'm finished.'

'Well, don't be too long, skipper, because I'm not going up with those carrying the bombs.' He left without bothering to drink any coffee.

Schrader sipped from his cup. 'Is he right?'

'The quality of the metal does leave something to be desired, yes,' said the weatherman.

'I'll have a look at it. What did you want?'

'Just to ask you for a debrief on last night's weather and an exact note of the route you took. Tonight is meant to be exactly the same conditions.'

'Then we won't have any trouble.'

'Maybe. Jackermann's Gotha never returned.'

Schrader's stomach flipped. There but for the grace of an unpredictable God.

'Well, we were pretty scattered by the end of

208

the raid. Some had trouble forming the diamond for the home run. Do we know what happened to him?'

Trotzman shook his head. 'Could be enemy guns, fighters, but . . . '

'Yes?'

'Oberleutnant Drezler swears he saw him over the sea, a little north of him, well clear of the English defences.'

'Engine trouble?'

'Jackermann has the best maintained plane in the fleet, you know that.'

This was because Jackermann was an engineer by training. He was all over the mechanics, all the time, making sure everything was done by the book. He had never had to send up a flare and return to base.

'If he was well to the north of you, he may have run into weather,' said Trotzman, 'You said last night that you flew into nothing untoward.'

'No. Slight headwind, nothing to worry about.'

'So we'll run yours as preferred course.'

'Very well, I'll write it up for you before the briefing.'

Satisfied, Trotzman left, also not bothering to drink any coffee.

Schrader helped himself to a second cup and allowed a warm glow to spread through him. The same conditions meant London would be laid out like a panorama. Never mind about the blackout, it was as clear as a dancer under a spotlight at the Apollo. The British guns couldn't reach them if they flew high enough and there had been no sign of any night fighters. Like shooting birds in a cage. Sometimes, at moments like this, Schrader thought he might even survive this war.

The warmth inside cooled a degree of two when Rudy von Kahr entered, boots, belt and buttons polished to a rare brilliance.

'Ah, there you are. Can you try to shut Deitling up? He's making everyone nervous.'

'You're the boss,' Schrader reminded him.

'I don't think anyone has told that Swabian prick,' von Kahr said, sitting down. 'If he weren't a decent flyer . . . '

'Coffee?'

'Yes, thank you.' Von Kahr poured himself a generous cup and drank, smacking his lips after he had drained half of it. 'Good. That's not the usual swill. You celebrating something?'

'Being alive.'

'Here's to that.' Von Kahr refilled his cup.

'Does Deitling have a point? About the bomb racks?'

Von Kahr nodded. 'I've ordered them strengthened.'

'Then what's he complaining about?'

'We're increasing the bomb load for tonight. By order of the Air Ministry. So we'll have trouble gaining height.'

Schrader said nothing. It was a foolish decision. Operating at a lower ceiling made them more vulnerable. But he could tell from the von Kahr's expression of regret that it wasn't his choice. Eventually Schrader said: 'In my opinion, it is better to drop fewer bombs and get home to fly another day.'

'I agree.' Von Kahr looked over at the orderly, but he was intent on his glass polishing. 'Which is why I am telling every commander, off the record, to ditch some of the load over the North Sea.'

'Jesus. You could be shot for that.'

'As leader of this squadron, my duty is to my men. Not the Air Ministry.'

Schrader put his coffee down and looked at von Kahr with fresh eyes. Von Kahr squirmed a little. 'What is it?'

'You know, some of us thought you were mainly interested in getting a Blue Max to pin at your throat.'

'Including me. I suppose it's like fatherhood. You don't appreciate the responsibility until you have it. I don't want the England Squadron to be known as a suicide league. I shall have to trust every man to keep quiet about this.'

'They will.'

'They'd better. Or they'll all get an invite to my execution.' He gave a wry smile. 'Now, certain people were very pleased with your efforts the other day. The flight to England.'

'Nobody said.'

'They are not the sort of men to send flowers.'

'No, I imagine not. Cigarette?'

'No, thanks.'

Schrader lit up. 'Well, I will consider myself patted on the head.'

He knew what was coming next. 'They'd like you to do it again. Sometime soon.'

Schrader had always suspected this might happen. Once he had established it could be

211

done, then they were bound to ask for a repeat performance. And perhaps another, and another until . . . the British slammed that particular door in his face.

'Another drop-off?' he asked.

'No. Pick-up.'

That was trickier. More to go wrong. 'All right.'

'There's just one problem.'

'Well, I'd be surprised if it was just one. What is it?'

'This particular passenger might not want to come.'

29

Under Miss Pillbody's watchful eye and her Browning pistol, two men, including the one who had given him the tap with the cosh, had frogmarched a shivering, blinking Watson out of the cold storage to a small, windowless room lit by a flickering electric bulb. Miss Pillbody had said nothing to him, simply gave a thin smile when he had hissed her name, with as much disgust as he could manage. They led him along a corridor to the room that was to be his next prison. In it was a cot bed, a gas ring and kettle, and a stack of magazines, none of them newer than 1915. Some kind of nightwatchman's hidey-hole, he assumed.

His two gaolers were also silent. They simply threw an Ulster blanket onto the stained mattress and locked the metal door from the outside. Watson tried the handle anyway. The door didn't budge. He banged a fist against it and it gave a dull ring. There was no way his shoulder could come out anything but second best against that. At least this room was warm and he wasn't likely to freeze to death.

But *Miss Pillbody?* Of all the evil creatures in the world, he didn't expect that one. Was she behind the abductions and mutilations? But why? She might be a monster, but there was always some sort of method in her savagery. Some benefit to Germany. He simply couldn't compute this one.

A wave of tiredness broke over him, and he sat on the bed, aware of how much his body ached. He doubted he could fall asleep, but he wrapped the blanket around himself and closed his eyes to rest them and the next thing he knew he was being shaken awake. The two men were there, one with a revolver pointed at him. Where on earth did they thing he was going to run to?

'What time is it?' he asked. 'How long have I been asleep?'

No response.

The mute pair led him past the meat locker where he had been imprisoned to a large, warehouse-like space. There, they chained him to a metal chair. He looked around. It was a white-tiled room filled with wooden benches, each bearing the scars of a million cleaver blows and coloured by the wine-dark stains of old blood. Along one wall a bench held a variety of mincers as well as some machines he didn't recognize. In front of him, beyond two rows of benches, was a long black gas range, upon which an enormous vat of soup or stock was bubbling away, filling the air with the scent of spices.

It was here that Miss Pillbody stood, sharpening a selection of knives with a few deft strokes on a steel. She was wearing a white high-necked blouse and a black skirt, which ended, as was the fashion, some inches above her ankles. Her dark hair was up, held in place by clips and two gold-headed pins that could double as rapiers. Watson had been trying to pierce her skin with his glare for several minutes, but she seemed immune to the daggers he was

214

flinging across the room.

He heard the footsteps of the men as they retreated. It was just him and this caricature of a woman now.

'You have a lot of nerve coming back to England,' said Watson.

There was no response. She turned and surveyed the block in front of her, which held a variety of cuts of meat, glistening red. She took one of the largest knives and sliced through the flesh, producing a thin escalope. Then she looked up.

'Good, sharp knives. A joy to use,' she said in a sing-song voice.

'What is this place?'

She turned back to the stove. He couldn't see what she was doing but he heard the flame of a gas ring. Heating one of the knives, perhaps?

A stab of fear momentarily swamped the hatred that was burning inside him for this woman. No, not woman, that did her sex a disservice. A she-devil.

'It was the German butchery centre. It's not far from Smithfield. Because we Germans like our meat jointed differently from you British, and, of course, we like our sausages, this was set up to supply the restaurants of Charlotte Street.'

Parts of Fitzrovia had been so popular with her fellow countrymen before the war that the main street was nicknamed Charlottenstrasse. It had, therefore, become the focus of Londoners' rage at the Belgian atrocities, the Zeppelin and now the Gotha raids. There were few overtly German businesses left north of Oxford Street now.

She turned again, a cleaver in her hand this time, and brought it down with such force it passed through a lump of beef and buried itself in the wood. 'You must hate me.'

Watson had to laugh. 'The word can hardly encompass what I feel for you.'

Miss Pillbody reached underneath the block and fetched an apron, which she slipped over her head and tied at the back. It had once been white; it was now stained with splodges, looking like a map of a strange remote archipelago. 'I won't apologize.'

'You think that would do any good? You think I would accept an apology from you?' In his anger Watson began to rock against the chains. He could feel spittle forming on his lips. 'Why don't you just get on with what you are about to do to me and have done with it. Oh, I forgot. You like your work. You like tormenting and maiming and torturing and pain, don't you?'

Miss Pillbody levered the cleaver free of the wood and brought it down again. 'On the contrary. I'm not saying those things don't have their uses. But as a means to an end. Not for any enjoyment they might bring.'

'You killed . . . ' Watson could barely bring himself to say the words.

'Mrs Gregson. Yes. I shot her on the bridge. Now that — ' she waved the bloodied cleaver at him ' — was an emotional act, I'll grant you. And it didn't have the effect I had anticipated. I had thought by shooting her, I would have all the time in the world to pick off you and Holmes. To do what the Broomway couldn't.' This was a

216

reference to the treacherous mudflats off the island of Foulness, where she had once left Watson and Holmes to drown. 'I have to say, Holmes moves swiftly for a man of his age.' She shook her head as if in disbelief. 'And I did not expect the submarine.' There was admiration in her voice.

'We thought they would imprison or kill you. Your own side, I mean.'

For a second, Miss Pillbody looked the picture of innocence, the prim schoolteacher she had once pretended to be, with her milk-and-honey complexion, bright guileless eyes and dimpled cheeks when she smiled. Only the gore-flecked blade in her hand and the specks of fresh blood on her apron spoiled the image. 'I can be very persuasive when I need to be, Major.'

'I am fully aware of that. But the way you have murdered — '

'Major!' Her exclamation, coupled with the slam of the cleaver into wood stopped him short. She took a breath. 'I was a young widow who was asked if I would serve my country. I was chosen to train for the Sie Wölfe, an elite branch of Naval Intelligence — '

'I know all this.'

She carried on as if he hadn't spoken. 'Thirty-two of us were selected. Eighteen qualified. The rest? Well, we used live targets and live ammunition. We were taught how to fight naked, how to slit throats effectively — not as easy as you might think — how to suppress any silly qualms about what we were doing. We toured the hospitals to see for ourselves what the

217

British and French were doing to our men.'

'No more than you to ours.'

'We see our task as an extension of war. The same as if we were in the trenches. There will be casualties, on both sides. But compared to the number of bodies out on no man's land? A drop in the ocean.' Again, she brought the blade down, this time catching herself with the edge. She sucked a finger. 'I convinced my old employers that my passion was still for the cause. That I could be of use, especially as a German who can pass as an Englishwoman. So, here I am, in London to report on the impact of our bombing raids on the population. And very devastating they are, too.'

'Then what do you want with me?'

Miss Pillbody picked up a wicked little boning knife and began to cut away at some sinew. Dissatisfied, she gave it a few more strokes along the steel. 'Well, this time it's a personal matter. I need to ask you a question. I need an honest answer.'

Holmes. She's come for Holmes. Unfinished business. 'You can go to hell. Slit my throat in your expert way and have done with it.'

'You haven't heard the question yet.'

'Go on then,' sneered Watson. 'Waste your breath.'

She held up a glistening fillet of beef. 'How do you like your steak?'

30

Sir Gilbert's eyes were still bandaged. He had not been told the full extent of the damage. Bullimore knew he had to tread carefully. He stood at the foot of the bed while Lady Hastings finished reading a letter from an aunt, wishing him well, and then asked her for a moment alone with her husband.

'You're going to catch the men who did this?' asked Lady Hastings.

'With your husband's help, yes,' Bullimore said softly.

'And hang them?'

'That's not up to me.' In fact, the perpetrators hadn't committed a capital crime. Not yet.

Lady Hastings' voice dropped to a growl. 'Actually hanging is too good for them.'

'I agree,' said Bullimore. 'But let's catch them first.'

She nodded at this sentiment, her lips tightening into a bloodless slit and she left the private room. Bullimore couldn't blame her for being so angry, one look at Sir Gilbert with his heavily bandaged eyes made him want to go around tearing doors off until he located the men who had sliced into him so brutally.

He sat down on the wife's newly vacated chair. 'Sir Gilbert, I'm Inspector Bullimore. I am part of the investigation into this dreadful affair. Rest assured that the police, Special Branch and MI5 are all putting every resource behind it.' Every meagre resource, he thought. 'I need to ask you some questions, if you feel up to it.'

The head turned on the pillow, and for a second Bullimore felt as if the man could see through him, like one of those X-ray machines he had seen in action at the front. When he spoke, it was with a slightly muffled quality, probably due to the morphine. 'What about the others?'

'Others?'

'Holbeck, Powell, Arnott, Carlisle? They were there with me.'

Bullimore hesitated and then decided the truth was the best option. 'We have found Dr Powell.'

A spasm of anguish passed over Sir Gilbert's face. 'And what had they done to him? The truth now.'

'Deafened.'

A sigh escaped his lips. 'Five men. Five senses. Are they to rob us of one each, do you think?'

'Possibly.' But there was a chance it could be worse than that. 'But I need you to go back, if you can, back to the room where you were held. I know it will be painful . . . '

'Not if it helps catch him.'

'Him? Them, surely?'

'But there's one man, one they defer to. The leader. The man who, although he tries, cannot hide one thing.'

'What's that?'

The voice was a croak as he pointed to his damaged eyes. 'That he enjoys this.'

'Enjoys?'

'I could hear it in his voice, his breathing. No matter what he claims his ultimate motive is, this barbarism is part of the appeal for him.'

'What can you tell me about him? Can you describe him?'

'They always wore masks — gas masks. I never got a clear look at all. It's a hospital of some description, of that I am certain. There's an operating theatre, you see . . . How is Dr Powell?'

'Not as well as you, sir.'

'Meaning?'

'I think the balance of his mind has been affected by his experience.'

Sir Gilbert managed a nod. 'I won't see again, will I? I can feel, even beyond the drugs they have given me. There's nothing there.'

'I'm not a doctor,' said Bullimore cagily.

'But you are a policeman. With a crime to investigate. I suspect you know the nature of this crime. It's severity.'

'Yes.'

'Will I see again, Inspector?'

'No, I don't believe you will see again, sir, not as you did, at least. Not unless there is a miracle.'

Sir Gilbert took a deep breath. 'I'd weep if I could, but I am not sure all that is working. Blind or deaf? Which would you choose?'

'Luckily, we rarely have to make that decision. Is there anything else you can tell me?'

'There was something about the way he spoke, even behind the rubber and canvas of the gas mask. Something . . . '

Bullimore waited while Sir Gilbert composed his thoughts.

'A brogue of some description. Lilting, that was it.'

'Lilting in what way?'

'Well, I can't swear to it, but I have a feeling the man is Irish.'

★ ★ ★

Watson did not feel like steak of any stripe. His stomach was a sea of corrosion, eating itself out through the walls, to flood acid through him. Miss Pillbody ignored him and set about frying a piece of meat in a skillet on the range, humming as she did so, like any carefree housewife.

'You think I'll poison you. Is that it?'

The thought hadn't occurred to him, but it was a distinct possibility.

'But, if I am as wicked as you think I am, where would be the fun in that?' She considered the scenario for a second. 'I suppose to see your eyes bulge, your tongue loll from your mouth.'

'Some might call it entertainment.'

She laughed at that. 'But, surprisingly, not I. You might find that hard to believe. But there is no gain from murdering you. The world might mourn the chronicler of Sherlock Holmes, but it will advance our cause — Germany's cause — not one jot.' She cut a piece of steak and popped it in her mouth. 'Are you sure you won't join me?'

Watson shook his head. 'If I am of such little importance, why have you gone to such lengths to bring me here?'

She swallowed another piece of meat, a thin line of juice escaping from the corner of her mouth until she dabbed at it with a cloth. 'First things first. You have to say thank you.'

'For what?'

'Rescuing you from those men who kidnapped you.'

It was Watson's turn to laugh.

'What's so funny?'

'That I should consider being taken from Captain Trenchard to you any kind of improvement in my situation.'

'I told you. I mean you no harm.'

'I am not convinced Captain Trenchard did either. But we'll never know now because your men shot him through the head. Who are they, anyway, your tame Alsatian dogs?'

'South African, mostly. All men with a good reason to hate the British. Look, Major Watson, you are chained to that chair because I know you hate me for the death of Mrs Gregson. I am going to try to persuade you to put that aside for the moment.'

'You think I can forget who or what you are?'

'I think you can take a pragmatic decision to ignore it for a short period of time. You are welcome to continue hating me. You are even welcome to try to kill me if you must, at some later date.' She savoured the final piece of the steak. 'If you think you're man enough.'

Watson saw the twinkle in her eye at the prospect. Now that would be entertainment for Miss Pillbody.

'You have to park your pain. At the moment,

you look at me, you see her. And that hurts. Physically. I know, I felt it every time I saw a Zeppelin and thought of my husband, falling to earth in flames. But that hatred for me might also blind you to something that is important. Important to you, I mean.'

Watson kept his eyes on her face, but it was as devilishly hard to read as ever. She could be telling him the results of a scone-baking competition. But she could equally have killed him by now or reduced him to a ball of pain. 'I'm listening.'

'Major Watson, I have been following you for some time.'

'Following me?'

'Not always personally. But on occasion.'

A light went on in his head. 'It was you outside the Diogenes Club?'

'It was. I had to leave in rather a hurry when the other Holmes spotted me. But I know what you discussed.'

'How?'

'It doesn't matter. You discussed the sinking of the *Dover Arrow.*'

He inclined his head in admiration. Miss Pillbody was indeed a formidable agent. Perhaps even Holmes would appreciate that, in a detached way.

'Mycroft Holmes was warned off looking further into it. By his own government. There is to be an inquiry into the loss of the boat-train. The results of which I doubt will ever be made public. Not in our lifetime, at least.'

That had a horrible ring of truth to it. He

224

might never learn the true fate of poor Jennings. 'You are very well informed. You have a man at the Diogenes, I assume?'

She ignored his assumption. 'I want you to think very carefully before you react to the next statement. Given the correct response from you, I do believe we can get rid of those chains.'

'Very well.'

'Germany did not sink the *Dover Arrow*.'

★　★　★

'Irish?'

Amies was pacing the floor of the old dining-club room, clearly agitated by the news that Bullimore had delivered.

'Is he certain?'

'No,' said Bullimore. 'Sir Gilbert's not certain about anything. He's been pumped full of morphia. But he is fairly certain he was in a hospital. I've put some men on checking every abandoned hospital in London.'

'What if it isn't in London? Have you thought of that?'

'Then we'll work outwards.'

'Good.' Amies walked to the window and looked at the gathering dusk. 'Any news of Watson?'

'No.'

'You think these GODS have him?'

'It is a distinct possibility.'

Amies punched the wall with a force that must have hurt. 'Go and get that sleep we talked about.'

'What's wrong?'

Amies turned. 'If the Irish are involved then perhaps this isn't as straightforward as we thought.'

Bullimore had never considered it straightforward but didn't voice the opinion. 'He said he thought he might be Irish — there was no indication that this was in any way political.'

'Everything is political with the bloody Irish — '

He stopped talking as they heard the sound of footsteps coming up the stairs. With barely a knock, Rush, one of Amies's colleagues, burst in. He looked pale and sweaty.

'They have found Holbeck.'

Bullimore had read up on the man. One of the finest surgeons in England, by all accounts, renowned for his delicate touch.

'Where, man, where?' demanded Amies.

'Sorry. On a barge in the Thames.'

'Is he intact?' asked Bullimore impatiently.

'They say something has happened to his hands.'

Bullimore cursed under his breath. 'What? What has happened to his hands?'

'They've gone.'

★ ★ ★

Later, after he had been told there was no way he could question Holbeck that night, Bullimore went back to the station house, bathed, and slipped into the single bed. The room was flickering to the glare of the searchlights

226

prowling the sky. He could hear the distant thud of guns, presumably from somewhere down the estuary.

He wondered what Marion was doing. Perhaps also lying down, hands on her stomach, waiting for the signs of the life within to manifest themselves. The thought of her made him restless and he tossed back and forth, unable to settle. It was torment, the thought he might never see her again.

The light in the room changed. It was orange now. He threw back the covers and went to the window. To the east, flashes of red. Bombs were falling. Again. And out there was the man who had mutilated three talented people and still had two more to go.

He felt a stab of guilt. His little woes were nothing compared to Holbeck's. To remove the hands from a surgeon . . . it suggested a very twisted mind indeed. He shuddered when he thought of Sir Gilbert's conviction that the devil of a butcher had actually enjoyed this. Despite Amies's new conviction that Irish rebels were behind this, it was difficult to see how these depraved acts could further their cause.

He knew sleep wouldn't come. From the top drawer of a chest he took a tube of Dr Fischer's Energy Tablets, swallowed a handful, and began to dress again. He would sleep when this was over.

★   ★   ★

Miss Pillbody was cautious enough to keep her pistol within easy reach once she had loosened

227

the chains. She need not have worried. Watson was in no fit state to start tussling with the woman. He accepted a cup of coffee from her, his mind buzzing with what she had just told him.

'Why should I believe that Germany did not attack the *Dover Arrow?* It wouldn't be the first hospital ship to be sunk by German U-boats or mines. The *Donegal*, the *Asturias*, it's a long list.'

'Mines, we can do little about. Both sides lay them. They're a blunt instrument of war. But we know what the public thinks of the sinking of hospital ships by submarines. And what they think in Milwaukee and Pennsylvania. You British have done your best to keep it in the newspapers over there.'

'It's too late to stop the Americans coming to fight.'

Miss Pillbody stirred sugar into her coffee. 'We know that. But there is still a large anti-war contingent over there. One that will grow once the first Americans come home in wooden boxes and when the first news reports filter back about exactly what trench warfare involves. We need to win that propaganda war. U-boat captains are, therefore, currently expressly forbidden to fire on hospital ships. No torpedo sank that ship. No German one, anyway.'

'Well, it can't have been a mine; those lanes are kept mine-free.' Watson sipped his coffee and wrapped his still-chilled hands around the cup. 'But suppose you are right . . . '

'Let me give you another quandary. Gothas were heard over London the night before last, the 23rd of September.'

'And last night. And probably tonight.'

'Perhaps. But consider this. No German aircraft flew against England on the 23rd. There were gales in the North Sea that were blowing planes into neutral Holland. All activities were cancelled.'

'You're certain of this?'

'I'm a spy, Major; it's my job to be certain.' She fluttered her eyelids at him and he felt physically sick at this coquettishness.

'But my — an acquaintance of mine was killed in that raid. Porky Johnson.'

'Not by a German bomb. Maybe shrapnel from a British antiaircraft shell.'

'No, he was blown to pieces.'

'Not by us.'

Was it possible a British bomber had done this? Confused and off course? It seemed unlikely to Watson. London could hardly be mistaken for a German city. The pilot would have to be deranged rather than simply befuddled. And as far as he knew, Great Britain didn't yet have heavy bombers to rival the Gotha.

Miss Pillbody walked around the benches, scooping up the gun as she went, and stood before Watson. He had a fantasy for a second of reaching up and grabbing that pretty swan-like neck . . .

'For what it's worth, and it isn't worth much, I regret killing Mrs Gregson now. All I can say is, the alternative was you or Holmes.'

'You didn't have to kill anyone on that damned bridge.'

Miss Pillbody looked slightly shocked at the

suggestion. 'No, I suppose I didn't, did I? But, as I said, it's what I am trained for.'

'Why me? Why tell me all this?'

'Who do you think I should tell? Lloyd George? Churchill? I know you have good reason to hate me, but you are a man of logic, too. I would not risk exposing myself as being in London for nothing, for a mere diversion.'

'What's in it for Germany? Apart from some propaganda value.'

'That ship was sunk for a reason,' said Miss Pillbody. 'The air raid was for a reason. We'd like to know what those reasons are.'

'I'm not sure what I can do. I'm in the middle of a terrible scandal — '

'The War Injuries Compensation Board?'

'You know about that?'

She inclined her head slightly in a way that said 'of course'. She took a step closer and looked down at him. 'I would like to make you an offer.'

Watson drained his coffee. If he shattered the cup, he might have a shard that would open a vein quite easily. 'You can try.'

'Let me take that,' she said, prizing the cup from his grip. 'I will help you discover who mutilated these men. If you help me find out what happened to the *Dover Arrow*.'

'Team up, you mean?'

'A temporary alliance.'

Watson laughed at her audacity. 'You must be mad.'

'While you were sleeping, Professor Holbeck was found. On a barge in the Thames.'

Watson felt bile burn his throat. 'Had he . . . ?'

'They'd cut his hands off.'

'Damn them.' He stood so quickly that Miss Pillbody leaped back, her grip on the gun tightening. He brought his clenched first down onto one of the benches, causing knives to clatter to the floor.

'I need hardly remind you that there are two men left. They have blinded, deafened, taken away a surgeon's sense of touch. I would imagine the next man might turn up without a tongue. Or a nose.'

Taste and smell, of course they would be next. They were literally rendering the five poor men senseless.

'What makes you think you can help me?' he asked her.

'You're no Sherlock Holmes.'

'And you are, I suppose?'

'No. But I have skills you lack.'

'Such as?'

The gunshot made his heart jump. The report rang off the hard, tiled surfaces. The spent cartridge case pinged onto the cement floor. Miss Pillbody's face was wreathed in smoke from the barrel. Watson looked up at the hole in the ceiling. 'You are sentimental, Major. I am not. I will use this and other weapons to get to the truth where you might dilly or dally.'

'I think we would have to lay some ground rules about your methods.'

'So, you will accept my help?'

'If it means saving the two remaining men, yes. But I fail to see how I can assist with the *Dover Arrow*.'

'With some questions.'

'Of whom?'

She laid the gun down, sure now he wouldn't make any move against her until the business at hand was resolved. 'Didn't I tell you? We have a survivor.'

31

Holmes was sitting up in bed when Watson came in to visit. Watson had changed from his soiled military uniform into civilian clothes, a rather fine dark chalk-stripe number that pre-dated the war. He came alone. The sight of Miss Pillbody, he reasoned, might well have triggered another cardiac incident in Holmes. Watson was not the only Englishman with good reason to loathe the German spy. He would have to break the news carefully to Holmes that the woman who had once tried to drown them was his new, if temporary, ally.

'Watson! A sight for sore eyes as always.'

'I've been told I can't be long,' said Watson. 'Matron made that very clear.'

'Sit down, sit down. The police were here, looking for you.' There was just the slightest pause, almost imperceptible, before he pulled the name out of his memory. No other man might have noticed this hesitation, if that's what it was, but Watson did. 'Inspector Bullimore.'

'I have sent a message that I am well, and for him to meet me.'

'Have a care. I feel the police are not entirely to be trusted. There is pressure for results. It can lead to hasty assumptions.'

'How are you feeling, Holmes?'

'Impatient to be out of here, I can tell you.'

As Holmes peered at him, Watson felt the gaze

of old, the one that seemed to pierce your innermost thoughts. There was colour on his cheeks and those dark smudges under the eyes had softened somewhat. 'You need to rest, Holmes. You were lucky.'

Holmes reached over and patted his knee. 'Lucky to have you, Watson. Now, where have you been? On the *Dover Arrow* case? Or chasing those villains who kidnapped the Compensation Board? Did Mycroft tell you about the nightwatchman?'

The colour on the cheeks had deepened and a flush appeared at the collar of Holmes's pyjama jacket. 'Calm down, Holmes. All in good time.'

He resolved not to mention Miss Pillbody after all. He would work around it. He gave an account of his evening, omitting the kidnap, making out he had been rescued from Trenchard by members of MI5.

'It is you who were lucky, then Watson. You knew this Trenchard?'

'I did.'

'Did he strike you as the sort of man who would cut the hands off a famous surgeon? Or, indeed, be party to this?'

'No.'

'The man with the false hand? What news of him?'

'None,' Watson admitted.

'If the hand was porcelain, then I could direct you to the two men who have pioneered the casting of realistic hands. Alas, non-articulated, but better than painted wood. One is in Stoke, the other is Reginald Coates at Sidcup.'

'I have heard of Coates.'

'He also practises at St Thomas's.'

'What are you thinking, Holmes?'

'All in good time. There is something else you want to tell me.'

Watson explained to Holmes about the sinking of the *Dover Arrow* and the mysterious phantom bombing raid. He kept Miss Pillbody's name out of it.

'The assertion is that the Germans did not sink the boat-train?'

'So I understand,' Watson said cautiously.

'And this came from?'

'The MI5 men.'

'Names?'

'Names?' Watson repeated.

'Yes, what are the names of the MI5 men? Your saviours. Come, come. Surely it is good manners to ask the names of the men who have just killed to save you?'

'If you do not stop getting agitated and relax, Holmes, I shall leave this instant.'

'With me snapping at your heels until you tell the truth.' He sunk back onto the pillow, and touched his fingertips together. 'You really are the most frightful liar, Watson. It's what I admire about you. You wear your integrity like a badge of honour.' He thought for a few moments. 'Who would tell you that the Germans are not behind the sinking of a boat carrying an ambulance train but . . . someone with German interests at heart. And who would know that no German plane flew that night. Not MI5. They are not party to the Imperial German Flying Corps's bombing schedule. So this points to a German. A German

235

agent here in England, perhaps. Are you in touch with a . . . ' His jaw dropped as the synapses fired. 'That woman? You have seen that woman?' It was as if he could not bear to say the name.

'Miss Pillbody, yes.'

'So-called Miss Pillbody,' Holmes reminded Watson. 'Frau Brandt, as she is more correctly known. It was she who rescued you from Trenchard? Yes, she would kill without compunction. I thought it strange that MI5 had taken to hiring cold-blooded executioners. But Frau Brandt . . . murder is in her blood.' A long finger lashed out at him, coming to rest a few inches from his nose. 'Have a care, Watson. I know, somewhere in the back of your mind, you'll be thinking about what she did to Mrs Gregson.'

Watson didn't argue the point. He reached over and poured two glasses of water, handing one of them to Holmes.

'She would crush you like we might step on a cockroach,' said Holmes. 'But, I grant you, there is something not quite right about the Dover Arrow affair. The fact that Mycroft was put off the scent doesn't sit easy with me. Nor does a secret inquiry. So, whereas I am inclined to disbelieve every word uttered by that woman, she might just be telling the truth this once.'

'And she claims to have a survivor from the Dover Arrow. A nurse, she said.'

Holmes's right eyebrow arched up. 'Has she indeed? Your nurse?'

'She doesn't know the name. All she knows is that the survivor will not speak to the Germans about anything.'

'And where is this survivor?'

'Belgium.'

'Which side of the lines?'

Watson drank some of his water. He was hungry, too, he realized. Perhaps he should have had some steak after all. 'Their side. In a German hospital. But Miss Pillbody has a way to get me over there. The same way she came in. By aeroplane.' He shuddered as he said it.

'But you hate flying.'

'Needs must, Holmes, needs must. But I have told her we need to clear this affair of the Compensation Board up first.'

'As I said, have a care. She wants you to fly into German-held lands. You have been there before. It didn't go well.'

'Don't I know it,' Watson said glumly. 'But if this nurse can give us answers . . . '

The pictures of the King and Queen on the walls rattled as the guns in the park barked once more. The glare through the windowpane told them the companion searchlights were scanning the skies. 'If your spy is right and there was no air raid the night poor Porky was killed, then the explosions were not real German bombs. Which means, as we suspected, it was really was murder, Watson.'

'I still consider it rather an elaborate ploy to disguise murder.'

'Perhaps. But also perhaps it is not the first time the air raids have been a convenient cover. It might be that the next step is to provide your own sham air raid as a distraction. I suggest we look at the names of all those killed in the air raids — the newspapers have published them — see if anything strikes us as odd.'

'Us?'

'You'll need help, Watson; you can't do this alone.'

'I have Bullimore.'

A roll of the eyes. 'A policeman? Have all your years with me taught you nothing?'

'Even a policeman can read lists of the dead.'

Holmes tapped the side of his head impatiently. 'But can he make connections? Eh? He can read, but can he understand?'

'I think this Bullimore is a cut above, Holmes. And I have Miss Pillbody.'

Another moment of hesitation before he gave a great guffaw. 'What strange bedfellows. The doctor, the policeman and the enemy spy.' The finger wagged at Watson again. 'You will keep me informed or I shall be out of this bed in a trice.'

'I will, of course. I shall leave you to it now.' The metal bed rails jangled as more guns fired. 'Try to get some rest. If the Germans let you.'

'Where are you meeting Bullimore and Miss Pillbody?'

'Well, Holmes, I think it best we avoid 221b. We don't want to add a journalist to our little coterie. So, Wimpole Street.'

'My cuttings are still there, I hope.'

'I would expect so.'

'Mrs Turner struck me as someone who wouldn't idly throw such things away.'

'No.' Watson stood to leave. 'One thing, Holmes,' he said. 'The nightwatchman?'

'What's that?'

238

'You told Mycroft to tell me something about the night-watchman. John Crantock, who was killed in the school raid.'

'I think we can be fairly certain that, whoever was found dead at that school site was not John Crantock. This Bullimore, perhaps he could be persuaded to get an exhumation order?'

'If we think the body has been misidentified, then, yes. Was that it?'

'No, I wanted you to remind me where he worked. If you ever told me.'

'I don't believe I did. He was at St Luke's, the mental hospital on Old Street.'

'Ah.'

'You think it important?'

'The little details are usually by far the most important things about a case. Go. I expect you back here tomorrow, with news of progress.'

With that Holmes rolled on his side and appeared to fall fast asleep.

* * *

The severed finger lay on the low table in the sitting room of 2 Upper Wimpole Street. It was, for a few moments, like a frozen tableau, a gruesome version of the Adoration of the Magi as all stared at the digit, which Bullimore had unwrapped from a handkerchief. Bullimore was crouching next to the table, Watson was standing in front of the fire, Miss Pillbody — whom Watson had introduced as his 'companion' — was sitting and Mrs Turner was holding a tray with a teapot, four cups and some biscuits on it.

Watson scooped up the finger and the cloth and allowed her to put the tray down.

'That gave me a turn, I can tell you,' she said.

'It is very realistic,' conceded Watson. 'Where was it?'

'After I couldn't sleep,' Bullimore explained, 'I went back to the park, to where we found the dead men. I borrowed a flashlight from a bobby . . . didn't take me long. I can't imagine how we missed it.'

Watson turned the porcelain object over in his hand. 'It must have been shot off when . . . ' he sensed Miss Pillbody stiffening, ' . . . when those men pulled me out of the taxi and then fired after him when he was fleeing.'

'I'm intrigued by this, Major,' said Bullimore. 'You say you were kidnapped by one lot of men, one of whom you knew, and then taken from them by other men who never actually gave their names, who detained you but then, equally mysteriously, let you go.'

'That is about the size of it. Baffling.'

Bullimore certainly looked baffled and not a little disbelieving. Watson could feel a pulse of doubt coming from him. Maybe Holmes was right and he could be read like a book.

'Do you take sugar, Miss . . . ?' Mrs Turner asked.

'Adler.' Watson had almost given the game away when Miss Pillbody had given her new pseudonym to Bullimore, by blurting his outrage at her co-opting of that surname from that scandal in Bohemia. 'But please, call me Elsie.'

Nobody but Watson saw the fast wink Miss

240

Pillbody gave him. A wink! From a woman. It was very unsavoury. But it simply signalled that Ilse had become Elsie. At least she hadn't gone the whole hog with Irene.

'So,' said Watson, 'we can ask Reginald Coates and his team if there is any way we can trace the owner of this finger. Thank you.' He took his tea from Mrs Turner. 'Coates is the leading expert on false limbs of this sort,' he explained.

'The chances are he will have asked for a replacement,' said Miss Pillbody as she sipped her tea. 'After all, a man with a missing real finger might arouse suspicion in a hospital. Someone with a damaged prosthetic simply asking for a repair . . . '

Bullimore turned his puzzled expression towards her. 'That's very true.'

'So a telephone call to Coates might suffice to confirm if any such enquiry has been made.'

'I shall do that first thing,' said Bullimore through pursed lips.

'St Thomas's and the new facility at Queen's, Sidcup, are where he is based,' said Watson.

'And the exhumation order,' added Miss Adler, in the voice of someone used to being obeyed. She followed it up with a sweet smile.

'If you think it relevant,' Bullimore said to Watson.

'Mr Sherlock Holmes thinks it is relevant,' Miss Pillbody said.

'And how is Mr Holmes?' Mrs Turner asked before Bullimore could answer.

'Recovering well, I would say. He wondered if you had kept the clipping he made?

241

She nodded and put down her cup. 'Just a moment.'

The landlady returned with a brown folder, which she handed over to Watson. The advertisements were in there, plus something very strange. A flick book Holmes had made up, by cutting some diagrams from the newspaper, and gluing them to card. They were pictures of hands making shapes. 'Sign language,' he said to himself.

'Pardon?'

'Holmes knew the next man would be deaf because they announced it with these, published in several newspapers. The black square previously heralded the blinding of Sir Gilbert.' It explained those strange movements with his fingers he had been doing for Mycroft. He had been trying to demonstrate sign language.

'So did they announce the cutting off of . . . ' Mrs Turner almost couldn't bear to say it, ' . . . that poor man's hands?' A thought occurred to her. 'Mr Holmes asked me to collect all the morning and evening newspapers until further notice. I'll fetch them.

They found it in the *Evening News* of the previous day. It was a square box, bordered in black. Inside were three words:

INCULCATE
HOLBECK
LUMBAGOED

'Lumbago?' asked Mrs Turner. 'It was a little more than lumbago they did to him.'

'It's a telegraphic code,' said Watson. 'But which one?' He looked around the room for suggestions.

'ABC?' asked Bullimore. The telegraphic codes were a way of reducing the cost of sending a telegram. By using an agreed codebook, people and companies could communicate with the minimum of words on paper, thus often saving a fortune. 'It's the most popular.'

They all looked at Mrs Turner. 'I have no use for telegram codes. I could ask the neighbours. They're probably out of the cellar now the raid is over.'

She returned with an *ABC* and a *Universal Telegraphic*, but, as Bullimore had suggested, it was the *ABC* version that the kidnappers had used.

'Inculcate . . . ' Watson turned the pages, ' . . . means 'Regret to inform you'. Holbeck we know.' When he turned to the key for lumbagoed he gave a snort of disgust.

'What is it?' asked Bullimore.

'It's a code for shipping and insurance companies. It stands for: 'Lost with all hands'.'

'Good grief,' said Miss Pillbody. 'That's wicked even by my — ' She quickly drank the rest of her tea. 'By my understanding of the Germans' standards of behaviour.'

'That a man could be so flippant about such things,' said Watson slowly, 'is almost beyond belief.'

The clock struck and Watson checked his wristwatch. 'We should just search today's papers for any hint of the next outrage.'

They spent thirty minutes combing the classifieds of Mrs Turner's trove of newspapers, but, despite a few false alarms, turned up nothing.

'Well, it could be good news, maybe even a reprieve, for Carlisle and Arnott,' said Watson. 'Or we could have missed something.'

'Or they could have tired of playing games,' offered Miss Pillbody.

The mantel clock struck the half-hour. 'I think there is little more we can do tonight. I suggest we reconvene at midday. If that is agreeable to everyone?'

All nodded, apart from Bullimore. 'I have to meet my contact with the security services. They are going after the Irish angle, which I think is a waste of time.'

'Irish angle?' asked Watson. 'What Irish angle?'

'Oh, just something Sir Gilbert said. He thought the main abductor had a touch of the Hibernian to his voice.'

The little details are usually by far the most important things about a case.

Watson walked to the window, pulled back the curtains and lifted the lower sash. The smell of smoke was on the air, not domestic, but the stench of burned buildings. Somewhere off in the distance guns were still firing. He turned back to the room. 'There is a man who, so we heard, is back in London. We know that he can make trouble. He was born in Ireland, but brought up here, although he still affects an Irish accent. Holmes was convinced he was up to no good, but we lost sight of him.'

244

'This man's name?' asked Bullimore.

'Shackleton.'

'Ernest Shackleton?' the detective asked, his voice laced with surprise.

'No, his feckless brother, Frank, the man who, allegedly, stole the Irish Crown Jewels.'

'And you have no idea where he is?'

'None.'

Miss Pillbody snatched up one of the newspapers she had previously examined and flicked the pages, finally holding one up for them all to see. It was a picture of Ernest Shackleton, standing with his wife, Emily, on a London street. 'Why don't we ask his more famous brother?'

32

'Armed police! Come out with your hands up!'

Walter Birchall was sitting down to a boiled egg when he heard the muffled cry from outside. It was followed by the thumping of something heavy and hard against the front door of his Fulham house and the splintering of wood.

Birchall leaped to his feet, knocking over his tea, pulled up his braces over his shirt and was across to the French windows in a few strides. But he could see uniformed figures climbing over the garden wall, at least one of whom had a rifle. Another of them spotted him and raised an arm to point him out to his companions. A whistle blew.

There was a gun, his ever-reliable Smith & Wesson, sitting in the drawer of the sideboard in the dining room behind him, but he had the feeling that even so much as waving that at the policemen would result in his being shot.

Glass shattered out in the hallway. They had smashed the etched panes out of the door. He couldn't even make it up the stairs: they could and probably would shoot him as he ran by, firing through the empty frames.

Perhaps he should do just that. It might even give the cause more publicity than he could alive, perhaps as much as those mutilating thugs that had hijacked the whole campaign.

The door to the street gave a final groan and

swung back with a crash that sent the last of the glass to the floor, and he heard the drumbeat of boots on his carpet. A high-pitched whine started in his ear, so debilitating he could only just hear the plain-clothes man who came in behind the two constables with pistols, but ahead of two others with Lee Enfields rammed into their shoulders.

'Walter Birchall, I am arresting you for kidnapping, blackmail and inflicting grievous bodily harm — '

One of the policeman produced handcuffs. He held out his arms to them and almost laughed when he saw the look on the copper's face. How do you handcuff a man who only has one hand?

★ ★ ★

Bullimore lit a cigarette and handed it over to the young man before him. Amies sat in the corner of the interview room at Bow Street, legs crossed, already smoking.

Birchall took the cigarette with his left hand and tapped the stump of his right on the table.

'Will I be able to get the new hand? It'll be ready tomorrow, so they said at the hospital.'

'Let's see how this goes, eh?' said Bullimore softly. 'Because up till now, I am not sure I believe a word of what you've said.'

'It's the truth.'

'So you say.' Bullimore sat down. 'But I am not going to get a stenographer in here to take a statement until I am convinced by this story of yours. This organization you belong to . . . '

247

'Yes.'

'GODS.'

'No, I told you, I have no idea who they are — '

Bullimore banged the table with the palm of his hand. Birchall jumped. The lad was twenty-six and he had lost his hand trying to throw a German grenade back over a trench top to save his men. He had also lost three toes on one foot after he had lain in a waterlogged trench for hours before a medical team could reach him. He was lucky not to have bled to death. 'Yet these GODS seem to have the same aims as you.'

'But not the same methods.'

'And you don't know who they are?'

'No.'

'Some friends of yours who decided that throwing flour wasn't aggressive enough, perhaps? That you had to take more affirmative action? Animals who thought you had to maim these people into understanding what you are going through?'

Birchall's voice was very small now. 'No. We thought we would act like suffragettes — early suffragettes before they started attacking property and people. Letters, throwing flour or eggs, advertisements.'

'And Captain Trenchard was one of your number?'

'Yes,' Birchall admitted.

Bullimore cursed softly. He had sent Trenchard to find Watson. How was he to know that the man had an agenda of his own? And would the super believe him? He was beginning to wish he had just put out the arrest warrant as he had been asked.

'How many of you altogether?'

'Fifteen. Thirteen since you shot Captain Trenchard and Myrtles in that taxi.' He held up his stump. 'And nearly killed me.'

So, he assumed the rescue of Watson had been carried out by the police. 'And you can provide names of these thirteen?'

'Yes. We are not GODS. We are called — '

'Were,' said Amies languidly from the corner. 'Now, you are just a young man in serious trouble.'

A nod from the prisoner. 'We were called the League of Unfortunate Gentlemen. L-O-U-G. You can see it in the classifieds we put in the paper.

'That's a terrible name,' said Bullimore.

'It took four weeks just to agree on that. Then we started by writing to the members of the Compensation Board, arguing that the proposed settlements were unfair. Not so much to me, you understand. But Captain Trenchard has a badly maimed brother. Myrtles, the cabby you killed, has a son who has gone soft in the head. Spends all day singing the same nursery rhyme, over and over again.'

'So you decided to move things up a peg or two,' said Amies.

'No, sir, it wasn't like that. When we realized that these GODS were pursuing a similar line to us, we decided to distance ourselves. Trenchard said we could talk to Dr Watson — '

'Talk? At gunpoint?'

'We needed his attention. We wanted to explain to him that we had nothing to do with these terrible crimes. Of course, as you know, we didn't have a chance. Your thugs came charging in, guns blazing like it was a Broncho Billy picture. Your people executed Myrtle and Trenchard, you know. A cold-blooded execution. By the State.'

Bullimore said nothing. He looked over at Amies, who shook his head. It wasn't MI5 or Special Branch who had rammed that taxi and shot those men. So who was it?

And just as importantly, why was Major John Watson lying to him?

★   ★   ★

Watson could smell the drink on the man's breath from twenty paces. And it was not yet midday. He was fairly sure there was more than coffee in Ernest Shackleton's cup. He sat down in the lobby of the Hotel Cosmopolitan, a place Watson hadn't been in for close on a quarter of a century. It was still grand, with gold swags of fabric at the windows, and marbled pillars with gilded caps, but like many of the best establishments, it was looking a little faded in places, another victim of the war.

Shackleton rose as Watson approached and ordered him a coffee from the waitress and one for himself while she was at it. They shook hands and Watson felt his coarse skin, the result of a life on ships and ice and the frostbite he had suffered on the *Endurance* trip after famously giving away his mittens to his photographer. 'Sit yourself down, Major.'

There was an Irish accent there, Watson noted, but worn away by the years so only a nub, albeit an attractive one, remained.

'Thank you for seeing me, Sir Ernest,' Watson said.

'Oh, how could I refuse the man who kept us entertained on board ship for so many hours? Both *Discovery* and *Nimrod* had copies of your Holmes stories. Maybe if *Endurance* had had them, we might not have got into so much trouble, eh?' The voice was smooth and comforting, in sharp contrast to his rugged, lived-in face. His eyes glistened as he laughed and when he smiled the face transformed. 'And you can drop the Sir, Major. Ernest will do fine. Mick if we get to know each other a little better. Ah, here we are.'

Two coffees arrived and Shackleton was very particular about which one he had. The signs of a hard-drinking man were all present and correct — the slight shake of the hand, the web of veins over the nose, the broken blood vessels under the eyes.

'Actually, Major Watson, before we get going, there might be something you can help me with.'

'Me?'

'You're an influential man, Major. Is that not so?'

'Well, my name carries a little weight in some quarters. In others . . . '

'Ach, Sherlock Holmes is not forgotten and

251

neither is his Boswell.' Shackleton leaned forward, giving Watson a blast of brandy-laden breath. 'You're a man of a certain age, are you not? Yet here you are in that smart uniform, when you could be tucked up in a cosy armchair in Baker Street. Am I right? So how did you do it? How did you get back in the army? Me, with my big, important 'Sir' in front of m'name, I haven't managed it.'

'I became a specialist. In blood transfusion.'

The explorer nodded his great head thoughtfully. 'I can see that they'd need that. But I have a specialism, too.'

'What's that?'

'Leadership. I didn't lose a man out there, not one. They could do with some more officers who try to keep their men alive.'

There was only one way to guarantee keeping men alive, Watson thought, and that was to stay away from trenches, machine guns and poison gas. 'How old are you, Sir Ernest?'

The explorer drank his coffee. 'Forty-three. I know I look older, but that part of the world, the cold and the wind ages a man. Jesus, there's winds that'll strip your skin like a barber's razor.' He cleared his throat and quoted:

O you that are so strong and cold,
O blower, are you young or old?
Are you a beast of field and tree,
Or just a stronger child than me?

'Robert Louis Stevenson,' said Watson.

'Aye, another fine writer. But forty-three, I ask

you, is that an age to tell a man he can no longer serve?'

'I am afraid I have no influence . . . '

Disappointment flitted over the iceman's face.

' . . . But I'll see what I can do.'

'That's all I can ask. I'm off to Buenos Aires next month. A sort of performing pony, to try to get some of these South Americans to join us against the Germans.'

'A diplomatic mission?'

'You could call it that.'

That didn't strike Watson as an appropriate use of Shackleton's talents. He was a man of action and work, and although he clearly loved a slice of poetry, the language of diplomacy was arcane and deceptive. Maybe the Government could find the explorer something, perhaps in training others to survive in harsh conditions.

'So you'll be back when?'

'Early next year. Perhaps we could talk about it by then.'

'If the war is still on,' said Watson.

'Amen to that. It's a fine sentiment. But I wouldn't wager a pound on peace right now. Not with the submarines and the bombers — the Germans still have some fight left in them.'

'I'm afraid you're right.'

'Now we've got my future army career out of the way, how can I help you, Major?'

'It's about your brother.'

The man stiffened and suspicion clouded his features. 'You're not still after him on that crown jewels business?'

'No, not at all. But we need to find him.'

253

'We, Major? Who is we?'

'I am working on behalf of . . . ' Who was he working for? 'Scotland Yard. We need, as they like to say, to eliminate him from an on-going inquiry.'

'In my experience that means we'd like to fit him up for something he didn't do.'

'We believe he is in London.'

'You believe wrong.' Shackleton drained the coffee with a small shudder of pleasure. 'Let me tell you, Frank is a bad boy. Not good with money. None of us Shackletons is. Look at me, I still owe thousands to my investors. Frank, well, he's worse than me. Declared bankrupt a few years back. Debts of £85,000.'

Watson whistled at the enormity of the sum.

'And there was that fraud business. But he did his time.' Frank had persuaded a young woman called Mary Browne to let him look after her inheritance. He had burned through it in a matter of weeks.

'Fifteen months, wasn't it?'

A nod. 'Hard labour. When he came out, I got him a job. A job, mind. And a house in Sydenham.'

'So he is in London.'

'More coffee?'

'No, thanks.'

Shackleton signalled for a refill. 'Frank Shackleton is dead.'

This was news to Watson. 'Dead?'

'To all intents and purposes. Goes by the name Mellor now. Lives as quietly as a man with his tastes can.'

254

'His tastes? You mean his criminal tendencies.'

Shackleton's voice flowed like honey from him, as if to soften the sordid words he was speaking. 'Tastes he shares with a gentleman once of your acquaintance. Mr Oscar Wilde. I think you take my meaning.'

'Ah. Indeed.'

'Some months ago, he picked up what some call a social disease, although if you ask me it's an anti-social disease. He is in New York, at the Osler Clinic, as we speak.'

Watson knew that a very effective regime to treat several types of venereal disease had been trialled in the city.

'I see.'

'And what, out of interest, do you think he might have been involved with?'

Watson explained about the kidnappings. 'No, that doesn't sound like Frank. I'm not saying he's an angel, but I don't think he would be doing this sort of mutilation. And besides, it's all in a good cause. The only good cause Frank believes in is Frank Shackleton.'

'Your father is a doctor. We thought perhaps . . . '

'That Frank had some surgical skills? He's like me. Has trouble sharpening a pencil.'

'In which case, I'm sorry to bother you.' Watson rose to leave.

'Wait a minute, Major.' The next coffee arrived and Shackleton waved him down. 'I know who stole the Irish Crown Jewels.'

Watson sat.

'It wasn't Frank. It was a Shackleton. Actually,

that's not true. He's a Garavan, on my mother's side, but he likes to use the Shackleton name. He looks like one of us, y'see.' He traced a circle around his face with a finger. 'Same looks. Well, if he parts his hair like this and you squint a little, he can pass for a Shackleton. He stole the jewels and it was him who put it around that it was Frank, to keep the authorities wrong-footed.'

'I see. And you think he could be doing the same here?'

'I just mention it in passing.'

'What is his name?'

'Garavan. Michael Garavan. A bad sort.'

Watson wrote it down in his notebook and then stood. 'Well, thank you, Sir Ernest. I wish you well in Buenos Aires.'

'If those U-boats don't get me.'

'They wouldn't dare.'

Shackleton hooted at this. 'You could be right. I will see you next year, perhaps, Major.'

'If I manage to secure something, I will let you know.' They shook hands once more and Watson turned to leave.

'One other thing, Major. Might be important.'

Shackleton had the coffee in his hand now, poised to drink.

'This Micky Garavan. He did three years of medicine at Trinity before he was kicked out.'

'For what?'

Shackleton took a slug of coffee. 'Unauthorized vivisections.'

★ ★ ★

256

The smell at Old Street Tube station made Miss Pillbody gag. It wasn't just the bleach that clawed at the throat but the underlying stench of human excrement. The platform was lined with tottering piles of rags, blankets and newspapers, as well as the occasional folding 'privacy' screen, similar to ones used in hospital, to preserve the modesty of those bedding down for the night and others answering a call of nature in the small hours. There were even rumours of people risking the live rail to go about their nocturnal business.

Miss Pillbody took all this in as she hurried along to the exit in search of fresh air. She might have, for the moment, thrown her lot in with Watson, but to her very core she was still a Sie Wolfe, an agent of Imperial Germany. And this panic, this fleeing for the underworld of London, was a sign that the bombers were succeeding the way the ungainly and vulnerable Zeppelins never had. 'Send more!' she wanted to shout. 'Send more Gothas and Giants!' Along with the U-boats sinking thousands of tons of material, the bombs could crush Londoners' morale and make them sue for peace.

The term 'fresh air' was highly relative, she decided when she emerged into Old Street itself and stood on the corner. The air was tainted with the soot and stink of a hundred small industries operating in the yards, warehouses, basements and attics of Hoxton and Shoreditch. The entire street was streaked with grime, the atmosphere laden with dust and grit. It might be doing this whole area a favour to burn it down and start again.

Along from the Tube, a gang of roughly dressed men was erecting two enormous wooden beams, designed to stop the frontage of a shop and the rooms above collapsing into the street. A system of ropes and pulleys was being used to manoeuvre them into position where they would be fixed with steel plates and bolts. There was the sharpness of coal gas in the air. The bombers were getting through, all right, she thought with satisfaction, although they would have to do better than targeting places like *E. Sheldrake, Boot Repairers.*

She took four steps forward along the pavement and then quickly stooped to refasten a boot button. A slight stumbling behind her confirmed what she had thought from the beginning of her journey. She was being followed. But she mustn't allow herself to notice. If she gave away that she knew some street craft, then people might become curious about Miss Adler.

She walked until she could see the building that had brought her to Old Street. It was enormous. Perhaps 200 metres long, she estimated. The vernacular of St Luke's Hospital for Lunatics was more like a grand country house than a mental asylum. There was a grand porticoed central section, topped with pediment and a brass-roofed belvedere and two wings, faced in what had once been a coloured brick, now blackened and sombre. These two wings had a row of triple-height windows and each ended in a square structure, like the keep of a castle, complete with crenellated tops. It was

258

almost as if the British thought being a lunatic was nothing to be ashamed of.

A high, spike-topped wall ran around the entire building, but the poplars and planes that poked their heads above the elaborate capstones suggested there were gardens within, most likely for the inmates to exercise. Although fresh air was not an option for every one of the incarcerated. There were three hundred tiny cells, she had read, many of them containing men and women too deranged to be ever let out of confinement. Surely it would be better just to end their suffering, humanely, than leave them strapped in restraining jackets to rot?

Miss Pillbody crossed the road, careful to avoid the trams, and approached the main gate. It was locked shut by a hefty chain through the bars. Beyond it she could see steps — adorned with white stripes for the blackout — leading up to the columns, beyond which were three-metre-high panelled doors, once painted in black gloss, now fading and cracked. A plaque directed men to one wing, females to another. Leaves were piled up at the foot of the doors. It looked as if they hadn't been opened for some time. When she touched the bars of the main gate, though, she could feel a vibration through her fingertips.

'Can I help you, miss?'

The man who approached was not yet forty, but wore an old man's mutton-chop whiskers. He was dressed in crudely made corduroy trousers, a waistcoat and collarless shirt, with some sort of kerchief at his neck. In his hand he held a wide wooden rake, with several missing teeth.

'All closed up here now,' he said.

'I see. I used to have a relative in here,' she began tentatively, frantically weaving the lie in her head. 'I wanted to see where she was kept.'

'All gone to Muswell Hill or Colney Hatch now,' the gardener said. 'All the records, too, if you're interested in tracing someone, are at Colney. Just us gardeners here now and the caretakers.'

'Can I come in and take a look. Just for a minute?'

He gave a firm shake of the head. 'Built in 1750 this place was. Not safe now.'

She felt the Tube rumble under her feet.

'I'll take my chances with that.'

'I don't think so, miss.' There was a slight steeliness to his voice. She gripped the bar, felt the vibration again. Was it the Tube? But no, the train had passed.

'I'd best get on,' he said, but didn't move.

'So, Colney Hatch, you say.'

'Yes. Up in North London. They'll be able to help.'

She looked up at the forbidding façade and felt a shiver. Who knew what horrors had gone on beyond those soot-stained bricks. If it was built in the mid eighteenth century, more than a hundred of years of suffering had taken place within. 'Well, thank you for your help. Nice meeting you.'

The man touched his forehead and she could feel his eyes on her as she turned to cross the road back to the Tube. She waited for a gap in the traffic as a number of drays and a bus

260

clattered by, the latter driven by a cheerful-looking ruddy-faced woman. The rather more sour-faced conductor standing at the rear platform was a female, too. Enjoy it while you can, my dears, Miss Pillbody thought. One day the men will return and they'll want their jobs back.

Directly opposite her was a man in a bowler hat almost reading a newspaper, but she avoided staring at him directly. Clumsy, she thought. Too obvious to take seriously.

She had just taken a step into the road, careful to avoid the consequences of horses being used in large numbers once more, when a vehicle swerved towards her from the opposite side.

She took a step back and instinctively reached for the clasp of her bag before stopping herself. She wasn't carrying a gun. She had felt naked without it at first, but the neat little Italian pistol she favoured might take some explaining.

The car drew to a halt with a squeal and then settled into a sort of rattly coughing. The rear door opened.

'Get in, Miss Adler,' said an authoritative voice from within.

She did as she was told.

★ ★ ★

It was early afternoon by the time Watson arrived for a new post-mortem at the mortuary at the Poplar Hospital for Accidents. As his taxicab had woven its way through the East End, his mind was reeling from what Shackleton had told him about this Michael 'Micky' Garavan, who had a conviction for his illegal vivisections. He was a strange mix by all accounts: thief, blackmailer, possibly a rapist, certainly an adulterer, but also a man who enjoyed inflicting suffering, both physical and psychological. Was it likely this man would become champion of the maimed and shattered?

There were signs of recent bomb damage along the streets they drove through on the way to the East India Dock Road, with gaps in the terraced frontages, the odd dwelling with its front blown off to reveal the meagre possessions of the occupants within. Watson looked away. It was like the wind catching a woman's skirt and blowing it up. Bad manners to stare.

The hospital itself had also been hit, a new wing looking as if a giant creature had taken a bite out of the upper corners of one of the towers. An inadequate tarpaulin stretched over the hole snapped in the breeze.

The mortuary was hidden out to the rear, beneath the isolation block. This hospital, Watson recalled as he walked under the main arch and past the porter, was where the victims of the Silvertown munitions explosion had been brought on that terrible night in January 1917. He had been a POW in Germany then, but people still talked about the strange glow that spread over London, as if the devil had left the door to hell ajar.

A hollow-eyed soldier on crutches watched him pass, and Watson almost saluted, forgetting he was in his civvies. Instead he touched the brim of his bucket-style fedora, even that coming as a shock after the unyielding peak of his major's cap.

He descended the steps and passed into the world of formaldehyde and Eusol. The walls were painted dark green, the floors tiled. Trolleys, some with bodies hidden under sheets, were lined up like buses in a garage. A nurse was busy mopping the floor nearby.

'Professor Elroyd?' he asked her.

'Room three, sir,' she said, pointing with the mop head.

'Thank you.'

'There's nose plugs in a bucket outside. You might need them.' She waved a hand in front of her face and wrinkled her button nose to signify there was a stench. Of course there was. They had dug up a dead man in a state of severe decomposition.

Watson eschewed the plugs but collected a cotton facemask from a rack before he rapped on the door and stepped in.

Just for a second panic engulfed him and the earth wobbled beneath his feet. The decay of the flesh reminded him of the trenches and the liquefied organic mush that would ooze out of the trench walls; 'hero juice' the more callous called it. He took three deep breaths and the vision faded.

'Come in, man, close the door; you want to stink the whole hospital out?'

Watson pushed the door shut with his heel and pulled on the mask. He was aware of circling flies and the smell from the air freshener burning

263

in the corner, almost as sickly as the one rising from the corpse that was laid out on the metal table. A pile of musty clothes cut from the body lay discarded on the floor.

'You might want to gown up. You'll ruin that nice suit.'

Professor Roger Elroyd was Assistant Supervisor of Medico-Legal Post-Mortems at Scotland Yard. Almost totally bald, with a beak-like nose, he always reminded Watson of a buzzard pecking at flesh.

'Forgive me for not shaking hands, Watson. Hope you don't mind, I made a start. Although I'm not sure what I am looking for. He's in worse shape than the last time he was up in the fresh air, I can tell you.'

Watson didn't need telling. The damage from the explosion that had killed him had stripped away a lot of skin from the face and what was left was grey and spongy. Most of his jaw had been pushed up into the sinus cavity. The chest had been split and the organs reduced to mulch. There was no glistening flesh of the newly dead to be seen, just a colourless mass.

'Thank you for agreeing to do this.'

'You said on the phone something about mistaken identity.'

'We think he was misidentified, yes.'

Elroyd pointed a scalpel at the face. 'Well, it is hardly surprising.' He picked a maggot from the eye socket with the forceps in his other hand. 'You know I have done a number of bomb victims. Professional curiosity about causes of death. Sometimes it is just the compression

264

wave, leaving the victim relatively unscathed.'

'I have seen that at the front.'

'At other times there is more extensive external damage, as we see here. But the blast pattern in this one . . . odd. I've also become rather an expert in German bomb cases.' He held up a piece of metal. 'And this isn't one.'

'Could it be a British anti-aircraft shell case?' Watson asked.

Elroyd shook his head. 'No. It's tin.'

'Like from a can?'

'Judging from the amount of it in the chest, more like an oil or petrol can.'

Watson stepped forward. Yes, now he looked closely he could see the glint of jagged metal under the lights. 'What are you thinking, Roger?'

'I'm thinking you owe me a large whisky after this, John Watson.'

'There might be a bottle in it.'

Elroyd chortled. 'I warn you, I like a Johnnie Walker White. Not so easy to find.' He paused. 'If I had to hazard a guess I would say this man had a device of some description strapped to his chest and detonated, to mimic the effect of a bomb.'

'Post-mortem?'

Elroyd shook his head. 'I can't tell at this stage. Let's hope so, eh? How was he identified?'

'Clothes, boots. By his wife. Who wouldn't have wanted to linger over the sight of her husband like that.'

Go on, Watson. Go on.

'Let us assume someone wanted us to think this is John Crantock. They mutilate the body

265

and dress him in the real Crantock's clothes.'

'Yes,' said the pathologist. 'The boots, by the way, were probably a size or two too small, from what I can make out. But nobody pays too much attention when the cause of death is so readily at hand.' He pointed to the sky.

'If you were going to do that, how thorough would you be in preparing the body? Knowing the explanation for death is so obvious.'

'How do you mean?'

But Watson was still taking his thoughts to a logical conclusion. 'The Crantocks wouldn't have had the money for a fancy undertakers who might try to rebuild the features. And no open coffin — '

'I should think not.'

Watson walked passed the professor, kneeled down and sorted through the dead man's clothes, ignoring the smell of earth and musty pine that rose from them.

'You think his real name might be in the clothes?' Elroyd asked.

'No,' Watson said with a grimace. 'I don't think we'll be that fortunate.'

After a few minutes of gruesome sorting of material stained by the inevitable processes of biological decay, and colonized by creatures that made him shiver when they slithered through an aperture or rip, he found what he was looking for on the remains of a pair of silk-merino drawers with a Jaylex waist. 'Expensive for a nightwatch-man.'

Elroyd said nothing.

'Ah, here we are. Thank the Lord local

outfitters still like to sew their own labels in the garments they sell.' He looked up at Elroyd. 'We'd be in trouble if it just said Selfridges. But it says Donovan & Co., York Street, and a telephone number. Crantock was a Poplar man. Why on earth would he go all the way to Colchester for his underwear?'

★ ★ ★

'Who are you, Miss Adler?' Bullimore asked as he tapped the driver on the shoulder. 'Montague Street. Is that right? You'll be going to your rooms?'

'Until we reconvene later, yes.'

She leaned back in the seat as the driver pulled away, bag placed on her lap, ignoring the policeman's question. How much did he know? He knew where she was lodging. He might even have searched her rooms. But the gun was well hidden and there was nothing to suggest her name wasn't Adler. Although the look on Watson's face had suggested he thought she had plucked it from thin air, she had created the alias before leaving Germany. He must have thought the name referred to that woman he had mentioned in his stories. In fact, she'd borrowed it from her Klein Adler typewriter.

'So, Miss Adler,' said Bullimore, twisting slightly in his seat as if to examine her more closely. 'Who are you, again?'

It was she who did the appraising. Late thirties, perhaps early forties, jawline firm, hair mostly dark but for a peppering of silver threads, dark lines under his eyes suggesting fatigue. And the eyes themselves . . .

'Well? Where did you come from?'

'Cambridge, originally.'

'That's not what I meant.'

'I am a friend and companion to Dr Watson.'

'He's never mentioned you.'

'You know him well, do you?'

'Not that well. By reputation, mainly.'

'I have known Major Watson for some years.' True. 'We have become very close.' Laughingly false. 'A gentleman would enquire no further.'

'At the moment I am being a policeman, not a gentleman. Dr Watson has made you privy to a very sensitive investigation. I need to know why.'

'Have you asked him?'

The car braked suddenly for a brewer's dray, then swerved around it.

'I'm asking you, Miss Adler.'

'We have found, over the past few years, that we compliment each other rather well.' She swallowed as she said his Christian name, as if it had stuck in her throat. 'John has some attributes I do not possess. I, on the other hand, bring a different perspective to some scenarios.'

'A woman's perspective?'

'You sound like you don't approve, Inspector.'

He stroked his chin. 'Forgive me for asking this, but do you have any proof that you are Elsie Adler?'

'Such as?'

'A letter from your bank.'

The car lurched again and kangarooed for a few feet.

'How about a driver registration document?'

From her bag she extracted the mustard-coloured document and handed it over. 'It still has my old address on it.'

'You drive?'

'Rather better than your man.' She watched the driver's shoulders stiffen.

Bullimore laughed. 'I know horses that drive better than Radcliffe. But he's learning.' His face took on a serious cast once more. 'Why did you go to that hospital?'

'Why did you have me followed?'

'What makes you think I did?'

'I don't believe in coincidences. You pitching up like that. And I would wager Old Street is off your normal beat, Inspector. Therefore either you or someone else followed me.'

'I was curious about you,' he admitted.

'I went to the hospital, with John's blessing, because it was where a man called Crantock was a nightwatchman. The man was thought to have been killed in an air raid, but there is some doubt. I thought it might be significant. Also, from what you said, Sir Gilbert was certain he was held in a hospital or somewhere with an operating theatre.'

'Which St Luke's Hospital for Lunatics never had.'

'Oh,' she said.

'Cold baths, electroconvulsive machines, strait-jackets, yes. Plus, it is a D-Notice building . . . you probably don't know what that is.'

But she did: requisitioned for war purposes under the Defence of the Realm Act. Another

269

fact to be tucked away. 'No, I'm afraid I don't.'

'Put it this way: we know these people aren't operating from there. They couldn't be.'

She nodded, as if feeling rather foolish.

'I think it is best if you don't rush off on your own to investigate anything, Miss Adler. Leave it to the professionals.'

If only you knew the half of it, she thought. 'Yes, I can see that. I'm sorry.'

His expression softened slightly at the apology.

'I think I might have read too many of Major Watson's stories.'

'You would be surprised what a detrimental effect on Scotland Yard's reputation they have had over the years. We can't all be Sherlock Holmes.'

'No, I suppose not.'

'And clear anything you are going to do with or without Major Watson through me, please.'

'I shall, of course.'

Sadness. That was what she could see in his eyes. Pain and sadness. Well, perhaps that was all a policeman's lot was. No, she suspected this was something outside of the job. A lover, wife or mistress, perhaps. She considered for a second what it could possibly be. Then she wondered at what point she would have to kill the inquisitive Inspector Bullimore.

33

By the time Mick Garavan had finished with Professor Carlisle, the man barely looked human. Barely alive, too. He had passed out during the rhinectomy. Lord Arnott, who had been forced to watch, had also fainted. Now the man who all and sundry assumed was a Shackleton removed his gas mask and let the sweat run free.

His men had absented themselves, too, although by physically leaving rather than fainting. Once he had the fever on him, they knew it was better to be scarce. Most of his assistants were Canadian deserters he had picked up from the camps they formed in the thickets of Hampstead Heath and Epping Forest, men who supported themselves by petty robberies across London, mostly during the blackouts, but doing the odd bank or post office when the opportunity presented itself. It hadn't been difficult to persuade them that there were bigger fish to fry in the city, if you knew how to go about it. Ernest Shackleton wasn't the only one in the family who could inspire men to follow.

Garavan walked out from the operating theatre and into the corridor. The German Hospital had been smashed by rioters early in the war, but had carried on going, serving the expat population of London: the numerous waiters, nurses, brokers and barbers who had

271

been a prominent part of London life before the war. It was hit by Zeppelin raids in 1915 and had moved underground, to the bunker where he was now. The first Gotha raids in early '17 had caused further anti-German uprisings and the main building was torched, with patients and staff inside. By some miracle nobody had died, but the wards and theatres were gutted. To anyone inspecting the blackened shell, it would seem there was virtually nothing left. But the *Notfall Unterirdische Krankenhaus* had remained relatively unscathed. Complete with generator for electricity and running water.

In the former prep room, he washed the blood off his hands, watching it swirl down the plughole. Would Carlisle survive the butchery he had performed? It hardly mattered. He had already placed the advertisement that would keep the police wrong-footed. We are GODS and we want justice for all. How high and mighty it sounded. Whereas, in truth, their slogan should be: we are mere men and we want to be as rich as Croesus.

It ran in the family, this lust for money and glory. Oh, they worship Ernie Shackleton out there, but in truth he often left England one step ahead of his creditors, off to pursue these fine ideals. Let's walk across Antarctica, nobody's ever done that before. Perhaps with good reason, Ernie. That's why you end up travelling 800 miles in an open boat and then crossing some God-forsaken rock of an island.

And yet they call you a hero.

Once he had stripped off the bloodstained gown, Garavan returned to the operating theatre and looked down at his handiwork. An eye

272

flickered open and he instinctively reached for the gas mask but stayed his hand. This one wouldn't live to describe him to anyone. That was fine. Carlisle could stand in for all those Englishmen who lay shattered out on no man's land, waiting for a stretcher-bearer who would never come. That was his role in this charade.

At least, that was what Garavan told himself in the quieter moments. Sometimes it was difficult to unravel his motives.

A mumbling behind a gag told him that Lord Arnott, too, had come to his senses. Garavan turned and, again, decided not to put the gas mask on. He knew his face was a powerful weapon when it came to persuasion. It was hard to show conviction from behind a wall of rubber, canvas and glass.

The last of his victims had been propped up so he could get a clear view of what had been done to Carlisle, with a strap threaded through the bars of the bed holding his head in place. Garavan reached over and undid that and Arnott shook his head as he did so. The words coming from him were unintelligible; the eyes, however, were very eloquent.

'I know, terrible business, isn't it?' said Garavan, as if he had been given no choice but to carve pieces off Carlisle and drop them in a kidney dish. 'Terrible. And still, the Government doesn't respond. How many more people have to be treated like that?' He took out a cigarette and lit it. 'And all this just for money. The most inconsequential thing about human achievement. Pieces of bloody paper.'

The smell of congealing blood was powerful, and flies had appeared and were buzzing around the wounds on Carlisle's face, some settling to suck at the carnage. He walked over and waved them away but, like a flotilla of warships standing offshore, they merely backed off until the opportunity arose to return.

'We need to talk, Lord Arnott. I need to be able to remove that gag in the knowledge that you won't merely hurl abuse at me. That we can talk like reasonable men. Can you do that?'

There was no response. Lord Arnott clearly did not trust his self-control.

Garavan pointed at Carlisle. 'Look, I've been thinking. There just might — might, mind you — be a way we can avoid that happening to you,' he said, his voice like soft velvet. 'There might just be a way we can both live happily ever after.'

34

While Watson waited for the others in the sitting room of 2 Upper Wimpole St, he sorted through the latest pile of letters addressed to Sherlock Holmes that he had brought from 221b. He split them into two piles, one he thought of no interest, the other he reckoned might engage Sherlock's brain while he was recuperating. He didn't want the man to get so bored he would go wandering through the hospital corridors in search of a drugs cabinet. That wouldn't do his delicate, damaged heart any favours.

To his surprise there was one letter — more of a parcel, really — addressed to John Watson, MD. He did get letters from people who had enjoyed his stories — and sometimes otherwise — but they normally came through the publisher of the collections or the editor of the *Strand*. A letter addressed to him at 221b was a rare thing.

It was a monogram, privately published, by the look of it. He checked the back page: 'F. Norman & Sons, Torquay, Publishers and Printers'. Yes, probably a small run with this tiny local press. The title, though, intrigued him. *Alkaloid Poisons and their Detection Post-Mortem*. It was attributed to Mary Westmacott (Miss). He turned to the title page to see if more biographical information was offered on Miss Westmacott by way of her qualifications, but there was none. A few lines on the final page stated that Miss Westmacott had served as a nurse and was a qualified dispenser.

As he flicked through, a sheet of paper fell out. It had the publisher's masthead on it, and a single scribbled line. 'I hope you find this of some use, either in fact or fiction.'

A present, then, from someone who thought he needed to brush up on his strychnine, morphine and nicotine.

There was the sound of the bell and footsteps on the stairs. Miss Pillbody entered the room, removing her hat and gloves as she did so. Mrs Turner was two steps behind. 'Is Bullimore here?'

'No.'

'Good. Mrs Turner, may I have some tea?'

'I know it's an easy mistake, but it's not a tea room, Miss Adler.'

She turned and caught the landlady in a beam of a smile. 'I'm sorry. Perhaps I could make some for you?'

'No, that's all right, I'll do it.'

Miss Pillbody gave an irritated huff once she had left. 'Watson, there is no operating theatre at St Luke's Hospital for Lunatics.'

Watson shrugged. 'It was a long chance.'

'But something is going on there. I could feel it.'

'In your bones?' he asked.

'In my fingertips.' She explained about the vibration through the gate.

'Is this relevant to this case?' asked Watson warily.

'You'll have to ask Bullimore. Where is he, anyway? I couldn't get rid of him earlier. And now he doesn't show.'

'He sent a message that he was detained at a meeting.'

'How did you get on?' Miss Pillbody asked Watson.

'I was going to wait until Bullimore was here, but . . . '

She sat. 'Go on.'

'The man we are looking for is called Michael or Micky Garavan. He is a relative of Ernest Shackleton. By some quirk of nature, the resemblance is close enough for him to claim to be Shackleton's brother, Frank. In this way he has often cast suspicion on Frank, when, in fact, he is the perpetrator.'

'Sounds like a nice chap,' said Miss Pillbody.

'The thing is, this is not a man in the business of altruism. All this is some kind of screen, I am sure, to mask a more nefarious motive.'

'Money?' she asked.

'I would say that is most likely.'

Miss Pillbody slumped forward and frowned as she thought long and hard before asking: 'The exhumation? Did that yield anything?'

'It is not John Crantock buried in the coffin that bore his name. It was a man who either lived in or visited Colchester.'

'That should be easy, then.'

Mrs Turner arrived with tea. 'Here we are. And some biscuits.'

'Thank you, Mrs Turner. You are a treasure,' said Miss Pillbody, as if she meant it.

There was a rap at the downstairs door.

'Bullimore?' asked Watson.

'That or the evening papers,' said Mrs Turner. 'I'll go.'

As soon as she had left, Miss Pillbody hissed: 'Bullimore suspects me.'

'Of what?'

'Of not being what I seem. You will have to show some affection towards me.'

'Affection? Watson asked, looking as if he had just been asked to kiss an eel.

'Hand holding. Let me put my arms through yours. Be like my lover.'

'Madam!' Heat rose up to Watson's skin and he felt the colour spread over his neck and cheeks.

'Are you quite well, Major?' Mrs Turner had entered with a stack of the evening papers. 'You look flushed. Shall I open a window?'

Watson ran a finger around his starched collar. 'No, no, I'm fine, just a rush of excitement.' Miss Pillbody gave one of her damned winks. Women shouldn't wink, he thought once more. So unseemly. But then she was no ordinary woman. 'At the feeling we are *this* close to a solution but can't quite grasp it.'

Mrs Turner handed out the newspapers. It didn't take long to locate the latest pronouncement from the GODS:

FORTY SHILLINGS OR LESS WHILE WE SUFFER
PAY UP!

凌遲

THE GUILD OF DISAFFECTED SERVICEMEN

'Why are they spelling out their name now?' asked Miss Pillbody. 'Why not before?'

'I suspect we are moving towards the

endgame,' mused Watson. 'On the face of it, after they dispose of the next person they have mutilated, then there is only one to go. The Ministry of Pensions and the War Office have not relented. What do they do next?'

'But we don't believe that, do we?' said Miss Pillbody. 'We don't really believe this is about the welfare of soldiers?'

'No,' Watson said firmly. 'This is an elaborate illusion. Like something from Devant or Maskelyne.'

' "It consists admittedly in misleading the spectator's senses, in order to screen from detection certain details for which secrecy is required." '

Both Mrs Turner and Watson looked at Miss Pillbody. 'Maskelyne said that.'

'What about the . . . what do you call them . . . ?' asked Mrs Turner.

'Pictograms? Chinese, I believe,' Watson said.

'Do you read Chinese?' asked Miss Pillbody.

'No,' said Watson, standing. 'But I know a man who does.'

★ ★ ★

'Ling-ch'ih,' said Holmes without hesitation.

'I knew you'd know.'

'My knowledge is hardly complete, Watson, but I know this one, for it is evil indeed.'

'Evil how?'

'All in good time. Tell me of events since we last met.'

Watson recapped everything he knew of the situation, adding in the most recent happenings.

279

For his part, Holmes, closed his eyes and touched his fingertips together, as if in repose. But Watson was well aware that he was processing each fact, turning it over and examining it as a Hatton Garden diamond merchant might a precious jewel. At least, that's what would have happened in the old days. At several points Watson worried that Holmes had simply fallen asleep.

When he had finished, though, the eyes snapped open once more. 'And you are convinced we are dealing with a man, this Garavan, who is creating an illusion to fool us?'

' 'It consists admittedly in misleading the spectator's senses, in order to screen from detection certain details for which secrecy is required.''

'Bravo, Watson, I didn't know you were a student of Maskelyne.'

He gave a sheepish grin. 'Actually, Miss Pillbody said it.'

Holmes gave a shiver. 'Please do not mention her by name again. To me, she will always be *that woman*.' He looked at Watson, his eyes as hard as drill bits. 'You have not softened towards her, I hope.'

'No.'

'After what she did — '

'You have no cause to remind me, Holmes.'

'My apologies.'

In truth, he had almost forgotten what *that woman* had done on the bridge. He felt a flush of shame. The shade of Georgina Gregson had walked with him every day for months, but in the heat of the current chase she had faded somewhat, fallen behind a step. He must not allow it to happen again.

Be like my lover.

Never, he thought. Never.

'You must act quickly, Watson. I shall come with you.'

'No.'

Holmes had already thrown the covers back. Watson put a hand on his shoulder. 'No. I will never forgive myself. If you insist I shall call Matron. And then where will you be?'

Holmes slumped back into the bed and pulled the blankets up. 'Listen carefully. Fetch me an express messenger boy.'

'They are difficult to find at night, Holmes. The raids, you know.'

Holmes looked irritated. 'Where is that policeman of yours? Bullimore. They have their own messengers.'

'I left word to meet me here. I assume he is still detained.'

'Then for pity's sake get me a telephone!'

Watson did not like the grey tinge to Holmes's skin. He reached for the oxygen mask but found his hand slapped away.

'Never mind that now. I shall call Mycroft. Or Churchill. Or Vernon Kell at MI5. We must find out what St Luke's is being used for.'

'You think it's important?'

'I think it vital. It has always been so. What use is a night-watchman? Why, he is someone who knows all the exits and entrances, for he has to check them on his rounds. No, Watson, we should have realized this earlier.'

'I didn't know the asylum had closed.'

281

'Nor me. We have both been . . . distracted.'

'I was a prisoner of war,' protested Watson.

Holmes smiled. 'Granted, some have been more distracted than others. I shall shoulder the blame entirely. Who still remains in captivity?'

'Carlisle and . . . Lord Arnott.'

'Doctors? Medical men, are they?'

'Carlisle. Not Arnott.'

'What is Arnott?'

Watson thought for a moment. 'A banker, I think.' He considered for a second. That didn't sound right. 'No, he works for the Treasury. And is a major stockholder in the Bank of England. That's right, he was seconded onto the Compensation Board to advise on how much the country can actually afford to pay its crippled.'

Holmes's eyes widened. 'The Bank of England! Then Carlisle is a dead man first.' He picked up the newspaper and thrust the pictogram at Watson. '*Ling-ch'ih*. Better known here as the lingering death or death by a thousand cuts. One of the execution methods used by the Chinese up until a dozen years ago. We are dealing with twin urges here, Watson. Your man Garavan is a psychopathic sadist and a thief. Carlisle will provide the satisfaction of slicing through a human being. Arnott will provide the cash.'

'But how?'

The thump of a maroon fired from nearby made them start. A warning rocket. They heard a second detonation, some way off, the echo seeming to pulse on for several seconds before diminishing. There would be a raid tonight. Both men listened carefully, but there were no engine

282

noises. The authorities were giving plenty of warning this time.

The two men could feel the change in the mood of the city, the sudden paralysis, followed by frantic activity. 'Take cover!' the policemen would be yelling. And, driven by fear of what the night sky might bring, London would flee underground, leaving the blackened streets deserted.

Holmes slapped his forehead with his palm. 'How? How? With that.' He pointed through the window.

'What?'

'The Gotha Hum.'

Bullimore arrived, breathless and wan before Watson could ask Holmes to expand. The policeman was in no mood for small talk. 'They've found Carlisle.'

'Alive?' Holmes asked.

Bullimore shook his head.

'How did he die?' asked Watson.

The face wrinkled in distaste and horror. 'They sliced him into pieces.'

Watson and Holmes exchanged glances. '*Ling-ch'ih,*' said Holmes bitterly. 'Gentlemen, whatever is happening here, I feel tonight it will reach its climax.'

'I am not at all pleased!'

It was the matron, her fist-like face underlining her words. 'This is a hospital, not some sort of detection club.'

'We were just leaving,' said Watson.

'You can't,' said Matron.

'Why not?'

'A phone call. You are to stay here. A car is on

283

the way to fetch you.'

'A car? From whom?'

'From a Miss Adler.'

Holmes started at the name. 'What? Here?'

Watson put a hand on his shoulder. 'Not that Miss Adler.'

Holmes realized what Watson was trying to convey with his eyes. 'Oh, *that* woman. Will we never be rid of her?'

Bullimore said nothing, simply made a mental note of the exchange. Now he knew there was more to Miss Adler than met the eye.

★   ★   ★

'I am here to see Mr Mycroft Holmes.'

The words seemed to flee along the corridor like a swarm of bats, swerving this way and that, filling every alcove and every crevice, growing in strength as they went.

The response was a great groan of dismay from within, underpinned by the snap of newspapers and the sudden ejection of half-swallowed drinks.

'I am sorry,' said the porter of the Diogenes Club. 'The Conversation Parlour is closed for the evening.'

Miss Pillbody stepped closer, forcing the double doors open a few more inches, allowing her voice the opportunity to penetrate even deeper into the marbled vestibule and beyond.

'Is Mr Mycroft Holmes in?'

'I am not at liberty to — '

'Yes or no?'

'That's all right, Bishop, I'll deal with this.' Mycroft came striding out into the hallway, face like thunder. 'I'll take the lady outside.'

Mycroft brushed past her and walked down the steps, lighting a cigar as he did so. London was unnaturally quiet. The maroons had been fired, but as yet no enemy aircraft had appeared. The city had closed its eyes and was praying for deliverance.

Mycroft turned. 'What is the meaning of this, madam?'

'I come from Major Watson.'

'You have the advantage of me.'

'Elsie Adler, at your service.'

'At my disservice. There will be questions about this.' He pointed at the club.

'I thought there was no speaking in there.'

'*Written* questions, madam.' He peered through the curtain of cigar smoke he had created. 'Do I know you?'

She was fairly certain he didn't. She couldn't think of an occasion when the brother had actually laid eyes on Miss Pillbody up close. He knew her by reputation only.

'I'm a niece of Major Watson's wife.'

'Which one?' Mycroft asked gruffly.

'Emily. Look, the major is with your brother. But there is something he desperately needs to know, even if he doesn't yet realize it.'

'What's that?'

'There is a D-Notice on a building near Old Street. St Luke's. You know it?'

'Of it.'

'Whatever is happening with the War Injuries

285

Compensation Board, it has something to do with the asylum and its current use. Someone like you could find out what that use is.'

Mycroft's eyes narrowed. 'Are you sure we haven't met?'

'Positive. Look, sir, we don't have much time. Can you help or no?'

Mycroft puffed on the cigar for a few moments. 'If this is some sort of trick — '

'Trick? There are men's lives at stake here. Englishmen's lives.'

They both felt the change in air pressure and involuntarily glanced up into the clear night sky.

'And it is something to do with the bombers,' she said.

'Bombers? How? Give me facts, madam.'

'I can't. All I can do is ask for your trust.' She held her breath, wondering if she had gone too far. Nobody in their right mind would trust Miss Pillbody. They might just trust the plucky, wide-eyed Miss Adler.

'Wait here.'

Mycroft disappeared inside, leaving Miss Pillbody to listen to the distant crack of anti-aircraft guns. A faint red glow, like a smear of rouge, had started to grow from the east. The first fires had started.

Mycroft returned, the cigar abandoned, his features set into a frown. 'You can drive?'

'I can.'

'You strike me as the sort of woman who might.' There was no suggestion of approval. 'There is a car coming round. Take it at once to Watson. I am going to ask Sir Francis to send the

286

Bank Guard reserve to meet you at the premises in Old Street with a view to securing the building.'

She knew Lloyd was effectively the governor-general of London. 'Why, what is it?'

Mycroft handed her a sheet of paper. 'Robbery, madam. Robbery on a grand scale.'

35

'Why would he play games?' Bullimore demanded. 'Why go to the lengths to obfuscate?'

Watson was in the front seat of the car. Miss Pillbody was driving with a speed and precision that both impressed and terrified her two male passengers. He turned to look at Bullimore, who was busy checking two revolvers, one of which was for Watson's use. 'I know his type,' said Watson. 'Sometimes the crime isn't enough. It's the game. It's not enough to steal from somebody, you have to make them look and feel ridiculous.'

'Is that all?'

'That, and a love of causing pain, I suspect.'

Bullimore cursed as the Crossley's solid tyres failed to grip on a corner and the vehicle slid around the bend.

'Sorry,' Miss Pillbody shouted.

Bullimore handed Watson the gun. 'Mycroft is sending troops?'

'From the Bank of England,' she said.

'Precious few other soldiers left in London,' said Watson. Ever since the Gordon Riots of 1780, the Bank of England had been guarded by a 'picquet' of armed men, a military detachment that stayed on the premises overnight. There were always two units on rotation, and Mycroft would have asked Sir Francis Lloyd — the man who controlled all military matters in London — to release the reserve.

They had already passed the mighty edifice of St Pancras Station. Now they were on the City Road. The moonlight and the slit beams of the Crossley gave Miss Pillbody enough to navigate by. There was precious little other traffic on the road and it thinned significantly as they passed Angel. The pavements, too, were deserted, apart from the odd scurrying pedestrian or a policeman still wearing his 'Take Cover' placard around his neck. It wasn't difficult to see why London had disappeared. The sky ahead of them was glowing scarlet and, although they couldn't hear it over the clatter of the Crossley's tappets, they knew the air was thrumming with the sound of German engines.

Watson wondered what the city would look like if you could see all the prayers being uttered at that moment. They would stream upwards, like a reverse rain, a never-ending procession of pleas and petitions, to what? Fall on deaf ears? Perhaps all the prayers filling the skies above Berlin, a negative to London's positive, asking for the survival of young Fritz and Frieda, cancelled each other out. Perhaps God thought they all deserved whatever they got. Perhaps God didn't play favourites. Or maybe there was nobody to listen after all.

'Miss Adler,' Bullimore announced, 'once we are there, I want you to retreat to a safe distance.'

'We'll see,' she said softly.

Bullimore leaned forward. 'I'm serious. You're a civilian and a female at that. I cannot take responsibility — '

'You are not responsible for me.' She put a hand on Watson's thigh. 'And I go where my beloved John goes.'

Watson gave Bullimore the thinnest of smiles. In truth, Miss Pillbody was probably worth two of him and Bullimore put together, but he couldn't admit that. 'She's very headstrong.'

Bullimore slumped back in the seat, brooding with unease.

They reached the junction of City Road and Old Street just as a canvas-sided army truck turned into the road ahead of them. Watson leaned across and parped the horn of the Crossley until the lorry's driver pulled up and Watson leaped out, with Bullimore on his heels.

An elderly captain appeared and saluted Watson. 'Sir.'

'I'm Major Watson, this is Inspector Bullimore of Scotland Yard. You've been briefed, Captain?'

'My orders are to secure the building.' He pointed at the darkened hulk of St Luke's, which looked like a grounded ocean-going liner, in scale if not design. 'Until further notice.'

'How many men?'

'Twenty.'

'Very well, we'll . . . ' The thrum that began to agitate the air meant Watson had to raise his voice. 'We'll follow you in.'

'Sir.'

'Good Lord,' he said to Bullimore as they returned to the car. 'That damned hum.'

It wasn't just the noise, it was the resonance in his chest, as if it were trying to swamp his heartbeat. He began to feel nauseous and he

290

could see by the look on Bullimore's face that he was suffering the same effect. There was little respite inside the Crossley, which had began to rattle in sympathy with the vibration.

The lorry moved off and Miss Pillbody followed.

'Those bombers,' began Miss Pillbody, glancing up the sky, 'they seem awfully close.'

The first explosion was at the far end of the street, a cylinder of flame like a biblical pillar, stretching upwards. Watson saw something flicker and spin away, and ducked as a manhole cover bounced in the road and whirled overhead with a malevolent whoosh.

A second explosion, orange and red, more ragged this time, burst out from the corner of St Luke's. An overhead tramline snapped, whiplashing across the road, spitting sparks.

'Stop!' yelled Watson to Miss Pillbody.

He steadied himself as she braked, watching helplessly as the third detonation lifted the truck carrying the Bank Guard off the ground. It seem to hover there for a second, before its back snapped in two and the world turned a harsh unforgiving white and he felt the Crossley rear up like a bucked horse. It twisted as a second explosion hit it broadside on and a concussion wave battered Watson's head, robbing him of consciousness.

When he came to his groggy senses, the car was on its side. He could hear liquid gurgling and could smell oil and petrol. Miss Pillbody had fallen on top of him, pinning him against the door. He was aware that they were covered in glass. He shook Miss Pillbody, but there was no response.

'Bullimore.'

A groan from the rear.

'Bullimore!'

'Yes. Yes.'

'You hurt?'

His response was lost in the crump of another explosion.

'Can you smell petrol?' asked Bullimore.

Watson could. 'We have to move. But Miss Pillbody here is pinning me somewhat.'

'Hold on.'

There was the sound of his struggling to get out, of the rear door slamming back, and then Bullimore was tugging on the unconscious Miss Pillbody.

'Careful,' said Watson as he managed to get his arms under her armpits.

'Is she alive?' asked Bullimore.

Watson gripped a wrist. 'There's a pulse.'

It took a good five minutes to extricate firstly Miss Pillbody and then Watson from the car, by which time Bullimore was dripping with sweat. They then carried Miss Pillbody to the pavement and laid her down on Watson's tunic. Bullimore draped a raincoat over her. Only then did they look at the carnage surrounding the truck.

It had almost separated into its component parts, the chassis twisted and torn, the wooden benches matchwood, the canvas shredded and flung onto streetlamps and what was left of the tram wires. The soldiers from inside the lorry had been cast aside like puppets, limbs splayed at unnatural angles. Not a man moved. Watson did a quick check, kneeling at each body in turn. All were dead, including the driver and the captain he had spoken to.

'Bastards,' said Bullimore, shaking a fist at the sky.

Watson, though, was kneeling, examining a manhole cover that had embedded itself in the road. 'No German bomber did this,' he said. 'This was what the trial run with Porky was for.'

Bullimore looked puzzled. The air was still lively with the noise of German aero engines. 'How do you mean?'

But Watson wasn't listening. He pointed to the shadowy building on the north side of Old Street. 'Look.'

Bullimore turned. One by one, the lights of St Luke's Mental Hospital for Lunatics were coming on.

★ ★ ★

'Generators are back on,' said John Crantock, striding back into the basement space that had once housed the electroconvulsive treatment centre for St Luke's. 'Any minute now.' The overhead lights flickered and steadied, settling on a dull yellow.

Micky Garavan turned off his flashlight and signalled for the Canadians to do the same. There were eight of the deserters, all in khaki, each with a Lee Enfield and a kitbag on his back. Every man had round his neck what looked like a pair of earmuffs, but was in fact a cleverly

293

designed acoustic device designed to keep out the worst of the hum whenever they were in the open.

Garavan himself was dressed as a captain in the Ulster Volunteers, which appealed to his sense of the absurd. As if he would ever serve. And if he did, with scum like the UVs.

'You haven't put all the lights on?' Garavan asked the night-watchman. 'Just down here.'

Crantock's expression told him he had.

'For God's sake, man. We don't want to be lit up like a Christmas tree. Eventually, someone will come looking for those soldiers. Let's buy ourselves time.' Garavan watched Crantock go. He should have killed him when he learned the bloody idiot had contacted his wife. Still, there was time for that. He was useful for the moment.

He looked down at Lord Arnott, who was crouching at his feet, a broken man. He prodded him with his boot. 'Come on, now, it's time for you to keep your part of the bargain.'

Arnott's face was streaked with tears, his voice small. 'I can't.'

'Now, now, we've been through all this. Of course you can. We're only talking about one day's production from these things.'

He pointed to the three gleaming printing presses that now dominated the subterranean space, each capable of churning out many thousands of pounds worth of crisp notes every shift. There were other machines of varying size and shape, for the production of pension books, war saving bonds, postal orders and foreign notes, but it was the sterling machines Garavan was interested in.

'And it's all in a good cause. Come on now. All you have to do is give me the combination to the key safe and we'll take it from there. And you can go home. In one piece.'

He reached down and pulled the man to his feet. He was like a Guy Fawkes dummy, but with less stuffing. He would have no trouble with him. And once in the vault . . .

'Gentlemen, if you'll just put the weapons down.'

Garavan looked up to where two men were descending the iron steps from the upper level of the hospital. One held a Lee Enfield and the other a Webley pistol and each had a clear shot at any of the Canadians. Garavan had posted a guard at the top of those stars, just beyond the door that led into the main entrance hallway of the building. One had clearly not been enough.

'Dr Watson,' he said to the man with the pistol. 'I was hoping you'd be a few steps behind me.'

'Weapons down,' said Bullimore. Conversation was the last thing he was interested in.

Garavan raised his arms to show he was not carrying a weapon. 'Do as they say,' he said.

Rifles clattered to the ground.

'Move away from them,' instructed Bullimore.

The Canadians shuffled towards Garavan and Arnott.

'You there. Step forward!' shouted Watson.

Crantock emerged from a doorway, also with his hands up.

'The nightwatchman?' asked Watson.

Crantock nodded.

'Then who was the poor soul buried from the school?'

It was Garavan who answered. 'A man called Bradford.'

'From Colchester or thereabouts,' said Watson.

Garavan smiled and Watson didn't like that one bit. He was enjoying himself.

'Very good. Our acoustician, who had reached the end of his useful life.'

'Follow me,' said Bullimore.

Together the two men continued to descend the stairs, keeping their weapons firmly focused on the group.

'Lord Arnott!' shouted Watson.

'Sir.'

'Come to us, please, slowly and steadily.'

The man actually looked to Garavan, as if seeking permission. Garavan nodded and Arnott scuttled across like a wounded animal.

'Where's the staff?' asked Watson. 'Killed them too?'

'I didn't have to.' He pointed to a metal door, painted green and barred across the outside. 'Children and old men, for the most part. They have a little funk hole where they take shelter from the bombers. All we had to do was lock them in.'

'That other door, there,' said Bullimore to Arnott, nodding at a newly installed slab of steel. 'I assume it's a vault?'

'To the cash room, yes.'

'How do you open it?'

Arnott hesitated.

'We must lock these men away,' said Bullimore

296

as they finally reached the floor. 'Where they can do no harm.'

'To access the vault, I need to open the key safe,' said Arnott. 'In the office. Two vault keys are kept in there.'

'Combination lock on the safe?' asked Watson.

'Yes.'

'Which you know?'

'Yes,' confirmed Arnott.

Having confirmed his suspicions, Watson spoke to Garavan. 'So this was merely a robbery. A way to terrorize Lord Arnott here so he would give you access to the vault?'

Garavan shrugged. 'Don't expect chapter and verse from me, Watson.'

'But how would he know about all this?' asked Bullimore. 'A D-Notice building? A new installation for printing notes?'

'An insider,' muttered Watson. 'Like the nightwatchman. Lord Arnott, go and fetch those keys.'

'Yes, Lord Arnott, do as he says.'

The new voice came from behind them. 'Steady, now, gents. Twelve-gauge shotgun coming through. Not likely to miss from this range. Guns down. Now.'

Watson twisted his head. He didn't recognize the man standing above them holding, as he had said, a hefty double-barrelled shotgun.

Bullimore, though, clearly did. 'Amies. What the hell are you playing at?'

The dapper MI5 agent took a step down. 'As your friend here so succinctly put it, being an insider.'

36

I think I have been here long enough.

Watson looked at the inscription, playing the candle over the wall, wondering what anguish lay behind those words. St Luke's had been famed for its robust treatment of the insane — purging, shocking, near-drowning. How long was long enough of that regime? A year? Ten? Twenty?

More to the point, how long would he be in that tiny cell, with but a single, high-barred window? Bullimore, he knew, was in a cell on the same level, although not immediately next door. Both had been incarcerated while Garavan got on with his plan. St Luke's had been converted by the Treasury at considerable cost, but money must have run out before they could modernize these upper attic rooms on the sixth floor. Which left them as a ready-made prison for Garavan's use.

But why hadn't the Irishman killed them?

Because once they had cleared out the vaults, what use was Watson and Bullimore's evidence? Yes, they knew who did it, could piece together the methodology, but the men involved would be long gone, back into the criminal ether from whence they came.

Besides, surely, Garavan wanted them to suffer for coming so close to stopping him.

Watson moved to the wall opposite the door and sat down on the hard floor, which was covered with a few strands of the straw the inmates had once had to lie on. There was also a rusty bucket, which he had no intention of using unless desperate. The smell was of cold, damp stone and brick, with top notes of desolation.

With the adrenalin gone, he could now feel the effects of the explosion out in the car. His knee had taken a knock, right shoulder crunched, elbow grazed, bruises about his body and a cracking headache.

Don't waste this time, Watson. Think, man. Start with the acoustician.

So the dead man who took the place of the nightwatchman had been an acoustician. A physicist, an expert in acoustics. That was where the Gotha Hum out in the street came from. It was how there had been a phantom bomber raid. The Gotha Hum, artificially engineered by that man to send London underground, to keep them away from Old Street while the crime was committed.

Very good.

The explosions outside in the street had not come from bombers at all. Just as in the case of Porky's death, when a phoney raid — and doubtless a trial run — had covered up the murder. In this instance, the detonations had come from the sewers. Hence the manhole covers. One of them had been designed solely to breach the walls of the asylum, enabling Garavan and his men to get access.

And what of the nightwatchmen, firemen or police who would have been on duty?

They had taken cover in their 'funk hole',

meaning it was simple to lock them all in one place.

And what about the five members of the War Injuries Compensation Board? And the GODS? A smokescreen, a piece of distraction, designed to hide the fact that they only wanted one of the board, the moneyman, Arnott, in charge of the new facility for printing the one-pound and ten-shilling notes that were replacing the sovereign.

Very likely.

But Garavan was clearly a man who, nevertheless, revelled in the mutilation of the abducted men. And for what? A hundred thousand pounds? A million? Who knew how much was in the vault awaiting distribution? But surely that depended on how much they could carry away?

The voice in his skull spoke softly, tentatively, as if not sure it was correct.

Leather Lane.

Leather Lane, running parallel to Hatton Garden, was another street of specialists in precious metals and jewellery, including . . . engravers.

The street of engravers. Holmes had heard that Frank Shackleton — or the man they had thought to be Frank Shackleton — had been spotted in those very streets. They had assumed he was there to try, finally, to sell the Irish Crown Jewels. But what if he was having plates made up? Not easy — each heavy square plate was designed to print twenty notes at a single press, but the actual design of the pound note was relatively simple. What if it was his intention to swap the bogus ones for the real thing in the vaults? So that . . .

300

So that the Treasury would be producing the forgeries, and he would have the genuine article. The cash taken would be another diversion. Once he had the plates, Garavan could make as much money as he liked for however long it took the Treasury to notice the switch had been made. Or Garavan announced, once he had amassed enough genuine notes, that the Bank's efforts were the real forgeries.

His head spun with the audacity of it. Not a simple robbery, but a sleight-of-hand undermining of the whole financial system. He banged on the wall of the cell, hoping to attract Bullimore's attention, but there was no response. The walls were too substantial to allow much sound through, at least not from mere flesh.

Watson stood, took the bucket and hammered it against the wall, harder and harder until a rage took hold. It distorted and disintegrated in his hands into a series of flakes, until only the handle was left.

Could he make a weapon out of that? In time, perhaps, but he suspected time wasn't on his side. He had no real idea how long he had been locked up. An hour perhaps? Probably less.

The candle was guttering now. Soon he would only have whatever meagre light might come from the barred window many feet above his head. The glow of London burning, perhaps. Some of the raids might have been false, but not all. There had been real bombs falling that night.

And what of Miss Pillbody? They had abandoned her on the pavement. She could easily have died. Why should he regret that? The woman was a murderess and a spy. She had shot and killed Mrs Gregson. Surely, the Hippocratic Oath didn't apply. She deserved to die, either on the gallows or prostrate on Old Street, no matter.

The Dover Arrow.

Ah, yes, the *Dover Arrow*. She held the key to that. And the fate of Nurse Jennings —

The bolt on the outside withdrew with a sharp scrape and Watson was on his feet, holding the handle in front of him, crouched and ready to jump.

'Really, Watson,' said Holmes coolly, 'I expect a better greeting than a mere snarl.'

At that moment they both heard the boom of a twelve-gauge shotgun.

⋆ ⋆ ⋆

Micky Garavan watched the last of his men pass through the double doors that led to the platform of the St Luke's underground railway terminus. Once used to transport the mad and the dangerous to and from the hospital away from prying eyes, it ran from the west to join with the Post Office line at Bunhill Row and south to Bank. It was this link that had helped it being selected as a site for the new printing works, because people and cash could be transferred below ground from the Old Lady of Threadneedle Street.

Now, though, no trains ran because the power to all rails was turned off while so many people colonized the Underground. No matter, the group would walk along until they reached one of the ventilation shafts on City Road, where a lorry was waiting for them above ground.

It was a pity he wouldn't be going with them.

Each man had filled his kitbag with the new notes from the vault, their reward for the months of work. Some were rich beyond their feeble imaginings. And because of that, they would all be caught within hours or days. They were not conditioned to have such wealth. Dizzied by it, they would make the most basic errors. If they weren't shot in these tunnels first.

'Keep going, come on,' barked Garavan. 'We don't have much time before all hell breaks loose here. Start walking along the platform. Make room there.'

When the last of the Canadians was through, he nodded to Crantock and Amies and they swung the steel doors shut, trapping the deserters on the other side. Before they could throw themselves at the metal, Crantock pushed the heavy bolts into place. They could hear shouting on the other side, and the ring of rifle butts, but the doors could withstand an artillery shell.

'What about the prisoners?' asked Crantock.

He meant Watson, Bullimore and Arnott. They had locked up Lord Arnott only once he had gained them access to the shelves of notes. While the men had gone into a money-frenzy, Garavan and Crantock had unbolted and substituted the plates on the pound-note machine, a hefty slab of metal that now sat at Garavan's feet in its special reinforced case, of the kind artists used to transport their bulkier works. It was far from lightweight, but he didn't have to carry it far. Next to it was a Gladstone containing his own stash of cash. Well, it had seemed a waste not to take some to be going on with, until his friends in Ireland could get to work producing genuine treasury bills, while the real presses cranked out very good forgeries.

Amies snapped the safety off the shotgun. 'Leave them to me.'

'No time,' said Garavan. 'They don't matter now.'

'They know who I am,' said Amies. 'Well, Bullimore does. Let me kill him at least.'

'Very well,' said Garavan. 'But we won't be waiting on you.'

'Won't take me two minutes.'

★   ★   ★

Inspector Bullimore stood up when the door to his cell swung open. Amies stood framed in the doorway, shotgun held at waist height.

'You can't murder a policeman,' he said. 'Not one of your own.'

'You're not one of mine,' said Amies. 'You persecute my kind.'

His kind? 'And that's reason enough to kill me?'

'No, you see, I want to go back to my old job. Just to make sure that the trail is cold. And kept that way. It was all part of the plan. Which means you have to go, because you know the truth. And didn't I hear you shout my name to the good Major Watson?' His eyes went along the

304

passageway, to where Watson was imprisoned. 'So he'll go next. Sorry.'

Amies placed the shotgun stock against his shoulder.

Bullimore closed his eyes and thought of Marion and the child he would never see, the child Arthur would believe was his own. He found himself laughing.

'What is there to smile about?' asked Amies, momentarily perplexed.

'Just that, although you don't know it, you'll be doing me a favour.'

'Well, then,' said Amies, still puzzled. 'Always happy to oblige.'

Two shots filled the cell. The first, from a small-calibre pistol, sent a bullet through Amies's skull; the second was the reflexive discharge of a single barrel by a dying man, which blew pellets across the wall and peppered Bullimore, who barely managed to lift his arm to protect his face in time.

Amies stood swaying from side-to-side for a moment, the force of the tiny bullet not quite enough to knock him off his feet. His jaw worked as if he was trying to say something, but the light was fading from his eyes and he finally crumpled to the floor, the shotgun clattering beside him.

It was Miss Pillbody, ragged and bruised but still with a defiant grin on her face, who stepped over the dead man into the cell. 'Lucky I was in the vicinity.'

Bullimore's cheek was stinging where pellets had caught him. 'Who the hell *are* you?'

She looked down at Amies and the blood pooling around his head. 'Right now, it looks like I'm your guardian angel, Inspector. Coming?'

37

Watson looked at the group gathered around the polished table of the Club Room of St Luke's Hospital, a space originally designed for the recreation of the Treasury staff, most of whom had gone to war. There had once been portraits on the wall, but now only ghostly outlines remained. The carpet, too, had gone, revealing the floorboards, and the chandelier was running on three-quarters of its electric bulbs. The organ and stage at one end were dusty and neglected. The drapes were pulled shut. Outside, with the German planes gone, there were only the flames the bombers had set to see.

Holmes, Sir Francis Lloyd, Mycroft, Sir Gerald Huxley of the Treasury — Lord Arnott having been sent to hospital — Bullimore, Miss Pillbody and himself were seated around the oval of mahogany. Downstairs, a detachment of the Volunteer Defence Force was scouring the building for any remaining interlopers. Elsewhere, Sir Francis had sent men from the London Regiment down into the Underground in pursuit of the thieves. Another group were exploring the nearby rooftops, looking for the acoustical machine that had generated the false Gotha Hum.

There was a burble of subdued conversation around the table. Miss Pillbody and Bullimore were speaking in low tones, Watson noted, not a

307

situation he liked. Bullimore had a series of sticking plasters on his face, marking where the pellets had caught him. He looked like a particularly clumsy shaver.

'I heard you say,' she said to the inspector, 'that he would be doing you a favour if he shot you.'

'Did I?'

'I think you'll find that you did.'

'I simply meant that it would be a blessing to get it over quickly.'

'No you didn't.'

Bullimore shook his head. 'Who are you again?'

'What is it? What's caused that sadness in your eyes?'

'Why do you care?'

Miss Pillbody hesitated. Why did she care? She didn't, not really. She must be getting soft. Either that or the old instinct of trying to discover a man's flaws and weaknesses was as strong as ever. 'You're right. It's none of my business.'

'No. But that doesn't mean I'm not grateful that you saved my life up there.'

She smiled as sweetly as she knew how. 'It was a pleasure.' Now *that* was the truth. Killing MI5 men, rogue or no, was definitely part of her job.

As Watson was wondering exactly what Miss Pillbody was smiling about, Mycroft tapped him on the shoulder. 'Who is that friend of yours again? Quite a remarkable woman.'

'Miss, er, Adler? Oh, I've known her for some time. And, yes, she has some peculiar talents.'

308

'Vernon Kell at MI5 could use the likes of her,' Mycroft suggested.

In the aftermath of the tank affair in Suffolk, Kell had wanted Miss Pillbody hanged or shot, Watson thought, but said nothing. He resolved to get her away from there as soon as possible. She caused too much curiosity. She couldn't help it. It was as if there was an energy crackling off her, not sexual exactly, but some sort of animal magnetism. It was like being drawn to the ledge on top of a high building or bridge, looking down, wondering if you'd have the nerve to jump. Something about Miss Pillbody pulled you to the edge.

It was Sir Francis who brought them to order. 'Gentlemen, Miss Adler. I think first of all it is Miss Adler whom we have to thank, for raising the alarm and browbeating — his words, not mine — the desk sergeant at City Road police station to contact both Holmes and myself.' He turned to Watson. 'And the major, for realizing that there was more to the War Injuries Compensation Board business than met the eye.'

Watson glanced guiltily at Holmes, but he had his eyes shut. His dash across London seemed to have quite drained him.

'I am sure we will get to the bottom of this affair eventually, but for the moment . . . ' He turned to Sir Gerald. 'Do you have any idea of how much might have been taken?'

Sir Gerald looked down at his notepad. 'There was close to half a million pounds in the vault. We estimate about half of that is missing.'

'I fear that is a distraction,' said Watson.

'A quarter of a million pounds a distraction?' asked Sir Francis, incredulously.

'How often do you change the plates on the machine. The actual pound-note ones?'

'Depends. Every six to eight months. We can print up to four million notes a week and there is a pressure of four hundred tons applied. They don't last for ever.'

'When did you last change them?' Watson asked.

'Three or four weeks ago.'

'Difficult to change?'

'Six bolts, four screws.'

'I would check them carefully. I suspect the plates may have been switched. My guess is that Garavan intends to forge pound notes. Or rather reproduce them using the genuine plates while the bank makes forgeries. Good forgeries, mind, so it would be a while before you noticed. In the meantime, he will be making perfect notes and exchanging them, for say, Swiss francs or US dollars.'

'I'll be damned,' said Sir Gerald.

'Perhaps,' suggested Holmes, 'the plates should be removed and locked in the vault each evening, as I believe happens at Portals Printing.'

'Surely you can just change the design?' asked Sir Francis.

'It isn't as simple as that,' said Sir Gerald, glumly. 'You have to declare the current design null and void. There are over forty million pounds in paper currency in circulation at the moment. Confidence in the Treasury and the Bank . . . ' He fell quiet for a moment, thinking of the economy and the damage that could be done to it during wartime. 'But of course, it isn't just the printing plates that matter. You need the correct machines. One to print the notes, one for the serial numbers, one for the signature. Another to cut and trim from a panel of twenty to single notes. And there's the paper.'

'Paper?' asked Watson.

Sir Gerald rubbed his thumb and forefinger together. 'It's a unique cotton-linen blend, made by Spicer Brothers and water-marked. It's the wavy line watermark that makes forgeries so difficult. People have used grease or picture varnish, but it's nigh impossible to copy. Only the Amsterdam forgeries have come close. Even with the plates, there is a long way to go. And they didn't take any of the paper, as far as I can tell. The rolls are too big and heavy to simply carry off. We use trolleys to move them around.'

'How is it delivered?' asked Holmes, suddenly alert. 'The paper?'

'Delivered? Here?'

'By the underground railway?' Holmes asked.

Sir Gerald thought for a moment. 'No. The same way we got the presses here. By barge. Direct from the manufacturer.'

Holmes and Watson exchanged glances. 'You stay here,' said Watson to the detective. 'Bullimore, come with me. Sir Francis, may I borrow a soldier or two?'

'By all means. But where are you going?'

'To get the Treasury's paper back.'

★ ★ ★

311

The fighters were waiting for them as they crossed back over the English coast. Someone, somewhere was learning something, thought Schrader. Instead of trying to gain height when the bombers first appeared, the British had realized they could take their time in climbing, and they would be at an attacking altitude once the bombers returned. True, they had to let London be hit, but the idea was that at least some of the bombers would not be returning the next night. It was taking the long view.

The first Schrader knew about the ambush was the tracers that arced through the sky, as lazy as drugged fireflies until, at the last moment they seem to accelerate to the speed of shooting stars.

A green flare burst among them, the signal to close up into a diamond formation. But even before Deitling could shift the giant plane towards the silhouettes flying around him, the Parabellum MG14 in the nose opened up as forward gunner Rohrbach let loose at something.

A beam swept towards them, passing a few metres off the port wing.

'Stay out of the lights!' Schrader yelled at Deitling.

'You don't have to tell me,' Deitling replied. 'Sir.'

Rutter had lowered the ventral ramp and had slid down into the lower gun position. Now he let off a burst into the night sky. He poked his head back up into the cabin.

'Sopwith Camels, I think,' he said breathlessly. 'Swarms of them.'

'Damn it.' These planes were small, fast, manoeuvrable and normally found only on the Western Front.

Now the Giant's guns front and ventral fired in unison and the airframe trembled from the recoils.

A small sun burst into life to their left, growing in intensity, trailing sparks. It was a Gotha. Tracer bullets continued to stream into it, just to be sure of the kill. The streak of flaming bomber tipped onto one wing, seemed to slow, and then began a sickening spin earthwards. A section of the upper wing detached and made its own spiral, like a crazed sycamore seed. The sudden red bloom as a fuel tank went told him that at least the crew's suffering was over.

'OK, let's get — ' Schrader began.

The Giant rocked, like a boat struck by a rogue wave. Shrapnel splinters rattled against its underside. He felt it crabbing through the air. A coastal battery or an ack-ack ship had their range and height now. All they needed.

'Man all guns!' he shouted.

Rutter slid back down into position. His gun began its staccato bursts almost immediately. Borschberg opened the upper hatch and cold air punched into the cabin with a roar, causing Schrader to grab at his charts as they swirled off his table. The gunner/engineer climbed out onto the upper wing, and kicked the hatch shut behind him. Soon, they could hear and see the muzzle flashes from his MG14.

The moon, which had been their friend over London, was showing another, more treacherous face now. The silvery beams were picking out the bombers for the fighters and Schrader could see the frantic winking of the Gotha and Giants' machine guns as they tried to catch one of the dark shapes that were flitting among them like crazed bats. It had only been a matter of time before the British came up with a response. A leapfrogging war; he'd said it himself.

Another burst of orange sparks smearing across the sky marked a second Gotha in trouble. Like sharks smelling blood the little Camels turned on it, pouring more and more rounds into the flames. The entire upper wing broke free of its moorings and the nose dipped. Still the bullets punished it until it was just a wreckage of canvas, wire and wood, falling to earth.

Schrader's Giant appeared to give a screech of pain and two hot balls of metal splintered part of the cockpit glass and thudded into the floor. A small fire started and Schrader grabbed the extinguisher, dousing the flames before they could take hold.

'Jesus, she's gone fuckin' heavy,' said Deitling. 'Rudder?'

'Aerlions. Something must have bent.'

Schrader stepped up the small ladder and opened the upper hatch, bracing himself as the slipstream tried to pluck him out. Up there was the harness for Borschberg, and the dorsal machine gun. The MG had gone, the mounting blown away. So had Borschberg. All that were left was two ragged straps. Something sticky sucked at Schrader's gloves as he pulled himself further up, squinting into the night. The top of the fuselage was dotted with blood and gobbets of the gunner. Schrader could only hope the man had been dead before the wind threw him into empty space.

Up above him, even over the roar of the wind and his own growling engines, he imagined he could hear the distinctive throb of a Sopwith's radial engines. More tracers stitched beautiful patterns across the heavens. He heard rounds puncture the wood and canvas upper wing, and a wire pinged free with a high-pitched whoosh, biting into his cheek as it snaked free.

Schrader slid down the ladder and pulled the hatch closed behind him. He took off one of his gloves and touched his face. The fingertips glistened red.

'See anything?' asked Fohn.

'Borschberg's gone.'

'Shit.'

'Take her low,' he shouted to Deitling.

'How low?'

'All the way.'

'We'll lose the defensive diamond.'

Schrader pulled his glove back on. 'That was the defensive diamond hitting our wing. We're shooting at each other. Take her down. Kiss the waves, if you have to.'

I've lost one man, he thought. I'm not losing another. We aren't going to die. Not tonight. It sounded like wishful thinking, with the night air whistling through the holes in the Giant's skin and the pilots sweating as they fought with damaged control surfaces.

Schrader stumbled back to his seat as the nose dipped. It was a risk. If the Camels noticed him breaking formation and decided he was a lame duck, they'd come after him. And now he had no dorsal gun with which to defend himself. But even if they did swarm down on him, at least his actions might save the rest of the squadron. The British didn't have unlimited fuel or bullets, so by coming after him they might use their last gasp.

On the other hand, firing tracers in the dark tended to blind the pilots. Perhaps they wouldn't see a shadowy shape breaking free and diving down towards the sea. And even a Giant was difficult to spot against the waves, far more difficult than with a star-filled sky as a backdrop.

Schrader held his breath, expecting at any moment to feel the impact of the twin Vickers the Camels had mounted on their stubby noses.

Above, another plane, friend or foe, it was impossible to tell, turned into a flaming comet, describing a slow arc as it fell towards the waiting sea, turning over and over as it did so.

Dear Herr and Frau Borschberg — it is with great regret that I have to inform you —

Schrader felt a buffeting as a small, nimble plane came past them, close enough to hear the engine note and feel its prop wash make waves for the Giant. The front gun gave several short barks. Schrader looked out through the side panel of the cabin.

He could see the RFC biplane clearly, hooked at the port side, running parallel with them. It was impossible for either of the remaining machine guns to fire at him without risking stray rounds splintering their own frame. On the top wing of the British plane he could make out the silhouette of a Lewis gun. Camels usually had Vickers firing through the propellers. So that was how they stopped the blinding of the pilots, by putting the muzzle up above, out of sight. Clever. But what was pilot playing at?

Below, he could see the glint of the sea, the spume of waves. He looked back at the Camel. The pilot, he realized, was waving. A gloved hand, penduluming back and forth in the moonlight. Perhaps he was out of ammunition. Or the Lewis had jammed. Either way, he was letting them know that God was on their side. Such chivalry was once the norm, but gruelling conflicts like Bloody April had swept away any foolish notions of honour between pilots. It was kill or be killed. But clearly, there was at least one British flyer who thought otherwise.

Schrader pressed his own hand against the cockpit glass. The Camel waggled its wings and then banked away, gone, as if plucked on a string.

Schrader let his breath out and replugged his heated suit in as the Giant levelled out. He smoothed out his charts and picked up a pencil.

Maybe it hadn't been wishful thinking. Maybe they weren't going to die that night.

★   ★   ★

The canal tunnel that ran from the rear of St Luke's Gardens to the Wenlock Basin was not marked on any map. It passed, in a straight line, under East Road, Nile Street and Shepherdess Walk, before it connected, through a barred gateway that could be locked shut, with an arm of the Grand Union Canal.

Garavan let Crantock navigate through the tunnel, while he checked that there were indeed half a dozen of the giant rolls of bank paper underneath the tarpaulin, as the nightwatchman had promised. Enough to print thousands and thousands of pounds, far more than they had been forced by weight and bulk to leave behind.

He made his way to the rear of the barge once he was satisfied, crouched low as the boat chuffed on through darkness. Ahead there was only a tiny arch of grey, as small as a postage stamp, suggesting that this black passage had a terminus.

Garavan could feel water dripping on his face from the dank bricks above them and he wiped it away. It had been a shame to abandon Amies, but once he had heard voices and shots, he knew the game was up. They had locked shut the gates to the canal wharf from the outside and steered the barge into the tunnel, its engine masked by the machines still generating the Gotha Hum and the blasting of the anti-aircraft guns.

Now he had to trust to luck. That nobody would expect him to make a getaway at four miles an hour. He was banking on their going after the Canadians in the Underground. The deserters would put up a fight. That would keep the Bank's soldiers busy.

Garavan knew he had been too clever. And too

318

greedy. He could have carried out the robbery without the kidnappings and the mutilations, perhaps. His plan had been to send a full account of how he had done it to the damnable Watson and Holmes, the men who had, off and on, dogged his footsteps — or Frank Shackleton's — ever since he had lifted the Irish Crown Jewels. A little gloating was in order. It had always been his weakness. Hell, it was a Shackleton family weakness. They loved a drama, loved a tale to tell.

But the love of pain, inflicted and sometimes even received, that one was all his own.

But other people had let him down. Crantock and his bloody wife. Well, all he needed Crantock for was to unlock the gate at the far end of the tunnel — the man had been canny enough not to reveal where the key was hidden — and then Garavan could dispose of him. There were men at the wharf on City Road — good men, Irishmen — who would help him unload the barge and transfer the paper bales to a truck.

Then Mrs Crantock could get on with being a real widow.

The pale half-circle of the exit grew larger and Garavan could make out the bars now. Crantock cut the throttle to idle and nudged the bow towards the wall of the tunnel.

'Take the tiller,' he said to Garavan. 'I'll open the gate.'

Garavan did as instructed and the nightwatchman scampered to the front of the barge. Garavan heard the scrape of a key and the squeal of hinges as the gate was swung back. 'Bring her up,' Crantock shouted.

Garavan gave the engine a little more power and the barge moved forward, scraping the wall as it went.

Crantock relieved him of the tiller and Garavan stepped away.

'Tricky bend out of this basin,' said Crantock. 'Then we'll be fine. About four hundred yards to the wharf.'

Garavan wasn't really listening. There was sporadic gunfire from the anti-aircraft batteries but he was aware that the Gotha Hum had stopped. They must have found the machines that generated the noise, the devices designed by the acoustician Bradford. Under duress, that was. He had proved most uncooperative when confronted with his task. It had taken all Garavan's powers of persuasion to cajole him into creating the Gotha Hum machines.

One thing was for certain, the German raids had made disposing of bodies like Bradford's relatively straightforward. They had used the bombings to get rid of the acoustician and then that private detective Watson had put on the tail of Crantock and his Mrs. After all, who questioned too much about the circumstances in which a man had clearly been killed in an air raid? Well, it turned out that Watson and Holmes did, he thought bitterly.

The nightwatchmen leaned hard on the tiller and throttled back, bringing the barge round to clear the bend into the main canal. Some way to the east, Garavan could see flames on the water. A warehouse was burning.

Once they were straight, Garavan reached over and killed the engine.

'What you doing?' asked Crantock.

'This is where you get off.'

'What?' Crantock looked disbelievingly at the gun in Garavan's hand. 'I can't swim.'

'You won't have to worry about that. You'll be dead before you hit the water.'

'It's not fair — '

'Neither was you contacting y'bloody wife.'

'I love her. I was doing all this for her. I told you I should've stayed on in place till tonight, but you didn't trust me not to act suspicious. It's your fault. But you wouldn't understand that.'

'No. I wouldn't.' Garavan lifted the pistol and Crantock was about to close his eyes when he saw the Irishman's skull shatter and watched his blood and brains escape into the night air.

38

The acrid smell of burning hung across all of London, even penetrating the sitting room of 2 Upper Wimpole Street, where Sherlock Holmes and Dr Watson sat, having finished a late breakfast. Holmes had been given the spare room by Mrs Turner and had spent the night there, while Watson had eventually located and boarded the stolen barge, which had been found drifting, jammed at the entrance to Wenlock Basin.

'So,' said Holmes, 'there was only the body of Garavan on board?'

'And the rolls of special paper. And the plates.'

'And money?'

'No, all the cash had disappeared.'

'It's no great amount for the Treasury to lose,' said Holmes. 'It's more important that they know counterfeits will not be flooding the country. I have suggested to Bullimore that they put a watch on Crantock's wife. He will come for her sooner or later.'

'Yes, he seems the only loose end now the main perpetrator is dead. Bizarre, though. Garavan's death.'

Holmes shook his head. 'I think not. As I said . . . '

'What goes up . . . ' offered Watson.

'Exactly.'

Watson's examination of the mutilated body

had indicated that Garavan had been struck by a falling piece of shrapnel, probably part of an anti-aircraft shell. It had sliced into his cranium, killing him instantly. Crantock had been saved by the country he and Garavan had set out to rob.

Holmes lit a pipe. 'I have a theory.'

'About?'

'The events of the past few weeks.'

Watson leaned forward in anticipation. 'You think there is more to all this than meets the eye.'

'I am certain of it. Germany has a plan to force Great Britain to the negotiating table. To starve her. To bomb her. To sink her ships, burn her warehouses, terrorize her people.'

'You think Garavan was working for the Germans?'

Holmes nodded. 'Perhaps, through Irish intermediaries. I think the Germans would have won whatever the outcome of his scheme — the aim of which was not to make Garavan rich but to destroy faith in the new paper money. Given that Britain's gold reserves are perilously low . . . our credit with the Empire and the Allies would reach rock bottom.'

'A German plan? Are you sure?'

Holmes shook his head. 'Certain, no. Suspicious, yes.'

Watson felt a sudden chill. 'You are thinking that . . . that I've been played for a fool? That somehow Miss Pill — '

'I would put nothing past *that* woman.'

'*That* woman is meant to arrange for me to fly to Belgium tomorrow.'

'To speak to the survivor of the sinking? I

think it best if you let the *Dover Arrow* go, Watson. I fear she is dealing her own hand in all this. And she is a better player than either of us when it comes to espionage.'

Watson slumped back and let a cloud of gloom settle over him. Could it be? He ran through the sequence of events in his mind, trying to see where Miss Pillbody might fit as puppet master. But he couldn't create a convincing case for any duplicity on her part. 'I am not so sure, Holmes.'

'It pains me to say this, but if you insist on pursuing the matter, there is only one sure way to find out.'

'What's that?'

'Go along with her scheme. Go to Belgium. Talk to this witness, who may or may not exist. But be aware . . . '

'That?'

'You might not make it back with whatever knowledge you glean.'

★ ★ ★

Rutter, the other gunner/engineer, had offered to do the job, but Schrader felt obliged to scrub the blood from the upper part of the Giant himself. It seemed disrespectful to delegate the task to another. He was Borschberg's commander. It was his way of paying respects to a brave man.

Using a stiff scrubbing brush and a bucket of bleach, he stood on the ladder and worked at the stained canvas, scooping off the lumps of skin and gristle that had somehow avoided being dislodged by the slipstream, and throwing them over the side. Not even a body for the parents to bury.

He examined the area where Rutter must have been standing. The upper wing had absorbed a lot of punishment. The engine nacelles were holed, too, which meant they would have to strip them down to make sure no damage had been done to the mechanicals within. One of the wooden propellers looked as if termites had been at it, and another was missing the last quarter of a blade. A day or two's work, at least.

He felt a tug at his ankle and crouched down to peer into the cockpit. It was von Kahr, his squadron leader.

'Sir?'

'You were right. Camels. They transferred a squadron back from France last week. They were refitted with top-mounted Lewis guns. 'Sopwith Comics', they are known as.'

'Why didn't we know this yesterday?'

'Would it have made any difference?' von Kahr asked.

Schrader thought about this. 'Perhaps not. But we'll have to change our game.' He glanced upwards. 'I don't think Borschberg was hit by any Sopwith. I think one of our own got him.'

'I'll pretend I didn't hear that,' said von Kahr irritably.

'It doesn't change the facts. The flat diamond is not ideal when the British planes are fast and able to come among you. Gunners panic. They don't think about what happens to the bullets that don't hit. We need a new formation.'

'I was there, remember?'

325

'Then you know. We were lucky to get back. They form another squadron of these Comics and it will be no laughing matter up there.'

'I agree. We'll have to rethink tactics. But I'll not have you saying we shot our own. Understood?'

'Sir.'

'And you won't have to worry about being hit by either side tonight.'

'No?'

'We lost three Gothas in that fire-fight. Another two to engine failure. We have another eight dead, including your Borschberg, and most of the surviving planes have some damage. Including mine. We skip tonight, get back up to strength.'

Schrader wiped his forehead. 'Then when we go back, we'll be ready for them.'

'You might be excused tomorrow, too.'

'How's that?'

'Tomorrow afternoon. You have to fly to England.'

Schrader sighed. He knew it was no use arguing. 'I don't want anyone else taking this plane up while I am gone.'

'You will follow orders. You can't do everything.'

'I can be over there and back before we take off for London.'

'Not necessarily. You'll be flying heavy on the return trip.'

'Why, who am I bringing in? Clara Butt?'

Von Kahr frowned at the levity. 'You have new orders.'

'New how?'

'When you land, there will be a man with the woman you took out waiting. Originally, just the man was to come. Now, they want both.'

'Three up in that Bristol?'

'If anyone can do it, it's you, Schrader.'

'If anyone is stupid enough to do it, it's me, you mean.' Schrader dropped the brush in the bucket. 'If you'll excuse me, sir.'

'Where are you going?'

'To church.'

'I didn't know you were religious.'

Schrader opened the door of the cabin and stepped out onto the folding ladder. 'I wasn't, until about thirty seconds ago.'

★ ★ ★

'Miss Adler, would you get dressed and come with me, please?'

Miss Pillbody pulled the dressing gown tighter around her waist. She was peering around the door of her rooms at the policeman on the landing. 'I think I deserve some rest after last night's exertions.'

Inspector Bullimore nodded. 'I'm sure you do. But there are other pressing matters. By the way, I have a constable with me at the foot of the stairs here and one posted at the rear of the property. Just in case, you understand.'

'I am under arrest? What for? Saving the Crown a pretty penny? Oh, no, forgive me. Saving your life.'

'I am making allowances for the fact you shot

327

Mr Amies. I'm not handing you over to his colleagues. Not yet.'

'And you'd trust his colleagues, would you?'

It was a fair point. How many more bad apples were there in MI5, he wondered. But that wasn't why he was showing her some clemency. He knew that once the secret services got hold of her, he would be sidelined. Having been comprehensively taken in by her, he wanted to make sure he was the one who got the credit for unmasking a German spy. Having been made a fool of by this woman, arresting her might just save his career.

'Can we please step inside?' he asked.

'What about my reputation?'

'Miss Pillbody, your reputation is why I have my hand on a pistol right now.'

She pulled the door open and allowed him in, closing it behind her. She let the dressing gown fall open. His eyes flicked down, but she pulled it shut when she realized what Bullimore was really looking at. Not her underwear, but the weight of the gown's pockets, just in case she, too, had a gun. But the tiny Beretta was back in its hidey-hole in the bathroom down the hall.

Bullimore allowed himself time to examine the room. It was spartan: a single bed, a rug, showing signs of wear, over-painted and stencilled floorboards, a gas fire, a table with a mirror on it and a padded stool. Various creams and powders were arranged on the table. The view from the window was of a light well. There was another, small room off to one side.

'What's in there?' he asked.

'Dressing room.' She took a step towards it. 'It's just where I hang my things. Take a look, if you wish.'

He shook his head. 'Stay where you are. I want you to get dressed. Out here.'

'You've got the gun. What do you imagine I might do?'

'I've read your file. I can imagine lots of things you might do. Plus I have seen you in action, remember? I know you have a gun somewhere.'

She shrugged, walked over to the table and sat at the stool.

'What are you doing?'

'You expect me to go along with you looking like this?'

'It's not a beauty parade.'

She unscrewed the lid of a jar of oxygen face cream and began to apply it to her cheeks. 'Won't take a minute. Even spies like to look their best.' She half-turned. 'Tell me, out of professional curiosity, how did I slip up?'

'Not you. Watson. When we were in the car at Old Street, when I was trying to get you off him. He called you Miss Pillbody, not Miss Adler.'

'Did he indeed,' she said flatly, not letting her irritation at the doctor show. 'And you knew of that name?'

'No. Pillbody rang a bell, but I couldn't place it. I wasn't in London when you escaped from Holloway. But the moment I mentioned it at Bow Street . . . seems you are something of a legend, if that is the right word.'

She met his gaze and spoke directly to him. 'Inspector, what if I were to tell you that, at this

329

moment, I am working for the British Government?'

He pulled the gun free from his jacket pocket and waved it at her.

'Get on with it and stop wasting your breath.' She wiped some of the excess cream away with a cloth and leaned in to examine her eyes. She gave each one a few strokes of Verdi's eyelash pomade.

'It's true,' she said as she applied it. 'You can ask Watson.'

'I wouldn't trust anything Watson said. He is clearly besotted with you.'

She laughed at this. 'On the contrary, he wishes me dead. He's in love, all right, but not with me. With the memory of a woman.'

She swivelled again, examining his face. 'Like you, Inspector. That's what I see in your eyes. Did she die? Marry someone else? Perhaps she is already married — '

'Shut up!'

Apparently satisfied that she had the answer she wanted, Miss Pillbody applied a light dusting of colliandum powder to put colour in her cheeks.

'I'll need a dress from in there.' She waved towards the dressing room.

'I'll fetch it. Tell me which one.'

'There is a floral one, with matching jacket, on a coat hanger, just behind the door. Possibly a bit too summery for this time of year, but I suppose it's not a fashion parade either. You can reach in without taking your eyes off me if you wish.' She flashed him a beaming smile.

'You are a very strange woman, Miss Pillbody.'

'That's been said before. But it's why I am still alive, Inspector.'

Bullimore backed up to the anteroom and, with the gun in his right hand, began to grope along the door with his left. He found the dress and worked his way up the material to where he could unhook the hanger. He had no time to react when something gripped his wrist and yanked him hard. His head caught the edge of the door, splitting the temple, and sending him to a heap on the floor.

Miss Pillbody was on him in a second, tying his arms while he groaned.

'He's hurt,' said Watson.

'A scratch. Get me something to gag him with.' She glanced up at him. 'Thank goodness you called on me before he did.'

Watson felt sick to his stomach at the sight of the policeman. 'Perhaps I should have just let him take you in.'

'We had an agreement, remember?'

'Yes, but I'm not sure you told me the full picture of why you're in London.'

'The full picture? Look, Major, can we play this little game of truth or dare later? Once we have hog-tied our policeman?' The old metal came into her voice. 'Or do you have another solution, as this mess was your doing?'

'Mine?'

'If you hadn't called me Miss Pillbody . . . '

'Slip of the tongue.'

'The kind of slip that in my business can prove fatal. Are you going to help?'

When Bullimore was suitably bound and Watson had made sure the blood was from a superficial cut, he leaned in close to him. Bullimore's eyes were flickering into consciousness. 'I know you will find this hard to believe,' Watson assured him, 'but for the moment, Miss Pillbody really is on the side of the angels.'

She shrugged off her gown, pulled the dress over her head and began buttoning it. 'Otherwise I'd kill you and have done with it.'

Watson stood. 'Enough of that, you vile woman. You heard what he said. He has a constable downstairs. One out the back. And I'm not going to let you shoot your way out. What do you suggest now?'

She feigned disappointment. 'Much as I might like a good gunfight, you forget one thing. I am a She Wolf. You can never paint a She Wolf into a corner. Give me a hand.'

'With what?'

She pointed at a tallboy. 'This. Oh, do keep up, Major. It's not just a wardrobe. There's a window behind here.' The cupboard moved under her shoulder and a strip of grey daylight entered the room. 'What we spies call an escape plan. Are you going to stand there gawping, or help?'

39

'I have a good mind to arrest you for obstruction of justice.'

Sherlock Holmes looked unmoved by the threat. He was sitting in Watson's chair, in front of the fire, a medicinal whisky in his hand, courtesy of Mrs Turner. He stared at the coal flames, counting the seconds between a flare of gas, glowing yellow, that was erupting with the regularity of Old Faithful.

'What do you say to that?' asked Bullimore.

'I am returning to the country tomorrow, first thing. The city has not really agreed with me. Besides, the bees need preparing for over-wintering.'

Bullimore strode over and addressed the detective as if he were hard of hearing. 'Mr Holmes, do you know how much trouble Major Watson is in?'

Holmes tore his gaze away from the dancing flames. 'I suppose there is a hue and cry out for him?'

'If we could raise a hue and cry, we would put one out, I can assure you. My own career is at risk. I was instructed to put out an arrest warrant and your brother persuaded me — '

'Mycroft can be very persuasive.'

'That he was an innocent. Now we find out he is consorting with an enemy agent. So what forces we do have at our disposal are on alert to look for Watson and the German woman and detain them both. By force, if necessary.'

'I can't say I approve.'

'Of the use of force?'

'Of the German woman. But Watson is quite adamant. He has become somewhat stubborn in his advancing years, I have found. The only bees he seems interested in are the ones in his bonnet. Of course, he hasn't been the same since that affair in Holland. It was *that* woman, are you aware of that?'

Bullimore sat down. A black and blue discoloration had formed around his right eye and his head still thumped from the blow against the door of the dressing room, and, although he had been bound for less than twenty minutes before One of the constables had come to check on him, both wrists and ankles were very sore. However, she had not actually cut the circulation off and most of the damage came from his struggling to get free. Which he had manifestly failed to do. Knots were clearly another Miss Pillbody speciality.

'I am not entirely sure what I'm aware of. All I know is that, leaving aside the events at St Luke's and the Garavan fellow, we have a dangerous spy loose and she is loose with your companion. And I believe you know where they are.'

'Believe away, Inspector, believe away, but it will not alter the facts. My part in this is done. I now know that Frank Shackleton was, in fact, this Micky Garavan. I also know that my instinct regarding his appearance in London was correct.

334

Something was afoot. That is all I ever wanted.
Watson, however, has his own agenda.'

'Which is?'

Holmes swivelled his head towards Bullimore.
'I am an old man. I have lapses. He did explain
what he was up to, but, to be honest, it was
singularly uninteresting. It involved a woman. I
find it often does with Watson.'

'The German woman?'

'No, one of his old colleagues. The name is in
here somewhere.' He clicked his fingers and then
gave a defeated smile.

'There is treason here, Mr Holmes. Treason.'

'And having been a protégé of Mr Amies, you
would know all about that.'

Bullimore bristled. 'Damn it, I wasn't his
protégé. I was taken in by him.'

'And by Miss Pillbody, it seems.'

'We have all been taken in by Miss Pillbody at
some point.'

Holmes nodded at this. 'Amies had debts.
Large debts. He moved in the same circles as
Garavan. Amies was almost certainly homosexual. Garavan was not. But as part of his
affectation of being Frank Shackleton, he
inhabits, or rather inhabited, that shadowy world
that runs through London like seams of coal
through the Welsh valleys. It would be simple for
a man like Garavan to entice a man like Amies
over to his scheme with promises of money.'

'But, surely, MI5 wouldn't employ a man who
was . . . '

'A gambler and of . . . singular tastes?' Holmes
pursed his lips. 'You would be surprised. Both

335

vices are dangerous in the world of espionage, granted. But there is also something about it that attracts both sorts. A habitué of the tables has to gamble, to take risks. As does any spy. A homosexual, by his very nature and the rigour of this country's laws on such matters, has to live a double life. Lying and deception become second nature. Again, perfect for a spy. But, all that aside, I suspect that if you ask at two or three of the more discreet gaming establishments around Mayfair and St James's, Amies's markers will come up.'

'Such as?'

'The gambling clubs? The Park for one, the New Crockford, the Orinoco and Henry Black's. I'd start with the latter. It has a reputation for its handsome young men. Or, at least, it did before they were all taken off to war.'

'How do you know all this?'

Holmes raised an eyebrow. He wasn't about to let slip his methods, even it did consist of nothing more than a few well-placed telegrams and the services of his brother. 'It was once my job to have an exact knowledge of London.'

'Yet you claim to know nothing of Watson's movements?'

Holmes returned to staring into the flames. 'I have nothing that can help you, Inspector, even if I wanted to. I bid you good evening. I shall probably dine at Goldini's tonight, if you need me.'

'Is that Mayfair?'

'Gloucester Road. And if you are intent on arresting me at some later date, I will leave a

336

forwarding address with Mrs Turner.'

'And how do I know you won't run off to warn Watson the moment my back is turned?'

Holmes put down his whisky, dug into his inside pocket and extracted a small bottle. 'This tells me my days of rushing about are over. Nitroglycerine. For my angina.' He touched his left arm. 'I am to avoid excitement, apparently. I am to relax. Chasing off after Watson and *that* woman is not on my agenda. Not if I want a few more years on this planet.'

Bullimore nodded, fetched his hat and left without another word.

Holmes waited five minutes before he sprang to his feet and walked purposefully to the top of the stairs. 'Mrs Turner. Mrs Turner!'

'Yes, Mr Holmes?' Was that a weariness he detected in her voice? No matter. 'Can you fetch me something?'

'More whisky?'

'No, although most welcome that was. I need a Bradshaw's, Mrs Turner, the most up-to-date you can lay your hands on.'

'Are you leaving us, Mr Holmes?'

'Try not to sound so pleased about it, Mrs Turner. I know your routine has been somewhat strained by my presence, for which I apologize. But yes, it's time I moved on.'

★   ★   ★

Watson imagined that Miss Pillbody hadn't stayed alive as long as she had without forward planning. The bolt hole she had prepared in case

337

of discovery at her rented rooms was just four streets away and was little more than a lean-to attached to a terraced house, accessed from the rear alley. Miss Pillbody fetched the key from beneath a plant pot and let Watson in.

The furnishings consisted of a single bed with a stained candlewick bedspread, a paraffin heater, a velvet wing-backed armchair that had lost most of its nap on the cushion and headrest, a chest of drawers and a narrow wardrobe. The room smelled musty and unused, and what light entered was filtered through the soot and grime on the windows. There was, he noted, no connecting door to the main house. She could come and go as she pleased.

Miss Pillbody walked to the wardrobe and opened it. She stripped off her blouse, apparently unconcerned about Watson's presence, and pulled on a fresh one. She also selected a hat from one of the boxes on the top shelf.

'I have to go out.'

'They'll be looking for us soon,' he said.

'Us. Not me. I have to make sure the flight is arranged.'

He groaned. 'We are wanted by the police. I think we have to re-examine our options.'

She put her clenched hands on her hips. 'Please sit down, Major. There are cigarettes in the top drawer there if you have none. I shall be thirty minutes.'

'Where are you going?'

'To do what Sie Wölfe do. Which means, I can't tell you. Sit, relax, they won't find you here.'

He carried out the first part of her instructions.

'I won't be long.'

When she had left he lit one of his own cigarettes and lay back in the armchair. What a pretty pickle, he thought. A fugitive in his own country, running from the very organizations he and Holmes had helped so often. And running with a woman who was an implacable enemy of the British Empire and all it stood for. He could see the headlines now: 'Author tried for Treason' or 'Author to be shot at Tower'.

And all because she had dangled the promise of the *Dover Arrow* before him. But what if she was playing her own game? What if somehow she was involved in thwarting Garavan for her own ends? Or that it had been a German plan all along? And where was she at that very moment? No doubt with other foreign agents planning her next move.

There was something else worrying him. His hatred of Miss Pillbody had burned bright for months, with the heat of emotional phosphorous. But he was finding it impossible to keep up the intensity of loathing. Sometimes he almost forgot who and what she was — a trained killer. He had to find a way to keep that at the front of his thoughts.

There had been many occasions in his dealings with Holmes when he had felt like man drowning in a sea of contradictory facts and theories. He felt it now, the cold waters of uncertainty and panic closing over his head.

Miss Pillbody was absent for the time it took

him to smoke two cigarettes, a duration that offered him no great insights into his dilemma. To follow Miss Pillbody or simply turn her over to the authorities? Perhaps he could solve the *Dover Arrow* problem using Holmes's methods? There must be another approach to discovering what happened to the boat and the fate of Nurse Jennings.

The door opened and Miss Pillbody bustled in, carrying several bags, which she immediately dropped so she could turn the key behind her in the lock. 'You were right. There are police out there, stopping and questioning people.'

'Were you stopped?'

'No.'

'And you weren't followed here?'

She simply raised an eyebrow at that, as if he was a child asking an impertinent question.

'No, of course you weren't.'

She shrugged off her coat and placed her hat on the bed. 'So, have you reached the point yet where you are thinking about turning me in to the police?'

'It's bad luck.'

'What is?'

'Putting a hat on a bed.'

'I don't think you're a superstitious man, Major. Don't duck the question. Are you thinking of simply handing me over to your countrymen?'

Watson shrugged. It was no use lying. 'I admit, I have considered all possibilities.'

'In many ways it's the sensible option. Things are unravelling somewhat.'

'Unravelling how?'

'Well, should you decide still to come along, we have to make our way to Colchester with Scotland Yard on our tail.'

Bullimore is out of Bow Street, he thought, but didn't say.

'And by now, you are wondering if there really is a survivor from the *Dover Arrow*. If, in fact, I have been running circles around you.'

'And have you?'

She bent down and began rummaging in one of the bags. 'Tell me, did you bring a revolver with you?'

'Sadly, I did not,' he admitted, although he had considered it.

'I thought as much.'

When Miss Pillbody stood, he saw the glint of a cut-throat razor's blade as it flicked out of its housing. 'Then I'm afraid this is goodbye, Major Watson.'

40

'Why are you and all your people followed everywhere you go? It is most disconcerting.'

Mycroft pulled the drapes of the Conversation Parlour in disgust.

'Oh, that is only the policeman Bullimore or one of his associates. While they are trailing after me, I know they aren't running Watson to earth.'

Mycroft gave the fire a stir and sat down opposite his brother. 'You look well for a man who has been yanking on the bell-pull at death's door.'

Holmes nodded. 'Well, I felt as if I had my hand on its handle at least. Can you ring for a decanter of brandy?'

'Brandy?'

Holmes lit a cigarette. 'I think this might be a three- or four-glass problem.'

Mycroft stood and yanked on the velvet pull rope. Within a few minutes they each held a balloon glass of cognac, with a half-full cut-glass decanter waiting on a side table.

'What are you up to, Sherlock?'

'Well, I was on my way to the coast, but then I thought, I need a sounding board, someone who will either support my conjectures or shoot them down in flames.'

'Conjectures about what?'

'The *Dover Arrow*.'

He caught Mycroft on the swallow and his

brother suffered a coughing fit, almost ejecting the brandy across the room. 'Good Lord, Sherlock, I thought I told you — '

Holmes leaned forward to emphasize. 'We are too long in the tooth to be intimidated, Mycroft. Between us we could summon support from ten, twenty, fifty of the great and the good. The very fact that someone does not want one to find out the truth is a pressing reason to go after that truth. Don't you agree?'

Mycroft wiped his lips with a napkin. 'I suppose so.'

'Do you remember 'The Lost Special'?'

'I do,' Mycroft replied. 'I remember discussing it with . . . what was her name . . . Mrs Gregson.'

'A train disappears between stations, the public are agog for a short while, and then lose interest. They were so concerned with *how* a train could disappear, they forgot the more important point.'

'*Why* someone would want a train to disappear.'

'Precisely!' said Holmes, flinging himself back in the chair and taking a puff on his cigarette. 'Why! We were almost fooled by Garavan's clever if barbaric distractions from his real purpose in kidnapping Lord Arnott. Perhaps, in the *Dover Arrow* case, we are too outraged by the thought of a German submarine's callous action to consider other possibilities. So, why would anyone else want to sink a hospital ship?'

'What do you mean by 'anyone else'? Other than the Germans, who would want to perpetrate such a thing?'

'The British,' said Holmes, and braced himself for the storm of protest.

343

When his brother spoke, though, it was more of a light breeze. 'You think we could sink our own ship?'

'I am asking you to consider the possibility.'

Mycroft sipped at his brandy once more. 'The Lost Special didn't actually disappear, of course. It was driven down a mineshaft.'

'And the *Dover Arrow* was sent to the bottom of the sea,' said Holmes flatly, but Mycroft raised a questioning eyebrow. 'Wasn't it?'

'The *Dover Arrow* cost some four hundred thousand pounds to build,' said Mycroft. 'If you count in the cost of its docking pontoons and the railway lines, perhaps more. I am not sure even the British toss away that sort of money.'

'Mycroft, what are you thinking?'

A slight smile played over Mycroft's lips. 'Have you heard of Richborough?'

'The town?'

'The scheme.'

'No.'

'Let me enlighten you.'

Slowly, two great minds, not as magnificent as they once were perhaps, but still wondrous pieces of cerebral machinery, applied themselves to the case of 'The Lost Ferry', until the decanter of brandy stood empty and the policeman outside had long grown bored.

★ ★ ★

A casual observer might not think anything remiss about the two gentlemen seated in front of the fire in the parlour room at the King's

Hotel, Colchester. Both were nursing tumblers of whisky, more to try to purge away the memory of an indifferent meal than anything else, and enjoying a small cigar each.

Someone with a trained eye, though, might notice the air of tension between them. The older man in particular was sitting bolt upright, rather than relaxing, and he was in the habit of nervously stroking his upper lip with a forefinger.

The younger of the pair played with his cane, needed because of a shattered knee, a war wound that explained his civilian clothes, a dark lounge suit that appeared to be a size too big for him. But many young men had come back from the war as mere shadows of their former selves.

'I haven't not had a moustache for nearly fifty years,' said the elder in a low voice, finally allowing himself to sink back in the seat. 'I feel naked.'

'You look younger,' said his companion.

'And you look frighteningly convincing,' said Watson, once again brushing his unadorned upper lip.

Miss Pillbody smiled. After trimming and then shaving Watson's moustache, she had cut her own hair short, strapped her breasts and assumed the role of Hubert Swannell, who, after service in France, travelled with his 'uncle', selling diesel engines to businesses. Somehow, in her time out of the bolt hole, she had secured them the use of a small van, in the back of which was a working model of a Paxman engine. Whether this was preplanned or a piece of improvisation, she wouldn't divulge.

'I have in my time been soldier, sailor and priest,' she explained. 'We She Wolves were trained in the art of disguise by Max Schneider.' She couldn't keep the pride from her voice.

Watson shook his head to show it meant nothing.

'No? Very famous actor in Germany. The Human Chameleon, they call him, The Man of a Thousand Smiles.'

'Holmes was partial to a disguise,' Watson said wistfully.

She nodded. Watson had forgotten that she had witnessed this for herself, on the bridge in Holland before she shot Mrs Gregson. It wouldn't be wise to remind him of that.

'What will you do?' Watson asked.

'Finish the brandy and get some sleep and hope breakfast is an improvement on dinner. We have to be at the field by eleven.'

'I meant after the war,' he said.

Her brow furrowed. 'I've never thought about it.'

'Really? I find that hard to believe. Surely, we all look forward to the day when the killing stops and we can go back to our old lives.'

'My old life went when my husband died. Do you think your old life will be waiting for you?'

'Something that isn't this life, I hope. One where men are mutilated and killed by the millions, and bombers roaming free over our cities. I'd like to survive long enough to be able to look up at a night sky and think of stars, not incendiaries.'

Miss Pillbody took a long pull on the whisky.

'I am not sure the average soldier in the trenches dares think he'll survive. It's almost like tempting fate. I'm much the same. I don't think much past the mission. Beyond that is just darkness.'

'So why do you keep doing this? You've more than done your part. Just say no, I'm finished.'

'Why does a German or British soldier go over the top when the whistle blows? Why does he walk across the mud and bones, knowing he is likely to be cut down by machine-gun fire at any moment? Why don't they just shoot their officers and go home?'

Some French units had, in fact, mutinied after the Nivelle Offensive, but Watson knew from Mycroft that the extent of the disaffection — and the reprisals — was kept secret from the Germans. He had no intention of spilling the beans to an enemy spy. 'Duty?' offered Watson.

'They feel it is their duty to die? Well, perhaps I feel the same.'

Watson didn't believe this. 'Yet you have gone to extraordinary lengths to survive.'

A shrug. 'Which is what I am trained to do.'

'Trained or mesmerized in some way? It seems to me that taking the fairer sex and turning them into . . . ' he struggled for the correct phrase.

'Into me?' she offered.

'Into what you have become, yes, which is monstrous. It's a perversion of everything womanhood stands for — caring, nurturing, the givers of life.'

She guffawed with laughter at this and he marvelled at how she managed to make even that

347

sound masculine. 'You didn't really notice the world passing into the twentieth century, did you, Major Watson?'

'Oh, I did,' he said, swirling his drink, 'I just didn't wish to join it.'

'Evening.' A fellow guest wandered into the parlour, looked around, picked up an evening paper and left again.

'Holmes has a theory,' Watson said.

'About me?'

'About Garavan. He thinks Garavan's real mission was to dent confidence in the new paper currency or to force the Treasury to withdraw the existing notes. A form of economic warfare.'

'Surely, Garavan was simply a thief?' she said. 'A deranged one, perhaps, but greed was his ultimate motive.'

'And perhaps he saw a way of combining larceny with a blow against the British Empire. Two paydays — one from the Treasury, one from his sponsors.'

Miss Pillbody considered this. 'So Holmes was suggesting that Garavan served two masters. Himself and Germany.'

'And he implied that you would know if this was true.'

She leaned forward and gave the fire a poke, releasing a shower of sparks. 'You don't understand how Germany works. We are a relatively new country, younger than you, Major, used to doing things in compartments. We don't yet think of ourselves as a whole nation and that is reflected in the way the government's various departments work. If someone in one branch of

348

intelligence decided to attack Britain through its currency, they wouldn't share that with the She Wolves.'

'Even though there was every chance of one group treading on the other's toes?'

She frowned. 'Each department is mainly concerned with enhancing its own reputation, in making sure they are the sole recipient of whatever glory is available. Sharing is not in their nature. In fact, the very opposite.'

'So, it could have been a German undertaking, or at the very least, funded by them.'

This time when she poked the fire, it was as if she were striking it through the heart with a rapier. 'It could have been, yes.'

'And you helped disrupt it,' he said with some satisfaction.

'I wouldn't look so smug if I were you. If I have managed to tread on toes, as you put it, for a serious strike against Great Britain . . . '

'There might be awkward questions for you to answer.'

'No.' She put down the poker and drained her whisky. 'If I did manage to help disrupt an operation like that, Major Watson, and they learn of my involvement, then, She Wolf or no She Wolf, I am a dead woman.'

41

Major Shandling of the Royal Engineers needed some persuading to show Sherlock Holmes around the Richborough port site. Even Mycroft's letter from the War Department asking for all assistance to be freely given was questioned — which it deserved to be as it was a forgery — and it was only when Holmes insisted the major speak to Winston Churchill himself that the man relented. Fortuitous, because Churchill, although familiar with Holmes, knew nothing about this undertaking.

Holmes knew he had been followed and this time he was certain it was by Bullimore himself, who had been picked up at Sandwich station by an unmarked police car with driver and had trailed Holmes's taxi to the site. Unable to enter the restricted area, Bullimore was most likely waiting outside for Holmes to leave.

'The correct name of what you are looking at,' said Shandling, his words almost drowned out by the gulls whirring overhead, 'is the War Department Cross-Channel Train Ferry. It will connect to Calais, Dunkirk, Dieppe and, eventually, Cherbourg.'

They were standing on a small bluff that overlooked what had once been a natural amphitheatre on the shoreline, but which had been marooned as the sea had retreated over the years. Now it had been extended, with a wide canal-like cutting that once more would connect it to the Channel, although a new harbour wall would protect it from the worst of the waves. Immediately below them it had been transformed into a churned plain of dirty-white chalky soil with a tangle of railway tracks and sidings laid out for completion. Battalions of men, many wearing shirtsleeves despite the sharp wind coming off the sea, were laying sleepers or hammering in spikes. Others were constructing elaborate gantries for signals, and a control tower to oversee all the expected activity was taking shape. At the area closest to the sea, quays were being constructed for ferry berths. Two of the boats, equipped with four railway lines on their decks, with funnel and bridge positioned to one side to allow rolling stock to be driven on unobstructed, were riding at anchor beyond the incomplete harbour wall. They had been freshly painted in the disorienting 'dazzle' geometric camouflage pattern, designed to make it difficult for a U-boat captain to judge range, course or speed.

Looking closely, Holmes could see that there were several nationalities at work across the site — English, Caribbean, Australian — their distinctive hats gave them away — Chinese in tunics and Sikhs in turbans, along with Hindus, Gurkhas and probably Mussulmans. The Empire was at work.

'What about the railway gauge?' asked Holmes. 'If you want to drive the train straight onto the ferry, aren't Continental and British railway gauges different?'

'Indeed they are,' said Shandling, pleased that someone took an interest in such matters. 'We have adopted the English standard, four feet eight and one-half inches for here and the ferry. The continental standard is four feet nine inches.'

'Which means you can take a train right through from, say, the factories of Birmingham to Ypres.'

'Quite.'

'When do you expect to be fully operational?'

'Not until January. As long as those German bombers don't notice us. But they haven't come calling yet. Probably not enough women and children to kill and maim here.'

'And the steamers out there, specially built?'

'They have been adopted from the Dover-Calais service that operated before the war. One existing ship and another completed from the blueprints.'

'Very good. Well, I won't detain you.'

'Mr Holmes, you haven't actually explained why you are so interested in our train-ferry system.'

'I had some small part to play in the development of the tank.' It wasn't the truth, but it wasn't entirely a lie either.

'Did you?' Shandling looked surprised.

'And I suspect that a lot of them will be coming through here.'

'Yes, yes, they will. They are buggers — excuse my French — to load and unload using conventional train and ferry transport, as you can imagine. But if they can stay on there while

352

we put them onto the ferries or the towed barges we'll use in calm weather, they'll be at the front that much quicker.' He smiled proudly at this.

'I just wanted to be sure they weren't going to end up at the bottom of the sea. I think you have done splendidly. I'll sign out, shall I?'

Holmes had left his cab waiting, but once they had let him through the gate at the facility, he marched past it to the police car. As he had anticipated, Bullimore was in the rear seat, a plain-clothes constable behind the wheel. The inspector pulled down the window as he approached and folded up the newspaper he had been reading.

'Inspector.'

'Mr Holmes.'

'Might I ask why you are so keen on pursuing me?'

'Not you. Your friend Watson. My superiors have made it clear that my career is in jeopardy because of him. You all played me for a fool, convincing me he was above suspicion. I still maintain consorting with Miss Pillbody, a sworn enemy of this country, is highly suspicious.'

'That's as may be, but you are wasting your precious time following me, Inspector,' Holmes said. 'I made it clear that I will not lead you to Watson. Or to *that* woman.'

'Perhaps not, but you are up to something peculiar.'

'Government business. For my brother. Have you found the missing nightwatchman yet? Crantock?'

'We have not. My superiors tell me he is small beer.'

'My instincts tell me he is a loose end.'

Bullimore refused to be goaded by this. 'And my instincts tell me you are helping Watson in some way. Wherever you are, he is bound to turn up sooner rather than later.'

'As I said, I am on government business.'

'Well, tell me, where will your government business lead you next?'

'So you can prepare to follow me?'

'If need be,' insisted Bullimore.

'Well, you had best make sure your papers are in order, Inspector, for tonight we sail for France!'

'France? Why France?'

'Because, Inspector, after my visit here, I know what really became of the *Dover Arrow*.'

★   ★   ★

There were men with tapes and poles busy crisscrossing the cricket pitch when they pulled up in the van. Three of them, one pacing out distances, the other taking notes, the third hammering in the tall wooden stakes. One man wore a bowler hat, the other two flat caps; all three had on wellington boots.

'What the hell are they doing here?' Miss Pillbody asked. 'The plane will be landing in thirty minutes.'

Watson wasn't sure where Miss Pillbody had picked up the compact Colt pistol she now held in her hand. Most likely she had acquired it on her little excursion. She pulled the slide back to chamber a round.

354

'What are you doing?' he asked as she opened the door.

She pointed to the low white building at the end of the field. 'I'll put them in the cricket pavilion. Tie them up.'

'And if they won't go?'

She looked around. There wasn't a dwelling in sight. She held the small pistol up. 'I'll shoot one of them. That'll concentrate their minds.'

With a speed that surprised even him, Watson snatched the gun from her grip. 'You bloody woman. You will not kill any more innocent men. Leave this to me.'

He managed to get the gun into his left hand and behind his back before she encircled his right wrist and squeezed. A stab of pain shot up to his elbow. 'If we are seen struggling, how will you explain that?'

'Give it back, Major.'

A white-hot locus of pain began to burn in his joint. It was all he could do not to cry out. 'When you learn to behave like a reasonable person.'

Anger clouded her face. 'I could snap your neck in a second and take it.'

He tutted. 'That's a long way from reasonable, Miss Pillbody. Didn't they teach appropriate levels of response at the She Wolves?'

She released her grip. 'I must have been absent that day.'

He pocketed the gun and massaged his throbbing arm. He waited for a renewed attack, but none came. Doubtless she was curious to see what he did next. 'You wait here,' he instructed, without much hope she would obey.

Watson stepped from the van, straightened his suit and walked across towards the men, who stopped what they were doing to watch him approach.

'Good morning,' he said.

'Mornin',' replied the bowler-hatted one without much enthusiasm, thumbs hooked into his waistcoat. 'What can I do for you?'

'Major Watson,' he said. 'Royal Flying Corps.'

'Oh, aye.'

Watson looked from one to the other. The man who had spoken was bull-necked and ruddy, about forty, with a drinker's web of veins under each eye. The other two men were older by five or ten years and showed signs of having been outdoors for most of their working lives.

'I'm sorry, you are . . . ?'

'Hugh Garber. Essex County Council.' He looked Watson up and down. 'RFC, you say?'

'Yes, not in uniform. People tend to get alarmed when the RFC come walking onto their land.'

'Why's that?' asked one of the other men.

'In case they want to build one of their air-fields,' said Garber. 'But you're too late. Vegetables.'

'I beg your pardon?' asked Watson.

Garber waved a hand over the pitch and beyond. 'Whole thing's going to be turned over to growing vegetables. Not much call for cricket these days . . . '

'First team's mostly dead,' offered the man with the notebook.

' . . . so we are going to plough it up for the duration,' said Garber.

356

'Ah. Well, we are looking for a forward air defence base. Somewhere to put the new night fighters that will go up against the bombers.'

Garber looked puzzled. 'What, as well as North Weald and Rochford?'

Watson remembered with dismay that Rochford in Southend had been an important base for anti-Zeppelin sorties. In all likelihood it was being used by the RFC to try to intercept bombers, too. His cover story was crumpling.

'As an overspill,' he improvised. 'For aeroplanes low on fuel or lost.'

'St Michael's College has a flying club at West Bergholt. Still got a grass strip there. Why not use that?'

'I'm just following orders,' Watson said with a shrug.

'Aye, me, too.'

'The thing is, Mr Garber, there is a test landing due at any moment. If you could just pull up the stakes over there.'

'Took us all mornin' to get 'em in,' said the third man tetchily.

'Test landing?' queried Gerber.

'To check the . . . um . . . ' Watson stomped a foot on the grass,' . . . consistency of the surface.'

Garber shook his head so violently he almost lost his bowler. 'Look, Major, this is highly irregular. Even the RFC can't just take land willy-nilly. There are proper procedures for this sort of thing. One, I need to see some sort of authorization. Then, I suggest you and I go to the town hall — '

His younger ears picked up the sound a few

moments before Watson did. The distinctive note of an aero engine, no louder than a distant gnat for the moment, but growing in strength steadily. The three men shaded their eyes and looked up into the sky.

When they looked back, Watson was pointing the pistol at them.

'What's your game?' Garber asked.

He heard the door of the van slam as Miss Pillbody exited the vehicle.

'Do as you are told and you won't get hurt. Do anything stupid and I'll be forced to make an example of one of you.'

'You . . . ' Garber began. 'You're bloody spies!'

All three men clenched their fists and Watson brought the pistol up to head level. 'No, we are not.' Well, not both of them. 'But I don't have time to explain the niceties of the situation. I want you to turn and walk while you still can.'

'Walk where?'

'The pavilion.'

The three men stood their ground until Watson flicked the safety off with a loud snick.

Garber spoke. 'Come on, it's not worth getting killed for, whatever it is.'

The trio turned and began to trudge across the grass towards the hut, each mumbling threats or curses under their breath.

Watson was aware of Miss Pillbody at his shoulder. There was an amused sparkle to her voice when she spoke. 'Well done, Major. We'll make a She Wolf of you yet.'

★   ★   ★

358

Miss Pillbody took over the task of tying and gagging the men — she clearly hadn't been away on that day — and Watson moved across the field gathering up the marking poles and wrapping up the cotton tape they had been using to mark out plots. The Bristol came in low at one point and Watson waved to the pilot, who lifted a hand in response.

The pilot took the plane round in a large shallow loop and by the time he was back on the approach the obstacles had been cleared and Watson and Miss Pillbody were standing on the perimeter of the improvised landing strip.

'What will you do?' Watson asked as the Bristol lined itself up for touchdown. 'While I am over in Belgium with this witness?'

'Return to London. I'll have to make alternative arrangements for you to come back across.' She inclined her head at the pavilion. 'I think we might have trouble using this strip again.'

'I'm afraid you're right,' he said. 'You know that, however I get back to England, our alliance, such as it is, will be dissolved.'

'I realize that. You'll do everything in your power to bring me to justice.'

'Yes,' he confirmed.

For Mrs Gregson's sake. Quite.

'Pity.'

'I think you only have yourself to blame.'

'No, I mean a pity that our partnership will be no more. I've quite enjoyed working with you, Major. You're a good man. I'd almost forgotten what they are like.'

'Perhaps that's because you have a tendency to kill most of those you meet.'

'You say the sweetest things.' She leaned in close and kissed him on the cheek. Watson scuttled back, horrified. 'Relax, Major. You're safe from me.'

'Nobody is safe from you,' Watson said with some feeling.

She slapped him playfully on the shoulder, as if this were some kind of compliment.

The handsome Bristol throttled back and drifted down towards the earth, bouncing twice before spinning round and coming to a halt. Watson and Miss Pillbody ran to the plane, holding on to their hats. As they reached the wings, both became aware that a gun was pointed at them.

'*Who are you?*' the pilot yelled, waving the Mauser at Miss Pillbody. Even at idle, the prop wash was snatching his words away.

'The same person you dropped off here, Oberleutnant Schrader.' She took her hat off. 'Only with rather less hair.'

Schrader lifted his goggles and peered at her before nodding. 'Get in.'

'Major, let me give you a hand,' she said.

'I want him in first, you on his knee,' said Schrader.

'*Ich werde nicht*,' she protested.

'I'm sorry, but my orders are to bring both of you or neither,' he said.

The gun, they both realized, was still pointing at them. Watson had the small pistol in his pocket, but it was no match for a 'Broomhandle' Mauser.

Miss Pillbody closed her eyes for a second, as if to keep the blast from the propeller out of them, but Watson knew she was running through her options. When she opened them again, he could see something like defeat in them.

'After you, Major.'

Watson found a stirrup-like foothold and, as he gripped the rim of the cockpit, allowed himself to be pushed up by Miss Pillbody to the point where he could hook a leg over and climb into the observer's seat.

'Hurry up, please,' said Schrader impatiently. 'Take off your hats. There are goggles in there, two pairs.'

'This is going to be cosy,' Miss Pillbody said as she followed him in and then slid down on top of him. 'Open your legs, Major.'

Watson ignored her and slid to one side, his knees pressed together so hard that they began to ache.

'As you will.' She wriggled a little until she had part of her bottom on the uncomfortable metal-and-canvas seat. The rest of it Watson didn't care to think about.

Watson found the straps had been lengthened so they could pass round two people and he fed them through to Miss Pillbody, who snapped the buckle shut. It was not so much cosy as compressed and he found it difficult to breathe. There were also parts of his body still tender from the car being tipped over in Old Street. However long the flight, it was bound to feel like an eternity.

The engine note increased and a storm of air

buffeted them. Schrader gave a thumbs up, increased the throttle and the Bristol lurched forward, bouncing over what suddenly seemed a very rough, corrugated surface. Watson realized he should probably have gone to the lavatory before he set out, a feeling reinforced when Miss Pillbody twisted round to speak to him. Her expression was glum as she shouted over the increasingly raucous whine and clatter of the Rolls Royce engine.

'Like I said, Major. She Wolf or no She Wolf, I'm a dead woman.'

42

Within twenty minutes of takeoff, Watson's lower body had gone numb and his face felt like it had been rubbed raw with pumice, such was the constant blast from the propeller. The pilot, Schrader, said nothing — not that they could have heard much — nor made many hand signals. Once airborne, he had made directly for the coast, climbing all the time at a steady pace. Only once did Miss Pillbody turn, a rather strange smile on her face.

'What?' he yelled.

'Nothing. Just funny how life turns out. Here we are, two peas in a pod.'

'Peas in a pod? Hardly. It suggests we are alike, Miss Pillbody. Nothing could be further from the truth.'

She had fallen silent then. Watson had examined the patchwork of English fields once or twice, but as they left land behind, decided he wouldn't bother looking at the relatively featureless mass of water below, which only made him feel sick. Lord, how he hated flying. Never again, he swore. They could not use the field again after what happened with the surveyors, so they'd have to feed him back to the UK another way.

If they allow you to return home.

That cheery sentiment caused him to shudder. He had no desire to see the inside of a German POW camp again.

They were almost touching the few clouds that dotted the sky now, stray wisps were stroking the upper wing of the Bristol. The sea, from their altitude, looked like a flat expanse of grey Welsh slate, hewn from a single piece, the only veins in it provided by the razor cuts of white left by the cross-channel ships ploughing those dangerous waters. Ahead must be the Belgian coast, but Watson couldn't see much past Miss Pillbody, Schrader and the blur of the spinning propeller.

Schrader watched the two planes rising towards him, small mottled specks against the waves. He could make out the undulating line of the coast. Soon he would spot the first of the giant British tented hospitals that seem to run in an unbroken line from close to their front line, all the way to Boulogne and beyond. No such concentration of beds existed for the Germans, who had no need to park up their wounded before they could be shipped over the Channel or returned to the war. But he doubted the number of injured and sick Germans was any fewer than the thousands upon thousands that the British had under canvas.

One of the escorts began winking a light at him, and for one second he tried to read the message, but it was far too fast. Only when the whine of a bullet sparked against the metal tip of his prop did he realize he was being fired at. Schrader glanced down into his cockpit. He hadn't even turned on the homing radio signal yet.

They were Germans, all right. Albatroses, although which variant, he couldn't be sure from

364

this distance. No matter, they were all very handy little fighters.

More winking, this time from the plane on the right, but they were at the limit of accuracy and apart from one thud at the tail, nothing seemed to come close. Probably new boys who hadn't learned the lesson about waiting until you could do some damage before firing. He checked the controls, making sure they were free and unsnagged. He hadn't really put this Bristol through its paces. It was steady, easy to fly and he suspected it would absorb a lot of damage. He might be about to find out.

He reached up to the Lewis gun, and checked the safety was off. The gun was fired by a Bowden cable, which ended in a loop next to his hand. He pulled once on the makeshift handle. The gun stuttered briefly. He was in business.

He dipped a wing and then turned to his passengers, pointing down at the fighters, so they understood, then levelled and pushed the nose up and began to claw his way into the heavens.

★   ★   ★

'This has absolutely nothing to do with me!' Winston Churchill fixed Holmes with one of his famous stares, then rose to his feet to point at the enormous map pinned to the wall of his office. 'This is my domain now. The National Filling Factories, the National Explosive Factories. Glasgow, Chilwell, Banbury, the Arsenal . . . machine guns from Birmingham, rifles from Enfield, howitzers from Coventry. The outcome

365

of the war depends on these establishments giving us the means to fight. And you come to me about a boat? One boat? Champagne?'

'No, thank you, Minister.'

Churchill, now the Minister of Munitions, walked over to a side table, yanked a bottle of Pol Roger from an ice bucket and filled up two glasses. He walked back and handed one to Holmes, who took it, albeit reluctantly. Churchill, he knew, didn't entirely trust a man without a drink in his hand after five p.m.

'Why haven't you gone to Kell? Surely this is MI5 business.'

'I fear I am not in Kell's good books after exposing one of his agents. Amies.'

'Heard about that. Peculiar business all round. But I suppose anyone can be bought if the price is right. What? What's so funny?'

'I couldn't imagine bidding on you, sir.'

Churchill looked suspicious. 'Don't flatter me, Holmes. Politicians are as venal as the next man. Except you bribe them with power and prestige. I wouldn't be so bold as to call myself immune to such blandishments. What is it you want from me?'

'I need to travel to France, to look into the log for this ambulance boat-train. It will have been signed off by the French railways before sailing. So the log will also have the name of the man responsible for handing over the train to the ship . . . '

'Which was then sunk by a German submarine,' Churchill said firmly.

'Possibly not.'

366

'One of those damned torpedo boats, then.'

Holmes said nothing.

'I am inclined to refuse you.'

'Why?'

'Because you are a bloody nuisance. It takes one to know one, Holmes. You are meddling for meddling's sake.'

'I am meddling for the sake of my friend Watson.'

'So you have come to me for . . . ?'

'If I turn up at Dover or Ramsgate or Folkestone asking for passage to the Continent without good reason, I shall be turned away. As Minister of Munitions you can issue me with a munition inspector's travel permit, ostensibly to check the stocks of shells . . . '

'But, in reality, a permit to poke around where you are not wanted.'

'Isn't that the only way we uncover the truth? By poking around where we are not wanted? Something is wrong here, something about this boat worries me. I am in the twilight of my career now. I have served you well. Watson served you well in the tank business.'

Churchill grunted. 'I paid that off with the submarine in Holland. Wouldn't have done it if I didn't feel I owed him something. Had to call in a lot of favours for that. Too many.'

'Then we will be in your credit.'

'A man at the twilight of his career is no good to me. One, I hear, with a heart problem.'

For a man who claimed his sole interest was explosives these days, nothing much escaped the minister, Holmes thought, but held his tongue.

'So it's a no, then?

Churchill peered at him through hooded eyes. 'Are you going to drink that or cuddle it till it goes flat?'

Holmes took a gulp of the champagne.

'An ordinary man, in the twilight of his career as you put it, is no use to me, is what I mean. But a man like you, Holmes, can still do great service. I ask you this, however. If what you discover about this affair is detrimental to this country, what will you do with that information?'

Holmes sensed not one trap, but several, waiting to snap closed on his ankle no matter which direction he stepped in. 'I would come back here and discuss it with you before I took any action.'

Churchill gave a wolfish grin. 'That, Mr Holmes, is the only answer I would have accepted.' He scribbled a note and held it out. 'See my secretary.'

'I need two passes.'

'I thought Watson was busy with his own foolish activities.'

'It's for a policeman. An Inspector Bullimore. He has been charged with following me and I thought I might make it simpler all round for him to know my exact whereabouts by being at my side.'

'And for you to know his?'

Holmes inclined his head.

'Very well.' He added a sentence to the instructions and Holmes took it. 'Be aware, Sherlock Holmes, that one day, perhaps not tomorrow or next week or next year, but one day, I will be calling that note in.'

Once Holmes had left, Churchill drained his glass of Pol Roger and poured another, before placing a call to Vernon Kell of MI5.

'I told you,' he said without preamble when Kell was on the line, 'that this *Dover Arrow* business would come back to bite your backside.' He explained quickly what Holmes was up to, then listened to Kell's reply. 'Well, that's straightforward enough. Make sure all the paperwork is destroyed at the French end.' He took a sip of the fresh glass. 'And then, I would imagine, you are going to have take care of the bloody idiot whose idea this was. What do I suggest? What do you think, if the Germans are on to what happened and looking for proof? EXTO, man. EXTO.'

★   ★   ★

Watson found himself gasping at the cold, thin air as the Bristol continued to gain height. Both he and Miss Pillbody had seen the fighters climbing towards them when Schrader had dipped the wing, but now they were invisible to the two passengers. He wondered what the pilot was thinking. He could hardly engage his own side in combat. His best chance was to try to out-climb or out-run them. But was the British plane good enough? The Germans had devastated the RFC in the 'Bloody April' campaign, until the British had introduced new planes with better firepower. He hoped this Bristol was one of them.

The answer came in a series of holes punched through the lower wing, sending scraps of material spinning away, and a steady whistling noise added to the laboured wheeze of the engine. The sky spun as Schrader flung the plane to one side. Watson felt his body pushed this way and that, and he and Miss Pillbody left the seat and pressed against the straps as Schrader twisted the machine through the air, losing height all the time. So he couldn't out-climb them. He was going to try to outrun them.

The plane fell with all the stability of a dropped handkerchief, apparently floating this way and that. Watson felt as if his ears were going to explode in his head. He was aware of another pressure, something strange. His hand. Miss Pillbody was squeezing his hand. His first instinct was to snatch it away. But then he squeezed back before removing it. It was comforting to know that someone else was terrified as they plunged towards the waiting sea. Even if that someone was Miss Pillbody.

The Bristol shuddered along its length, crabbed through the air sideways, and then it was flying straight and level. Watson had no idea at what height — there were no ships for him to judge scale. They could be at five hundred or fifty feet above the Channel. The wind was tugging at Watson's face and pulling back his lips. Even if he wanted to shout in terror — and he did — he doubted he could make the requisite shape with his mouth.

Schrader looked back at them. Although Watson was sure he was mainly looking for his

370

pursuers rather than worrying about his charges, he made a signal with his hand. *Get down*, it said. *Make yourself small.*

Miss Pillbody slid further towards the floor and Watson lowered himself so that the top of his head was barely poking above the rim of the cockpit. But what use was that? All that stood between them and a bullet was wood and canvas. Any form of armour would slow the aircraft down, he supposed. Speed was everything in combat.

His ears popped. They were still descending. The engine noise had increased to the point where it sounded as if it were shaking itself apart.

A streak of hot air hissed by, almost parted his hair and he looked up in time to feel a splinter of wood embed itself in his forehead, just above the goggles. He swivelled as best he could to take a look at what was happening. One of the German planes was gaining on them and he could see the short bursts of fire it was issuing, trying to gauge range. Part of the Bristol's tail tore away, leaving a long streamer of material trailing behind them.

The Bristol drooped a few more feet, quickly enough to bring his stomach into his mouth.

The air above them zinged and he felt the buffeting impact of the rounds on the fuselage.

Miss Pillbody began to squirm and he put a hand on her shoulder, but she carried on twisting. It was a moment before he appreciated she was trying to climb out of the cockpit.

'No!' he said. 'Stay where you are.'

But she continued to scramble up him, all

elbows and knees, until her weight was pressing down on him. She pushed harder, and he grabbed onto her coat. He wouldn't let her go.

Her face came close to his. 'Get down, you stubborn old fool!'

'What?'

'You have to live. I'm a dead woman anyway. It will be Admiral Hersch waiting for you. He will take you to the survivor.'

'Hersch!' he exclaimed, moments before the plane rose once more and threw Miss Pillbody's full weight against his chest. Hersch had been part of the plot to exchange Watson for Holmes on that cursed bridge in Holland. A spymaster. The creator of the She Wolves. 'You've been lying to me,' he managed to gasp.

'No. But I haven't been entirely candid — '

Her body arched as a bullet spun an eccentric path through the flimsy sides of the Bristol and passed into her chest cavity.

'*Gott*,' she whispered. '*Gott verzeih mir.*'

She coughed blood, wet and hot on his face, splattering his goggles, and then slumped down on top of him, pinning him into the seat. He was aware of a shadow above them, one of the two German planes, and then the sound of a machine gun loud and close, and then smoke and cordite streaming past him.

He closed his eyes and waited for the end.

★　★　★

They were saved by the Fokker escort that came up to protect the Bristol in response to the radio beacon. The noise Watson had heard was Schrader pulling the gun down on its Foster Mount so it could fire upwards. He had inflicted enough damage on one Albatros for it to break off and the Fokker managed to convey to the remaining one that he was escorting the by-now battered Bristol back to German-held soil.

Watson managed to slide Miss Pillbody down a little and wriggle upwards. He could see the coast; dunes now, a long low line of solid land, as welcome a sight as he could recall. Something else warm spotted his face and goggles. At first, he thought it must be blood from a wounded pilot, but when he examined it on his fingertips it was black.

Oil.

He was no expert on engines, but it was clear this one was running rough, with what seemed like the occasional spasm before it picked up again. A thin flume of the lubricant was bleeding out of the system.

Schrader turned and Watson made signs that they had a dead body on board. The pilot nodded and pointed to the sea.

'What?' Watson mouthed. 'We're going to ditch?' He mimed the plane going in.

Schrader shook his head. There was a few more seconds of charades before he understood. The engine needed all the help it could get if they were to make it home.

He refastened the straps that Miss Pillbody had undone when she had climbed on top of him, pulling them as tight as he could around his body. Then he lifted the spy up, under the arms, until she was back laying on him. Then he gave the thumbs up.

The port wing dipped and Watson pushed and heaved until the corpse, with the help of gravity, slowly slid from the cockpit. He had just a moment before Schrader corrected the angle to watch Miss Pillbody spin, her lifeless limbs flailing in a parody of flight, down towards the sea that would take her as it had so many others in this war.

★ ★ ★

If the footman who opened the door recognized Bullimore, he didn't let on. It wasn't surprising. Bullimore had been sequestered in the East Wing, along with the other war damaged. Staff from the main house rarely entered. Bullimore remembered this one, though, Jepson, who never met any soldier's eye.

'Can I help you, sir?'

Bullimore showed his commission book. 'Inspector Bullimore. Bow Street. Is the gentleman of the house in?'

'I am afraid not. On active service.'

'The lady?'

'Can I ask exactly what this is about, sir?' *And why you have come to the front door?* was the unsaid component.

'It's rather a sensitive matter.'

'Of course, sir. If you'll wait here.'

The door closed firmly on him and Bullimore turned and looked along the long, tree-lined drive he had driven down. It was dusk, and he could see the jittery movement of bats, making a last frantic feast before winter. The jerky movements were reflected in his stomach. This might be the biggest mistake of his life.

To his right there were lights on in the East Wing, where he had been housed. If he strained his ears, he could hear voices and the scratchy sound of a gramophone. Clearly, there was fresh batch of patients in residence.

The door opened. 'If you'll follow me, sir.'

He walked across a vast, echoing hall, a circular sweep of marble columns with a series of double doors running off it. Jepson opened one set and announced gravely, 'Inspector Bullicore, ma'am.'

Bullimore didn't bother correcting him. His eyes were drawn towards Marion, seated next to the fireplace in a room decorated as if any free space on wall or floor was an anathema. The walls were crowded with jostling portraits, there were four sofas, twice as many armchairs and two grand pianos. They must be items from the East Wing, he thought, emptied to make space for beds when the wounded came. Two four-foot high porcelain dragons in the Asian style guarded the fireplace, an elaborate confection of wood, tile and glass. There were also, he noted, some silken wall hangings with Chinese or Japanese — he couldn't tell — garden scenes.

She stood as he entered the room and held out a hand. 'Inspector. This is very exciting. How can I be of assistance to the police?'

He barely brushed the tips of her outstretched fingers for fear of being swept away in the sensation of her touch. 'It concerns some robberies in the area.'

'Robberies.' She put a hand to her throat. 'Goodness.'

'Well, burglaries to be more precise.' Idiot, he really hadn't thought what to say while servants were present. 'Specializing in fine jewellery.'

'How awful. But I don't think we've had any problems. Have we, Jepson?'

'No, ma'am.'

'It's my job to make sure you don't, ma'am, said Bullimore. 'A few simple rules to follow.'

'Well, sit down and tell me all about them.'

'Shall I bring some tea?' Jepson asked.

Bullimore turned. 'Not on my behalf. I won't be staying long. Just some advice on security.'

'The inspector won't be staying long,' she repeated. It sounded more flinty when she said it. 'But tell Cook to put dinner back by half an hour, would you?'

'Ma'am.'

The door closed and he listened for the man's retreating footsteps.

'Burglaries?' she asked.

'Yes. The jewels being replaced by excellent forgeries.'

'So it is someone who would have access to the originals?'

'We believe so,' he said, going along with the charade.

'And where did you get this from?'

'C. L. Pirkis did a story about it. In the *Ludgate Monthly*.'

Her voice dropped to a croak. 'What on earth

376

are you doing here?'

His mouth was suddenly very dry. 'I needed to see you.'

'And I,' she hissed with some venom, 'said I never wished to see you again. For crying out loud, you stroll up to the main entrance, announce you are the police and then offer some penny dreadful excuse. What do you think the staff are talking about at this very moment?'

'I know. I'm sorry. At least you still have staff to talk about you.'

'Don't.'

'What?'

'Try to make me laugh.'

'I wasn't. I'm surprised you have staff.'

'Jepson there, who has a heart murmur he can turn on and off at will, is butler, footman and valet rolled into one. I have but one cook, a scullery maid and two housemaids, a nanny for Charles, and a gardener who thinks it is always time for a good prune. The garden looks like those pictures of the Somme. Oh, and thirty-eight gassed soldiers in the East Wing to visit like Florence Nightingale each morning. Keeps their spirits up, apparently.'

'Certainly kept mine up.'

The lighter tone disappeared as suddenly as it had arrived. 'You are very trying. I am so angry with you. What if Arthur had been here?'

'Then I would be discussing how to keep valuables secure with him.'

'Over a stiff brandy.'

'Not while on duty, ma'am.'

'I wasn't talking about you.' She gave a sigh. 'I

had a telegram. He is on his way back.'

'So soon?'

'He's a senior officer, Inspector. They get a decent amount of leave.'

'Is my name out of bounds?'

She frowned. 'I wouldn't call a visiting policeman by his first name. Ever.'

'I suppose not.'

'And before you go, I want you to go downstairs and talk to the staff about making sure they lock doors and to my maids about never leaving jewellery out unnecessarily. Understood?'

'Yes, ma'am.'

She stood and he did the same. 'Well, you've seen me now. Was that all?'

He looked down at her stomach. 'I was wondering — '

He never finished the sentence. She stepped in and kissed him on the lips, pressing harder until his mouth opened slightly and she let the tip of her tongue dart out. Her hands gripped the sides of his head, pressing hard as if she wanted to burst his cranium. When she pulled away, he found himself breathless. His cheeks glowed as if a furnace had been lit beneath them.

'My goodness, where did that come from?' she said. 'My apologies, Inspector.'

He wasn't sure what to say. She seemed to be sending conflicting messages. Although that last one was as clear as semaphore on a sunny day. But was he dismissed now? With the most passionate kiss she had ever given him?

'Marion — '

378

She put a finger to his still-glowing lips. 'It's all fine, the baby, I mean. I feel fine. No sickness.'

'Good. Look, I am going back to France tomorrow.'

'Not to fight?'

'No. Police business, after a fashion. But I can't say I'm looking forward to it. I wanted to ask you something, before I left.'

'Yes?'

'When you decided against me, was it money you were worried about? Or status? Is it about giving up all this to live with a policeman who shouldn't even go to the front entrance of a house like this?'

She shook her head. 'It isn't you. It's Charles — '

There was a tap at the door and they stepped apart.

'Yes?'

A young woman in a starched uniform appeared. 'Excuse me, ma'am, but Charlie would like to see you before bath-time.' The nanny, Bullimore assumed.

'Of course,' she said. 'We had just finished. Perhaps you could show the inspector the staff quarters for me? He needs to have a word with you all about house security.'

'Yes, ma'am.'

'And how many times have I told you, Nora. It's Charles. Not Charlie.'

'Yes, ma'am. Sorry, ma'am.'

As Bullimore walked towards the door, a young boy swept past him in a blur and leaped into Marion's arms and the look on her face told him everything he needed to know.

'She sacrificed herself to save you? I don't recall that in the She Wolf manual.'

Watson was sitting on a leather button-backed couch in what had once been the library of a wealthy merchant's house on the outskirts of Ghent. The shelves were devoid of books, many of them lined with empty champagne and wine bottles, the contents consumed by the German officers who were now billeted in the mansion. Admiral Hersch was standing before the fireplace, glass of schnapps in hand. Watson contented himself with a cigarette. He had bathed and been given a change of clothes, and some warmth had come back into his body. But he couldn't quite shake the unbidden image of Miss Pillbody's lifeless body plunging seaward.

'She thought you were going to kill her anyway.'

'Me?' Hersch looked genuinely surprised.

Watson said nothing. It was all too easy to fall into chit-chat with a German who, on the face of it, seemed sympathetic and civilized. He knew what Hersch really was.

'Come, Major, you owe me an explanation. Why would I want to kill the woman I created?'

Watson sighed. He had started the ball rolling. Now, he supposed, he had to run with it. 'Not you. But whoever ordered the raid on the Treasury building at Old Street.'

'I don't know what you are talking about.'

Watson explained how they had thwarted Garavan and his plans to print thousands of pounds worth of notes from stolen plates.

'I know nothing of this. Will you excuse me?'

Hersch left the room and Watson stood to stretch his limbs. He caught sight of himself in the mirror above the fireplace, still shocked at the lack of a moustache. He must grow it back. If he lived that long.

He heard Hersch's boots ringing on the parquet floor of the hallway and the admiral entered, closing the doors behind him. 'As I thought, nobody has heard of this Treasury business, not even the Department of Economic Warfare. I am afraid the enterprise seems to have been this man Cavan — '

'Garavan's.'

'His alone.' He chuckled. 'Although I think the Department of Economic Warfare wished they had thought of it.'

'So why was she ordered back?'

A shrug. 'Her job was done. We knew what effect the bombers were having on the population. Besides . . . '

'Yes?'

'Well, you'll find out eventually. Tonight and tomorrow the largest bomber fleet ever assembled will descend on London. I expect it to be nothing but rubble and flames within forty-eight hours.'

' "The Englishman is a patient creature, but at present his temper is a little inflamed, and it would be as well not to try him too far." '

'Is that a quote, Major?'

Watson gave a thin smile of acknowledgement.

'She told me that she had not been truthful with me about the sinking,' said Watson, returning to the matter in hand. 'Just before she died.'

'Ilse said that?'

'Not in so many words.'

Hersch shook his head. 'But what she told you is absolutely true. There are no games here. We have a survivor who won't speak to us. But might to you.' Now he frowned, deep grooves appearing in his forehead. 'I am still puzzled by her actions. Self-survival is everything for a She Wolf.'

'Perhaps it was for the good of the mission. So I might live to see this through. Or perhaps it was an act of kindness, of self-sacrifice.'

Hersch's look told him he was being ridiculous.

'Admiral, it seems to me you take people, women in this case, who are shattered, emotionally and physically, and you put them back together, using their grief and sorrow as glue. From what's left of them you fashion monsters, who think that by doing your will, they can somehow bring their husbands back or honour their memories.'

'You make me sound like Dr Frankenstein.'

'Perhaps without his humanity.'

Hersch plucked his drink off the mantelpiece and drained it. 'Pious poppycock, Major Watson. I am proud of what Ilse and the other She Wolves have achieved. You win wars by any means necessary.'

'Yet it is possible, is it not, that you failed to extinguish one last spark of decency in your subjects, even in Miss Pillbody?'

382

'Sentimentality, Watson, British sentimentality. I think you are right. She saw that of the two of you, the mission was best served if you survived. Don't fool yourself, Doctor; it was logic, nothing else, that dictated her actions. Now, do you want to discover what really happened to the *Dover Arrow* or not?'

'Before we go, I have one question I need to ask.'

'You can try.'

'The survivor. Do you know her name?'

'*Her* name?'

'Yes. She was a nurse, Miss Pillbody said.'

Now Hersch realized what Ilse had meant when she told Watson she had not been truthful. Or rather, what she had omitted to say. 'You knew a nurse on the *Dover Arrow*?'

'I did. Staff Nurse Jennings. Is that who you have?'

'The survivor is a nurse, or, at least, what you call a VAD.'

Watson felt his heart press against his ribcage and his stomach soured. 'VAD?' Jennings was a QA, a fully qualified nurse, not a volunteer. 'Are you sure?'

'Positive. And there's one other thing. It's not a 'she'. It's a 'he'.'

43

The smell hit Nurse Jennings as soon as she stepped into the carriage and heard the door locked behind her. The stench was thick, ripe and diseased, carried on a wave of heat from febrile bodies. It was all she could do not to gag and she placed a hand over her mouth. Dozens of eyes stared at her, but the rush that the colonel had been anticipating never came. Even if they had wanted to, rushing was beyond most of the men. Some were crouched on the floor, knees drawn up to their chests, others stood next to them, holding onto straps that dangled from the ceiling. A third group lay on the floor, curled like commas around those sitting. The men were all dressed in simple blue trousers and tunics, the majority of which were filthy and encrusted with what looked like a mix of vomit and blood.

The coughing sound she had heard from outside was more pronounced in here, and those who had an attack of the hawking and gasping screwed up their faces in pain. Many, she could see, had soiled themselves where they lay or sat, and pools of vile brown liquid had puddled in the dips and grooves in the wooden floor. Others, she noted with alarm, had rivulets of blood oozing from them, some from their nose, others from their ears. Jennings had served for two years on the Western Front and thought she had seen every degree of human suffering, every manifestation of disease, but she had never been confronted with symptoms like this.

She held up the water container that the lieutenant had fetched from the station, and hands grabbed greedily at it. Within a few minutes it was empty, poured down throats so hastily that a good portion of it was spilled, and greedy eyes looked at her for more. The stares made her uneasy.

There was something else that made her want to turn and run screaming from the carriage. She could see from the features of the men that they were all of Chinese origin, as the colonel had said. But for the majority of them it was only the shape of the eyes and face that indicated this. Not the skin.

Because the majority of these very sick men had turned blue.

'Does anyone here speak English?'

Jennings' voice sounded thin. It lacked gravitas. Once the shock of her sudden appearance among them had faded, some of the men had found the strength to start jabbering at her. Several had pressed in close, poking at her with angry fingers. It was with great reluctance she pulled out the revolver the colonel had given her and waved it at the poor souls. They weren't out to harm her, she knew. She could tell in their eyes they just wanted answers.

'Anyone? English?'

'Me. I do.'

There was a reluctant movement in the crowd and she sensed, rather than saw, someone making his way towards her. There were sharp protests from people on the floor, clearly being trodden on. Eventually, the last of the bodies parted, and a young man appeared. His skin, she noted, was still the usual colour, only one ear lobe had a tinge of blue. But there was blood on his tunic.

'Who are you?' she asked.

'When you let us out of here?' the man demanded. 'We need to get out. I have dead men back there. Lot of dead.'

'My name is Staff Nurse Jennings. I am — '

'Let us out!'

He stepped forward and Jennings brought the gun up, quicker than intended, catching him beneath the chin. He staggered back in shock. A murmur of anger flared through the onlookers.

'Sorry, sorry. Jennings,' she repeated, banging her collarbone with her fist. 'Jennings.'

'Jiang Yutang,' the man mumbled, rubbing his chin. She couldn't help notice the sweat pearled on his brow.

'Where are you from?'

'Shandong. Mostly Shandong men.' He indicated his companions. 'All Chinese Labour Corps.'

A man close by began to vomit and the others shuffled away from him as best they could.

'Yutang, what is wrong with these men?'

'You nurse,' he said. 'You tell us.'

'Has a doctor seen you?'

The man laughed. 'Doctors said we had to be quarantined. Chen Dien first man to go blue. Doctor put all of us who travelled here with him in hut in a hospital at a place called . . .'

'Noyelles-sur-Mer.'

'Yes. Then put onto train. They lock doors! We trapped here.'

'What are the symptoms? The first symptoms. The blue colour?'

Jiang shook his head. 'Headache. Cough. Fever. Shivers. Bone ache.'

That could be any number of things, she thought. The body had a generic response to many infections.

'Then cough so bad, break ribs. Sick.' He mimed vomiting. 'Then shit.' A wave at his backside. 'Then blue. Then dead.'

'How many dead in here?'

'Twenty, I think, maybe more. What is it? What we have wrong?'

Something new, she thought, something I have never seen before. It was as if all the worst elements of typhus, flu, tonsillitis, trench fever and scarlet fever had been mixed together into one toxic super-brew. But the blue colour, that was a completely fresh symptom. The last time she had seen a hue like that had been at the Casualty Clearing Station with Watson, where men were being deliberately poisoned. But that was unlikely to be the root cause here. Wasn't it?

Jennings leaned against the wooden and metal partition at her back. Her own head was thumping now. Could she have picked up whatever it was already?

'I want the gun,' said Jiang.

'No. I need this,' she said.

He held his hand out. 'Give me the gun.'

'What for?'

'We will shoot off the locks. Then get out.'

Jennings could understand the desire to break out of this hell, but she also knew letting these people flee would be a mistake. If this was contagious, then they could be releasing an epidemic on the British side of the lines, devastating the army. On the other hand, the way they were treating these men was barbaric. They wouldn't do it with Englishmen, that much was certain.

'Wait, think about this. It might only be contagious in close contact. You all travelled together, yes?'

'Yes. Across sea. Across Canada.'

In, she imagined, unsanitary conditions. 'But it might just require passing exposure, like a cold. I know it's hard, but I expect they are taking us to Netley. There is an isolation unit there. They'll do tests.'

'They'll leave us to die.'

'They will not,' Jennings insisted. 'You are British subjects, for God's sake.' Were the Chinese British subjects? she wondered. As guest workers, they must be under the protection of the British Empire, at the very least. 'No harm will come to you.'

He laughed at that. 'Give me the gun.'

'I can't — '

It wasn't Jiang who slapped her across the face, causing her to reel sideways, but it was Jiang who twisted the revolver from her grip. 'Sorry,' he said with some sincerity.

She held her stinging face as he moved her gently to one side and stepped up to the door

388

through which she had entered. He peered between the bars and the cracked glass before taking three small paces back and pointing the revolver at the lock.

Jennings and the men also took a step back, and several put their fingers in their ears. Jennings placed the palms of her hands over her hair and pressed it to the side of her skull.

At first, she thought the gun had been fitted with some sort of device to muffle the sound of the discharge, in that the report seemed feeble. She had been close to guns before and knew they hurt the ear in a confined space, no matter how you tried to protect them.

But then Jiang staggered back and dropped the gun, hand to his chest as the glass fell free from the window. He had been shot from outside.

Another man rushed to pick up the gun, but ended up tripping over Jiang and crashing into the solid bulkhead of the carriage. The train had jerked backwards as aloco had connected. Now it gave a long, low moan and a few squeals and began to move forward with increasing purpose. They were on their way to wherever they were going.

44

The survivor told Watson his name was Stephen Harrow, and then he refused to say anything else until the major explained how he came to be in a German hospital. Harrow was in a private ward, one of his feet shackled to the bed by a long chain, which enabled him to move around the room but not much more, unless he wanted to take said bed with him.

He had recovered from most of his injuries, the majority of which were due to exposure and hypothermia, although a gash on his head had been slow to heal. He was in his mid-twenties and Watson wondered why he was a VAD, rather than in khaki. The Volunteer Aid Detachments took men as well as women, but the former were normally of more advanced years. This was a lad, prime material for the trenches and mud, blood and death of Flanders.

However, it wasn't Harrow's story Watson was interested in, but a few hours in the life of the *Dover Arrow*. And perhaps in the death of Staff Nurse Jennings.

Watson pulled up a chair and sat down. 'Well, Stephen, I'm Major Watson of the Royal Army Medical Corps.'

'You a prisoner, too?' The accent was north of London, but south of Birmingham.

'In a manner of speaking.'

Harrow looked him up and down. 'Can you prove it?'

'That I am a prisoner?'

'That you are who you say you are. You aren't in uniform.'

'I don't have any identity papers on me, if that's what you mean. Not genuine ones.' He had left Major Watson's papers hidden in the van Miss Pillbody had procured, in case they had been stopped and searched by the police. 'You think I am a German?'

Harrow sat up on the edge of the bed, swung his legs over and dangled his feet. Watson realized he was only about five foot five or six inches tall. Still, they would have had him in a 'Bantam' battalion of under-height men. 'Germans would love to know what I know.'

'How can I convince you I am not one of them? The third verse of 'God Save the King'? Name the fourth in line to the throne?'

'Not by memory tricks, no.'

Watson considered for a moment. He played a card he was always loath to draw from the pack. 'Well, I do have some small fame. It was I who wrote the Sherlock Holmes stories.'

Harrow's eyes widened. 'Really?'

'Yes,' Watson said.

'My dad loved those. I've never read them. I prefer Buchan, Childers and the like.'

Watson tried not to show his disappointment. 'I see. So it is no good me answering questions on, say, *The Hound of the Baskervilles*.'

'No. Was it a real dog, by the way? The Hound?'

Watson gave a thin smile. 'You'll have to read the book, young man.'

'Hold on, I've seen the pictures. Watson had a moustache.'

Watson ran a finger along the site of an absent friend. 'Not quite the ultimate sacrifice for getting to see you, but close. Look, we are both here because of the *Dover Arrow*. Me, because I am interested in the fate of a friend of mine whom I suspect was on board, you because you appear to be able to answer the question of what happened to her.'

'Her? A woman? A nurse? A white woman?'

The mention of her race puzzled Watson. There were some nurses from the colonies working in Europe, but precious few of a different skin colour; the majority were from Canada or Australia or New Zealand.

'Yes. Staff Nurse Jennings. You knew her?'

'I saw her,' he said glumly. 'In fact, I was probably the last man to see her alive.'

Watson let the dread at what was to come build and slowly transform into acceptance. The poor woman was dead after all. 'So she died when the *Dover Arrow* went down?'

Harrow leaned in very close now, as if there were eavesdroppers next door with glasses pressed to the wall. 'Oh, no, Doctor. You see, the *Dover Arrow* didn't go down at all.'

45

It seemed to Staff Nurse Jennings that the ambulance train gathered velocity with indecent haste. Within a few minutes the men on board were being tossed around like rag dolls as it rattled over points and took bends at breakneck speed. She had never heard of a loco pulling a Red Cross transport travel at much more than a walking pace.

She retrieved the gun and tucked it in the waistband of her skirt. She was sweating now, and risked unbuttoning the top of her blouse. When she wiped her neck, her hand came away wet. Sweat or fever?

She took a deep breath to try to calm herself. All her training told her that developing a fever was impossible in such a short space of time. But why did her throat feel scratchy and swollen? Because she needed water — she should have drunk from the container herself before passing it over. Pull yourself, together, Jennings. Imagine what Sister Spence would do in this situation.

She swallowed a few times and then tried to yell over the rattle of bogeys on the track. 'Anyone else speak English? Anyone?'

'Little,' said one of the men standing close by, holding up thumb and forefinger and pinching them together. 'Only little.'

He was older than Jiang, judging by the gaps in his teeth and thinning hair, and had the build

393

of a scrawny chicken. Again, his skin was still mostly its natural colour, but the whites of his eyes showed blue flecks.

'Name?' She pointed to herself. 'Me Nurse Jennings. Jennings. What's yours?'

He pressed a bony fist to his chest. 'Lau.'

Was that a first or last name? No matter. 'Right, Mr Lau, we have to get organized.' She indicated the men on the floor. 'We need to make room. Lay out the dead properly. Make space. Understand?'

He nodded, but she wasn't sure he did. Nevertheless she got to work, pushing her way through the hollow-eyed workers and issuing orders for them to sit in seats, lay in vestibules or stand out of the way. The smell was by turns cloying and piercingly sharp, like a slap to the sinuses. She quickly tore up a handkerchief, wadded the material and pushed it up her nose. She would breathe through her mouth from now on.

She soon gathered that this was British rolling stock and consisted of coaches that had been converted into SIC — Secure Infectious Carriages — used to transport men suffering from typhus or measles. These could be opened only from the outside, to prevent the sick going walkabout with their germs. The barred windows, though, were a new addition.

Of the six carriages, three were kitted out for lying-down cases, with a stack of stretcher-like berths suspended from the ceiling at either side, and a narrow corridor running between the two stacks. She managed to convey to Lau what she wanted, and the men who had enough strength began piling the dead, one on top of another, onto the berths. The amount of bodily fluids spilled in the process was alarming, but soon she was so soaked with blood, pus and piss that she no longer cared. The main battle was to stay upright as the speeding loco dragged them onward.

At the front of the train, in one of the sitting-up carriages, she found a canister of water under a seat. After guiltily helping herself, she told Lau to pass it along. 'One mouthful each. Yes?'

Lau raised the square tin to his lips and she watched his throat work, then pulled it away. She held up an index finger. 'One for each man, yes?'

'Yes.'

Oh, how she wanted to pour the whole contents over her head and rub at her face and hair. She watched it disappear with regret.

'Right, we need men sitting here. You, there. You, take that one.'

Someone began to retch after drinking and she heard vomit — and the precious water — splatter on the floor and protests from some of the men splashed by it. 'Take him to the rear. There's a free berth in coach five.'

The train began to tip from side to side and she steadied herself on a seat back, watching the shapes of trees turn solid black in the twilight. A hand gripped her wrist. She looked down at a moon-faced man, who tried to smile. He said something low and, of course, unintelligible, closed his eyes and let out a long, last gurgling breath. His head dropped onto his companion's shoulder, but he, in turn, was leaning against the window, too weak to move.

She felt a mixture of anger and shame curdle her stomach. How could they treat men like this? She supposed it was because they didn't see them as men. They saw them as Chinese. *Chinkies*, as that colonel had said. What was that phrase the lieutenant had used? EXTO? What on earth was that? Ex-something. Another term for what they considered sub-humans?

She had to admit she had possessed a wide streak of xenophobia when she had arrived in France. She might have spent time in the West Indies but, even on St Kitts, she and her family had treated the locals like backward children, certainly not as equals. The thought that God had created them to be on a par with Englishmen and women would have made her father explode with rage. But exposure to the Sikhs and Gurkhas and other groups over the past two years had made her realize that the old certainties about the superiority of the British race in all matters was just national arrogance.

And ignorance. Where was Shandong, the place where these men apparently originated? And what calamity or need would drive them overseas to work for foreigners at the most menial of tasks? She didn't know the answers. Growing up, to her, China had been a place of opium, foot binding, white slaving and, latterly, Fu Manchu.

She heard the raised voices and screamed insults of an argument building in the next

396

carriage. As she walked along the passageway, swinging from seat back to seat back like a monkey in a zoo, she noticed that the wall of trees had disappeared, replaced by the outlines of warehouses and other industrial buildings and, silhouetted against the deepening blue of the night sky, in the distance, skeletal cranes. The docks. They were nearly at the quays, where they would be unloaded and then transferred to an ambulance boat. She felt sure it would all be all right once they got to England.

46

'It was odd at the time. We were meant to be performing tidal experiments at Richborough.'

'Where?' asked Watson.

'It's in Kent.' Harrow's voice was still low, barely above a whisper, but there was hardness to it, the tension of suppressed anger perhaps. 'The *Dover Arrow* was not a normal ferry. It had been designed before the war for the trains to drive straight onto it, so the passengers didn't have to disembark. It was deemed perfect for transporting the badly wounded. Which is why we VADs were on board, to help with the medical side. Four of us. But suddenly, we are told we have to undertake docking trials at this new installation. You know that if you are taking a train directly onto a boat, you have to make sure the tracks are level in a tidal port. They were using pontoons and a levelling system at Richborough.'

Watson wasn't interested in the technical details of a roll-on-the-train, roll-off-the-train system. It wasn't relevant. 'Go on.'

'So we crossed the Channel to Calais, which was always nerve-racking, especially as we had minimum crew and a new captain. No VADS needed on the voyage, we were told.'

'Why were you on the *Dover Arrow* in France then?'

'I wasn't meant to be. Just as we were

disembarking at Richborough, the captain — Owen, his name was — managed to jam his hand in one of the ramp systems. Mangled a couple of fingers. He was determined to carry on, but someone had to splint it up, so I volunteered to do it while we sailed across.'

'Did any of this strike you as strange?'

The VAD gave a cynical laugh. 'Have you been over there, Major Watson? The whole damn war is one strange thing after another. I'm sure the average day in Bedlam makes more sense than what happens over there. Criminal.'

'You're a conchie?' Watson asked, trying not to sound too judgemental.

Harrow nodded. 'A conchie with a very influential father. I am an artist. A sculptor. I object to the war, to the waste of human life, and I refuse to kill another human being.'

'It's a brave decision.' Conscientious objectors were roundly reviled and persecuted, and often either imprisoned or sent down the mines to do the most disgusting and dangerous jobs. Others were dispatched to the front as stretcher-bearers, not a recipe for a long and peaceful life. Watson knew that, had he been thirty years younger, no matter how uncertain he felt about war, he wouldn't have had the gumption not to fight. But then again, he was a soldier by profession, a veteran of the Afghan Wars. He wouldn't have faced the dilemma of this young man.

'So the local Military Service Tribunal allowed me to join a VAD unit. I don't know what it cost my father, in money or promises or favours, and I'll probably never find out because he swears, having done this, he'll never talk to me again.'

'I'm sorry to hear that.'

Harrow smirked. 'You wouldn't be if you knew my father.'

'So you docked at Calais,' Watson prompted.

'And everything seemed fine there. The train came on, a locomotive and six carriages, and then we were told to get underway. I said at the time, we had four rail lines on deck, we could get another three trains on. The captain just ordered me below.'

'And then?'

'And then we laid off the port for perhaps twenty minutes, wallowing, as if giving everyone time to get thoroughly seasick. I'm perfectly fine if we are moving or if I can see the sky and the sea. But I was in the cabin I usually share with the other VADs, which doesn't have a porthole and stinks of oil. So I went up on deck. I heard the noise before I got there.'

'What noise?'

'Shouting, screaming, banging. A terrible, inhuman racket. It was as I was halfway up the gangway, I felt the ship shift.'

'Shift how?' asked Watson.

Harrow swung his legs back onto the bed, pulled the covers over them and poured himself a glass of water from the side table. There was a stubborn set to the jaw when he had finished drinking.

Watson gripped his arm. 'It shifted how, lad?'

Harrow turned and stared at him. 'Let me ask you a question: Do you know what an EXTO is?'

'No,' said Watson truthfully. 'What is it?'

400

'I have no idea.'

'You're playing games with me, man,' Watson snapped. 'Why have you stopped?'

'Because this is the part you won't believe is true.'

47

Staff Nurse Jennings was relieved when, finally, the driver applied the brakes and the train of sick and dying men slowed. The rhythm became the familiar, comforting one of slow clicks over joints as the platforms approached.

'Not long now,' she said to Lau, who simply blinked several times in response. She wondered if he was concussed. He had lost a tooth in the fight over the water, which Jennings had resolved by firing a shot into the ceiling. It had done the trick, but not before Lau had managed to get in the way of a flying fist or two.

The train decelerated some more, until you could count to four between the thumps over the expansion gaps in the rails. A platform finally hove into view and Jennings found herself pulling at her hair, as if it could make any difference to how stained and dishevelled she looked.

The train kept rolling.

All the men who could manage it stared out of the window, watching the station slide by. Now they were down to the jetties and the loco was barely crawling along. 'We're going straight onto the boat,' she said, and made a series of signs to Lau, who barked out an explanation in his own tongue. 'They are bound to let us out once we are on the ship.'

She moved to the very front of the carriage

where there was room to squeeze past the seated Chinese and put her face against the window. A stream of salty air came through the cracked glass and she pulled out the makeshift nose plugs. There were people standing on the deck, watching as the train, as gingerly as threading a fine needle, inched its way onto the ambulance ferry.

She waved to the blurred figures, but they were clearly intent on making sure nothing went wrong with the loading and didn't acknowledge her. After some long, slow grinds, the train finally came to a halt. She heard a great exhalation of steam from the loco like a sigh of relief.

She rapped on the window with a knuckle, but the men were hurrying away, towards the stern of the boat. There was movement as chains rattled and a sudden sense that the boat was floating free.

'Thank God,' she muttered.

'We get out now?'

It was Lau, standing behind her. Engines thrummed into life, screws turned and the boat wallowed, causing a few shouts of dismay.

'I don't know,' said Jennings. 'If they could just open the doors and get some air to blow through.'

'They frightened?' he asked.

She looked around at the pitiful men, their cyan skin, stained clothes and blood-encrusted faces. Of course the British were scared. Scared that they might catch whatever this plague was. Scared of the unknown. But fresh air, fresh sea

403

air purging the carriages, was that too much to ask?

'I think, yes, they are frightened of this.'

He gave a freshly toothless grin. 'Me too.'

Jennings gave him a squeeze on the shoulder, turned and banged on the glass again. 'Hello! Anyone there? Hello!

'*Ràng wŏmen chūqù!*' shouted Lau.

Another took it up, feebler. Then a third. Soon they were all chanting she knew not what. But the sentiment was clear. They wanted out of there.

Hands and fists started to rattle the windows and there was the sound of more and more breaking glass as the occupants realized that once the panes had broken, cold, bracing air was driven in by the boat's forward motion. Those who could stamped their feet to increase the cacophony.

'Shush!' Jennings yelled as she felt the vibration of machinery through her feet change note. 'Quiet!'

The racket throughout the carriages gradually subsided. She looked out of the window and beyond the ship. The few lights on the shoreline were moving up and down, but stayed where they were laterally. 'We've stopped.'

Lau repeated this, then asked her: 'Why?'

'Perhaps because of the . . . ' She had to steady herself as a decent sized wave hit them. They were beyond the breakwater. 'Perhaps we were making too much noise. Let's see if we can get some lights on in here.'

There were electric lamps, but she could find

404

no way of turning them on. In the end, she lit the single oil lamp that was provided for each carriage. Still, there was no sign of help. The ship was pushed this way and that, the motion unpredictable and disquieting. Some of the men began to groan as seasickness and nausea took hold. There was more vomiting, but she couldn't be sure whether it was from queasiness or the illness.

She had just reached the front of the first carriage when she felt the main engine boom into life once more and the low vibration as it built up power. The carriages began to thrum in harmony as the screws turned, and the ship swung in a wide arc, more purposeful this time.

'How long England?' Lau asked.

'How long to England?'

'Yes.'

'How long was it last time? Did you come Dover — Calais?'

'Not been England. Canada.'

So the workers were shipped direct to France. 'Well, it normally takes less than two hours, but sometimes they zigzag.'

'Zigzag?'

She was about to explain about avoiding submarines, but decided better of it. He had enough to worry about without fretting about torpedoes. 'Nothing.'

Lau started to bang on the window again and stamp his feet. She didn't join in. Her limbs felt like great fluid-filled sacks, almost too heavy to lift. She needed to lie down. She was still sweating, despite the cool breeze leaking through the broken glass. Others, though, began to shout until the noise settled down to what sounded like a sea shanty with added percussion.

Again, the sensations transmitted through her feet told her that something was up. 'We're slowing.'

The clank of chains was close by, just the others side of the solid bulkhead. 'Hello!' she yelled again. 'Anyone there?'

Another sort of engine started up, one with a fast, rhythmic thud. Water gurgled, as if someone were emptying a bath. Jennings was aware that she was having to press down harder on her left foot than her right to keep her balance. It was as if . . . as if the boat were listing.

There came a low grunt, then a metallic screech. The carriage was clearly at an angle now. The ship was sinking.

She reached through a broken window and gripped one of the bars. With a squeal like a pig being slaughtered the carriage began to roll, back the way it had come on board. Now Jennings screamed as it gathered speed, heading for the waters of the Channel.

★   ★   ★

'I felt the boat tip. I thought we were sinking.'

'But you weren't?' asked Watson.

'No, but by the time I got on deck, it was at quite an angle. Boats like the *Dover Arrow* have ballast tanks at each end, so they can adjust their height. By flooding or emptying the tanks they can raise or lower that end. Clearly they had

406

flooded the set at the stern.'

The monstrosity of what Harrow was describing finally sank in. 'So the train was . . . ?'

'Not the whole train. They had chocked the loco, I reckon. Because it didn't move. But the carriages, they were rolling down off the end of the ship.'

Watson closed his eyes, trying to stop the images forming in his brain. 'What then?'

'I ran forward. As if I could stop the momentum. Me. Alone. I did actually grab onto a handle on the side, but my feet just slithered along the deck. But then I looked up. There were lamps lit in the carriages. I could see there were yellow faces pressed against the glass and bars, staring down at me, shouting, shouting and screaming.'

'Yellow?'

'Well, Chinese, but there was one white woman. A nurse . . . ' His voice tailed off. 'She wasn't shouting or screaming. She was just staring at me, as if this were all my fault.' The tears came suddenly, rolling down his cheek to the corners of his mouth. 'As if it were my fault,' he repeated.

Watson put a hand on his arm. 'Go on. What happened next?'

★　★　★

Jennings braced herself against the bars as the first carriage crashed into the water. From the far end came the screams of the living as water poured through the smashed windows. A huge bang suggested that something structural had given way. The forward motion halted for a moment, but then, with more ominous creaks, the ambulance train carried on its descent. She could hear the greedy inrush of water, creating a log jam of bodies.

And then, with a jolt and a spine-numbing crash, they were free of the boat.

Their carriage remained upright, but began swaying from side to side. The front carriages had to be already submerged and now they were pulling them down.

Ahead of her, men were coming like locusts, climbing over seats and each other as if they had six or more limbs. Behind them grey water swirled and foamed. She felt something touch her hand and turned. There was a man, a boy, on the outside, shouting at her. 'You've got to get out!'

He was tugging at the bars, his feet pressed against the side of the carriage, as if he could tear the bolts free. 'Push with me.'

She stood, frozen, staring at this apparition.

'Miss, please. I'm trying to help. Push with me.'

She did as she was told, but she knew the bars were securely fixed. Now the mass of frantic bodies was nearly on her and she could feel the icy chill of the rising sea. 'Go!' she said to the would-be rescuer. 'Go.'

'No! Help me.'

The floor tipped beneath her and she scrabbled for a foot-hold. The carriage was turning turtle and as it did so, she fell backwards, her skull smashing against a seat back. Jennings gasped as the water came over her, retching as it filled her nostrils, but somehow managing to expel it with a snort. Her sinuses burned but she managed not to fill her lungs. The light had gone. All was darkness. All was cold.

But her arms and legs worked automatically and she found herself swimming through a tangle of limbs, some intent on pushing her down, others thrashing with no purpose. Surely a wall of the carriage might split? The roof come off? Something to get them out of this sinking coffin. And what then? A slow death bobbing in the Channel?

Stay alive, woman, stay alive.

She kicked off a seat arm and propelled herself upwards. There was an inch or two of air between sea and windows, disappearing as, with moans of what seemed pain, the Channel took the train. Reaching out she found the bars and gripped as tightly as she could, but her hands were already numb. She pulled herself up, her mouth finding that ribbon of air and gulping at it. She could see her would-be rescuer's outline, blurred by the seawater in her eyes. The brave lad was still there, still clinging on, still pulling at the bars. But it was no good . . . no good . . . She shouted the one word that might help him make sense of this, this massacre. Then she reached a hand up towards him, and was pleased she could still feel the grip, the warmth, the care, of another human being, however briefly. Staff Nurse Jennings opened her mouth and gulped water as the sea flowed over her face, hoping it would be over quickly.

★ ★ ★

Watson wiped his eyes with the back of his hand. The sorrow sat heavily on him. The rage, the fulminating, would come later.

'Deliberate, do you think?' he asked, rummaging for a handkerchief. 'This ditching of the carriages?'

'Oh, yes,' said Harrow with conviction. 'Otherwise the loco would have rolled as well, surely. The carriages were uncoupled, the boat's tanks flooded to an angle where they would move, the stern gates lowered so they would slide unimpeded into the sea.'

'Murder,' said Watson.

'Hardly does it justice.'

'And you are sure this is what she shouted? EXTO?'

'EXTO or EXMO. It sounds like a military term, don't you think?'

'Or an acronym. Had a lot of those lately. And you, what happened to you after the train went down?'

Harrow held up a bandaged wrist. 'Like an idiot I got my hand stuck in the bars. I couldn't free it. I was dragged down some way. I . . . I closed my eyes. I didn't want to see. And then it was too dark. But part of the carriage panelling finally gave away and I floated to the surface. There was no sign of the *Dover Arrow*. I have no idea how long I was out there before a German fast torpedo boat picked me up. But here I am. Alive, at least.'

'It was a remarkably courageous thing to do. To try to rescue her.'

'Courageous for a conchie, you mean.'

'I never said that,' insisted Watson. 'Nor thought it.'

Harrow gave a hollow laugh. 'I apologize. You get very used to being called a coward. And worse.'

'I would strike any man I heard utter that word in your presence,' said Watson.

Harrow looked at him, head tilted to one side, as if examining an exotic specimen unknown to science. 'You know, I really do believe you are that Dr Watson.'

'I was that Dr Watson once,' he said wistfully, before blowing his nose.

Harrow shook his head. 'The man I just saw then, he was real enough. I believe who you say you are. I suppose I won't be needing this now.'

From beneath the pillow he produced a curved scalpel, of the sort used to unpick stitches. 'Manage to get it off a trolley,' Harrow said apologetically.

'You would have used that on me?'

'If I'd had to.'

'How does that square with your values?'

'It's senseless war I hate. When it comes to survival, I'm beginning to think I have to reconsider.'

Watson looked at the wicked blade, which could easily slice through a carotid artery or jugular vein. Death would take a very few, very

411

messy minutes. 'What made you think you might have to kill me?'

'Dr Watson, if men are prepared to do that to a group of fellow human beings, to drown them in cold blood, think what they'd be prepared to do to keep their actions a secret.'

48

'You aren't going and that is the end of it. Look at you.'

Schrader stared at his squadron leader and then at Trotzman. They were in the weather hut. Conditions, according to the charts on the wall, looked fine for bombing. Outside he could hear the cough and splutter of engines starting.

'I'm fine. It's not like I have to fly the damn plane.'

'No, but you do need your wits about you,' said von Kahr. 'You are exhausted. You need a hot bath . . . '

'And a hotter woman,' added Trotzman.

Von Kahr glared at him. 'Look, the improved incendiary racks are in. We shall spend tonight fitting them to your Giant. Tomorrow, on the hunter's moon, you can lead the biggest wing of bombers ever seen in the skies over England.'

Schrader nodded his defeat. He was aching all over. The strain of the combat with the Albatroses had drained him, and his bad shoulder throbbed. His hair was still greasy with oil. Perhaps a ten- or twelve-hour night was asking too much of his body. 'Very well,' he said. 'What news of the Albatroses?'

'Don't worry,' said von Kahr, 'you didn't kill anyone. The pilot you hit got back to land. The plane is a wreck, but he walked away.'

Schrader sighed with relief. The last thing he

413

needed on his conscience was the death of a fellow flyer. 'No more of those trips for me.'

'That's not up to me,' said von Kahr, 'but the Bristol isn't in the best of health, either. That won't be flying for a while.'

'The device they have on it, where you can slide the Lewis gun to fire forward, or pull it down to fire up.'

'The Foster Mount. What about it?' asked von Kahr.

'Well, if I were a fighter and couldn't make the height of the bombers, I'd use it to fire upwards.'

'You know, Schrader,' said Trotzman, 'it's probably best you don't mention that to any Englishmen you meet.'

Another engine kicked into life, a Maybach. The hut shivered in the prop blast. The racket made Schrader's heart beat faster. He could fly, he could push himself, but he had to concede he had lost the argument. And his crew would enjoy a night off. 'How many?'

'Two Giants, including mine, fifteen Gothas. Tomorrow, if all goes well, four Giants, twenty-five Gothas.'

Schrader stood. 'Come on. The least you can do is let me watch you bastards take off without me.'

★ ★ ★

Admiral Hersch poured two inches of red wine into a glass and pushed it across to Watson. Then he repeated the action for himself. They were in a tiny, smoke-filled, dark wood tavern, close to

414

the hospital where Harrow remained chained to his bed.

'Cheers,' the spymaster said, raising his glass.

Watson drank without saying anything. There was nothing to toast as far as he was concerned. He knew he should eat, but the emptiness in his stomach could not be filled by food.

'So you believe us now?' asked Hersch.

'I believe you had nothing to do with the sinking of the *Dover Arrow*, yes. Quite what you expect me to do with the information is another matter.'

'I want you to tell me what the British are up to. Did they sink their own ship?'

'You think that's what it was? Self-inflicted? It could have struck a mine.'

Hersch lit a cigarette and pushed the pack to Watson, who waved them away. 'When he was picked up by a *Torpedoboot*, the survivor was delirious. He said things that intrigued us. About deliberate murder of the men on board. Once he recovered, he would answer no further questions.'

So Hersch knew only part of the story. He didn't know that the *Dover Arrow* didn't, in fact, sink at all. 'You cannot expect me to give you information that would aid and abet the enemy.' Especially information that suggested the British could be as barbaric as the baby-bayoneting Hun of popular imagination.

The admiral puffed on his cigarette. 'You know, I've been thinking about what you said. About me being a creator of monsters. There is some truth in it.' He flicked ash on the floor.

'But whether I am worse than Herr Maxim or Herr Haber is a moot point. Machine guns and poison gas have killed far more people than I have. But even I have my limits. I never agreed with sinking hospital ships, because these things work both ways. We have had ambulance trains bombed. So perhaps Allied hospital ships are fair targets. However, the thought of killing our own sick and wounded?' He took another drink of the wine. 'I cannot imagine any circumstances where I could condone that.'

'Nor me.'

Except, Harrow had described the majority of people trapped inside the train as of Chinese or at least Asian origin. Would they count as 'our own' sick and wounded to the British if they posed a threat? But what kind of threat justified murder?

'What are you thinking, Major?'

'Nothing yet,' he lied.

In 1900, San Francisco suffered an outbreak of bubonic plague. It was the 'third pandemic', and was believed to have started in Yunan. Watson vaguely recalled that there had been atrocities there against the Chinese population who took the blame for the deaths in the city. Something similar had happened in India, too, although it was Brahmins blaming the lower caste there and massacring a whole village. Yet there were simple hygienic measures to control plague, even before Haffkine created a vaccine. Maybe that's what this was. A 'cleansing' by ignorant, frightened people.

'Well?' prompted Hersch. 'Why would they

sink their own ship?'

'As my friend Holmes would say, there simply isn't enough data. I don't know.'

'So that's it?' the admiral said irritably. 'You just accept that these things happen in war?'

'Not at all.' Watson finally took a decent mouthful of drink. It burned like acid. 'A good woman was on board that ship, and if — if — she was murdered, I will rest at nothing to uncover the truth. You can't expect me to offer to share that truth with you.'

'No.'

'But once a truth has been dragged into the light of day, it has a way of becoming common knowledge.'

'Even with DORA?' the German asked.

It was a good point. DORA was a powerful tool that could effectively smother the dissemination of information. Watson thought it justified, mostly, but not if it was used to hide something as evil as mass murder.

Isn't this entire war mass murder?

Perhaps, Holmes. But you didn't think that at the beginning. None of us did in 1914. And if we didn't cling onto the belief that there was some justification somewhere for all that slaughter . . .

'You will have to take my word for it that I will endeavour to get to the bottom of this.'

'Even if the results prove detrimental to your country?'

'I am an old-fashioned man, Admiral. Out-of-date in many ways. I believe that the truth, while it might hurt, never harms in the long run. At least compared to the alternative of

417

a corroding soup of secrets and lies.'

Hersch stubbed out his cigarette on the table top. 'You are talking to a man who deals only in secrets and lies.'

'The answers to the *Dover Arrow* aren't over here, though, in Belgium. They are in France and in England.'

'You want to go home,' the German said.

'I do.'

'With your witness.'

'Yes.'

The admiral poured them both more wine. A low vibration filled the room as he did so, and both men looked up at the smoke-yellowed ceiling but neither acknowledged what they both knew. That was the sound of the bombers leaving for England.

'There is the small matter of how to achieve this. The idea of a white flag on no man's land . . . well, you've seen it. The days of truces are over. And even if you did get across without being shot by a sniper, there will be questions asked about how you came to be here. They might even shoot you as a spy.'

That was a good point. Commanders on the front line were understandably jittery and often trigger-happy.

'We could get you to Holland,' suggested Hersch.

'Where I am *persona non grata* after our last encounter.'

Hersch smiled a little at this. 'I can imagine.'

'And, again, there will be questions asked by the British mission there. I need to get back to

London as soon as possible.'

'Leave it with me,' said Hersch. 'I'll see what I can do.' He looked at his watch. 'It's too late to do anything this evening. I'll find you a billet for the night.'

'One other thing you can help me with. Are you familiar with British Intelligence terms?'

'I hope so,' he said, 'or I'd be a pretty poor spy. I might not be entirely current. You British think up new ones all the time.'

Watson hesitated, wondering if he was throwing away an important trump card.

'What is it you wish to know?'

'EXTO, I think it is.'

'EXTO? Are you sure?'

Watson nodded and the admiral busied himself with lighting another cigarette. 'You know what it means, Admiral?'

'I do.' He frowned in further thought. 'I was just wondering if it was what happened to your ship.'

Watson leaned forward. 'Tell me.'

'As far as we understand it, EXTO stands for Exceptional Termination Order. It is, in effect, an official licence to kill.'

49

Holmes and Bullimore managed to find passage on the *SS Dempster*, a troop ship out of Folkestone. The *Dempster* carried 400 members of the 5th Battalion of the South African Native Labour Corps, most of whom chattered in language — or more accurately languages — that the Englishmen couldn't understand. Most of the labourers stayed below deck as, according to one of the white officers, after their voyaging from Cape Town to Lagos, and then Plymouth before the hop to Folkestone, the ocean had lost its allure, especially after the Bay of Biscay crossing.

In truth, the Channel that day was as far removed from the notoriously choppy Bay as was possible, mirror-calm and benevolent, with a gloriously warm late-summer sun reflected off it.

Holmes and Bullimore stood at the rail, both men smoking.

'Days like this, you wonder why everyone doesn't just throw their weapons down, take off their shirts and lie down on a piece of grass,' said Bullimore. 'Have a day off from killing each other.'

Holmes didn't say anything.

'I'm going to get hell for coming with you, you know. And for failing to apprehend Watson. There was a message at the station house this morning summoning me to see the super. I ignored it.'

'You didn't have to come.'

There was an edge of sarcasm in Bullimore's voice. 'When will I next get to work with the great Sherlock Holmes?'

Holmes brushed the hair from his eyes. 'You are not working with me, Inspector. You are merely observing. And I suspect there will be precious little need for my powers of deduction. This is donkey work. But sometimes, it is the donkey work that uncovers what we seek.'

'Donkey work. That's what Amies called it. And look where that ended.'

'I suspect the *Dover Arrow* mystery has little to do with bombing raids and currency,' said Holmes.

'Perhaps not. But I am curious to see where your trail leads. And there is Miss Pillbody to hunt down.'

'You know, when you return I could always get Mycroft to tell your superintendent that you were working for him. In the national interest.'

'Am I? Working in the national interest?'

'One way or another, I believe you are,' Holmes assured him. 'In the long term, at least.'

'Then I may call upon you for that favour.'

'It would be my pleasure.' Holmes turned to examine the policeman. 'But there is something else. Another reason for your being here, to risk your very career. Something you aren't sharing with me.'

Bullimore gazed out to sea. 'You wouldn't understand, Mr Holmes.'

'You can try.'

'I have a feeling, no more than that, that this business of the *Dover Arrow* is somehow important to me, personally. But how it could be, I

421

have no idea. I am sure you think that is foolish.'

'Illogical, perhaps. But not foolish. Whatever that feeling is, it has a powerful pull. You would do well not to ignore it.'

'Thank you, Mr Holmes.' Bullimore caught a half-formed yawn. 'Sorry . . . those damn bombers and the guns kept me awake.' The raids had lasted for hours and first reports were that London had been hit across a wide swathe, with bombs falling from Islington to Camberwell. 'It's a disgrace they can get through.'

'I have given some thought to that,' said Holmes. 'I shall present a paper to the Air Ministry. You are right, London is not doing well. But we have all the elements in place — the observers, the acoustics bowls, the plotting rooms, the barrage balloons, the night fighters, the early warnings. But *ad hoc*. No one group talks to another. It is vital — vital — that they are co-ordinated. Because now the Germans have shown the power of the bomb, this threat will never go away. But, with the right system, I believe that the bomber can be, if not defeated, then at least to some extent neutralized.'

They watched as four biplanes crossed the blue sky in front of them, as playful as mayflies as they swooped around each other. Replacements, Holmes thought. With a life expectancy not much longer than the insects they mimicked.

'Have you ever been tempted in your line of work, Mr Holmes?'

'Tempted? I have known temptations, certainly. Did you have something specific in mind?'

'I was thinking, there we were at St Luke's,

surrounded by money. How easy it might have been to slip a stack of notes under one's jacket.'

'Ah! Money! The least interesting of the temptations in many ways. No, it has never been a weakness of mine. Perhaps because, while not rich, I have never wanted for anything.' Holmes threw his cigarette overboard, watching it spark before it hit the swell and fizzled out. 'Listen. Here that? The clicking?' He turned and walked to an open hatch. 'There are Xhosa men here. How fascinating.' Then he abruptly turned back to Bullimore. 'Who is she? This woman?'

'Which woman?'

'Come, come, Inspector. A man thinks wistfully about being rich . . . I see you dress modestly, even by a policeman's standards. You do not frequent any fine restaurants, for you do not know Goldini's. You do not gamble, because you did not know the main clubs, which, even if you couldn't afford them, any gambler worth his chips would aspire to. You live, by your own admission, in the station house, so do not crave property. Now, what would suddenly turn a man's thoughts to money? A woman. A mistress. No, if you live at the station house you are unmarried.' Holmes furrowed his brow. 'You are smitten with a woman above your station or at least above your income level.'

'Mr Holmes — '

'A child might also create this sudden desire for enough money to live comfortably. Does she have one or more? Or perhaps she is with child?'

Bullimore shook his head. 'What you do is so simple . . . '

'So I have been told, many times.'

'Yet can seem like sorcery. Her name is Marion.'

'And she is spoken for?'

'Married? Yes, very,' he said.

'But with child?'

Bullimore nodded.

'Your child, I presume. I can see it is a miserable situation.'

'It is. What do you suggest I do?'

Holmes laughed at the thought of him, of all people, dispensing guidance on matters of the heart. 'What do I suggest? Oh, you wouldn't want to hear that. I can offer but one piece of advice.'

'What's that?'

'Don't try to rob a bank. You have far too honest a face for such things. Look, I do believe that is the coast of France over there.'

★　★　★

'I think,' said Watson, as he finished his breakfast of sausages and bacon at the tavern where he and Hersch had talked the night before, 'that you must be pulling my leg.'

The admiral was opposite him, drinking a mug of tar-black coffee and smoking. Watson felt guilty about enjoying a meal in German-occupied territory quite so much, but the sausages were excellent, the bacon a little too fatty perhaps, but flavoursome, and the bread almost unadulterated.

'In German we say, *auf den Arm nehmen*. It means the same, I think. Playing a joke on someone, yes?'

'Yes. I do not think you can be serious.'

'It is the best I can offer. Do you mind?' He ground out the cigarette on Watson's empty plate and lit another. 'There are no crossing points where anyone is safe, even with a white flag. Not since your new offensive at Ypres. Which will not succeed, by the way.'

'I'll tell General Haig when I see him.'

The admiral smiled. 'Well, it would save a lot of wasted lives if you could. Landing by boat or submarine is possible, but we have, shall we say, a mixed record of success. Several agents we landed have been shot on sight. I don't think you want that.'

'Not if I can avoid it.'

'And even if they didn't shoot you, you would have quite a time explaining yourself. How you managed to catch a ride from a passing submarine or *Torpedoboot*. And then there are the mines . . . '

'I take your point.'

'To get you through Germany to Switzerland . . . complicated. It might take weeks.'

'I need to be back before the inquiry into the *Dover Arrow* is convened,' Watson reminded him. 'If our witness is to have maximum impact.'

'And we seem to be completely out of stock of captured British aircraft to ferry you over in. Also, as you discovered, that is not without its complications.'

'I never did get to thank that pilot. I was too . . . dazed, I suppose, by the death of Miss Pillbody.'

'Schrader, you mean? I can arrange for you to

425

go in his aircraft. He will be flying tonight.'

'So let me see if I have this straight. You intend to put us on a bomber, en route to try to destroy London, and to get Harrow and me to jump, willingly, out of the aeroplane at twenty-thousand feet — '

'Lower, I think.'

'And use one of those ridiculous parachutes to float down to earth, where we'll very likely break our necks.'

'Ankles are much more common.'

'And the failure rate of these giant hand-kerchiefs?'

'When jumping from balloons, very good. One in twenty.'

Watson helped himself to one of Hersch's cigarettes. 'And from an aeroplane?'

Hersch scratched behind his ear before answering 'I believe around a third of pilots or crew have died jumping from fighters or bombers.'

'A third?' Watson repeated. 'Hardly reassuring.'

'Ah, but you will have the new Heinecke harness and canopy. And remember, those pilots were jumping from burning or spinning planes. Very easy to get the shroud lines caught or burned through. You will be making the jump from a very stable platform.'

'Which will then go on and bomb my city.'

For the first time, Hersch looked impatient. 'Which it will do with or without you and your witness. Will you make the jump?'

That image came to Watson again, of Miss Pillbody spiralling down into the Channel, her

426

body breaking on the waves. If a parachute failed, how long would he have before his body smashed into the earth? Ten seconds? Twenty? And all the time knowing that there was going to be a terrible flash of agony as bones broke and the torso burst like a ripe fruit before oblivion fell. Or did some benevolent God strip your senses before that gory impact?

'Do I have any choice?'

Hersch's head moved from side to side, as if considering the options. 'Another prisoner of war camp, perhaps.'

'I'll make the jump.'

50

Watson was amazed by the size of the aeroplane. It looked ten or twelve times larger than the Bristol, a great hulking behemoth that appeared too heavy to take to the air. Physics would not allow it, surely? Even the Gothas that had so terrorized London looked puny next to it.

Hersch had driven him over to the airfield and reintroduced him to Schrader, who showed Watson around and indicated the section from where he and Harrow would jump. The German crouched down under the fuselage with an agility Watson envied. He bent his knees a little more gingerly and waddled in beside Schrader.

'This section can be lowered, like a child's slide,' explained the *Oberleutnant* in his excellent English. 'It is where the ventral machine gunner sits. We shall unclamp and remove the gun until you are safely out. To make sure there is nothing for you to snag on. The rails are quite smooth. You just have to roll your body over them and gravity will do the rest. But count to five when you are falling before pulling the cord, to make sure you are a good distance from the plane.'

Watson looked to the rear and the wicked metal tail-slide, which was like a blade positioned to slice him in half when he exited the belly of the bomber.

'Don't worry about that. You and the aircraft

will be travelling at the same speed. As long as you don't deploy the 'chute too early you'll be well clear of any part of the aircraft. Then once you're out of the plane, I'll get the hell out of there as fast as I can.'

'You don't seem too happy about this,' said Watson.

'I don't claim to understand what you and the admiral are up to or why a British citizen, two British citizens, enemies of Germany, should be chauffeured home by the air force. I do know that I will have to lose altitude to drop you. That height is precious; it will take me a long time to get it back. And while I am doing that, I'm vulnerable to British night fighters.'

Watson wasn't sure what to say. Part of him wanted to thank Schrader for what he was doing, another thought the damned monster deserved to be shot down by British defenders.

'Would you do it?' Watson asked.

'What, jump from an aeroplane putting my faith in a giant pair of bloomers to float down to the ground? I hope never to find out.' Something caught Schrader's attention and he swung out from under the fuselage. 'We have to go.'

Watson followed his gaze. Mechanics were wheeling several trolleys over to the plane. He could see they were stacked with what looked like toy bombs. Schrader grabbed his arm, pulled him from beneath the plane, spun him round and led him away from the Giant.

'I'll show you how the parachute fits when your friend arrives. In the meantime, Major, do you play chess?'

429

'Yes. Not very well.'

'Good,' he grinned. 'Let's have a little wager.'

'I have no money on me. None that you can use, at least.'

'Not for money. If you win, then I will come down to below a thousand metres to drop you. I win, I come to only three thousand.'

'So we are gambling with my life?'

'We are gambling with the odds of both of us surviving. At a thousand metres that thing is a sitting duck, but you are at a good height for the parachute. At three thousand, I'm able to get back up that much quicker. You, on the other hand, have a long way to fall.'

'Or float.'

'Yes,' agreed Schrader. 'Or float. What do you say?'

'Can I be white?'

★ ★ ★

For the first few moves, they mirrored each other. The queen's pawns faced off to each other on squares four and five. The white queen's knight came out, as did the black king's, to be confronted by Watson's bishop.

'So far, so conventional. We are very cautious men,' said Schrader.

'Lives are at stake,' said Watson, considering his options. His chess game was adequate, no more. Holmes, of course, was an exceptional player when he put his mind to it. Where was that phantom voice in his head when he needed it?

They were in the weather hut. Schrader had decided that Watson's presence in the officers' mess would generate too many questions and too much gossip and speculation. Trotzman came in from time to time, but if he was surprised by the presence of an Englishman, he didn't show it.

'*Er betriigt*,' he said at one point, wagging a warning finger at Watson.

Watson knew what that meant. He cheats.

'Only against him,' Schrader said to Watson, moving a rook's pawn out to intimidate the white bishop. 'And I don't really have to cheat to beat him. But it makes him feel better if he thinks I rely on devious means, rather than skill. Your move.'

Watson retreated, one square. 'I'm having trouble with you.'

'Not yet, surely.' Schrader's second knight came out. 'This is merely sparring.'

'No, I mean with you as a person.' Queen's pawn to d3.

'I don't understand.'

'Well, you seem like a decent chap . . . '

Schrader laughed. 'A decent chap? How terribly English.' The king's bishop broke out.

'Yet here you are, flying that, that aberration over London, killing innocent men and women.'

The smile faded. 'Are there any innocents in war?'

Watson advanced a pawn one square. 'I've seen them. Alive and dead. All over my city.'

'All of London is considered a military target,' Schrader said, repeating what he told himself on every mission. 'They should send the women

431

and children away instead of complaining about them being in the way.'

'Those that can afford to do so have done just that. Which leaves an awful lot of people at the mercy of your bombs.'

Schrader sighed. 'Above all, Major, men like us have to do their duty. Even if we don't agree with it or fully understand it. Otherwise, what is the point of an army, a navy or an air force?'

'Perhaps we should try to see how we get along without them.'

'Now you don't sound terribly convincing, Major.' A pawn was brought out to threaten Watson's bishop. 'I have to believe what I am doing will shorten the war in Germany's favour. You started this, remember?'

Watson moved the bishop to safety. 'To this day, I am not entirely sure how we got to this point from a bullet in Sarajevo.'

Another black pawn moved forward. There was a wall of them now across the centre of the board. Was Schrader playing chess like trench warfare, creating a miniature Hindenburg Line?

'You think perhaps we should have settled our differences over a game of chess?' asked the German.

Watson positioned his queen in front of the king. 'Better than bombing cities.'

Schrader pondered for a moment, castled his king, then looked up from the board. 'I hope you remember that when your bombers come over to Hamburg and Dresden and Cologne and Berlin. As they surely will.'

Watson slid his bishop out to threaten

Schrader's rear lines. 'Well, you started that one. The bombing campaign, I mean.'

The German gave a wry smile. 'I had hoped to finish it. Quickly.'

'With those little bombs?'

Schrader wagged a finger. 'I'll forget you said that. And don't say anything to anyone about them. Understood? Or they won't be sending you anywhere other than a cell. You saw nothing. All right?' A black pawn came forward menacingly, a white pawn or a knight in its sights.

Watson nodded his agreement and took the pawn. He had what he wanted from the exchange — if Schrader was touchy about the bombs, they had to be something new and secret.

The game moved on, not inspired, perhaps, but with a relentless logic. Schrader's queen came out like a marauding Dreadnought. Watson castled. Then, on move eighteen, his concentration lapsed and he was punished by Schrader taking his queen. Two moves later, he retaliated by wiping the black queen off the board. But by a dogged use of his knights and castles, Schrader surrounded Watson, and by move 35 the Englishman knew he was doomed.

Outside, engines were starting, disturbing the evening air and shaking the hut. Trotzman entered and told them the other *Engländer* had arrived from the hospital.

Watson used his index finger to topple his king.

Schrader held out his hand and Watson shook it. 'Three thousand metres it is, then.'

51

'I am afraid we have had a wasted day,' said Bullimore to Holmes as they each took a tin mug of tea from the makeshift canteen on the upper deck of the steamer back to England.

'Why do you say that?' Holmes asked.

Bullimore moved to the rail, watching the sun edge closer to the horizon, its colour bleeding into the water. 'All those hours looking at transit logs and arguing with French officials. Not a mention of the *Dover Arrow*.'

'Which tells us something,' said Holmes, pulling his scarf tighter around his neck.

'What's that? Is it the dog that didn't bark or some such?'

'Similar. It is the ship that vanished completely, even before it set sail. Somebody does not want any trace of the *Dover Arrow* left in the records. Even a ship that sinks has to leave port. Not this one.' Holmes sipped his tea.

'But you don't think it did sink.'

'No, it's been repainted as a dazzle ship and will continue to sail these waters as a boat-train. With a few helpful prods from my brother, that is what I surmised at the harbour works on the Kent coast. So, ask yourself, if the ship didn't go down, what did?'

Bullimore thought for a few moments. 'Its cargo.'

'Precisely. The train that was on board.'

'With the passengers inside?'

'I would assume so. For reasons we can't yet conceive. One hundred and thirty-nine unwanted and unnamed souls.'

Bullimore gripped the mug with both hands, the hot metal almost burning his palms. 'What sort of monster would do that?'

★ ★ ★

Colonel Arthur Hartford was on the same troop ship back to England as Holmes and the policemen, whom he knew had spent a fruitless day trying to find the log of the *Dover Arrow* and the origins of the loco and carriages that boarded it. There was not a sniff of any of that, Hartford knew, because he had been asked to expunge it from the record, which he had. No paper trail led back to Noyelles-sur-Mur; his name did not appear on any authorization.

He would not get a medal for what he had done. But, in his view at least, he deserved one.

The ship went through the usual zigzag routine as it left the harbour. It was another bright, star-filled night, with a friendly moon setting the surface of the sea aglow. It would be a perfect night for a romantic cruise, strolling on the deck with his wife, but instead he was sharing the boat with dead-eyed, battle-scarred men who were the beneficiaries of the Government's recent relaxation of the rules for leave from the front. They were mostly Geordies, which was bad luck for them — the five or six days' leave took no account of travelling time. Those who lived in the south might get several full days at home. Those from

435

the north or Scotland might find a huge percentage of their free time eaten up by long, tedious train journeys.

How long would he have at home, Hartford wondered. The unexpected order to return to Blighty came through along with instructions to cover the tracks of the Chinese incident.

Hartford had always considered the bringing of Chinese labour halfway across the globe a misguided idea. He had been there, working as a doctor in Tientsin, where he met Vernon Kell, who was then working as a correspondent for the *Daily Telegraph*. Kell had subsequently tried to recruit Hartford into the secret service once war was declared, but he had resisted the blandishments. He was a doctor. He would join the RAMC. Too old for the front line, they had said initially, and then changed their minds when the medical services almost collapsed under the weight of wounded, tossing him straight into the Ypres carnage and into the bottle. He drank, morning, noon and night, until he was as much a danger to the British soldiers as the enemy's Big Berthas.

After the breakdown, he was put in charge of the health of the labour battalions, which at first were British, Belgian, French and North African. Of late, the scale of the Allied fortifications, and the number of dead that needed burying, meant the net had been cast a lot wider. To China. And his time in that country and his ability to speak a small amount of Mandarin meant he had been given the task of screening the new arrivals.

He watched Holmes and the policeman at the rail, smoking and chatting. Holmes would be coming up with some theory about the lost ship. Not lost at all, of course, simply repainted and renamed, and would soon operating out of Richborough as the *Kent Flyer*.

If Hartford hadn't been there to spot the signs of the Blue flu, as he called it, disaster might have struck the entire British Army and, eventually, England. He had seen it before, of course, in Shandong province, when he was dealing with what he thought was a recurrence of Russian flu from the 1889 outbreak. But this had proved far more horrible, with the bleeding and coughing and that terrible tinge to the skin. The only way to prevent its spread was to isolate the victims totally.

When he discovered an infected man in a batch of labourers, Hartman had ordered them quarantined and had contacted Kell at MI5 to tell him of the threat. If the Blue flu got a foothold, and infected soldiers carried it home when on leave, the number of deaths could be enormous. Millions. Extreme measures were needed, he had insisted. Tough decisions had to be made. Kell had been there during the cholera outbreak in China; he had seen for himself what a stubborn disease could do in Qingdao. And Blue flu was far worse than cholera. Back then he had lost two nurses and a doctor to it, gone in twenty-four hours.

Yes, he had murdered people. And that nurse, he supposed. Idiotic woman, making herself a witness. He touched his breast pocket. He still had the scribbled note the nurse had written, absolving him of all responsibility for entering the carriage full of infected labourers. Yes, she

437

had signed her death own warrant, but he had saved a nation by his actions. And he had subsequently drawn up a rigorous series of health checks to put all the foreign workers through before they mixed with the British Army. If he was certain of anything, it was that diseases didn't give up and certainly didn't disappear. Blue flu, or some close relative of it, would be back. And he had arranged for compensation payments for the workers' families back in China, something he was under no obligation to do, as they were in no position to make waves in a British court.

He had a good mind to stride over and tell Holmes all this, to ask him what he would have done in his position. But then they were all distracted by the noise from above. Something that set the air pulsating. He peered up, but could see nothing, but without a shadow of a doubt there were bombers up there and they were heading for London.

★   ★   ★

There wasn't much space inside the Giant. Watson and Harrow had been placed against the low storage unit behind the two pilots. Within it was the compartment that held the parachutes. They sat, facing the rear, both tense as the plane lumbered along the runway and into the air. The racket was, thought Watson, unbelievable, but he was surprised by how quickly he became accustomed to it.

The climb was a long slow one and nobody spoke to the two passengers. The crew had been

438

told they were German spies being dropped into England. Schrader had plotted a course that would take them over northern Kent and a designated drop zone, before the bomber continued on to London.

Watson closed his eyes as the Giant dragged another few thousand feet from the sky. He ran Harrow's story over and over in his mind. A group of men — ignoring their nationality — are deliberately sealed in railway carriages and then dumped at sea to drown. Why?

Did they know something detrimental to the war effort? Unlikely: they were labourers. Were they some kind of threat? Mutineers, perhaps?

Mutineers, no. A threat yes. It is the only possible solution.

So they were carrying a disease, then. But what sort of Englishman would order such an outrage?

A frightened one.

It was possible. People have reacted irrationally when faced with something they don't understand. Especially if that something comes from a mysterious country, far, far away. Like China. There were incidents in history of whole towns and villages being sealed off when plague was suspected and of people being killed to stop them leaving. The thought that, perhaps, a medical man was responsible, though, was depressing in the extreme. Although doctors on both sides, with their toxicology experiments, had willingly helped develop poison gases. All you had to do was convince yourself that another group of people were less than human, and, it seemed, ethics flew out of the window.

Whatever the reason, it wasn't good enough. Not to stoop to murder. Not to kill all those men. And Miss Jennings. And in a few days' time an inquiry would quietly sweep the truth under the governmental carpet. He had to get back with Harrow, to let him tell them what really happened to the *Dover Arrow*.

He could feel the heat of anger in his face when something shook his leg. It was Schrader, crouching before him. 'Time to get the parachute on, Major. We'll be crossing the coast soon. I don't think there are too many guns at the spot I have chosen, but I might be wrong.'

Watson nodded and stood. Harrow was already struggling into his harness. 'You know, I thought this was an exciting idea when they told me. Now . . . ' He gave a wan smile.

Watson gripped his shoulder. 'At least you're young. I fear these old bones might just crumble when I hit the ground.'

The Giant wobbled and they heard a series of muffled explosions. 'That's an anti-aircraft ship,' said Schrader. 'Don't worry, they rarely hit us. The ones on land are a different matter. They're getting better,' he added ruefully.

What irony, Watson thought, to be blown out of sky by his own side. He looked out into the night, and tried to imagine jumping out into it, but couldn't.

Watson's ears popped. They were going down.

Schrader checked the harnesses. 'So, remember what I said. You pull this when you are well clear of the plane. A small canopy will pop out. The air will catch it, and it will drag out the main parachute. If it doesn't, you can reach over and pull this cord. It should do the trick and deploy the large chute.'

'Should' was not a reassuring word, thought Watson, as he wiped a clammy hand on his jacket. 'Thank you. For this. Not for what you will do later.'

'Deitling,' Schrader yelled. '*Nehmen sie bis zu tausend Meters.*'

Watson said. '*Tausend? Nicht drei?*'

Schrader winked. 'One thousand. As Trotzman said, I like to cheat.'

It seemed to take a lifetime for the plane to lose height, with one of the pilots shouting out the altitude every hundred metres. Watson could feel the tension in the crew. All of them were peering out of the cabin, scanning the stars for shadows flicking across them, the sign of a hunting British fighter, and for the sudden explosion of tracers that would mean they had been discovered. Off in the distance, they could see dancing searchlights, seeking the main fleet, which had continued on its way to London.

'Harrow, you go first,' Watson said quietly.

'Oh. You sure?'

'You go first.

'*Tausend Meters!*'

Schrader gave an instruction to cut the airspeed, made a hand signal and the rear gunner lowered the ramp. The increased roar of wind and engine filled the cabin. Somewhere below was England. All they had to do was go down the slide and roll over the rails that normally held the straps for the gunner and the machine gun itself. All they had to do.

'If I don't see you on the ground, I shall see you in London, Major,' yelled Harrow.

'If they leave any of it intact,' said Watson, staring at Schrader.

'Now,' said Schrader. 'Quickly.'

Harrow looked as if his nerve had gone, his legs were shaking as he stepped onto the ramp. But some sort of fatalism took hold, he smiled, crouched down onto his bottom and slid to the rail. Without a moment's hesitation, he flung himself over and was plucked away in the blink of an eye.

Watson felt a hand on his shoulder. 'Your turn, Major Watson.'

★　★　★

There were precious few lights at Folkestone in case the bombers returned, and the harbour navigation aids flared briefly as the ship approached. But docking went smoothly. As usual, the officers were allowed to disembark first before the troops were released, so Colonel Hartford found himself walking down the gangway some steps behind Holmes and the copper.

On the quayside he could see two military policemen, scanning the passengers as they disembarked. So, unless he was very much mistaken, it looked as if Holmes's meddling was going to be curtailed.

'I have your luggage, sir,' said a voice in his ear.

It was Terence, his batman, who was carrying his steamer trunk. It was clearly an effort, probably because of the half-dozen bottles of brandy in there. Hartford felt his stomach contract at the thought. He imagined himself sitting before the fire, matching the stare of the two dragon sentries he had had shipped back from China, drinking a large glass while Marion fussed over him before bringing Charles down to say hello to his papa. The evening would slide into a warm fug of an alcoholic blur and he could forget all about drowning Chinamen. Later, he would slide in beside Marion . . .

'Colonel Hartford?'

He snapped out of his reverie and looked up at the military policeman. He was six foot three or four, with a face as square as a spade. 'Yes.'

Holmes and the policeman had walked on along the jetty. He could see their heads above the crowd, heading away, unmolested.

'If you could come with us, sir.'

'What? Why?'

'We'll take your luggage for you,' said the shorter of the two, relieving Terence of the trunk and indicating he should leave. Terence, never a fan of MPs, scuttled off without an argument.

'What's this about?' asked Hartford indignantly. 'I have important meetings in London.'

'We have no idea, sir. We are just following our orders,' said spade-face.

'I need to get home.'

The words sounded futile and empty, and as soon he said them Colonel Hartford had an inkling that he might never see home, his wife, Marion, or his son, Charles, ever again.

443

Watson spent some time staring down into the void below the bomber at the spectral country-side. No sign of a parachute, but they had already travelled a considerable distance since Harrow went over, so that wasn't surprising. He put his feet on the ramp, sat down and looked up at Schrader 'I'm sorry,' he shouted, 'that we should have met like this.'

The German raised a hand in acknowledge-ment and Watson pushed himself down, hitting the rail awkwardly. He clung on, the roar of engines and air filling his skull, swamping any chance of rational thought.

Legs over first.

Yes, legs over the top rail first. Hook elbow around metal strut. Let go.

Watson hadn't imagined the sound could get any louder but it was as if demons were screaming in his ears. His legs flailed, and he began to oscillate in the prop wash, slamming his ankles into the fuselage. Up above, he could see Schrader shouting at him, but it was as if he were miming the words. The message was clear, though: he wanted him to let go.

Watson let his weight drop him down the pole he was clutching and used his right hand to rummage in his jacket. His strength was fading, he knew, there were only seconds left before he was snatched out into space.

His chilled hands fumbled the little pistol he had so assiduously hidden from the Germans. Miss Pillbody's little Colt, a mere peashooter

444

against this raging Giant. It fell from his fingers but caught in the lining of his jacket. Now he had it. Safety off. His thumb felt as thick as sausage and about as responsive as he tried to move the lever. He was aware from the twisting movement of the slide that Schrader — or another crew member — was coming down after him.

Watson forced himself down, ducking beneath the metal ramp, and raised the gun, watching it twist and buck in the airstream as he tried to steady his arm. Too old, too old. Too old for this nonsense.

His eyes were streaming from the wind slapping his face. His vision began to blur. He tried to recall exactly where they had been going to load the bombs and squeezed the trigger.

The pistol bucked wildly, but he swung it back round and fired again, the spent cartridge, bouncing off his cheek as it spun away, singeing the skin.

A pain shot through his left hand and arm and he felt his purchase slip and then fail. Schrader had stomped on him with his boot. As he fell away, he felt a moment of stillness, away from the shriek and growl of the engines and the battering of the wind. He gripped the gun with both hands, pointed in in the vague direction of the bomber, and fired until the slide jammed back. Then he let the weapon go, spinning away into the darkness.

The great beast carried on, chewing the air as its engines powered up to gain Schrader's precious height. Watson wondered if he should just close his eyes and surrender to what was inevitable, to give himself up to an eternal peace. There was weariness in his bones and he wanted it to end.

The survival instinct was too strong and his right hand decided it, at the very least, wanted to live and began scrabbling for the primitive handle that would release the chute.

Up above, something shone from the plane, like the sliver of light under a doorjamb at night. It was the outline of the bomb bay, glowing silver.

One pull.

Nothing. And then, a fantail of sparks, spinning away behind the bomber, like a spluttering firework.

Two pulls.

A light so intense it hurt his eyes blossomed from the belly of the Giant.

Three pulls.

A jerk as the canvas bag eviscerated itself and a tangle of material and cords exploded above his head before twisting and turning and finally resolving a lovely bell-shaped flower. The straps dug into him and for a few moments he felt as if he were rising back towards the stricken bomber. The movement stopped, the parachute steadied and he began to pendulum down towards the fields of Kent.

An orb, brighter than the moon, was falling to earth in front of him, a man-made shooting star, no longer discernible as an aircraft of any kind, just a blazing white sphere of thermite and magnesium, sending off hot globules behind it, as if it were giving birth.

The Giant hit the ground well before he did, creating a ragged-topped column of light that illuminated the fields where it fell as if it were day. The deep boom of the impact and the whoosh of flames reached him some moments later. He tried not to think of Schrader, Deitling, Fohn and the others. But he couldn't let the bomber go on to London with its firebombs. He would have felt complicit in its actions.

Far too many had died around him of late — not just the bomber crew, but Mrs Gregson, Staff Nurse Jennings, Miss Pillbody. Then there was Trenchard, Garavan, Amies. Some might have deserved to die, but that was enough bodies laid at his door. More than enough.

Watson reached up and gripped the lines, letting his weight relax into the harness. It was so damned quiet, apart from the occasional crackle and pop from the burning bomber, which reached up to him even at that height. It was easy to imagine this was what the world once sounded like, before man and his machines marched across it. Silence, he realized, was a precious commodity, especially in war. Now, at last, the appeal of the Diogenes was clear.

Watson looked down between his feet. He had no idea how far away the ground was. He could only make out the ghostly outlines of hedgerows, the black ink-spot of woods and copses. Not a light shone in a house. Still, gravity would do its work. He would be down soon enough. Yet, dangling there in the straps, Watson felt suspended not just by the harness, but in time

447

itself, and he wished that the warm feeling coursing through him, the calming sensation of being free from all the cares that awaited him below, could last for ever.

Author's Note

After a series of accidents and failures, the experimental Elektron incendiary bomb was withdrawn in the autumn of 1917 and the modified version was not introduced until the spring of 1918.

By that time, the British air defences had been formalized and streamlined. The system of observation, plotting and interception was essentially the same as that used just over two decades later in the Battle of Britain, apart from the fact that, by 1940, the far more effective radar had replaced the acoustic dishes built on the coast.

His service record states that Colonel Arthur Hartford contracted typhus in the course of his duties. He died at an isolation ward in Essex. After a period of mourning, his widow, Marion, married a former policeman in 1919. He took over the care of the couple's son, Charles, and daughter, Clara.

St Luke's Hospital for Lunatics, as it was originally known, was used by the Treasury and subsequently the Bank of England from 1916 onwards until the early 1950s. The building was demolished in 1963. The author would like to thank Margherita Orlando of the Bank of England's Archives Department for help in researching the wartime history of the printing works.

The body of Stephen Harrow was never found. Rumours of a German spy killed by locals in the north Kent village of Iwade have never been substantiated.

The origin of the Spanish flu epidemic that swept the world in two waves during 1918–20, killing 50–100 million people, has never been definitely established. Some researchers suggest it may have been a bird virus that mutated and spread to pigs kept near the front. Others contend that it first appeared in Kansas, which was certainly the location of the first big outbreak, but possibly not the site of its origin. Mark Humphries of Canada's Memorial University of Newfoundland is of the opinion that it was brought by some of the 96,000 Chinese labourers who were transported to the Western Front. He points to evidence that a respiratory illness that struck northern China in 1917 was identified a year later by Chinese health officials as being identical to the Spanish flu. The symptoms included the skin turning blue.

In the trunk containing Dr John Watson's papers in the vaults of Cox & Co. on the Charing Cross Road, there is a partial manuscript called 'The Adventure of the *Dover Arrow*'. Dr Watson's notes appear to indicate that the definitive solution to the case eluded Holmes, possibly because vital information was destroyed by individuals in senior positions in the British Government and further enquiries curtailed by use of the draconian DORA regulations.

Robert Ryan

We do hope that you have enjoyed reading this large print book.

Did you know that all of our titles are available for purchase?

We publish a wide range of high quality large print books including:
Romances, Mysteries, Classics
General Fiction
Non Fiction and Westerns

Special interest titles available in large print are:
The Little Oxford Dictionary
Music Book
Song Book
Hymn Book
Service Book

Also available from us courtesy of Oxford University Press:
Young Readers' Dictionary
(large print edition)
Young Readers' Thesaurus
(large print edition)

For further information or a free brochure, please contact us at:
Ulverscroft Large Print Books Ltd.,
The Green, Bradgate Road, Anstey,
Leicester, LE7 7FU, England.
Tel: (00 44) 0116 236 4325
Fax: (00 44) 0116 234 0205

Other titles published by Ulverscroft:

A STUDY IN MURDER

Robert Ryan

1917: Doctor John Watson is a prisoner in a notorious POW camp deep in enemy Germany. With the Allied blockade in force, food is perilously short; and when a new prisoner is murdered, all assume the poor chap was killed for his Red Cross parcel. But Watson isn't so sure. Something isn't quite what it seems, and a creeping feeling of unease tells him there is more to this than meets the eye. And when an escape plot is apparently uncovered in his hut and he is sent to solitary confinement, he knows he has touched a nerve. If Watson is to reveal the heinous crimes that have occurred at the camp, he must escape before he is silenced for good. All he needs is some long-distance help from his old friend, Sherlock Holmes . . .